PRAISE F

CLASH
→ OF ←
EMPIRES

'Fans of battle-heavy historical fiction will, justly, adore *Clash of Empires*. With its rounded historical characters and **fascinating** historical setting, it deserves a wider audience'

Antonia Senior, *The Times*

'Grabs you from the start and never lets go. Thrilling action combines with historical authenticity to summon up a whole world in a sweeping tale of politics and war. **A triumph!**'

Harry Sidebottom, author of the *The Last Hour*

'The word **epic** is overused to describe books, but with *Clash of Empires* it fits like a gladius in its scabbard. What Kane does, with such mastery, is place the big story – Rome vs Greece – in the background, while making this a story about ordinary men caught up in world-defining events. In short, **I haven't enjoyed a book this much for ages. There aren't many writers today who could take on this story and do it well. There might be none who could do it better than Ben Kane**'

Giles Kristian, author of *Lancelot*

'Exceptional. Kane's excelled once again in capturing the terror and the glory . . . of the ancient battlefield, and this story is one that's been begging for an expert hand for a long time'

Anthony Riches, author of the Empire series

'Carried off with panache and Kane's expansive, engaging, action-packed style. A complex, **fraught, moving and passionate** slice of history **from one of our generation's most ambitious and engaging writers**'

Manda Scott, author of the Boudica series

'It's a broad canvas Kane is painting on, but he does it with vivid colours and, like the Romans themselves, he can show great admiration for a Greek enemy and still kick them in the balls'
Robert Low, author of the Oathsworn series

'Ben Kane manages to marry broad narrative invention with detailed historical research . . . in taut, authoritative prose . . . **his passion for the past, and for the craft of story-telling, shines from every page**'
Toby Clements, author of the Kingmaker series

'This **thrilling** series opener delivers every cough, spit, curse and gush of blood to set up the mighty clash of the title. Can't really fault this one – **pure man joy**'
Jon Wise, *Weekend Sport*

'A **powerful** and **vivid** historical novel that moves along at chariot-race speed'
Helena Gumley-Mason, *The Lady*

'Ben Kane's new series **explores the bloody final clash between ancient Greece and upstart Rome**, focusing on soldiers and leaders from both worlds and **telling the story of a bloody war with style**'
Charlotte Heathcote, *Sunday Express S Magazine*

'**A thumping good read.** You can feel the earth tremble from the great battle scenes and feel the desperation of those caught up in the conflict. Kane's brilliant research weaves its way lightly throughout'
David Gilman, author of the Master of War series

THE
FALLING
SWORD

BEN KANE is one of the most hard-working and successful historical writers in the industry. His third book, *The Road to Rome*, was a *Sunday Times* number four bestseller, and every title since has been a top ten bestseller. Born in Kenya, Kane moved to Ireland at the age of seven. After qualifying as a veterinarian, he worked in small animal practice and during the terrible Foot and Mouth Disease outbreak in 2001. Despite his veterinary career, he retained a deep love of history; this led him to begin writing.

His first novel, *The Forgotten Legion*, was published in 2008; since then he has written four series of Roman novels. Kane lives in Somerset with his wife and two children.

Also by Ben Kane

The Forgotten Legion Chronicles
The Forgotten Legion
The Silver Eagle
The Road to Rome

Hannibal
Enemy of Rome
Fields of Blood
Clouds of War

Spartacus
The Gladiator
Rebellion

Eagles of Rome
Eagles at War
Hunting the Eagles
Eagles in the Storm

Clash of Empires
Clash of Empires

THE
FALLING
SWORD

BEN KANE

ORION

First published in Great Britain in 2019 by Orion Books
an imprint of The Orion Publishing Group Ltd
Carmelite House, 50 Victoria Embankment
London EC4Y 0DZ

An Hachette UK Company

1 3 5 7 9 10 8 6 4 2

A CIP catalogue record for this book is
available from the British Library.

ISBN (Hardback) 978 1 4091 7342 7
ISBN (Export Trade Paperback) 978 1 4091 7343 4
ISBN (eBook) 978 1 4091 7345 8
ISBN (Audio) 978 1 4091 7346 5

Typeset by Input Data Services Ltd, Somerset

Printed and bound in Great Britain by Clays Ltd, Elcograf S.p.A.

www.orionbooks.co.uk

For everyone involved with Park in the Past*, in particular

Paul 'Whirlwind' Harston of Roman Tours UK, and all his team.

*Park in the Past is near Chester, north-west England; it's a place where a second-century AD Roman fort is being built. Interested? Check out the website: parkinthepast.org.uk – and please donate if you can at: localgiving.co.uk/park-in-the-past – thank you!

Asked how he controlled the Greeks, Alexander the Great replied, 'By putting off nothing that ought to be done today until tomorrow.'

A SHORT NOTE ABOUT GREEK CITY STATES

Ancient Greece contained a confusing plethora of similar-sounding city states and regions. Most readers will have known of Athens, Sparta and Macedon, but not necessarily of Aetolia, Achaea, Athamania and Acarnania. Thermopylae and Marathon will be familiar, but it's less likely for modern readers to know the towns of the Hellespont and the mountain towns between Macedon and Illyria. It took me some time to familiarise myself with these political and geographical entities, and so to increase your enjoyment of the book, I urge you first to spend a little time looking over the maps.

Ben Kane

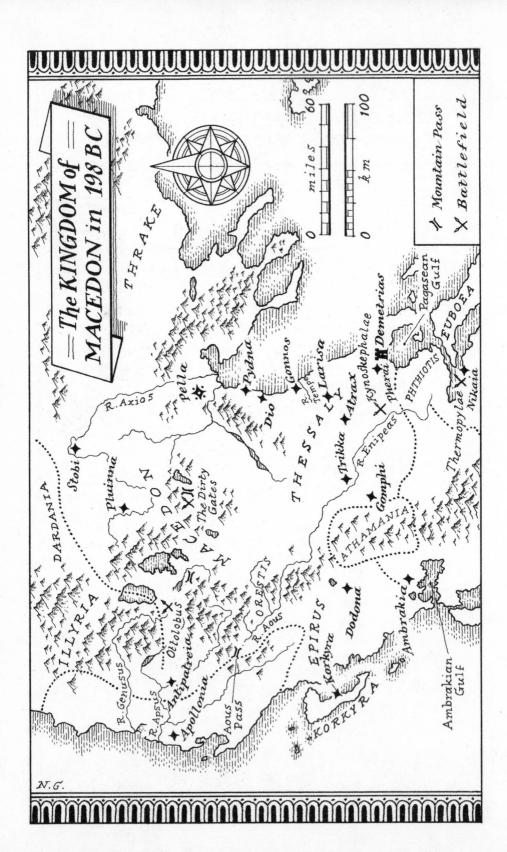

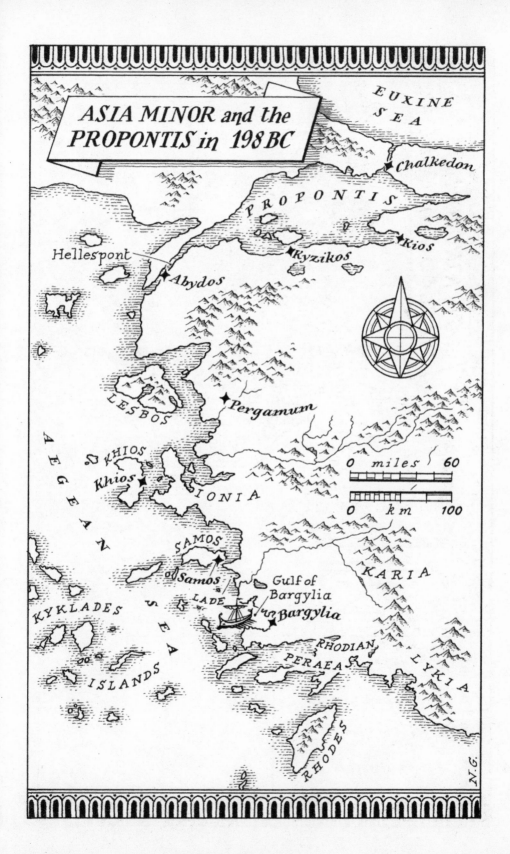

ASIA MINOR and the PROPONTIS in 198 BC

EUXINE SEA

Chalkedon

PROPONTIS

Hellespont

Kyzikos

Kios

Abydos

LESBOS

Pergamum

KHIOS

Khios

IONIA

0 miles 60

0 km 100

SAMOS

Samos

Gulf of Bargylia

KARIA

LADE

Bargylia

KYKLADES

AEGEAN SEA

RHODIAN PERAEA

LYKIA

ISLANDS

RHODES

N.G.

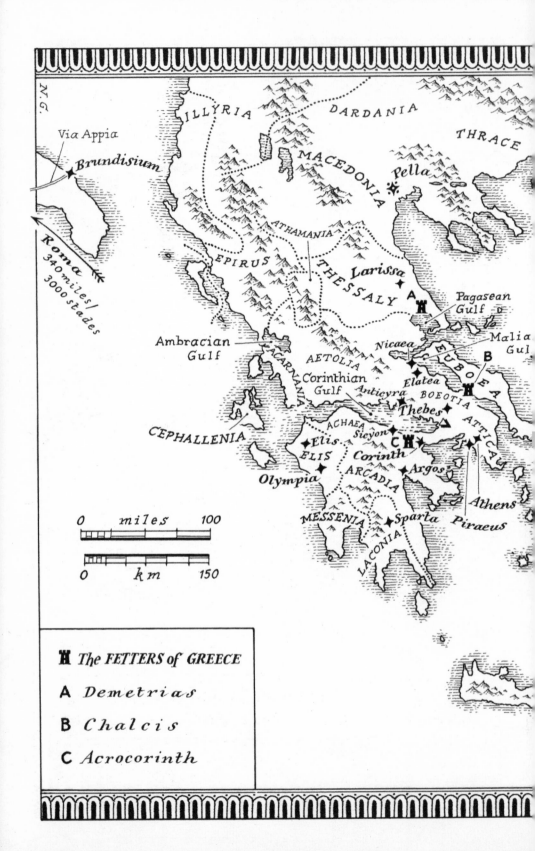

EUXINE SEA

PROPONTIS

Chalcedon

THASOS

Hellespont

Pergamum

LESBOS

CHIOS

IONIA

AEGEAN SEA

SAMOS

CARIA

LYCIA

CYCLADES
ISLANDS

RHODES

CRETE

MACEDONIA and GREECE
in 198BC

CHAPTER I

Near Elatea in Phocis, autumn 198 BC

Despite the waning year, the narrow Phocian plain was bathed in warm sunlight. It was bordered to the north by mountains, on the other side of which lay Thermopylae, the 'gates of fire' where Leonidas and his Spartans had fought and died. South of these peaks the flat ground sprawled, bisected by a road that was as important now as it had been during the Persian invasions almost three centuries before. South of here lay Athens, open to attack. Harvest time was not long past; the fields were yet full of golden stubble. Neat rows of vines lined the road in places, their heavy clusters of blue-purple grapes an invitation to the thirsty traveller, or soldier.

Long trails of dust hung in the air, marking the passage of Titus Quinctius Flamininus' army. Six days had gone by since its defeat at the Macedonian fortress of Atrax, eighty miles to the north-west. Its dead buried, the injured in wagons or left behind, it had come south-east to protect the Roman fleet, at harbour nearby. Other than the keen-eyed vultures following the legions from above, few creatures were abroad. The approach of such a host meant many things, none good. Local farmers had fled with their families and animals, most taking refuge inside Elatea, the town outside which the first of Flamininus' troops were deploying.

The Roman vanguard had spread out, forming a protective screen for the rest of the army to deploy behind. Among the *principes* stood a friendly-faced man by the name of Felix. Black-haired, sallow-skinned, he stood a head taller than most. He stared at the walls of Elatea with sullen resentment; so did his brother and his comrades. Elatea, with its defenders atop its walls, was a sharp reminder that the war wasn't over. More of them would die here, thought Felix grimly. Not many, perhaps, but some.

Wise to the proximity of their acting commander Livius, no one

1

complained. Instead the principes leaned on their shields, drank sly mouthfuls of wine and waited, for orders, for time to pass.

Nothing would happen before the next day, Felix judged. After the cavalry and scouts, who travelled in front of the army, his unit had been among the first to arrive, which meant that at least three more hours would pass before the last of the miles-long column caught up. The wagons, laden down with supplies and the dismantled catapults, travelled slowly, and the score of war elephants did too. Stragglers would still be trailing in after the sun went down, and until they were told otherwise, Felix and his comrades had to watch out for a sally by Elatea's defenders.

An attack seemed doubtful: this was no mighty fortress built to protect Macedonia's borders, but a small town with a fortified rampart. The majority of its garrison would be bakers and carpenters, smiths, leather workers and wine sellers, not soldiers. They would certainly not be the *phalangists* of Atrax, on whose *sarissa* spears the legionaries had broken like waves on a harbour wall. Their centurion Pullo had been the most grievous loss, but plenty of ordinary soldiers in the century had fallen too, among them Felix's always-laughing friend Mattheus. Others had died during battles earlier that summer. Felix's original *contubernium* tent group was down to three men: him, his brother Antonius and Fabius, the crusty old veteran who snapped whenever anyone asked if he was related to Fabius 'the Delayer'.

'Won't be long now,' said a voice.

Felix started. Livius was an *optio*, but he had the unnerving centurion's knack of appearing when one least expected it. He had been in command since Pullo's death. Felix threw him a curious look. 'Until what, sir?'

Livius grinned, revealing the gap between his front teeth. 'Until you can start digging. The second half of the legion is almost here.'

Constructing the defensive ditch that would surround their camp, and after that, the rampart, was better than fighting, but Felix was unable to muster any enthusiasm. 'Aye, sir,' he mumbled.

'It's been a long march. I'll see that there's a ration of wine issued tonight.' Livius walked off, leaving Felix open-mouthed. The journey from the fortress where Pullo had fallen had been simple, and through easy terrain. The only difficulty had been the grief weighing them down, and Livius had just acknowledged it, albeit indirectly.

'He's a good officer,' said Felix under his breath.

'More's the pity that he won't become our centurion,' said Antonius. Shorter, more serious than Felix, he was four years the elder.

Rumour had it that those in command had been impressed with Livius' holding-together of the shattered century after Pullo's death. Promotion to the centurionate wasn't unheard of for similar feats of bravery, but it was something that none of the principes wanted for Livius, for it would mean losing him as well.

'Gods will it that he'll stay with us,' said Fabius, giving his phallus amulet a rub. It was the norm for surviving junior officers to remain in place.

'Who's the new centurion going to be?' said Felix.

A chorus of I don't knows filled his ears, and he grimaced. There was no reason for his comrades to have any more idea than he. Don't let it be a cunt like Matho, he prayed. Both brothers had served in the legions during the war with Hannibal; five years before, they had been dishonourably discharged by the malevolent Matho after the battle of Zama. Civilian life had not worked out for the pair, and when war was declared with Macedonia, they had risked their lives by joining the army again. Capricious to the last, the goddess Fortuna had again crossed their paths with Matho. The only witness to their final confrontation with him, which had resulted in Matho's death, had been a Macedonian – a youth who was fortunately dead.

'We need new men too,' said Fabius. 'Who ever heard of a contubernium of three?'

'I don't see that happening any time soon,' observed Antonius.

'More likely that we get shoved in with another tent group that's in the same position.' Felix raised his voice so it could be heard. 'Let's hope it's not the shower of bastards in the next rank.' He grinned at the hail of insults and threats that came by way of response.

The next few hours were spent in similar fashion. Wise to their need for diversion from the grim reality of life, Livius let them be. Other than the occasional wink of sunlight off a helmet, there was no activity atop Elatea's walls. This was also heartening, as was Antonius' observation that the defenders were shitting themselves at what would happen in the coming days.

*

Darkness blanketed the Phocian plain. Inside Elatea, dogs barked at one another, in the annoying way dogs do at night. Peace reigned over the great camps built by Flamininus' legions. Sentries paced the walkways, checked on every so often by junior officers. A short way beyond the ditch facing the town stood the catapults that would soon wreak havoc on Elatea's defences. The hour was late, and most men were abed. Among the neat lines of principes' tents a handful of fires still glowed, including that of Felix, Antonius and Fabius. Orders had come in at sunset. An attack on Elatea was planned for the next day; the principes would be taking part. This unwelcome news had seen the wine procured by Livius left unfinished. No one was stupid enough to get rat-arsed drunk with a fight in the offing. By unspoken consent, the assault went unmentioned.

'What will you do after the war?' Fabius inched his toes closer to the glowing embers, and then eyed Felix and Antonius, who were lounging on their blankets on the other side of the fire. 'You left your farm once before – could you go back to it?'

'I'll give it another try,' said Antonius, as he had each time the topic had been discussed during the previous two summers' campaigns. 'By the time this war is done, I should have enough coin to buy mules and a slave. That will make life a good deal easier.' He glanced at Felix, trying to gauge his interest, but Felix pretended not to see.

Fabius, who knew only that their farming life had been brutally hard, grunted. His gaze moved to Felix. 'And you?'

'What will you do, old man?' countered Felix.

'Me? Same as I've always said. I'm going to buy a tavern and slowly drink myself to death.'

Felix snorted. 'How long will that take?'

'Many years, I hope.' A rare smile appeared on Fabius' face. 'Why don't you two come in with me? You're young and strong – taverns need men like that around. With you there to keep me straight, I'll last into my sixties.'

'It could only be better than our last experience in the trade,' admitted Antonius. 'My ribs hurt just remembering it.'

Felix rubbed his jaw, which had ached for days after a fight with a brute who'd nearly had the better of the two of them. 'Where would it be?'

Fabius gave him a look. 'I'm from Rome. Where else would a man want to open a tavern?'

'There are plenty of shitty areas in Rome,' challenged Felix.

'D'you think I came down with the last shower?' retorted Fabius. 'I know that. We would decide on the location together.'

Felix glanced at Antonius, and then at Fabius. 'Equal partners?'

'As long as you can come up with a third of the coin each, aye.' Fabius spat on his hand and shoved it at Felix.

Felix held back. 'What d'you think, brother? Running a tavern has got to be better than working a plough day in, day out. Better than breaking your back at harvest time too.'

Antonius' eyes met his, and moved to Fabius, who nodded encouragingly, before returning to Felix. 'Aye, why not?' he muttered. 'If it doesn't work out, the farm will still be there.'

The three shook hands, grinning. Fabius produced a skin of wine, an event so rare that Felix declared it to be another reason for celebration. Under normal circumstances, this acid comment would have soured Fabius enough to make him refuse to share, but tonight he merely grumbled about youngsters having no respect for their elders and betters. The skin travelled around the fire, and the three partners took small sips as they discussed their new enterprise.

Fabius was the first to nod off. One moment he was enthusing about the wines he could buy from an old contact with a farm south of Rome, the next his chin was on his chest and he was gently snoring. There was no response from Antonius, and Felix saw with amusement that he too was almost asleep. Felix prepared to stir himself. It wasn't that cold, but the fire had burned down to embers. Despite the wine-warmth coating him, the tent was only a few paces away, and was worth getting up for. Tipping up the skin, he swallowed a few last drops. It had been a decent vintage, he decided.

He nudged Antonius and Fabius into wakefulness and went to empty his bladder in the latrine trench, which was close to the wall nearest Elatea. Job done, Felix smoothed down his tunic and turned to retrace his steps. He aimed an idle glance at the walkway, thinking he hadn't heard a sentry's tread while he'd been pissing. There was no one in sight, which was curious. He moved back a little, to take in more of the earthen rampart, which stood tall as two men. Not a soul.

He felt a prick of alarm. Sliding his feet now so they made no sound, he paced twenty and then fifty paces along the base of the wall. There were no sentries visible, but a telltale prone shape made his mouth go dry. Felix studied the nearest tents, but could see and hear nothing to suggest that attackers had entered the camp. He warred with himself for a moment. Scream a false alarm, and he would be punished. Better to check on the man, he decided, stealing towards the nearest ladder.

He crept up it, heart pounding, eyes darting to left and right along the walkway. Halfway up, he noticed a second figure slumped in a sitting position. It had to be another sentry. Ill deeds *are* afoot, thought Felix, his pulse quickening. The Elateans weren't without spine after all. Crouching below the top of the rampart, he sped to the nearest sentry. The man lay face down and still as stone. A dark pool around his neck was grim warning of what had befallen him. Felix dipped his fingers into the liquid to be sure, and wished he hadn't. A grappling hook lay nearby, and from it a rope snaked over the rampart – this was how the enemy or enemies who'd killed the sentry had climbed up. He couldn't see a soul along the entire walkway, which meant this wall was undefended, but bizarrely there was still no sign of attackers within the camp.

He risked a look over the fortifications, and his eyes widened. Around the two large catapults that had pounded a hole in the walls of Atrax, dozens of figures loomed. Torches flickered in their hands; the distinctive tang of pitch carried through the air.

Felix leaped to his feet and bellowed the alarm with all his might.

Heads turned among the attackers, and their efforts to light the catapults grew more urgent.

Felix heard sentries on the other walls taking up his call; there were men stirring in the nearest tents. It was slow, however, too slow. Flames were licking up the side of one catapult, and the attackers had moved on to the second weapon. He wondered about rousing Antonius and Fabius, but that would also take too long. Cursing himself for a fool, Felix stripped the dead sentry of his baldric and sword. He tossed the man's javelin and shield into the defensive ditch, checked the grappling iron was secure and clambered over the rampart. Down he went, hand over hand, balancing his feet against the wall. He paused at the bottom to stare at the attackers. None appeared to have noticed his descent. Not that they'd worry about one man, Felix decided grimly. He peered into the ditch, thinking, one slip and I'll end up on a caltrop, if not two. There was nothing for it, though. Sitting on his arse with his hands on the edge, he eased himself down.

He gingerly found safe footing, and then crouched to spot the shield and javelin. Fortuna smiled on him; they had landed close by. Probing for caltrops with his fingertips, he retrieved both and heaved them over the lip of the ditch. Praying that no one was waiting to brain him, Felix scrambled out of the trench.

No one had noticed. Although there was good light now from the first burning catapult, the attackers were absorbed with trying to set the second piece ablaze. For some reason, it had not ignited with the ease of its companion, but given their frantic efforts it wouldn't be long going the same way. Felix wavered. He had raised the alarm; he could not put out the fire alone, and the attackers would soon be driven off. Why throw his life away?

One of the attackers turned and saw him.

Felix had time to think what an old bitch Fortuna was, and then he was beckoning to imaginary comrades and shouting, 'Come on, brothers! With me!' He threw the javelin, spitting one of the enemy between the shoulder blades. Then, roaring as if he were a century of legionaries, not one, he drew the sword and ran towards the burning catapults.

The man who'd seen him was nervous. His badly aimed spear hummed past, nowhere near Felix.

Felix was on him in another heartbeat. The shield boss slammed the man backwards, onto his backside. Felix left him behind, closing on a second man who, panicked by his wild face, turned to flee. Felix stabbed him in the back, and drove on. Two attackers joined forces, one going left of Felix, the other right. I'm dead, he thought. They'll have seen I'm alone. He made a snap judgement; the one to his left was no more than a youth. Dart forward. Punch with the shield. Stab with his sword, and the youth went down, mewling like a babe ripped from the tit.

Felix spun, wary of the second attacker. The man was hanging back, however. Paunchy, holding his shield and spear like a new recruit, he was no soldier. Felix felt a glimmer of hope. He charged, not seeing the discarded torch underfoot. Skidding, balance lost, he stumbled forward and fell flat on his face. A cry of triumph rose from his opponent, who stepped in, spear raised high.

'ROMA!' The cry was some distance off, but it was being made by scores of voices. 'ROMA!'

Felix flinched, still expecting a spear in the back.

The blow didn't fall. Feet pounded. Men cried to one another in Greek.

Felix rolled over, unable to believe his luck. A trained soldier would have killed him before running away, but the paunchy man had given in to fear, and saved his own skin.

An odd peace fell. Wood crackled. Heat radiated from the catapults. Felix got to his feet. Both artillery pieces were ablaze now; attempt to put out the fire and he would get badly burnt. He stood back, deciding that Fortuna had been tempted enough for one night.

The siege of Elatea was going to be more difficult than everyone had assumed.

CHAPTER II

Tempe, on the Macedonian border

Rolling hills marked the northern border of the Thessalian plain. They ran from west to east, all the way to the Aegean Sea. Cloud-wrapped peaks stood behind, part of the mountainous girdle that encircled Macedon. Some seventy *stadia* inland, far from any village, a defile marked a rare path northward. It was a mark of the times that scores of *peltasts* stood guard over it, fierce-faced Thracians, watchful Macedonians and Thessalians. Their horses grazed the short grass nearby.

Halfway through the morning, there was a flurry of activity as half a dozen horsemen emerged from the narrow pass. At their head, astride a feisty grey stallion, was Philip, fifth of his name, ruler of Macedon. Slim, bright-eyed, chin covered by a neat beard, he was dressed in a simple *chiton* and sandals. A plain-scabbarded *kopis* hung from a baldric over his shoulder. He acknowledged the sentries' salutes and cries with friendly waves.

'Anything to report?' asked the king.

The nearest man came running over. 'No, sire.'

'Berisades!' cried the king with genuine pleasure. The peltast was old enough to be his father; he had served in the army for perhaps two decades.

'Greetings, sire.' Berisades' grin was broad. Tall, lanky, with skin turned walnut-dark by the sun, he wore only a belted chiton and sandals.

Philip reached down to clasp Berisades' hand. 'It's good to see you.'

'And you, sire. Come to lead us south? Word of your latest success is on everyone's lips. Men are eager to have another crack at the Romans.'

'Nothing would give me more pleasure.' Philip put the back of a hand to his mouth and whispered loudly, 'But would you not rather be warming your bones by the fire at home?'

'No, sire, I would follow you,' said Berisades. Seeing Philip's grin, he said with a shake of his head, 'You make fun of me, sire.'

'I do so only because I know you have the heart of a lion, Berisades.' Philip glanced over his shoulder at his companions, and cried, 'See this man? He is the most valiant of all my soldiers. Threescore years he's seen, and still he marches to war. Faithful and valiant, Berisades shall always be honoured.'

Discomfited, Berisades shuffled his calloused bare feet. 'You didn't have to go saying that, sire.'

'Never have I spoken truer words,' said Philip warmly. 'I must take my leave now – forgive me, Berisades – but we shall talk again soon, gods willing. Keep an eye out for carts. Wine and venison for you all will arrive by nightfall. See to it that everyone knows it came from me – a small gesture of gratitude for the days you've spent here.'

Beaming from ear to ear, Berisades bowed low. 'A thousand thanks, sire.'

Raising a hand in farewell, Philip rode on. He reined in a short distance onto the plain. 'Menander?'

'I am here, sire.' A heavy-set nobleman in late middle age eased his mount to the king's side. 'That was well done, sire.'

Philip glanced at him. 'They don't come much better than Berisades.'

'And you've just bound him to you even tighter, sire. He'll be talking about you for days. So will his comrades. They would have done anyway, with you visiting, but the wine and the meat – it was smoothly done.'

'Show your men you care, and they fight better.'

'It has ever been your way, sire.' Menander's eyes were full of respect.

Philip waved an expansive arm at the vista, an expanse of stubbled fields and gentle hills. In the distance to the south-west, the walls of Larisa were just visible. 'A fine view.'

'It is, sire, and all the better for being empty of Romans.'

'Indeed.' Philip relived the satisfaction of hearing the momentous news from Atrax. After a summer of setbacks, the victory had been much needed. It was regrettable that the success had not been complete; the Roman general Flamininus' losses had been heavy, but by no means overwhelming. To make matters worse, the year's campaign, which should have been drawing to a close, was being prolonged. After the recent winds and rain, a period of unseasonal warm weather had set in, and seemed set to continue for a time. Consequently, the legions were still at large. Philip cast an eye at Menander. 'Has there been any word?'

'Yes, sire. As you know, Flamininus' army marched south. Latest reports indicate that it rounded the Malian Gulf and passed through the gates of fire two days hence.'

'He's set on besieging Elateia, just as I thought. Control the surrounding area, and it becomes impossible for us to launch an overland attack through Boeotia from Chalkis.' Chalkis, the king's fortress on the island of Euboea, was of vital importance. It seemed Flamininus was aware of this, thought Philip.

'You're thinking you should have sent more soldiers to Elateia, sire.' Mere days before, Philip had ordered a *speira* of phalangists to move south to reinforce the garrison.

'You know me well.' Philip's smile was rueful.

'And if you had, sire, and the town fell anyway?'

'I know, but it's galling to think of losing it.' A grimace. 'I suppose even if we'd held the town, the chance of moving troops over from Chalkis was a slim one.'

'With luck, there will be heartening news from Elateia, sire. The townsmen sent word a few days since that they intended to try and torch Flamininus' catapults in a night attack.'

'May the gods be with them. Even if they succeed, however, Elateia is no fortress.'

'It is not, sire, and the siege leaves the fate of Phokis in the balance. And Boeotia.' These two regions – historically friendly to Macedon – lay to the south, on the road to Athens.

'Everyone within five hundred stadia must be wondering when Flamininus will come knocking at their door.' Philip made a fist in frustration. 'There's precious little I can do to help either. Send more troops, and I weaken my own army.'

'I know, sire.'

Philip's mind was on the move again. He indicated the empty plain for a second time, impulse taking him. 'If we marched south, there's a good chance we could surprise the legions outside Elateia.'

'On flat ground, the phalanx would butcher the Romans, sire, but it might not be that simple. What if Flamininus leaves scouts to watch over Thermopylae, or a local seeking coin brought him word of our passage? If the legions contrived to ambush us the army would be far from home.'

'Level heads are ever the bane of surprise tactics,' said Philip with a regretful shake of his head. 'Yet in this instance, Menander, you are right again. If Elateia should fall, I will have lost a single speira and an allied town, but if the phalanx were to come to grief, Macedon would lie defenceless. That I cannot risk – not yet.' Menander looked relieved, and Philip laughed.

How he wished that he had listened more to Menander in times past than he had to Herakleides, the silver-tongued but treacherous Tarentine. At least Herakleides was no more. Unmasked as a traitor, the Tarentine had died under the torturers' hands, with him watching.

'I know,' he said again. 'I must forget Flamininus for the moment, and Phokis and Boeotia. He will not advance on Macedon before winter. It is time for us to consider our options, marshal our forces, and to prepare for spring.'

'Wise counsel, sire.'

'It would be fine to see Akhaian neutrality continue, eh? It will never happen, though. They are in an impossible position, with the Roman fleet on their northern coast and Flamininus not much further away. Meanwhile, Nabis of Sparta skulks about on their southern and eastern borders like a hungry wolf.' Akhaia and Sparta both lay on the Peloponnese.

'It would not surprise me if the Akhaians broke faith with Macedon soon, sire.'

'Enough of the filthy Akhaians. I will not waste my breath on Aitolia either. *It* will send every man that can be spared to join Flamininus when he attacks Macedon.' The city state of Aitolia was the bitterest of the king's enemies. Philip made an impatient gesture. 'As ever, we are surrounded by enemies, or those who will not commit one way or the other.'

'Let us not forget Akarnania, sire. It remains loyal,' said Menander.

'Harsh it may sound, but Akarnania is too far away to be helped. Gods forbid they ever ask for aid. All I shall be able to send are encouraging words.'

An unhappy silence fell.

'About this time last year, we went hunting together. Do you remember? I had Peritas with me.' The thought of his favourite dog brought a fleeting look of happiness to Philip's face.

'I remember, sire. The hounds brought a fine boar to bay.'

'And we were talking about the same thing.'

Menander saw Philip's mood blackening. 'You hadn't defeated Flamininus a year ago, sire. Atrax may not have won the war, but it revealed the enemy's weakness. On flat terrain, or in a confined space, phalanx can defeat legion.'

'More's the pity that the gods filled Greece and Macedon with mountains, eh?'

They both chuckled.

Philip swept his arm from left to right, over the plain. 'Thessaly has plenty of suitable ground. If Flamininus can be persuaded, or more likely tricked, into battle here, we have a chance of winning.' Despite his combative words, Philip knew he was in a weaker position than before. Shorn of almost every ally, effectively trapped within Macedon, he could do little but await Flamininus' return. That test would be far sterner than the clashes of the summer that had just ended. 'Flamininus is no fool.'

'Sire?'

'To make him deploy his legions here would require a ruse worthy of Zeus himself.'

'The portents have been good of late, sire.'

'The priests' fine words mean little, everyone knows,' said Philip quietly. 'We must make our own fate as best we may. The gods will do what they please, as they always do.'

A short silence followed, and then Philip said, 'There is another possibility that we have not discussed.'

'Sire?'

'Antiokhos.'

'The Seleucid emperor?'

'One and the same.' Antiokhos was the ruler of a vast empire spanning Asia Minor and Syria, all the way to India. No great friend to Philip, they had nonetheless come to secret agreement in the past. 'He will be well aware of Rome's intentions here and in Greece.'

'He's rubbing his hands together, sire, or I'm no judge. Your loss will be his gain – think of your spies' recent messages about his arrangement with the Rhodians. Between them they intend to capture every one of your towns and cities in Asia Minor and the Kyklades Islands.'

Ruefully, Philip admitted, 'That was bound to happen while I am caught up here with Flamininus. What I am thinking of will take Antiokhos' attention from Asia Minor. I will offer him a military alliance against Rome.'

'With respect, sire, he will judge your situation to be, let us say, precarious,' warned Menander. 'Even if he were to agree, is it not likely for him to promise much, deliver on nothing, and watch from a safe distance as the war with Flamininus progresses?'

'Of course it is.'

'In that case, sire, why consider entering into an agreement with him?'

'Even an emperor cannot rest on his laurels, Menander. Antiokhos' forebears lost half their territories to rebellion over the last century. It has taken him years to reconquer them. He must see that Rome's legions – fresh from their victory over Hannibal – are a fearsome enemy. He must also realise that if Macedon falls, Rome's attention will soon wander east, to his empire. Let Antiokhos send but a portion of his army to Greece, and together we would smash Flamininus' legions, thereby protecting his empire.'

Menander stroked his beard, his habit when deep in thought.

'Well?'

'If he agreed, sire, and you beat Flamininus, Antiokhos might then use his foothold in Greece to try and overthrow you.'

'Indeed he might. *That* is only a potential problem, however, whereas Flamininus' legions stand in Phokis this very moment.'

Menander sighed and said, 'If you are sure, sire. I never thought to see the day we allied ourselves with the Seleucids.'

'Nor I, and yet it might work. We have little to lose. If Antiokhos refuses, our situation remains as it is now – precarious. If he agrees, our position would be a good deal stronger, although we would have to be wary of his treachery later.'

'True, sire.' Menander bent his neck in acceptance.

Philip could picture the Thessalian plain filled with an immense phalanx – together, he thought, his and Antiokhos' phalangists could easily number twenty-five thousand.

Flamininus' legions would never stand before it.

CHAPTER III

Inside Elateia

Dawn had broken not long before. It was the second day since the legions' appearance outside the town. Demetrios was standing on the battlements, watching the enemy camp. Sunlight winked off a section of bronze breastplate visible under his cloak. Average in height, well-muscled, he had untidy brown hair and a wide, friendly face. His helmet perched on his *aspis* shield on the walkway; his long sarissa lay parallel with that of his friend Kimon, the next sentry to the left.

Demetrios stamped to and fro. It had been a long, sleepless night. After the success of the catapult burning, everyone had expected the Romans to mount a retaliatory assault; in anticipation, the garrison commander, a solid greybeard named Damophon, had ordered double sentries from sunset to sunrise. Nothing had happened, however.

Demetrios eyed Kimon, who was yawning. 'Your turn to buy the bread?'

'Nice try. It's yours, as well you know.' Kimon had longish hair, and an impressively sized nose. He regarded everyone as his friend until proven otherwise, a characteristic that Demetrios liked, although he did not share it. In his mind, friendship had to be earned over and again.

'No, it isn't,' he retorted. 'Antileon, it must be you.'

Antileon, the third member of their little group, snorted. Tall, brawny and with curly hair, he liked nothing better than to construct an argument from nothing. As Demetrios often said, Antileon would argue with a statue. Despite this tendency, he was brave, and a loyal friend. 'I'll buy it – with your coin.' He held out a meaty paw.

They laughed, glad of the light relief. Victory at Atrax had seen their morale soar; that their speira had been sent to Elateia by Philip himself seemed recognition of their role, but since the arrival of Flamininus' legions, the phalangists' mood had grown solemn. Tartaros beckoned again.

Trumpets sounded in the enemy camp, and Demetrios felt the familiar plucking of fear. Eager not to let it take hold, he admitted, 'You have me. It *is* my turn.'

'As if you were going to get away with pretending it wasn't,' said Kimon as Antileon jeered.

Demetrios had spied their replacements. It was safe to leave his post; eager to keep his mind off the legions beyond the walls, he decided to play a trick on his friends. 'Want me to buy the bread? Catch me,' he challenged, edging past Kimon before there was time to react. He broke into a run.

The pair gave chase at once. Being the furthest away, Antileon was at a disadvantage, but his sheer power soon saw him catch and then outstrip Kimon. Demetrios' head start was whittled away almost at once. The walkway was narrow and, thanks to loose bricks, treacherous underfoot. Every thirty to forty paces was a sentry, not all of whom saw him coming. He dodged around the first few, but a more alert one took him for a thief and grabbed his arm, calling to Kimon and Antileon that he'd caught the bastard.

Demetrios' protests were in vain; it wasn't until the do-gooder saw how hard his friends were laughing that he was able to break free. His lead lost, he was nearly caught then by Kimon, who put on an uncharacteristic burst of speed. Demetrios got away thanks only to a corner tower. Darting through its first door, past a trio of startled men sitting around a glowing brazier, he managed to half-slam the second in Kimon's face.

Along the northern wall they pounded, Demetrios shouting at sentries to get out of his way. A scrawny mongrel, one of the many that lived in the town's alleys, assumed he was after it and shot down a staircase, tail between its legs. Doves scattered into the cool air. A bemused greybeard come to survey the enemy gave him a solemn bow; grinning, Demetrios saluted in reply.

By the time he had cleared the corner tower that spanned the northern and eastern walls, Kimon had given up and fallen away. Antileon continued in grim pursuit, but any time he narrowed the gap, Demetrios broke into a sprint. Sure now that he had won the contest – he would still have to buy the morning's bread, but that didn't matter

– he slackened his pace. It was as well he did. A four-file leader he recognised appeared at the top of the next staircase, about to check on his men. Luckily, the officer's interest was drawn by a large group of Romans marching past the walls. Demetrios was able to saunter past, giving the closest sentry a broad wink.

Confident now, ever more aware of his rumbling belly, he imagined the sweetmeats on sale in his favourite bakery. Although the effect of the siege would soon bite, shortages hadn't yet become apparent. One honeyed pastry each for Kimon and Antileon, and two for him, Demetrios decided. If they wanted more, they could pay out of their own purses.

Reaching the spot where the race had started, he cast an eye towards the Roman camp. Little was going on, thus far anyway. He didn't see Kimon until it was too late. His friend leaped in, grappling him to the walkway. 'Who's the clever one now?' demanded Kimon in triumph.

Demetrios' grin was rueful as he clambered to his feet. 'Not I.'

Antileon arrived and gave him a couple of none-too-gentle kicks. 'Smartarse.'

'Neither of you pricks wants a honeyed pastry? Ah, you *do*?' Demetrios shoved Antileon. 'Best be nice to me then.'

'Here stand the dusty feet, bleating like the sheep they are,' said a voice. 'Nothing changes.'

'Piss off, Empedokles,' said Kimon and Antileon in unison.

'You're late,' sneered Demetrios. It was past the time to be relieved: Empedokles and the others must have been gossiping at the foot of the stairs while he and his friends had been sprinting around the walls.

He watched Empedokles climb, remembering how the wavy-haired, sturdy phalangist had taken against him the first moment they'd met. His dislike had been cemented by Demetrios' surprise victories in two of their five rounds of pankration. Some months later, Empedokles had tried to seriously injure him in training; then Demetrios had almost let Empedokles have his throat cut by thieves in an alleyway. Suffice it to say, thought Demetrios, their relationship had soured from there.

Empedokles looked up, and curled his lip.

'Last time I heard Simonides mention you, Empedokles, he said you were from a farm. That makes you a dusty foot as well,' Demetrios jibed. 'Or was Simonides lying?' Their file-leader was a quiet but ferocious soldier, and not someone to cross.

Empedokles muttered something.

'I didn't catch that,' said Demetrios, noting his friends' encouraging gestures.

'Simonides is no liar.'

'So *you* are a dusty foot too!' crowed Demetrios. He could hear Andriskos and Philippos, the two comrades who'd come with Empedokles, join in the laughter that followed. It warmed Demetrios' heart. Empedokles was one of the four front-rankers in the file, but his sneering, unpleasant manner meant he wasn't popular.

'Listen to the mouthy pup,' cried Empedokles. 'A round or two of pankration would sort you out. Fancy it later?'

'I almost beat you four years ago,' said Demetrios. 'I'm full sure I could now, and at boxing too. Name a time.'

A contemptuous noise. 'Simonides wouldn't allow it.' This was Empedokles' stock answer.

'He doesn't need to find out about it,' Demetrios shot back, pretending that he was not also wary of Simonides' response. Aware of their enmity, their file-leader had banned them from wrestling, boxing or fighting pankration with one another because, he said, the contest would end with someone maimed, or dead.

'Why can't you pair set your differences aside? Almost-neighbours in the file, a common enemy and all that.' Philippos, who was just behind Empedokles, boomed his great belly laugh. A big man with a big heart, he had become a father figure to Demetrios. 'Andriskos and me, we rub along well. Apart from his farts, of course, which I end up breathing every time we're in line.'

Even Empedokles laughed now.

Andriskos, a step below Philippos, grinned but made no attempt to deny Philippos' accusation. An excellent soldier, and handsome, Andriskos stood second in line, behind Simonides; Philippos was next and Empedokles after him. Then came the new quarter-file leader Taurion, the replacement for Dion, who had died at Atrax.

There was *no* chance of friendship, thought Demetrios, glaring at Empedokles glaring at him. Too much had happened. If there was anything to be taken from the unpleasant situation, it was that as sixth-ranker in the file, he stood behind Empedokles rather than the other way around.

It was scant consolation.

Demetrios was not surprised when the trumpets summoned every phalangist to the walls perhaps an hour after his race with Kimon and Antileon. Despite the loss of his catapults – perhaps because of their loss – the Roman general Flamininus was impatient to prosecute the siege. Other factors would also have influenced him. Heavy dew had blanketed every tent at dawn; the damp smell of autumn in the air was undeniable. Great banks of rain-heavy clouds swept in from the sea, a sharp reminder of the changing seasons. If Elateia was to be taken before spring, it had to be done fast.

The trumpets' peal had not faded when Simonides' voice rang out, telling his men to ready themselves at once.

Demetrios relished a final mouthful; he'd saved the sweet cakes until last. 'At least our bellies are full, eh?'

'Aye.' Antileon ran a finger around the plate, picking up the last traces of honey. 'A shame there weren't more.'

'Buy as many as you like for us when it's your turn,' said Kimon, winking at Demetrios.

Good-natured insults filled the air between the friends as they dressed and armed themselves. No one hurried. Whatever Flamininus intended, it would take time for the legions to march out of their camps. Kimon and Antileon wore the mail shirts they had stripped from Roman dead at Pluinna the previous year; simple *pilos* helmets protected their heads. Demetrios had had similar armour, but now he was the proud owner of a fine bronze panoply, a gift from Philip for saving his life.

Soon everyone in the speira was ready. Missing only those on sentry duty, the files formed, *aspides* and still-disassembled sarissae on men's shoulders. Led by their file-leaders, the phalangists tramped from the *agora*, the only space in Elateia large enough to accommodate their tents. Simonides' file had a position on the western wall, the one facing the largest Roman camp.

It was already a familiar walk, first passing the municipal offices and then a temple to Zeus. After came the paved street that led to the west gate; it was lined with businesses. Wine shops and open-fronted restaurants, both popular with the phalangists, stood beside ironmongers' premises and those belonging to potters, carpenters and leather workers.

The pavements were jammed; it seemed the entire population – apart from those already on the walls – had come to watch the phalangists march to the defence of their town. A sombre air prevailed. Some voices called encouragement, but most people just stared. Hunched greybeards muttered to one another. Hairy-chinned crones mumbled prayers, asking the gods for their blessing. Women of childbearing age, whose husbands were part of the garrison, watched in worried silence. Little girls half hid behind their mothers, staring wide-eyed at the intimidating lines of soldiers, while a few of the bolder boys strode beside them, offcuts of wood their pretend sarissae.

The subdued atmosphere was uncomfortable, and it was a welcome relief when a plump old woman shuffled out of the throng to plant wet kisses on any phalangist she could reach. Increasing his pace, Demetrios managed to avoid her clutches, as did the next few men. Kimon could not get away, however. Raucous cheers rose from his comrades as the crone embraced him; he managed a strained smile. Emboldened, she pinched his arse, declaring that if he had a moment later, she'd show him a good time.

The alarming image sent everyone within hearing into uncontrollable laughter; Demetrios and the rest gave Kimon no peace for the rest of the journey to the walls.

'The battle's worth winning just to see you two spend a night together,' Antileon chortled, wiping away tears of amusement.

'I like them well covered,' Kimon grumbled. 'I never said I liked grandmothers.'

The hilarity came to a halt at the top of the stairs, where the speira commander Stephanos was waiting, grim-faced. 'Intersperse yourselves between the townsmen,' he ordered. 'One phalangist to every three locals.'

No one liked being separated from his comrades, but the command made sense. Perhaps one in every ten Elateians was a trained soldier; few faces on the walkway looked anything other than terrified.

The townsmen's apprehension was understandable, thought Demetrios grimly as he found a spot halfway along the wall. The flat ground before the town was packed with the enemy. If even a fraction gained the ramparts, Elateia would fall. They were in dire need of the gods' favour again, yet there seemed no chance of such fortune befalling them. There was every chance that this place would be his graveyard.

His right-hand neighbour, a stout man with a badly fitting linen corslet, was at least ten years older than Demetrios and looked as if he hadn't used his rusty-bladed spear in many years – if ever. The man leaned it against the stonework and stuck out a sweaty hand. 'Eurykleides.'

'Demetrios.' He wrapped an arm around the two parts of his sarissa so they didn't fall, and took Eurykleides' grip.

'Was it this bad at Atrax?'

'It was far worse.'

Eurykleides gave him a disbelieving look. 'There were two thousand of you. We number less than half that.'

'Aye, but there was a cursed great hole in the wall. The Romans had only a short climb to get inside the fortress. With their catapults reduced to piles of ash, here they must rely on ladders and battering rams, if they have them. All *we* have to do is hold the gates and knock them off the walls, into the ditch,' said Demetrios, aware that however scared he might be, Eurykleides was in far worse shape. 'That's what we did for forty days in the Aous valley, and we could have kept doing it if the whoresons hadn't found a way round our defences.' He pulled a confident grin.

Eurykleides looked a little happier for a moment, then his expression grew dubious. 'They can always build more catapults.'

'Of course they can, but look – they're not. Time is against Flamininus. He needs a quick victory, so his men can settle into winter camp without having us at their backs.'

'What if they use the elephants?' Eurykleides shuddered.

Demetrios hadn't liked seeing the great grey beasts either, but he was confident they wouldn't be used here. He shook his head. 'Flamininus will keep them back for more important battles.'

'You think we can win?'

It was quiet on the rampart, and Eurykleides' tremulous voice carried. Men's heads turned.

A year and a half before, Demetrios might have faltered. Not now. A veteran of several brutal battles, a gulf separated him from the likes of

Eurykleides and his fellow townsmen. The awe and respect in the stout man's eyes was proof of this.

'We don't have to win, that's the thing,' Demetrios cried.

'I . . . I don't understand.' Eurykleides looked to the next men along, a spiky-haired type who looked just as nervous as he, and a snaggle-toothed greybeard who looked too arthritic to be on the rampart. He received shrugs by way of reply, and turned back to Demetrios.

'Our task is to stop the bastards from getting inside the walls, nothing more. Throw them back half a dozen times, kill enough of the filth, and they'll soon piss off.' It sounded good, but everyone knew that the number of local towns falling to the legions was growing by the day. There was nothing to say Flamininus wouldn't have new catapults constructed here, as he had before. The defenders' artillery consisted of two poorly maintained bolt throwers. Even if they didn't break, the weapons would wreak few casualties among the enemy. Yet the scared faces watching him needed to believe that all was not lost. Demetrios stared hard at each defender, willing them to believe his words. 'Every Roman out there was at Atrax too, remember. Hundreds of their comrades died there. They won't have the stomach for a prolonged fight. Hold fast – that's all we have to do.'

'Aye.' A light sparked in Eurykleides' eyes. He clapped Spiky Hair on the back and nodded fiercely at the greybeard. 'Aye. Keep them from gaining the rampart. We can do that.'

'That's the spirit,' said Demetrios, relieved that the men further away also seemed a little encouraged. The moment Eurykleides looked away, he caught Kimon's attention with a glance. His friend dipped his chin, to say yes, he understood what Demetrios had done, and that he would do the same, and pass the word on to Antileon, who stood further over to the right. Philippos, who was to Demetrios' left, was already talking to his neighbours.

Demetrios could have kissed the merchant who arrived soon after with a file of slaves in tow. They carried wine for every man atop the rampart. 'A small gesture of thanks,' cried the merchant. His timing couldn't have been better. A more settled air fell. Stephanos was next to make his way around the walls, checking that everyone had assembled his sarissa, and that the long, forked poles he'd ordered were in place. Like the good officer he was, he encouraged and poked fun at his men by turns, and exchanged a few words with each townsman.

'Demetrios.' Kimon's tone demanded attention.

Demetrios looked, and managed not to curse out loud. At Atrax, Flamininus had sent in his allies first, wild Epirote, Illyrian and Dardanian warriors. Only when they failed had the legionaries attacked. Today would be different. The closest units to the walls now were principes – some of the best soldiers in the legions.

Demetrios' father had been fond of saying a man should never plan his future, because each time he did, either the gods or the Fates would intervene. He could have been talking about this exact moment, thought Demetrios bitterly. His words to Eurykleides seemed hollow beyond belief.

Their fate would hang in the balance from the outset.

Another hour passed as the Romans deployed on all four sides of Elateia, proving that Flamininus *was* eager to take it fast. Only when the town was surrounded did the assault begin. Two battering rams presented the most serious threat; one was moved towards the west gate, not far from Demetrios' position, while the other was carried towards the north. Telling himself that fire arrows would see to the rams, and heated sand lay low their crews, Demetrios readied Eurykleides and his companions as best he could.

He had the arthritic greybeard, another Dion, change places with Eurykleides so that he stood directly to Demetrios' right. He had no idea if Eurykleides and Protogenes, the man with spiky hair, would hold their own, but at least they were able-bodied. Dion's breath rattled in his chest, and he struggled to keep his spear upright. A *kopis* in a simple scabbard hung from a baldric over his bony shoulder, although Demetrios doubted he had the strength to wield it.

Demetrios would have sent him down from the walls before the fighting began, but he hadn't the heart after Dion related the story of his son's death at Ottolobus the previous summer.

'A peltast, he was. Fine shot with a spear too.' A bout of phlegmladen coughing. Dion grimaced. 'And a good stonemason too. I do my best, but the workshop isn't the same without him. His wife didn't want me up here, but I told her my son is watching from the other side.

What kind of father or grandfather would I be if I didn't defend his family?'

Demetrios tried to imagine his feelings if he were untrained, like so many here, and had his long-dead mother and father in a house somewhere in the town. It didn't take long to conclude that he too would have been terrified.

'This is my only choice.' Dion fixed his rheumy eyes on Demetrios.

'You're doing the right thing,' said Demetrios, and meaning it. 'I would do the same. Together we will prevail.' Zeus, he prayed, let that be true.

'Here they come,' cried Kimon.

Demetrios licked his lips. In neat ranks, the principes were marching towards Elateia. At a rough estimate, there were three for every man atop the walls. The principes looked calm and determined; they were carrying dozens of ladders. At two hundred paces, the lone catapult on the west wall twanged. Its bolt hummed over the Romans' heads and vanished. The second shot missed as well. Demetrios wanted to shout his frustration. There was no chance of devastating the enemy, as at the Aous, but causing even a few casualties would hearten townsmen and phalangists alike.

Cheers rose as a third bolt punched through a shield and into the *princeps* carrying it. Several more fell to the bolt thrower's missiles, but the ranks of principes reached the defensive ditch looking as neat as if they were on parade. Officers shouted. Teams of men worked the ladders into the ditch, while others clambered down alongside.

Two ladders were about to hit Demetrios' section. Ordering Eurykleides and Protogenes to tackle the rightmost one with the forked pole they shared between them, he told Dion to stand ready for the left-hand one.

'What if a third appears?' asked Dion.

'Do your best to throw it down. Gods willing, you'll manage it. If not, either Eurykleides or I will get to you as fast as we may.' Demetrios turned his sarissa so its point faced downwards. He fed it hand over hand until it hung suspended over the enemy. The nearest principes quailed, and he grinned. The long spear could have been made for defending a wall. Moments later, he pithed the first princeps onto the ladder, but the blade stuck fast in the man's backbone. As he struggled to free it, another princeps reached up and hacked off the tip.

They remember what happened at the Aous, thought Demetrios grimly.

He managed to knock another Roman off the ladder with the splintered stump, but then, in a clearly prepared move, a pair of principes worked together to seize its end and cut off a lengthy piece. Demetrios hurled the ruined sarissa into the ditch with a curse and focused on the ladder instead. There would be no help from Eurykleides and Protogenes; they were still battling to push 'their' ladder out from the wall.

Splinters ran into Demetrios' fingers as he seized the rough-hewn timber, but he paid no heed. The princeps trying to climb was a heavy-boned, meaty individual; it took Demetrios a little time to shake him off. Quickly, he heaved the ladder to one side, watching with satisfaction as it injured a princeps at the base of the wall.

'Another ladder!' Dion's voice shook.

Demetrios darted to the old man's side. The ladder projected three hands' span over the top of the rampart. He grabbed hold and tried to wrench it towards him. Failing, he attempted to push it to the right, but couldn't. Peering over the wall, he saw that Flamininus' men had learned a great deal indeed. The ladder was being held upright on each side by a princeps wielding a forked stick, a shorter version of the poles being used by the defenders. Nothing Demetrios did shifted the ladder more than a few fingers' breadth. Abandoning this tactic, he grabbed Dion's spear and the moment the princeps climbing it was in range, stabbed him.

'Eurykleides!' Demetrios didn't dare take his eyes from the ladder. Another princeps was already two rungs up.

'Aye?'

'How are you faring?'

'Holding our own.' There was a note of pride to Eurykleides' voice.

Dion was babbling about a fourth ladder; Demetrios had seen it from the corner of his eye. Indecision battered him. Abandon his position, and the enemy would gain the rampart. Leave the new one to the frail Dion, who was only armed with his *kopis*, and he risked the same.

'Philippos!' he roared into the din of shouts, screams and from further off, trumpets.

A moment's delay, and then, 'What?'

'I need you!'

There was no answer.

Demetrios went with his gut, deciding that the princeps on Dion's ladder would reach the top before the one on his. He shuffled sideways, leaned out and killed the Roman. Within three breaths, he'd returned to *his* ladder. He was just in time. The princeps there had seen his chance and was already swinging a leg over the rampart. He screamed like a woman when Demetrios' spear skewered his right thigh. Raising his sword to fight back, he left his armpit unprotected. Demetrios tugged free his spear and ran it deep into the man's chest.

His fight had afforded fresh principes the chance to start climbing not just his ladder, but Dion's. Demetrios' skin crawled as he thrust down at the men on his; it was only a matter of time before the attackers timed their ascent so that they reached the top of the wall at the same time. He killed one princeps and injured the second, which made the man at the ladder's foot hesitate. Pulse hammering in his ears, Demetrios went to help Dion, finding to his relief that Philippos had arrived. It made no difference that two principes with forked poles were now supporting the ladder; Philippos was so strong that he had simply wrenched it free. Laughing, he used it to batter the principes with great sideways sweeps, over and back, like a giant swatting rats with a stick.

Using their forked pole, Eurykleides and Protogenes had heaved down another ladder; beyond them, the walkway appeared clear of principes. It was the same to Demetrios' left. In the ditch below, surrounded by their dead and wounded, the principes looked a great deal less determined than they had a short time before. Even better, the faces of the men in as yet undeployed units – those waiting a little distance away – looked unhappy. Wary. Fearful.

Hope flaring in his gut, Demetrios twisted to study the entire rampart. Not a princeps was to be seen. At the base of several staircases, groups of women were hauling wicker baskets of rocks up to the walkway, ammunition to hurl down on the enemy.

A brief grin creased his face. The gods continued to smile on Elateia.

CHAPTER IV

Anticyra on the coast of Phocis, northern shore of the
Corinthian Gulf

The harbour of Anticyra was small. A pair of semicircular walls reaching out from a quay at the town's heart, it held perhaps twenty fishing smacks. Too confined a space for large vessels, it forced the Roman *triremes* now stationed here to tie up just outside the harbour mouth.

Standing atop the tower that guarded one side of the port's narrow entrance, Titus Quinctius Flamininus was feeling impatient. Two days earlier, a report that his elder brother Lucius was leaving an important conference at Sicyon had brought him south. Leaving a senior officer in charge of the siege of Elatea – 'I won't be gone long,' Flamininus had said – he had hurried to Anticyra. Rather than find Lucius waiting, Flamininus had on his arrival that morning been greeted by a flustered trierarch, the officer commanding one of the ships at anchor. His brother was on his way – a letter in the trierarch's possession confirmed it – but when he would reach the port was impossible to say.

Flamininus had opted to remain, when he could have returned to Elatea – a frustrating affair that seemed set to drag on without a successful conclusion. He had chosen to believe the still-flustered trierarch's assurance that Lucius was bound to sail in with the afternoon tide. He hadn't.

Irritated, but more interested in what might have happened at Sicyon than taking yet another shithole town, Flamininus spent the rest of the day catching up on paperwork, penning letters to his many spies in Greece and Italia, as well as a smoothly crafted missive intended to keep the Senate in Rome happy. While the summer's campaign had not all gone his way – Atrax in particular was hard to ignore – it was impossible to deny that many advances had been made. Flamininus had repeatedly cited his successes. He had neglected to include mention

27

of Pluinna – the loss of one and a half thousand legionaries was a flesh wound, not a mortal injury – and underlined the importance of Gomphi fortress, the occupation of which opened a much shorter route for supplies to reach his army.

Lucius still hadn't arrived by sunset, testing Flamininus' patience further. He decided to stay in Anticyra, telling himself that while his brother's timing was rarely good, he *could* be relied on to do what he'd said. Lucius would arrive with news from Sicyon – eventually.

Flamininus returned to his post atop the tower not long after dawn the following day. A short, brown-haired man with protuberant eyes, a long nose and fleshy lips, he had none of his brother Lucius' looks. This had troubled the youthful Flamininus, but no longer. Truth be told, he would not have changed places with Lucius for all the gold in Croesus' treasury. His ruthless determination, unbreakable confidence and a refusal to accept defeat were of far greater value than an Adonis-like physique and a face that made women – or in Lucius' case, men – go weak at the knees.

'Whoring.' Flamininus' tone was distasteful. 'That's what he'll be doing.'

For the umpteenth time, he looked south. Thirty miles away, the coast of the Peloponnese was a brown smear on the horizon, the water between a mass of grey-blue flecked with white. There was little wind; weather hadn't delayed his brother. It was possible, thought Flamininus, that he had been attacked, or laid low by illness, but given his history, it was a great deal more probable that Lucius was dallying with a youth who'd caught his eye.

One day, something Lucius had done would come back to haunt him, Flamininus was sure of it. When that came to pass, he would distance himself from his brother without a qualm. Family ties were important, but not if the price was loss of power and political influence. Nor could his reputation as one of the greatest Romans ever – to be remembered in this fashion was Flamininus' heartfelt desire – be marred. Inevitably, an image of Galba came to mind. His political rival, enemy, and blackmailer, Galba was a sizeable obstacle on his path to everlasting greatness.

Even if Flamininus kept to the terms they'd agreed – a legateship here in Greece for Galba, and the payment to him of vast sums for the next ten years – there was still a risk that the malevolent ex-consul would make public Flamininus' secret and treasonous dealings with the Aetolians. If that happened, his career would come to a premature end; it wasn't impossible that the Senate might order him to commit suicide.

Flamininus had never been one for fighting, but if Galba had appeared in that moment, he would have beaten him to a pulp. Calm yourself, he thought. Brute force might subdue an aggressive dog, but a stealthier approach is required for a snake. Fresh letters of instruction needed to be sent to his spies in Rome. Every man had a weakness, and Galba was no different. It had proven impossible thus far to find his Achilles heel, but persistence paid off. One day, gods willing, he would be at Flamininus' mercy.

His attention drifted to the harbour below, where fishermen held shouted conversations with one another from their boats. Off-duty crewmen from the triremes watched pairs of local youths wrestle on the edge of the quay. Roars of laughter went up as the loser of each bout was unceremoniously tossed into the water. A trio of greybeards squatted on their haunches by the base of the tower, gossiping and repairing nets.

The ordinariness of the scene was reassuring. Life goes on, no matter what, thought Flamininus. A muffled sound from the stairwell made him turn. 'Pasion?'

There was no reply.

'Who's there?' demanded Flamininus, a little unsettled. 'Pasion?'

He hurried to the opening that communicated, via a wooden ladder, with the tower's interior. On hands and knees, he peered into the guardroom below, a simple chamber with bunk beds, a brazier, a table and chairs. There was no sign of anyone, least of all his Greek secretary. It must have been a rat, Flamininus decided, glad that no one had witnessed his unease but wondering if his impulsive decision to leave his escort at the tower's base had been wise.

What are you, he asked himself, an old woman?

Pretending that his heart wasn't beating a little faster than normal, he stood and smoothed down his tunic. Another study of the horizon revealed no sails. His enjoyment dampened, his irritation at Lucius simmering, Flamininus decided he'd wasted enough time. His brother would arrive no sooner whether he stood on the tower or sat at his desk, and doing the latter would keep Pasion off his back.

Flamininus felt a flicker of amusement. His secretary was a slave, but by the gods, he could be as annoying as a nagging wife. And as every sensible man knew, the best way to placate an unhappy wife was to accede to their demands.

Several hours later, Flamininus was at his evening meal in his tent. Night had not yet fallen; most Romans would not dine so early, but of recent years he had found that eating late gave him terrible indigestion. Various surgeons had been unable to remedy this affliction; by a process of experimentation, Flamininus had found this simple solution. In Rome, he often *had* to eat in the evening, formal dinners being the most common reason, but here he could suit himself.

As usual, his cook had done a fine job. The fish – sole, mullet and sardines – decorating the large platter at the centre of the table could not have been fresher. Lightly fried in oil with herbs, their white flesh was succulent and delicious. Boiled greens, something he had grown to like only in adulthood, made a fine accompaniment, and crusty, just-baked bread served well to mop up the juice left on his plate. A large cup of Caecuban washed it all down.

Flamininus eyed the jug, wanting more. He held off. It was too easy when on his own to drink more than was good for him. Although there was little that could happen in Anticyra – fresh news from Elatea would not arrive before the morn, and of Lucius there was no sign – he was at war. It was best he remain in full command of his senses, just in case. This resolve lasted long enough for Flamininus to consider that there was nothing to do apart from paperwork – his efforts had only reduced the mound on his desk – or retiring to his bed.

Curse it all, thought Flamininus, I deserve another cup. He poured a healthy measure, and then with a shrug, the same again.

'Master.' Pasion was framed in the entrance to the dining area.

'Enter.' Flamininus beckoned.

Pasion came closer, his eyes moving as they always did at such times, to the food on the table. 'A ship is approaching the harbour, master.'

Flamininus held in his excitement. 'What direction does it come from?'

'The south, master.'

'It's Lucius – it must be.' Flamininus permitted himself a little smile. 'How long until it docks?'

'Soon, master.'

'Bring him to me the moment he disembarks. No visit to a tavern, or anything else. Understand?'

'Master.' Pasion vanished as unobtrusively as he'd arrived.

Flamininus heard Lucius' voice long before he saw him. His brother was complaining about how tired he was, and how hungry and thirsty. Throwing back the last of his wine, Flamininus filled his cup and one for Lucius.

'There you are!' Lucius came striding in, cheeks reddened by the wind, his hair tousled. 'Is all well?'

Flamininus gave him a frosty look. 'The conference at Sicyon ended some days since.'

'What way is that to greet your brother? I've been travelling for two days.' Without asking, Lucius swept up the second cup and drained it. 'Not bad.' He poured another; eyeing Flamininus, he asked, 'Need a top-up?'

'No,' snapped Flamininus. 'What took you so long? Didn't you know I would be here, waiting for you?'

A vague, apologetic gesture. 'I was worn out. You know how boring politicking is, and gods, the Greeks love the sound of their own voices even more than Romans. I spent one night on the wine after the conference ended, that's all.' Lucius made a face. 'It took a day to recover, but that couldn't be helped.'

'Jupiter's prick, Lucius!'

Now a shrug. 'I'm famished.' Lucius sat and began loading food onto a plate.

Flamininus ground his teeth, but to demand more information straight away would prolong the agony. He watched in silence as Lucius ate his fill. Only when his brother had finished did he speak. 'Is your news good?'

'The fish is tasty.' A belch. A smirk. 'Apologies, brother. You wish to hear my tidings.'

'I do,' said Flamininus drily.

Lucius drained his cup. He stared at Flamininus, daring him to demand he reveal the details of the Sicyon conference, where the leaders of Achaea, a powerful city state on the Peloponnese, had met to discuss their future.

Flamininus refused to lose his temper. To play coy and then reveal that his news was bad would be too much, even for his wastrel brother. Showing none of his impatience, he said, 'Tell me.'

'My pleasure. It was clear from the outset that the Achaeans were beset by indecision. An hour spent in one of the better taverns – there weren't many, I can tell you – soon revealed that to a man, they felt caught between a rock and a hard place. Men were saying that if Achaea remained neutral, we Romans might prevail on Nabis of Sparta to join us.'

Flamininus made an amused gesture of acknowledgement.

'The presence of my fleet at Cenchreae has sharpened their aware-ness of how easily Rome could strike at Achaea. And then they had Philip to consider – their ally of old, and someone to whom many still feel obligated. The king of Macedonia is a good friend, and a bad enemy, I heard more than one man say.'

Flamininus chuckled. 'The same might be said of Rome.'

'True,' agreed Lucius with a smirk. 'When the assembly convened, our envoy Lucius Calpurnius was given the floor first. He waxed lyrical about the benefits of joining with Rome and its allies. Fight Philip to-gether, he said, and he will soon fall. When it was Philip's ambassador's turn, he spoke much of the old, long-standing alliance between Achaea and Macedonia. His speech went down well, but the Athenian envoy spoke last, in order that his honeyed words did not linger in men's minds. An entire day went by in this fashion, and gods, my arse hurt by the end of it.' Lucius leered. 'Because I sat from sunrise to sunset, you see – it wasn't for the usual reasons.'

'Spare me.'

Lucius sat back, allowing Pasion, who had reappeared with a fresh jug of wine, to refill his cup. After a large mouthful, he sighed with contentment. 'You have always had good taste, brother. Caecuban?'

'You know it is,' said Flamininus, but he was pleased.

'The second day's proceedings had to be seen to be believed. The Achaean assembly members were given the floor. This was their oppor-tunity to discuss their thoughts of the various emissaries' contributions, and to come to a decision.'

'And?'

'Not a man stood forward.'

'Eh?'

'After the herald spoke, beginning the proceedings, silence fell. Men looked at one another. You could have heard a needle drop.'

'No one wanted to be the first to make his opinion known,' said Flamininus, guessing. 'Children act thus – many adults are the same.'

'Even so. A decision had to be made, however. The Achaean general Aristaenus harangued his fellows for a time, and still none would speak. Frustrated, Aristaenus repeated the offers made by the various envoys the previous day. The benefits of joining with Rome and its allies were clear. Although old ties linked them to Macedonia, Philip was in no position to offer them anything more than words, barricaded as he is behind Tempe. Why, Aristaenus asked, should they answer Philip's request for troops when he could not offer them the same, to counter the threat of the Roman fleet at Cenchreae and the legions close to Achaea's borders? It was more important for Achaea to concern itself with its own interests. To reject the alliance offered them would be madness. Far better, Aristaenus said, to have Rome as a friend than an enemy.'

'That swayed them, surely?'

'So you might think. And you'd be wrong.'

Flamininus could not hold in his surprise. 'They rejected our offer?'

'A ballot was taken, which resulted in a draw. Five of the ten senior magistrates voted for Achaea to ally itself with Rome, and five against, for fear, they said, of breaking the terms of their agreement with Philip. The arguments around this went on for the rest of the day.' Lucius made a face. 'I could take no more. Retiring to an inn, I left Calpurnius to monitor the fools.'

Flamininus rolled his eyes, although he suspected his own patience would have been tested to the limit by the Achaeans' inability to agree. 'I take it that matters came to a head on the third day?'

'Indeed.' Lucius' tone was droll. 'The representatives of the three cities with the strongest links to Macedonia refused to go back on their word, and stormed out of the assembly. With their departure, the vote for an alliance with Rome was carried at last.'

'I swear the Greeks would argue with one another on the threshold of Hades.' Flamininus raised his cup to Lucius. 'But the result is what we wished for, so I suppose we must be thankful. The Achaean army . . .?'

'Is being mobilised even as we speak. Two to three thousand hoplites and several hundred cavalry will be at your disposal.'

'Excellent,' said Flamininus with a smile. 'I have a task for you, brother – the Achaeans can help you achieve it.'

Compared to Flamininus, Lucius was poor at concealing his emotions. He leaned forward, eyes glinting. 'Tell me.'

Instead Flamininus began a protracted explanation of his tactics for the following spring. The more impatient Lucius looked, the slower he went.

'Point made, brother,' said Lucius when he was done. 'I annoyed you by holding back with my news. You have done the same to me. Are you going to keep me in the dark for ever?'

Flamininus' lips twitched; this banter reminded him of their childhood, when Lucius had always got the better of him. No longer, he thought. 'I want you to besiege Corinth.'

'Corinth?' Lucius looked delighted.

'It will be a tough nut to crack. Take it, however, and we protect ourselves from surprise attacks to the south. The capture of one of the "Fetters of Greece" will humiliate Philip too, even more than the loss of the garrison and his influence over the Peloponnese. He will be incandescent to hear of Corinth's fall.'

'An enemy who loses his temper is prone to make mistakes.'

'You're not just a pretty face, brother,' jibed Flamininus. 'Or a wine sack.'

Lucius seemed about to come back with a biting retort, but thought better of it.

They exchanged a not entirely friendly glance.

Lucius was the first to look away, leaving Flamininus content.

As the elder of the two, it would have been usual for Lucius to be more senior – the consul, in this case – but he had little of Flamininus' ambition and even less of his ruthlessness. Lucius was a lover of wine and of flesh, a debauch who, from time to time, needed to know his place.

Which was precisely the lesson he had just delivered, thought Flamininus.

A discreet cough. 'Master?'

Pasion might have been listening to their conversation – in all like-lihood, he had been, but Flamininus didn't care. 'What?'

'I have a letter for you, master.'

'At this hour?' His senses a little dulled by the wine, it took Flamini-nus several heartbeats for the significance to sink in. He beckoned to his secretary. 'Where did it come from?' he asked, hating the sugges-tion of a high note in his voice.

'I don't know, master. I went to answer a call of nature. Upon my return, it was on my desk.' Pasion shuffled forward, a wooden message tablet in his hands.

Flamininus seized it. He longed to smash the thing into pieces, but he couldn't bring himself to. Galba, he thought. It's from that whore-son Galba. The noise at the tower earlier must have been his agent: I disturbed him before he could leave the letter there. It was one explan-ation, but Flamininus could not put from his mind the disturbing notion that the noise maker could have been someone like Benjamin. Galba's Judaean slave had seemed harmless, yet he had slain Flamini-nus' huge bodyguard Thrax with ease.

'Are you going to open it?' Lucius' voice, a little concerned.

Flamininus gave his brother a brittle smile. Breaking the wax seal – unmarked – he opened the tablet.

Atrax was a disaster. Now you waste time on Elatea, a town of no importance. Time marches on; Philip remains unde-feated. Must I stand at your shoulder to see this war brought to a successful conclusion? Remember: I am watching.

The note had no signature, just like the one Flamininus had received just over a month before at Gomphi. It was from Galba, of that there could be no doubt. He has men in my camp, thought Flamininus. How else can these letters be delivered to my very door?

'Brother?'

Flamininus did not respond. Hard as stone, his eyes slid to Pasion, who was hovering before him. 'This was on your desk, you say?'

'Yes, master.' Pasion's throat worked.

Could Galba have got to Pasion? Flamininus wondered. The Greek had been with him for years; he had come to rely on him as few others, freeborn or no. He was part of his household. Flamininus crushed the sentiment at once. Only a fool would think of slaves as trustworthy; Pasion *had* to be behind the letter's delivery. Who else could have sneaked past his sentries? The circumstances of the previous letter's delivery had also been odd. Flamininus observed the beads of sweat on Pasion's brow, and his suspicion hardened.

'What's in the letter, brother?' asked Lucius.

Never taking his gaze off Pasion, Flamininus tossed the tablet across the table.

'It's from Galba?' Lucius was aware of the ex-consul's hold over Flamininus, although not its full degree.

'Yes.'

'Cocksucker.' Despite the appositeness of the oath to himself, there was no trace of irony in Lucius' voice. 'His agents must be invisible to deliver them without being seen by a soul.'

'They must.' Flamininus jerked his head, dismissing a pale-faced Pasion. It was late, and he had not the energy to supervise a torture session. It mattered not if Pasion were to inform Galba that Achaea had allied itself with Rome; there was little else he could do before morning.

After a good night's sleep, Flamininus decided, he would see the ministrations of his bodyguards make Pasion sing like a bird. Or perhaps he would observe Pasion discreetly for a time, as a hawk hovers unseen over its prey. With the year's campaign almost at an end, there was no need to make a premature move.

Well-laid traps caught the most prey.

CHAPTER V

Corinth

Down the dusty track along the isthmus that linked the Peloponnese to Greece, an army was on the march. Southward it had come from Elatea, one legion of Flamininus' four, sent to help Lucius attack Corinth. The consul had acted the moment he'd returned from Anticyra five days prior; abandoning the attack on Elatea, he had moved to take other towns in Phocis, many of which were making overtures of peace. It was Felix's and Antonius' bad fortune to serve in the unit chosen to go south. Instead of easy marches between towns with open gates, they were wearing down their hobnails, eating once a day at best, and heading for yet another siege.

After the scouts and cavalry came the *hastati*, and then the principes and *triarii*. Losses since the spring had seen the principes' numbers whittled from a shade over eleven hundred to somewhere under nine hundred. These casualties weren't all dead – close to half were wounded. A decent number would return to the fight after the winter, but others still hovered somewhere between this world and the next in various makeshift hospitals left in the army's wake.

Felix and Antonius were marching close to the front of the principes. Recommended for promotion by Livius after he'd spotted the attack on the catapults, Felix was now a *tesserarius*. It had been a popular decision; indeed plenty of men had told him they thought it was long overdue. They didn't know that he had tried to refuse, or that Livius had laughed in his face and written the official document anyway. 'You can't keep a good soldier down,' Livius had said, and Felix had grimaced and thanked him, and prayed that the promotion would not cause someone to remember him from Scipio's army, and how Matho had had him and Antonius dishonourably discharged. Thus far, things had gone well, and he could only hope they continued to do so.

'We must have walked the length of fucking Greece by now,' said

37

Felix. 'Any further and we'll be at Olympia.'

'I've always wanted to see it,' said Dordalus, one of four men from another contubernium that had been amalgamated with theirs. 'Pity the games aren't on. What a sight they would be.'

Coming from Dordalus, a self-confessed pimp in Rome before he'd joined the legions, this was revelatory. Hoots of derision followed the comment, and Dordalus, a pock-faced individual with one blue eye and one brown, glowered.

'Here's me thinking your only concern was ploughing women, or should I say, selling women to be ploughed,' said Periplectomenus, another addition to the tent group. Quick-witted, but shorter than most and scrawny to boot, he was a natural target for bullies. In the short time since Felix and Antonius had known him, he'd been beaten up twice by men from other units. Periplectomenus, or Peri as he was known, waited until the laughter had died down before crowing, 'But no, you're an athlete too!'

More laughter and crude jokes followed.

'Fancy your chances at the wrestling or boxing?' Felix eyed Sparax and Clavus, the last additions to the contubernium. Sparax, whose name meant 'Mangler', and his close friend Clavus, whose name translated as 'Nail', were two bruisers from the roughest part of the Esquiline in Rome. Sparax had cauliflower ears and was a lot larger than Clavus, but both had the look of men who knew their way around an alley fight – Clavus wore two daggers rather than the usual one. 'You're twice the size of any Greeks I've seen, Sparax,' said Felix. 'You at least would place.'

'It'th not all about thize, thir.' At odds with his fearsome appearance, Sparax had a lisp. Few men were foolish enough to mention it – the last who had, a man from another century, had ended up one dark night with a broken arm and two black eyes. 'Technique is jutht ath important.'

'He's not wrong, sir,' rumbled Clavus. Blue-eyed, with dark brown, almost black hair, he had a small scar on the back of his right hand. He chuckled. 'I'd still fancy my chances, or Sparax's.'

'Non-Greeks are forbidden from taking part, as well you know.' Livius had materialised alongside their rank. 'Barbarians, they call us. And them, the ones who run, box and wrestle naked!'

Everyone laughed, but Felix caught Dordalus and Clavus exchanging a look. It added to his suspicion that there was more to their friendship than met the eye. The fact that they lay beside each other in the tent wasn't unusual, but he'd spied them sloping out of camp twice during the march from Elatea. Felix didn't care what they did in private, but if another officer found out – or even an ordinary soldier – the pair would be beaten within a hair of their lives, perhaps worse. He resolved to have a word about being less obvious.

'Look, brothers.' Livius was pointing to the south. 'There it is. Corinth.'

The jokes died away.

Thanks to their current elevation, the principes could see how, pinched in by the sea on both sides, the isthmus narrowed to just a few miles' width. Occupying a site where the land opened out again stood the city of Corinth. Even at a distance, the long wall marked by regular towers was an impressive sight. So too was the great rock of the Acrocorinth, the stronghold towering south of the centre; it defended the city from all comers.

'That's a big bastard of a fortress,' said Antonius, voicing the thought in everyone's heads.

Sensing the mood waver, and aware of his new position as a junior officer, Felix jumped in. 'None of that! There are four armies to lay siege to the place. Us, the crews from Flamininus' brother's fleet, the Achaeans and the Pergamenes. Word has it that there's no love lost between the Corinthians and the Macedonian garrison. A couple of good assaults and we'll take the place, you mark my words.'

The principes rumbled their pleasure at this prospect.

Felix wasn't sure if he was right, but keeping up morale was vital. Pullo had been good at doing that – even Matho had. And Livius, who was giving him an approving nod, knew its importance too. Felix grinned.

Whatever happened, he decided, they were together. Despite being a tesserarius now, he was still a comrade to his friends, and to the rest of the century.

By the time the sun was falling in the sky, and the air growing chill, the legion had set up camp close to the position occupied by the sailors and marines on the eastern side of the city. Five miles away at Cenchreae on the isthmus' eastern coastline, the Roman fleet lay at anchor. To the west, Attalus and his soldiers were attacking from Corinth's second port, Lechaeum, where their ships were moored. The freshly mobilised Achaeans had encamped in and around the road that led from the city to Sicyon. As Livius jubilantly declared, the Corinthians and their Macedonian garrison were surrounded by land and sea.

This welcome news bolstered the principes' morale, but there was little merriment around the fires that night. The imposing defences looked impregnable. Thorn hedges stood in front of each of the two deep defensive ditches, the first of which lay two hundred paces from the walls. The second was situated much closer. Not only were there catapults on top of the frequent towers; wooden-shuttered slits indicated the presence of more artillery. Hades would stalk among them on the morrow. Cackling evilly, Fortuna would roll her dice to determine who fell and who didn't, and so the principes concentrated on ordinary things: a good supply of fallen timber for their fire; eating a hot meal. They drank wine to dull the fear, but reminded by a newly responsible Felix, not so much that they'd have pounding heads at dawn.

Sleep evaded Felix for a lot of the night. Each time he did drop off, his old nightmare returned, the occasion when he, Antonius and their comrades had been subjected to the *fustuarium*. It had been a cruel irony that Ingenuus had been the least suited to army life among them. Horrific scenes filled Felix's mind over and again; his ears rang with screams and pleas for mercy.

Bathed in sweat, he jerked back to reality. In that moment, he would have given everything in his possession to forget Ingenuus' bloodshot eye, framed by strands of gore-sticky hair, staring at him. The image was seared into Felix's mind, however, deeper than any slave brand could go. He sucked in a ragged breath. Forgive me, brother, he asked silently. I wanted only to end your suffering. He felt no better after the prayer. Fed by the sneaking awareness that he would do the same again if forced to, Felix had concluded long since that his guilt was deserved. The alternatives – refusing, even killing Matho – would have resulted in his own death, and like as not, those of Antonius and the rest of his comrades.

'Night terrors, sir?' whispered a voice.

Felix started. He lay closest to the tent's entrance, at right angles to it. Antonius' spot was beside him, and *he* hadn't moved. 'Who's that?' Felix muttered.

'Peri, sir.'

In the silence that followed, Felix warred with himself. If his slain comrades had been aware of his nightmares, they had never said. Antonius knew, but he was Felix's brother. Now it seemed Peri had also realised. Felix didn't want to be thought of as weak. He was an officer now, and an impression of being strong at all times was vital. Before he had decided how to cut Peri down to size, however, his comrade spoke again.

'I get them too, sir.'

Feeling a little sympathy, Felix raised himself up on an elbow. In the gloom, all he could see of Peri across Antonius' slumbering form was the whites of his eyes. 'Aye?'

'Ever since Antipatreia. The things I saw there–' Peri's voice caught '–*you* know what it was like, sir.'

'I do.' Felix threw up a prayer that the girl he'd rescued was still alive, and that she hadn't been driven mad by her savage ordeal. 'Zama did it to me.' The lie wasn't so far from the truth. That battle had been the most brutal he'd ever fought.

'You killed an elephant there, sir.' There was a trace of awe in Peri's voice.

'My brother talks too much when he's drunk.' Fresh worries coursed through Felix. There were few veterans who could claim to have done such a thing; if the wrong person heard the story, he and his brother could be found out. He tried not to think about crucifixion, one punishment for men who rejoined the legions after being dishonourably discharged. It was even worse than the fustuarium.

'Is it true, though, sir?' Peri again.

'Venus' cleft, will you two shut up?' Antonius' sleep-fuddled voice, irritated.

Perhaps a hundred heartbeats went by. Antonius' snoring grew louder than ever.

Peri hissed, 'Is it, sir?'

'Inquisitive, aren't you?' retorted Felix. 'I did, aye, and it's no one's business but mine. Tell a soul, and I'll cut your balls off and stuff them down your throat.'

At dawn, Felix made sure to pin Peri with a vicious stare the first chance their gazes crossed. Peri gave him a cowed nod that said, my lips are sealed. Felix drew a thumb across his throat to underline the point and left it at that. Crouched around the fire, spooning down mushy, bland barley porridge – all they had to eat – he studied his comrades' faces for an indication that they had overheard the murmured conversation. If any had, they were experts at concealing it. Even when Antonius grumbled about being woken by Felix and Peri, the only responses were chuckles and comments about the foul bastard who'd been farting in the tent.

'They're a low lot, sir. Solid, though.' Livius rounded the corner of their tent, accompanied by a short, ruddy-faced man with a distinctly rounded head. Without a helmet or armour, it was hard to know his exact rank, but his tunic was of a finer cut than any ordinary soldier's. His fat lips were fixed in a sneer.

'On your feet!' barked Livius.

Felix and the rest scrambled up into a line and, nervous, saluted Livius and the stranger.

'This, maggots, is your new centurion.' Livius leered at their surprise. 'Gaius Atilius Bulbus.'

'Sir!' They all saluted again, and shot curious glances at Bulbus.

Bulbus paced along in front of the principes, looking down his long nose at each. 'They can fight, you say?' he asked Livius in a gravelly tone.

'Aye, sir. Three have been with the century since Apollonia. The other four have only been with us for a few days, but their previous centurion spoke well of them.'

'Even when at war, personal appearance continues to be of importance.' Bulbus' forefinger poked at the large, irregular discoloured area on the belly of Fabius' tunic. 'What is *this*?'

Fabius looked alarmed. 'Err, a stain, sir.'

Bulbus' *vitis*, which he'd been holding by his side, came up lightning fast. He struck Fabius on the head so hard that his knees buckled. 'Do you take me for a fool?'

'I . . . No, sir,' slurred Fabius.

'Explain it then.' Bulbus' voice cracked like a whip.

'It's a wine stain, sir.'

This time, Bulbus drove his vitis into the offending mark, and behind it, Fabius' gut. He smiled a thin smile as Fabius bent double, retching. 'Next time I see you, your tunic had best be clean.' Bulbus moved to stand in front of Clavus. 'Ugly bastard, you are, but at least

42

your garment is cleanish. Where's your helmet? Your mail?'

Hades, thought Felix as Clavus hurried to find his kit. We've got a kit-polisher for a centurion. He was right. Clavus was beaten because of rust spots on his mail, Sparax because a helmet strap had been repaired with a knot instead of renewed. The dull sheen to Peri's scabbard earned him several blows of the vitis. Antonius, a stickler for keeping his equipment and weapons in good order, escaped Bulbus' attention – there was no praise, however – and then it was Felix's turn.

'This is the new tesserarius, sir,' said Livius.

Bulbus stared at Livius. 'New?'

Livius explained what Felix had done.

Bulbus didn't look impressed. He peered at Felix as closely as he had done the rest.

By pure coincidence, Felix had cleaned his gear the night before; the mind-numbing task a way not to think about the impending assault. He took relish, therefore, as Bulbus poked and prodded at his mail shirt, helmet, sword and shield to no avail. Search away, Felix thought.

'Lift up your right foot!'

Surprised, Felix didn't react at once. Bulbus' vitis clattered him across the face, making him see stars. Swaying, he lifted his sandal-clad foot. The onion-headed prick is checking the hobs, thought Felix. The bastard is treating me no differently from the rest of the men.

'Look!' crowed Bulbus. 'That's two, three missing hobnails! Lift the other foot.'

Resigned – he knew the left sandal was a little worse – Felix obeyed.

'Four hobnails gone.' Bulbus swept the vitis sideways. It made meaty contact with Felix's calf.

Felix gasped with pain; unsteadied, he would have fallen but for Antonius' arm.

'What kind of tesserarius doesn't maintain his footwear?' Bulbus was right in his face; there was wine on his breath. 'What kind of officer do you call yourself?'

'A bad one, sir.' Felix took care to stare straight ahead. Onion Head, he thought. That shall be your name from now on.

'Correct.'

Half a dozen vicious swipes of the vitis came next, on Felix's shoulders, arms and head. He staggered, but managed to stay standing. Aware that men like Bulbus needed no excuse to deliver further punishment, he pulled himself upright the instant the last blow landed and came to attention as best he could.

'You're all on sentry duty for the next ten nights,' declared Bulbus with a curl of his lip. 'And a twenty-mile march every day that we're not fighting.' He turned to Felix. 'The only reason you're not demoted to the ranks is because I'm in a good mood.' To Livius, he said, 'If the rest of the men are as poor as this shower, I've been given the worst century in the whole legion. Lead on.'

Livius, who had never been insistent on spit and polish, kept his face blank. 'If you'll follow me, sir.'

Felix and his comrades watched in silence as the men in the next tent received the same treatment. Wary of the long ears possessed, it seemed, by every centurion under the sun, they said not a word until Bulbus was fifty paces and more away.

Then the tirade began; their new centurion was cursed high and low. By rights, Felix's new position meant he should have put a stop to it, but, incensed, he did no such thing. Unsurprisingly, he wasn't the only one to think of the nickname 'Onion Head' for Bulbus. It caused much hilarity, which Felix didn't join in with. As he muttered to Antonius, they seemed to be cursed with disciplinarians for centurions. Matho, who'd hounded them from the legions, hadn't cared about kit shining like new-minted coins, but he'd been a brutal taskmaster. Bulbus could have been his brother, or his cousin.

Once again, they had worries close to home – as well as the enemy – to contend with. The brothers' old worry, that their illegal re-enlistment might be found out, was once again in the forefront of their minds.

A day of back-breaking toil and death passed. Every soldier in the legion played his part, for to reach the walls, the ditches had first to be filled. That meant felling trees, chopping off the branches and hauling the trunks in wagons to where they were needed. Watched by the enemy, the Romans came under attack the moment they began to cut gaps in the thorn hedges. The wooden screens they'd built for this purpose afforded some protection, but direct hits, particularly from the stone-throwing catapults, wreaked a heavy toll. The first ditch was filled despite these setbacks, and the legionaries pressed through a vicious artillery barrage to the second. Bulbus' men weren't alone in seeing their initial efforts a miserable failure; waiting until the ditch was almost full of timber, the defenders poured down oil, and after, threw lit torches. Mocking laughter echoed from the walls as flames rose to the sky. Hours were then wasted as seawater was hauled from the coast to soak their remaining stocks of wood.

By sundown, their toil and the blood they'd shed had finally yielded results. Along the legion's allocated section of Corinth's wall, seven 'bridges' provided uneven but relatively solid access over the second ditch. Guards were set over them after dark, and when the inevitable enemy attempts to destroy the 'bridges' came through the postern gates hours later, they were beaten back with heavy casualties.

At dawn, the Roman attack began in earnest. Armed with a battering ram borrowed from Lucius Quinctius Flamininus' sailors, Bulbus' principes advanced to the base of the wall, pounded at every step by the enemy bolt throwers and catapults. Close in, they were subjected to rocks and bricks dropped from above, as well as lethal showers of hot sand.

After the ill luck of gaining Bulbus as their new centurion, the capricious Fortuna smiled on his men during this assault. Their casualties – five dead, seven injured – were lighter than in other centuries, perhaps because their task was to shield the principes wielding the bronze-headed ram rather than climbing the ladders. Success came sooner than they'd expected too. Sharp-eyed, Bulbus had noticed a hairline fissure in the wall and directed the ram's attentions to the stonework below. Ominous cracking sounds after a dozen blows were a portent of things to come. The ram's twentieth impact saw large sections of masonry collapse in a great cloud of dust. A dozen more, and the entire section of wall gave way. Screams rose from defenders who'd been trapped or injured in the fall. Their fellows watched in horror from the broken walkway on either side; the artillery fell silent.

'This is your chance, men!' shouted Bulbus.

Oddly for a centurion, and a disciplinarian at that, he never seemed to curse. It was as if, Felix maintained, he thought himself too good to sully his fat lips with bad language. 'The onion-headed cunt,' Felix would add, to the amusement of his close comrades. He took care not to use the insult in front of anyone else in the century.

Bulbus, who was standing behind a screen, pointed with his sword. 'Up!'

'Here we go,' muttered Felix, willing away his nausea, wishing he could take a piss.

'Just like Atrax,' said Sparax, his face working.

'Shut your trap!' Livius came stalking among them. Like everyone, he was coated in dust, the horsehair crest on his helmet turned a dull grey, but he exuded energy. 'It's a bastard of a job, but it's *our* job. Let's get it over with. The faster we get up there, the more chance of success.' Without a backward look, he began clambering up the fallen masonry.

Felix threw himself forward with an oath. Antonius and the rest were with him. The remainder of the century followed, but not Bulbus. He stayed where he was, shouting encouragement.

Peri prayed as he climbed: 'Mars, protect me. Mars, protect me.' Sparax and Clavus stuck close together. Dordalus, wily, climbed behind them. Despite his age, Fabius kept up with Felix and Antonius. 'I'm old, but not done yet,' he declared to the world at large.

'First to take a section of city wall gets a *corona muralis*,' Livius called over his shoulder. 'I've always wanted one—'

Felix had been glancing from the rampart to his feet and back, trying not to fall while watching out for the enemy. An odd, choking sound drew his attention; he glanced at Livius. To his horror, an arrow had driven through both the optio's cheeks. Not a lethal wound – at least, immediately – the agony of it still caused Livius to drop his sword. An instinct for survival made him hold onto his shield, raise it towards the archer who'd shot him. A second shaft thunked into the layered wood, and Livius staggered.

'Come on!' shouted Felix, memories of Pullo tearing at his conscience, when he had been powerless to do anything. 'To Livius!' Fear powered his legs; he heaved himself up beside the optio within a few heartbeats. 'You're all right, sir. The surgeon will soon have it out.' If we ever get to the cursed surgeon, he thought.

Another arrow dinked off a rock close to his head.

Felix wanted to help Livius to safety, but someone had to lead the attack, or men would hesitate, and when that happened, men died. He locked eyes with Antonius, on the other side of Livius. 'Someone's got to take him down.'

'I'm coming with *you*, brother,' muttered Antonius.

'I'll look after him.' Sparax's voice, just behind them. 'You can lean on me, thir.'

It was up to him now, thought Felix. This is what being an officer was about. He quickly checked that the remainder of his comrades were with him – dust-coated, shields held high, it was hard to tell, but they seemed to be – and left Sparax to it. Hobs scraping on the irregular footing, left knee smarting and missing a gouged-away chunk of skin, he clambered towards the breach. An arrow shot overhead; there was a yelp as it hit someone to Felix's rear. Balls tight with fear, knowing the archer's next effort could strike *him*, he peeked around the side of his shield. Thunk. The force of the strike halted him in his steps. His gaze moved; an arrow had lodged in the shield's edge, three fingers' breadth from his face.

Felix could see the archer now: a slim figure perched atop the breach. He was close, no more than a dozen steps upward. 'Bastard!' shouted Felix in Greek, adding in Latin, 'I'm going to gut you, arse-humper!'

His scare tactic worked. After loosing another shaft that shot wide, the archer scrambled to safety on the nearest walkway.

Panting with relief, and not a little fear – there were other archers shooting from the walls, and spearmen too – Felix worked his way towards the top of the shattered wall. ''Tonius?'

'Three steps behind you,' called his brother. 'Dordalus has taken an arrow in the leg, but the others are here. The rest of the century is too, bar a few.'

It's not so bad, thought Felix, taking heart. There are no phalangists with sarissae inside. We'll carve a way through, one way or another.

'Ready, brothers?' shouted a voice on the other side of the breach.

'Aye!' came the answering roar.

'With me!'

Latin. They're speaking Latin, thought Felix in confusion. ''Tonius! D'you hear that?' He twisted.

'Aye.' Lines of sweat had streaked through the dust coating Antonius' face. 'Romans, here?'

Together they neared the top. Swearing profusely, Fabius was at their backs, followed by Peri and Clavus.

Rocks moved. Hobnails clashed. Men hauled themselves into sight, formed a line along the breach.

'Fuck,' said Felix, not believing what he was seeing.

'That's right, cocksucker,' shouted one of the principes facing him – it seemed impossible, but *that* is what they were. 'We speak Latin.'

'Romans?' cried Peri, his face a pasty grey.

'You should be fighting with us, not the arse-humping Greeks!' roared Antonius.

The leader, an optio by his helmet crest, sneered. 'We Bruttians burnt that bridge a long time ago, didn't we, brothers?'

His men bellowed in reply.

Like much of southern Italia, Bruttium had gone over to Hannibal during the war, Felix remembered. The conflict might have ended, but Bruttians who'd fought in the Carthaginian army would receive short shrift from any Roman, which is probably why these men were fighting for Macedonia. Nonetheless, their behaviour rankled – it felt wrong. 'A cross each is what you'll get,' Felix shouted. 'That, or worse!'

Another sneer from the optio. 'You'll have to take us alive first.'

Clattering swords off their shield bosses, his men hurled abuse at Felix and his comrades.

With the advantage of height, and of a courage born of desperation, the Bruttian deserters had all the advantages in the fight that followed. It was brutal fighting up a slope, and only about a dozen principes could engage with the enemy at any one time. Felix shouted constant encouragement, much as he'd seen Pullo and Matho do. The remainder had to stand waiting as spears and arrows showered in from defenders on the ends of the shattered walkways. If anyone tried to clamber up to reach *them*, they were shot at close range by the archers.

After a time – it seemed like hours – Felix ordered the battered principes to retreat a little way down the slope. Behind the protection of their upraised shields, they conferred.

Felix looked around the filthy, sweaty, bloody faces. Alarm filled him. 'Where's Fabius?'

'Dead,' Antonius muttered.

'And Peri?'

'Gone as well, sir,' said Clavus.

Felix bottled up his rage and grief. To crumble now was to die, but their situation was grim. Livius had been helped to safety by Sparax. Bulbus' shouts from the bottom of the wall were incomprehensible in the din. He was the ranking officer; he had to make the decision.

'We've lost two men, sir,' said a princeps from another contubernium.

'Four for us, sir,' came a voice a little further down the slope.

Felix cast a look at the Bruttians, who hadn't moved a step from their position atop the breach. 'Shitty-arsed traitors.' Again his gaze moved over his comrades' faces. They were grim yet still determined. If I lead them forward again, he thought with bursting pride, they'll follow me. A fresh tactic was needed, however.

'Attack again,' said Felix, 'and more of us will die. We won't break those goat-molesting, sister-screwing whoresons either – I know it in my bones. It's time to pull back.'

No one argued.

'What about Fabius' body?' Antonius' voice was toneless. 'And Peri's?'

'We'll ask for a truce to retrieve them later,' declared Felix.

Their ears rang with the Bruttians' insults every step of the treacherous way down.

CHAPTER VI

Akraia promontory, north-west of Korinth, opposite Sikyon

Demetrios' eyes roved around the encampment. General Philokles had chosen the location with care, he decided, approving. He and his comrades, part of a fifteen-hundred-strong force, were on a scrub-lined peninsula poking westward into the sea from the narrow isthmus that joined Greece to the Peloponnese. In essence, it was surrounded on three sides by the Gulf of Korinth, Eastward, it was a short distance from the besieged city of Korinth, their destination. The peninsula's only inhabitants were simple shepherds, men happy to say nothing to the Romans after a little silver crossed their calloused palms.

Demetrios and his comrades had been busy since their arrival earlier in the day, seeking out every local fishing tub and hiring it with its crew. The small craft had been hauled up on the beach of a narrow inlet several stadia from the camp; there were enough to carry all of Philokles' troops. Unless an enemy vessel strayed a good way off course, they would not be seen. Before dawn the next day, Demetrios and the rest would embark and sail the short distance to Lekhaio, Korinth's western port. There they would lie low in the hills before making their way at sunset to the city. Delighted by their unexpected arrival, the Korinthians would feed and water them like kings, or so Philokles had told them. After that, he had joked, it only remained for them to defeat the Romans, Pergamenes and the treacherous Akhaians.

The witticism had raised a few laughs, but Demetrios was unamused as he wandered the shore with Kimon and Antileon. Most men's food had run out that morning. Scarce rations meant that few of his comrades had any wine either; those in the rest of the speira weren't sharing theirs. All Demetrios had was a quarter-filled bag of musty-tasting water, and he was saving that for the next day when there might be fighting. Catch some fish, went his reasoning, and he might fall asleep later without having to listen to his growling stomach.

'I'm going to try my luck here,' called Kimon from Demetrios' left. They had wandered away from the beach and the shallows there to the rocky outcrop that sheltered the fishing boats from being seen to the west.

Antileon had already secured himself a position above a deep-looking area of water and was about to toss in his line. Grumpy, wanting solitude, Demetrios waved at Kimon; he continued to clamber over the smooth, sea-washed boulders until his friends were out of sight. Happening upon a sheltered spot, he placed his drinking cup down, eyeing the worms within with distaste. There had been no other carrying container. He'd wash it out with seawater when it was empty – that would have to do. Slipping a fishing line from around his neck, he fitted a juicy worm to the iron hook. With a practised couple of twirls, Demetrios threw hook and bait out over the water. A small lump of lead at the line's end gave it weight; a patch of old leather prevented the shooting-outward line from stripping his palm bare.

Lead, hook and worm plopped into the water perhaps twenty paces away. Not as far as he would have liked, but not worth starting over again. Demetrios began pulling the line in, nice and slow, winding it around his hand. By the time the dripping hook emerged, the worm still writhing upon it, he hadn't felt even the faintest nibble. He wasn't discouraged. There were fish out there. Time was all he needed. His next throw was better, dropping into the sea half as far again as his first effort. This time, the gentle tugs on his line began almost at once. Picturing a fat bream roasting over the fire, he yanked – and lost the fish.

'Patience,' Demetrios told himself. 'Patience.'

A more measured approach yielded results. By the time the sun dipped towards the horizon, turning the western sky red-pink, six mackerel and several mullet lay at Demetrios' feet. Imagining the bread or cheese he might trade for a portion of his catch, he began to whistle. When Kimon shouted that he and Antileon were returning to the camp, Demetrios called that he'd see them back there. 'Make sure the fire's good and hot,' he added. 'Poseidon is in a generous mood.' He rebuffed their instant offer to join him, lying that there was no space amid the rocks for their fat arses. The truth was he was enjoying himself too much to want to share with anyone. Cold, muscles cramped no doubt, his friends didn't climb up to see.

If he'd had a drop of wine, thought Demetrios, life would have been perfect. The sunset was glorious, his cloak was keeping him warm, and soon he'd have enough fish to feed his friends in the file *and* to sell for extra provisions. Fishing was also a welcome break from the monotony of the previous few days' march. At least, he mused, he had only had to march from Elateia. Dispatched south from Pella, the rest of Philokles' troops had sailed down the coast of Macedon to Euboea and then had to cross the island to Boeotia, where they had met with Demetrios' speira.

The task set them by Philip was a double-edged one – it was a great honour for the unit to have been selected from all those in the army, but death beckoned again in Korinth – yet Demetrios would not shirk it. There was a strong bond between him and the king; Philip had saved his life once, and he had returned the favour, taking wounds from an assassin's blade that had been meant for his monarch. Nursed back to health by Philip's own surgeon, rewarded with magnificent armour and weapons, Demetrios' devotion now knew no bounds. Atrax, Elateia, Korinth – he would march wherever he was ordered.

Deep in thought, his concentration lapsed. A sharp tug on the line surprised him; he pulled it in to be confronted by a worm-free hook. Affixing another to the barb, he threw again. His luck had ended, however. Try as he might, the fish had stopped biting. A breeze sprang up, blowing into Demetrios' face. The sun had dropped below the horizon and the light was leaching fast from the sky; night would be here soon. It was time to return to the camp, he decided, starting to feed the length of springy branch he'd brought along through each fish's gills.

A noise made Demetrios turn. He peered into the gloom, unable to pick out anything among the jumble of rocks. 'Kimon?' he called. 'Antileon?'

No answer. Other than the gentle lap of waves, no further sound.

Demetrios shrugged and knelt again to attach the last few fish to the branch. Done at last, he glanced at the darkening sky, and regretted staying so long. With his catch to carry, it would be a job to reach the beach without turning his ankle between the rocks or falling into the sea. Eager for this not to happen, he stood to rummage in his purse, coins the only offering to Poseidon he could think of.

Deciding that a *drachma* was better than the potentially insulting alternative of two *obols* – the price of the cheapest whores – Demetrios twisted from the waist, right arm cocked to hurl the silver coin. From the corner of his eye, he saw a shape looming behind him, and managed – barely – not to throw the drachma. 'Hades, Empedokles, what are you doing, sneaking up on me like that?'

'Been fishing, have you?' Empedokles toed the line of fish.

'What does it look like?' Demetrios snapped, wondering if Empedokles meant him harm.

'Spare a few?'

'Catch your own,' said Demetrios, stooping to pick up the fish just as Empedokles grabbed the other end of the branch. 'Let go,' Demetrios cried.

Empedokles' reply was to pull with the hand on the branch and shove Demetrios in the chest with the other.

Caught off guard, Demetrios moved a foot, which met only air. Unbalanced, he fell. Wind rushed past his ears; his arms flailed, and an inarticulate cry escaped him. Before the water closed over his head, he saw a grinning Empedokles holding the line of fish.

Entangled, blinded by his cloak, and pulled down by its instantly saturated wool, Demetrios gave in to blind panic. He thrashed back and forth, unable to free himself from the voluminous garment's folds. Bubbles streamed from his mouth; he was already desperate to take a breath. Down he sank. Down. Down. I'm going to die, he thought. Drown, like a fool.

Overcome by despair, he let his arms and legs relax.

Then, by some magic, the cloak floated up and away from his body, attached now only around his neck. The new-found freedom struck a tiny spark of hope. Demetrios grasped the sodden fabric with both hands and lifted it over his chin. It caught a little on his ears, and then, unbelievably, it came away, off his head.

Frantic for air, sure that would he still sink to the bottom, he struck out for the surface, discernible from the enveloping gloom by a marginally greater amount of light. How deep he had sunk, Demetrios would never know, but his struggle upwards seemed like an ascent of Mount Olympos in a winter snowstorm. At last his head broke free of the water. He sucked in a sweet mouthful of air, and along with it a good deal of brine. By the time he had stopped coughing and managed to get his bearings, Empedokles had vanished. The cowardly bastard, thought Demetrios. He wanted me to drown.

Poseidon had been kind, however; he was alive, and the currents weren't strong. It was a short dog paddle around the rocks to the beach. Demetrios staggered ashore, arming himself at once with a sharp-edged piece of stone. If Empedokles was capable of leaving him for dead, he was also capable of trying to finish the job. He crouched for a time, listening, but the only sounds came from the men among the beached fishing smacks further down the sand. Eyes peeled for danger, he set out in the direction of the camp. Not until the points of light that marked men's fires came into sight did Demetrios allow his rage to take hold.

That bastard, he thought. I'll get him back.

Kimon's hoots of laughter at his bedraggled state and Antileon's jeers that he had returned empty-handed died away as Demetrios beckoned them into the darkness, away from the other men with whom they shared a tent. Safe from eavesdroppers, he told the pair everything. Anger chased shock across their faces.

'It was an accident, surely,' said the ever-reasonable Kimon.

'Maybe,' said Demetrios. 'But he didn't try to help when I went into the water. He took off, hoping no doubt that I would drown.'

'Treacherous whoreson,' said Antileon, fingering his dagger. 'I say we go and cut him a new arsehole.'

Demetrios shook his head. 'No. It's my word against his. When he sees that I'm alive, Empedokles can easily say that he saw me swimming to shore, which is why he didn't raise the alarm. The best I can do is take back my fish, and make sure *he* knows not to leave camp on his own.'

Kimon and Antileon glanced at each other.

'If I accuse him of attempted murder, Simonides might take it higher up. Gods only know what will happen if Stephanos gets involved. It's better to say nothing and deal with it myself. I'll get the bastard back in training, something like that.' Demetrios could still remember the dunt to his helmet from Empedokles' sarissa; head spinning, he had sunk to his knees.

Happy that there was no violence impending, Kimon nodded. 'If you're sure,' said Antileon reluctantly.

'I am,' said Demetrios.

He led the way to their file-leader Simonides' tent. Empedokles was one of the half-dozen who shared it. Since his promotion to sixth-ranker in the file, Demetrios could have been among them. He had cited not wanting to leave his friends as his reason for refusing, but every phalangist knew that his enmity with Empedokles was a major factor. Demetrios had assumed Simonides' silence on the matter was tacit recognition of the situation. The seventh-ranker, a block-jawed man called Skopas, had been happy enough to take Demetrios' place.

'Ho there!' boomed Philippos as they emerged into the firelight. 'You look like a drowned rat, Demetrios. Been swimming?'

'Something like that,' said Demetrios, casting about for Empedokles.

'You fell into the sea.' Simonides was a man of so few words that people said he had Spartan blood.

'I did. Is Empedokles about?' Demetrios could sense Antileon bristling beside him; Kimon's smile was forced.

'He's off somewhere with Skopas,' said Andriskos.

Simonides twisted to regard Demetrios full on. 'What's going on?'

'The bastard stole my fish.'

'Did he, by Zeus?' Philippos frowned, then he peered into the gloom. 'Ah, here he is, with Skopas. Empedokles – Demetrios wants a word.'

Surprise flashed across Empedokles' face, then he sneered. 'Been swimming?'

'In a manner of speaking,' said Demetrios. 'You've got my fish, I see.' The branch hung from Empedokles' hand. Demetrios shot a glance at Skopas, and seeing nothing sinister in his expression, concluded that he hadn't known about it, which signified Empedokles had meant only to steal his catch. That said, Demetrios thought darkly, the bastard had made no attempt to save him from drowning.

'What in Tartaros is going on?' demanded Simonides.

'Empedokles appeared as I was about to come back to the camp,' Demetrios explained. 'Being too lazy to catch his own fish, he grabbed for mine. We struggled, and I fell in the sea. I swam to the beach, while he sauntered back with what he'd stolen.' The bastard didn't try to help me, he wanted to add, but he kept to his decision about not getting officers involved in his quarrel, and held his peace.

'Well?' Simonides scowled at Empedokles. 'You haven't been gone long enough to catch that many.'

Empedokles spat a curse. 'Aye, I took his fish, but only because he wouldn't sell me a few. I didn't have any luck catching any, while

Demetrios had landed plenty. It's only fair that a man should see another comrade right, isn't it?'

'True enough,' said Simonides, adding, 'but shoving a man into the sea would make most disinclined to sell, however. What do you say, Demetrios?'

It was obvious that Simonides wanted the matter settled, so rather than protest that Empedokles was lying about asking to buy fish, Demetrios said, 'I'll give you two, for three obols each. I choose which ones.'

Simonides nodded; Empedokles could not refuse. He walked to Demetrios and glaring, handed over the laden branch. Demetrios slid off the two smallest mackerel, and took six obols from Empedokles, who stalked back to Skopas.

An uneasy air fell.

Simonides took the situation by the scruff of the neck. 'We are all comrades here. Dig out the wine you were boasting about earlier, Empedokles. Share it with everyone.' The command made his opinion of what had gone on clear.

Furious, Empedokles rummaged about in his kit, producing a mostly full wineskin.

Simonides produced a simple black and red *krater*, and an unhappy Empedokles filled it. A libation to Poseidon, the god of the sea, was poured, making the fire hiss, and then Simonides filled cups from the krater and passed them out. Toasts were made, as were loud comments about how tasty Empedokles' wine was, and how generous he was to share it. Simonides, who had caused the mischief, drained the cup and demanded it be refilled. Scowling, muttering under his breath, Empedokles emptied the skin to his comrades' cheers.

Demetrios took enormous satisfaction from the hatred in his enemy's gaze as he saluted him with his cup, and mouthed, 'Watch your back.'

A day later, and Demetrios and his comrades had achieved the task set Philokles by the king. Despite the numerous trips needed to ferry all the men to Lekhaio, no enemy vessels had come upon the little fleet of fishing craft. Attalus and his troops appeared to have left their ships at Kenchreai, meaning Lekhaio could be safely approached. The defenders' delight and surprise at their arrival had been memorable; even the sentries atop the paired walls that ran from Lekhaio to Korinth had cheered as the phalangists and light infantry had marched towards the city.

Best of all for Demetrios and his friends, Philokles had seen to their needs the moment they had passed through the great western gate. Ignoring the messengers from the garrison commander who descended on him, he had declared that Androsthenes could wait an hour. 'My soldiers are hungry and thirsty,' Philokles had chided the messengers. 'Do you expect them to fight on empty bellies, with parched throats? No? Then bring wine and bread. Bring cheese and meat, and olives!' That done, he had ordered space to be cleared in the agora for his troops' tents; only then had he departed to take counsel with Androsthenes.

Demetrios hadn't been party to the two generals' conversation, but the result saw first the light infantry and then the entire *chiliarchy* march out of the northern gate the following morning. Five hundred men of the garrison followed after. A sense of optimistic anticipation hung in the air. Some soldiers were singing the *Paean*, while others loudly discussed what they'd been told by the defenders: that the Romans had not ventured across the ditches since their defeat by the Bruttian deserters from Hannibal's army some days before.

A *stadion* beyond the first ditch, trumpets halted their advance. Stephanos and the other speira commanders bellowed orders. Smoothly, the files moved from marching formation – with each speira at half its usual width and double depth – to that used in combat. Another barked order saw sarissae grounded, pointing at the windblown sky. On either side, the light infantry were moving to protect the chiliarchy's flanks. Beyond them, the garrison soldiers moved into position.

A little time passed. Sentries ran along the wall of the enemy camp, which lay perhaps five stadia away. Trumpets signalled. Voices shouted orders; the heavy tramp of feet followed. Crested helmets appeared on the camp's rampart: officers, come to look at the Macedonians. The gates – nothing more than stacked bundles of fresh-chopped timber – remained closed.

'Two thousand of us against what, three and a half thousand legionaries,' Demetrios declared; memories of the victory at Atrax were vivid in his mind. Enemy numbers here were an unknown factor, but he was working on the rumours of three hundred men lost at the breach and the fact that no four thousand, two-hundred strong legion was ever at full strength. 'I'll take those odds.'

'And I,' rumbled Philippos. 'Let them come.'

Taurion chuckled. Empedokles glowered. Skopas remained silent, and Demetrios' skin prickled. Since the episode at the fire, he hadn't trusted the seventh-ranker. It was bad enough having Empedokles two men in front of him, without also having a friend of his right behind. Demetrios had to hope that Skopas truly hadn't been involved when Empedokles had stolen his fish. Antileon and Kimon were too far away to be of help. You're dwelling on it overmuch, Demetrios told himself. Skopas and Empedokles drink and gamble together, that's all.

'Here they come,' said Simonides.

Men were muttering with excitement. A tinge of nervousness was also palpable. Demetrios forgot about Empedokles. His eyes were fixed on the entrance to the enemy camp. First came the *velites*, swarming out in their usual undisciplined mob. Rather than move towards the Macedonians, however, they loped off to the east.

'Kenchreai lies that way,' said Demetrios.

Empedokles let out a contemptuous snort. 'And? They'll be sweeping around to cross the ditch further along and then take us in the rear.'

But they didn't. The velites disappeared. Curiosity rippled through the phalangists. Men began to say that perhaps the enemy had had enough, and few argued with them.

The cavalry attached to the legion emerged next. Stiff-backed, they rode off, following the velites. Incredulous, delighted, the phalangists watched as the hastati and principes marched out and took the same path as their comrades. By the time the triarii came out, guarding the legion's senior officers, it was clear that the Romans were withdrawing.

Riotous cheering broke out among the Macedonians and the garrison soldiers.

Philippos cupped a hand to his mouth. 'Call yourselves soldiers?'

Roars of laughter. More insults hurled.

Demetrios shouted as loud as the rest.

This was incontrovertible proof of the phalanx's superiority over the legion. Let the day come when Philip's entire army faced that of Flamininus, he thought.

Victory would be theirs.

CHAPTER VII

Temple of Zeus, Gonnos

It had been too long since he had worshipped here, Philip decided as he rode closer to the sanctuary, which lay on the north bank of the River Peneios, a short way from the town. Surrounded by tall cypress trees, four plain-stuccoed walls formed a long rectangle; the main gate was in the eastern wall, one of the two shorter sides. Simpler than Zeus' shrine at Pella, and half the size of the great complex at Dio, it was less dear to the king's heart than the Asklepion at Trikka. Yet it was close to his camp by the narrow defile of Tempe, and with Mount Olympos nearby, sure to receive the god's attention.

Unease tickled Philip, and he hoped his failure to sacrifice here in months hadn't angered Zeus. 'I have been busy with my army,' he muttered, 'and affairs of state.' Truth be told, the war occupied his every moment. Philip woke thinking about it; he discussed it with his generals and advisers for hours each day; when alone, he schemed and plotted ways to defeat Flamininus, and he dreamed of battle every night.

I also pray to the gods every morning and evening, he thought, and I'm here now, with a fine offering. The rope in his right hand led to a ram that trotted behind his horse; every so often a jerk signified its resentment.

Rather than come with a party of officers, and have fawning priests fill his ears with things that they thought he wanted to hear, Philip had come early and alone. Astride one of his Companions' mounts, wearing an old cloak and under that, a plain chiton, he would be taken as a king's cavalryman, not as himself. At least, that was his hope.

'Mind your horse, sir?' An urchin had materialised from between the cypresses. His bare feet made no sound as he ran alongside Philip. 'It'll be stolen while you're praying otherwise.'

'By the likes of you.'

'I'm no thief, sir!' The boy's thin face was the picture of wounded innocence. 'I'm the one as will *stop* any thieves.'

Philip's lips twitched. The spiky-haired urchin was eight or nine summers old. Ill-fed, puny-looking, he wouldn't be able to stop anyone from taking the horse. Whether he was trustworthy was far from certain either, but there was something to him, and the beast had to be left outside the sanctuary. Better to pay the boy than not, Philip decided. 'How much?'

'Three obols.'

'Do I look like a fool?' Philip slipped off and handed over the reins. 'One.'

The urchin's chin jutted. 'Two.'

Philip snorted. 'You'll get whatever I give. Know that if a hair on his mane is out of place when I return, I will tan your hide. If he's gone, and you with it, best ride for your life. When I find you, your death will be slow, and more painful than you can imagine.'

Cowed, the boy nodded.

Without a backward glance, Philip made for the entrance, the reluctant ram following. One of the great doors had been propped open. Several steps inside sat a collection box on a stone plinth. Philip didn't hesitate: he rummaged in his purse. Zeus' bearded face stared back at him from the first drachma he pulled out. Pleased – he had felt for the coin without looking – Philip dropped it and three of its fellows into the slot.

'Blessings on you,' called a soft voice.

He turned. Hidden in the shadows, an old man was watching from the colonnaded walkway that ran around the courtyard. His twig broom proved him to be one of the temple keepers. Given the sanctuary's quietness, perhaps the only one, thought Philip. 'Greetings.' He waited as the greybeard came shuffling over.

'You are here to ask Zeus for his favour.' His rheumy eyes moved to the ram.

'I am,' replied Philip.

'You are a soldier.'

'A cavalryman, yes.'

'One of the king's men, bless his name.'

'Yes.' Philip was even gladder that he'd come alone and in simple clothes. Being able to venture among his people unknown was a rare experience; it was a thing to treasure when he heard himself being talked about in good terms. 'Are any of the priests in attendance?' At quieter times of the year, shrines were often empty but for temple keepers like this greybeard.

'There is one.' The old man twitched his brush towards the main building, which stood in the middle of the courtyard.

'My thanks.' Philip had gone a dozen steps when the temple keeper spoke again.

'The Romans will return in the spring. Is that why you are here?'

Tartaros, thought Philip. He has no idea who I am, yet he sees through me with ease. 'A lot of soldiers must come for the same reason.'

'Aye, many. The ram is a worthy gift. Zeus will look kindly on it.'

Philip's worries about the war, which he'd been suppressing all the way from his camp, flared up. Zeus was no different from the other gods. He might accept the plentiful sacrifices being offered here, but whether he would intervene in anyone's favour, let alone Philip's, during the next campaigning season was far less certain.

One step at a time, he told himself. The ram, which had pulled on the rope all the way from his camp, now followed meekly. This was pleasing: an animal that went unwilling to its death could never be regarded as a suitable offering.

Crossing the courtyard, his eyes were drawn to Mount Olympos, which towered over the sanctuary. Clouds obscured the snow-capped peaks where the gods dwelt, but that didn't stop a shiver from running down Philip's back. He muttered a hasty prayer. Tethering the ram to an iron ring in a post by the altar, he studied the temple properly for the first time. Six Doric columns formed its frontage, stuccoed in white. On the portico above, a magnificent frieze depicted Zeus wielding his thunderbolts. Everything needed attention, thought Philip, noting the peeling paint and the cracked plaster. He would see to it.

A cat sat at the top of the three steps that led to the shrine, a neat, poised shape with its tail curled around its feet. The creature didn't move as he climbed up, regarding him with a calm, inscrutable expression. Although cats weren't sacred to Zeus, Philip still gave it a wide berth.

A dim gloom pervaded the shrine, at the back of which stood a mighty statue of Zeus, tall as two men. Entering, Philip dipped his head in respect.

'A fine likeness, is it not?' A portly, robed figure emerged from the darkness to Philip's left. Perhaps five years older than the king, he had straggling brown hair and an untidy beard. Despite his dishevelled appearance, the eyes regarding Philip were shrewd.

'It is. You are the priest?'

A dip of the chin. 'That is my honour. Have you come to make an offering?'

'A ram.' Silver glinted in Philip's palm. 'And this.'

The beginnings of a smile. The handful of coins vanished into the priest's purse. 'What is your request of the god?'

'I . . . I . . .' Hating how his voice had momentarily turned traitor, Philip cleared his throat. 'I seek to know the outcome of the war with Rome.'

'A common question.' Indicating that Philip should follow, the priest led the way outside.

It wasn't surprising that his soldiers were worried too, thought Philip, but it was unsettling. They must never see *his* doubts, or all would be lost.

The temple keeper was waiting by the altar, upon which sat a small wicker basket of wheat. The ram had lain down, a good omen. Philip stood close by as the priest chanted a prayer and the temple keeper lit a small fire on top of the altar. Without urging, the ram got to its feet as the rope was untied from the iron ring. Following tradition, the temple keeper poured a gentle stream of water on its head. Its neck bent, signifying acceptance of death.

From nowhere it seemed, a blade appeared in the priest's hand. Now the temple keeper lifted the ram's head, towards Olympos, the gods' home. Swift and sure, the priest reached down and cut its throat from underneath. The ram's legs buckled, but the temple keeper was there, holding its chin up and catching the gouting blood in a bronze bowl with his other hand.

Philip's mouth was dry as he watched the priest swirl the crimson-frothed liquid around the bowl.

'Zeus accepts the sacrifice,' intoned the priest.

Philip couldn't help thinking, of course he does. It's the best ram in Thessaly.

The dead beast was rolled onto its back. Blood continued to run from the gaping wound in its neck, staining the fleece and filling the cracks between the paving stones. With practised cuts, the priest opened the belly, easing out long loops of glistening, pink-grey intestine. 'I see no blemishes,' he said, running the guts through his hands.

Philip paid little attention. An animal had to be worm-ridden or at death's door to show disease there. It was the liver that mattered.

Working his blade inside the abdomen, the priest cut and tugged. A moment later, he lifted out the slippery, purple organ and standing, placed it on the altar.

Philip leaned forward, unable to contain his eagerness. 'Well?'

A sharp look from the temple keeper; the priest gave no sign of having noticed.

Philip had seen a thousand sacrifices over the years; he had heard the most outlandish things being promised, almost none of which ever came to pass. He had thus learned to regard prophecies with a good deal of scepticism. That didn't stop his heart from pounding now, or prevent the queasy feeling in his belly. The solitude of this sanctuary, the lowering, cloud-bound mountain, the strange cat – and most of all, the grim situation facing him – combined to imbue this offering with more significance than any in his life.

'The path ahead is fraught with danger.'

Philip's eyes darted to the priest, who was running reddened fingers over the liver's surface.

'Rome is a dangerous enemy.'

Philip stifled a savage retort to this statement of the obvious. Only a few hill-loving shepherds would have escaped news of his loss of western Thessaly and the fortress of Gomphi.

'Success can come from unexpected places – if only they can be found.'

Yes, yes, thought Philip. That's a vague comment that applies to everything and nothing.

'The man who commands the legions is determined. Implacable.'

Philip's cynicism faltered. Here in remote Gonnos, the priest could know little of Flamininus. Was he making an assumption because of Flamininus' successes, or was the liver actually revealing the future?

'The Romans can be beaten, however.'

'How?' The word had escaped before Philip could stop himself.

Again the temple keeper shook his head in disapproval; again the priest seemed not to have heard.

Silence fell.

Despite his burning desire to know more, Philip dared not interrupt again.

At last the priest spoke. 'Remain steadfast. Loyal to your king. Keep your face to the enemy. Macedon will prevail.'

Philip wanted to scream. These platitudes told him nothing; in all probability, the priest was a charlatan like most of his kind. To show anger or frustration might anger Zeus, however, and that was not something Philip was prepared to risk. Even his cynical thoughts might be enough to draw down the god's wrath. 'Is there anything else?' he whispered.

'When he wishes it, Zeus' cloak is impenetrable.' The priest's tone was final.

Philip put on a pleased face. 'My thanks.' He took a step away from the altar.

'The meat?' asked the temple keeper.

'Offer the best cuts to the god. Do as you wish with the rest, but make sure the boy outside – the one who watches over horses – receives a good lump.' Philip waved an acknowledging hand as the priest and temple keeper cried their appreciation. He had no further interest in the ram. It was time to get back to camp; if his memory served, he had a meeting with the quartermasters. The bane of his life, they were still some of the most important men in his army. Feeding and supplying his troops was as important as winning battles, for the one could not come without the other.

'Sire!'

His head shot up. A Companion came striding through the door-way at the far side of the courtyard. 'I am here,' called Philip, feeling his brief freedom slip away.

'I bring news, sire!' The Companion broke into a run.

Barely hearing the priest's gasp of surprise and horror – springing from the realisation that the man he'd taken for a soldier was in fact the king – Philip paced forward. Terrible images flashed through his mind: Flamininus' legions being augmented by the arrival of more from Italia; Korinth falling to the enemy; the fortress at Demetrias under attack; plots against him in Pella. Stop it, he told himself. 'Speak.'

The Companion skidded to a halt and executed a sloppy salute. He was grinning all over his face. 'It's good news, sire.'

'I see.' Philip controlled his surprise – and relief. 'Tell me.'

'Philokles has been victorious, sire. Korinth yet stands! The Romans and Pergamenes have withdrawn, and the Akhaians are skulking back to their holes.'

'This is a happy day,' cried Philip, turning to look at the priest, who pulled a sickly smile. The temple keeper went to one arthritic knee.

'There's more, sire,' said the Companion. 'Argos has come over to you.'

Philip spun, unable to believe his ears. After Korinth, Argos was the second most important city on the Peloponnese. 'Is it even so?'

'Aye, sire.' The Companion's smile broadened. 'The leaders of the assembly were so sure of their people's support that they sent word to Philokles, who entered Argos at night with several hundred men. A few Akhaian fools insisted on dying at their posts, it seems, but the rest of the garrison surrendered.'

'Cleverly done, Philokles.' Although Philip was delighted that Korinth was still his, he was less pleased about Argos. To regain a city in the middle of Akhaian territory was a hollow victory, and he could ill afford to have Philokles blockaded inside it. That was surely what would happen once the perfidious Akhaians reorganised. And yet, after the setbacks of the previous month – the loss of several towns in Phokis, and Elateia under assault for a second time – this was welcome news indeed.

'Sire!' The priest came hurrying across the courtyard. A few paces from Philip, he bowed deeply.

'Yes?'

Shame mixed with frank fear in the priest's face. 'Forgive me, sire, for not recognising you. If I'd known, I—'

'You would have told me victory over Flamininus would be mine,' said Philip. He raised a hand, cutting off the priest's protest. 'It matters not. Zeus accepted my offering, and for this messenger to arrive with good news while I am in the sanctuary, well, that feels like a message from the god. Does it not?'

'My very thoughts, sire.' The priest's double chin wobbled.

'In gratitude, my workmen will redecorate the temple. That is, if you wish it?'

'A thousand thanks, sire,' gabbled the priest.

Again, Philip's ears were filled with fulsome praise. Fresh ideas already coming to him, he had forgotten the priest and temple keeper within a few steps.

The urchin was waiting with Philip's horse right outside the entrance. Gone was his previous confidence: he had heard the Companion's shouts. Eyes full of terror, he dropped to both knees. 'I did not mean to offend, sire.'

Philip took gentle hold of the boy's elbow. 'Rise.'

The urchin stood. Trembling, he kept his gaze fixed on his dirty, broken-nailed feet.

'You have spirit,' said Philip. 'Have you a father? A mother?'

'They're both dead, sire.'

'So you fend for yourself. That takes courage.'

A tear fell to the ground. The boy wiped his face fiercely.

'You looked after my horse well.'

At last the urchin looked up. His gaze was nervous but proud. 'I did, sire. No one touched him.'

'A man who does his job must be paid.' Philip upended his purse into one palm, counting eight *drachmae* and almost twice that many obols. 'Here.' He tipped the lot into the disbelieving urchin's hands, knowing that it was more money than he had ever seen in his life. 'When you've hidden that away, go inside. The priest has meat for you.'

The boy's face lit up. 'Zeus bless and keep you, sire!'

Philip took the reins, and gestured to the Companion to mount up.

Three stadia from the sanctuary, he could still hear the urchin shouting his thanks.

Night had fallen over Philip's camp. Sentries stood guard round the perimeter, while inside, bursts of song and shouted conversations rose from around the fires. A discontented mule brayed; a moment later, it was answered by another. In his great tent, Philip sat across a table from Menander. Between them, a stack of writing parchment was weighted down by a little bronze figurine of Alexander astride his horse Boukephalos. An inkwell and several plain iron styli lay alongside.

Menander was filling his cup from a magnificent black and red krater decorated with diners reclining outdoors under vines.

Philip snorted.

Menander lowered the vessel. 'I hope you're laughing at the prick and balls, sire, and not me.'

'Of course I am,' answered Philip. They both chuckled. Rather than a simple circle of clay, the foot of the krater had been shaped into a phallus and testicles.

Menander made a rueful face. 'The fact that I'm holding it "tip" downwards, sire, would be about right. As they say, wine quickens desire, but does little for performance.'

'Our wives are far from here, so we have no concerns in that regard,' said Philip, waving at a slave to fill the krater again. 'We can drink to our hearts' content.'

They took turns to toast one another and drank again.

'I'm still thinking about Flamininus' face when he heard how his brother had broken off the attack on Korinth,' said Philip. 'Between that and Argos switching sides, he must have looked as if he'd swallowed a wasp.'

'You're right no doubt, sire,' said Menander. A heartbeat's hesitation, and he added, 'Yet he has renewed his siege of Elateia.'

'Curse him, he has. It will fall too, without my phalangists there. Would have fallen anyway, or I'm no judge. And here we are, safe behind Tempe, powerless to prevent him.' Philip thumped the desk, sending ripples through the wine in the krater.

'Difficult times, sire. Korinth may well stand with us, Argos too, but as you say, we can do little for them but send encouraging words. When taken with the successful defence of Atrax, however, these developments leave you in a strong position as winter approaches.'

Philip scraped a thumbnail across his teeth. 'That position might change come the spring. Argos will not withstand a prolonged siege from the Akhaians. Korinth is not invulnerable either.'

'Indeed, sire.'

Philip made an impatient gesture. 'Spit out whatever it is you're thinking, man.'

'May I be frank, sire?'

'You are one of my most trusted advisers. My *most* trusted adviser. Speak.'

Menander gave him a nod of thanks. 'Flamininus knows that despite his legions' numerical superiority, the battle for Macedon will be bitter, sire. In the right place – for us – he could be defeated. The successes at Korinth and Argos will have rammed home that point – they might make him more amenable to a negotiated peace. I know

67

that his terms were unacceptable before, sire, but leaving you as king of Macedon would suit Rome for many reasons, not least of which is the threat posed by Antiokhos.' Menander made to fill his cup again, but he was really taking refuge behind the upraised krater.

'Put that thing down. I'm not going to punish you for voicing your opinion.' Philip's tone was amused.

Looking a little embarrassed, Menander placed the krater back on the table. 'Sire.'

'You have read my mind.' Philip chuckled at Menander's expression. 'Are you surprised that you and I have the same thoughts?'

'I . . . No, sire, but I didn't expect you to be so . . . calm.'

'He who ignores what's staring him in the face is a fool. Let us pen a missive to Flamininus together. Now.' Philip eased a sheet of parchment from under the Alexander figurine, thinking that while the Lion of Macedon might not have treated with an enemy so, he hadn't had to face the legions. Nor was it admitting defeat to write this letter – it was buying time.

After Philip had finished the message to Flamininus, he would write another. The one he had been thinking of writing for months.

To Antiokhos.

CHAPTER VIII

Near Elatea

I t was nearing midday, and Flamininus was riding through his camp. He wasn't a keen horseman – the cursed creatures made him sneeze for some reason – but a better way to escape the mounds of paperwork in his tent, he hadn't found. An hour's ride through the surrounding countryside, pretending to ignore the *turma* of cavalry sent by his staff officers as protection, and a man felt more at ease with the world. Unwilling to return just yet to his onerous duties, Flamininus decided to have a hot bath when he got back. To Hades with anyone who thought it an odd hour for his ablutions.

'Salute the general!'

Flamininus didn't normally pay attention – this happened all the time – but for some reason, he turned his head. The officer – a centurion – who'd shouted at his men was ruddy-faced and round-headed. An unfortunate looking type, thought Flamininus. I'd wager his men call him 'Onion Head'.

Flamininus' lips twitched, imagining the jokes.

His good humour evaporated as he neared his tent and spied Pasion waiting for him. That was never a good sign – invariably, it meant extra paperwork to wade through. Flamininus could see his chances of a bath disappearing before his very eyes. Pasion had a way of sighing, and mentioning how important such and such a letter was. More often than not, because doing nothing only made things worse, Flamininus would give in and work until the pile of official documents was a manageable size. Curse him, thought Flamininus with a certain sneaking admiration. How does he do it?

Inevitably, thinking of Pasion, his mind turned to Galba's letters. Flamininus had held off questioning his secretary since Anticyra in the hope of catching him in the act of delivering an anonymous letter, but the tactic had failed. He suspected that Galba had not yet penned another, rather than Pasion suspected anything.

Interrogating Pasion carried some risk. If he was Galba's agent and Galba found out, his enemy's demands might become even more punishing, And yet, decided Flamininus with glee, Galba was far away in Rome. There was no reason for him ever to discover what had happened to Pasion – if that's what it came to. A new secretary might have to be found, but it was better to cut out a canker than leave it to fester.

It was time to act, decided Flamininus. He had left off dealing with the problem long enough.

He acted as normal when he reached his tent. Leaving his horse in the charge of his groom, he stalked past the sentries without any indication of having seen their salutes. He unclasped his cloak in his meeting room, a partitioned area towards the front of his massive pavilion, and a waiting slave darted in to take it.

Flamininus' belly rumbled, and he wondered whether to eat first. He wasn't of a delicate disposition, and even though he didn't wish to use violence, things might get messy. Better to eat later, he decided, after his bath. 'Pasion.'

'Master?' A stool scraped back in the small antechamber that served as Pasion's office. A moment later, he entered. Ink stains marked his fingers; he was clasping a bundle of documents.

'Set them down,' ordered Flamininus, tapping his desk.

This was not their usual routine. Looking confused, Pasion obeyed.

Straight to the point, thought Flamininus. 'Odd how that letter appeared in Anticyra, was it not?'

'Yes, master. I hurried outside the instant I saw it, but could see no one. The sentries had nothing to report either. Whoever it was must have lifted the tent leather and slipped under.'

'Whoever it was,' repeated Flamininus in an ironical tone. 'And the sentries saw nothing.'

Pasion's eyes flickered. 'Yes, master.'

He's nervous already, thought Flamininus, his suspicion increasing. 'Would this have been the same person who delivered the letter at Gomphi?'

'I have no idea, master,' said Pasion, quickly adding, 'that letter was given to one of the sentries. A dark-haired man, he said, who spoke Latin like a Roman.'

'So you said.'

'It's true, master.'

'Tell me what the sentry looked like, and I'll have him brought here to confirm your words.'

'I can't remember, master,' said Pasion nervously. 'It was more than a month ago, and there are so many sentries.'

'You must recall a detail about him. A scar, the colour of his hair. Something.'

Silence.

'Well?'

Pasion's hands fluttered. 'I . . . No, master. I cannot remember.'

Flamininus didn't believe him. Taking a deep breath, for he had never resorted to such measures, he dealt his secretary a meaty slap across the face with the back of his hand. It sent Pasion stumbling backwards.

Pasion clutched his cheek and stared at Flamininus with a terrified expression. This had never happened before, but he knew better than to protest.

'It's a little odd, don't you think, that two letters should come into your possession in such a mysterious manner?'

'I suppose, master.' Pasion's voice trembled. 'What I told you is true, however. The message at Gomphi was delivered to one of your sentries, the other—'

'Yes, yes, it "appeared" on your desk while you were answering a call of nature. How convenient.' Flamininus rubbed his fingers. He felt bad for striking Pasion, who, while acting suspiciously, hadn't been proven guilty. His loss of control was also lamentable. A surgeon had once told him how easy it was to break bones in the hand punching with a fist. 'Better to use an implement,' he'd said.

'I don't know what to say, master.'

The letters' appearances were more than coincidence – Flamininus felt sure of it. He decided with regret that more force was required. Having no desire to inflict further suffering on Pasion himself, he cupped a hand to his mouth. 'Guards!'

Pasion stood mute, eyes wide.

Two principes entered. They came to attention and saluted. 'Sir!'

Flamininus waved a hand at Pasion. 'Hold him.'

The principes glanced at each other, then one strode to Pasion, who allowed his arms to be seized from behind. The second princeps looked to Flamininus.

'It's not too late, Pasion,' said Flamininus, still hoping that his secretary would say something that proved his innocence.

'I am your faithful servant, master. I have done nothing!' A tear ran down Pasion's cheek.

'Who sends the letters? I need a name.'

'I don't know, master!'

'Hit him,' ordered Flamininus.

The second princeps punched Pasion in the gut.

A rush of air. A grunt of pain.

Flamininus waited. When Pasion's sobbing had eased, he spoke again. 'A name.'

'I work for you, master. Only for you. I am loyal, master.'

He's lying, thought Flamininus, and he's really good at it. Who would have thought it? 'Hit him again. Harder.'

Thump. Vomit spattered the carpet. The princeps' face twisted with distaste: a few drops had landed on his feet and sandals.

Pasion now hung from the first princeps' grip. A string of drool ran from the corner of his mouth. He coughed. 'I . . . loyal, master.'

'I know it's you who delivers the letters,' said Flamininus, deciding that this was what happened. He could think of no other plausible explanation.

'No, master,' said Pasion.

Pasion's continued protests made Flamininus certain of his guilt. The Greek was a liar, he concluded, like all slaves. Not for nothing was their testimony admissible to courts only if it had been obtained under torture. It was incredible to think he had ever trusted him.

He glanced at both principes. 'Move my stool away from the desk. Sit him down.' Flamininus picked up the pliers he'd demanded from a bemused carpenter the day before. 'Here.'

The princeps who'd been punching Pasion bared his teeth as he took them. 'Sir.'

'Start with his left hand,' said Flamininus, thinking, he uses the other to write with. He might yet survive. 'One fingernail to start.'

These words brought Pasion's head up. His gaze darted wildly from the pliers in the approaching princeps' fist to Flamininus and back again. 'No! Master! Please!' He struggled to rise from the stool, but the first princeps was leaning down on his shoulders. Using another tack, Pasion clenched his hands tight; the second princeps had to lay down the pliers to unpeel his fingers. When he reached down to pick them up, Pasion closed his hand again. The princeps didn't try a second time; instead he brought the head of the pliers down on one of Pasion's toes with immense force.

The shrill scream that followed brought the officer in charge of the guards running. He stopped at the entrance to the chamber, taking in the scene.

Flamininus stared. 'Yes?'

'Just checking all is well, sir,' said the officer.

'It is.'

'Sir.' Looking a little uncomfortable, the officer withdrew.

Flamininus' amazement at Pasion's duplicity and endurance had increased, but his patience was ebbing. 'Continue.'

The princeps bent to his task; another agonised cry rent the air.

'Pasion,' said Flamininus.

It took the secretary long moments to drag his pain-filled eyes up to Flamininus'. 'M-master?' he whispered.

'You work for Galba, do you not?' Let him confess now, thought Flamininus, and I will let him live. There was no question of the Greek remaining in his service, but someone would buy him in the slave market.

'Galba? No, master.'

Gods, but he puts on a good act, thought Flamininus. Galba must have put the fear of Hades into him. 'Another,' he said to the princeps.

Pasion could not stop crying and whimpering after the removal of a second fingernail. Angered, Flamininus ordered a third pulled out, after which he paused to let his secretary recover a little. Then, approaching with care – the carpet was now dotted with vomit, blood spatters and fingernails – he lifted Pasion's chin. 'The pain can stop. Admit that Galba threatened you into his employ. That you are sent his letters to me, so you can deliver them. That you write back to him, revealing everything you know about me, about the campaign.'

Pasion mumbled something.

Hopeful that his secretary was about to confess, Flamininus leaned closer. 'What?'

'L-loyal.' Pasion swallowed. 'I am loyal only to you, master.'

Frustrated, Flamininus almost struck Pasion again. Having no desire to get bodily fluids on himself, however, he leashed his anger, and buried the last of his regret. Pasion was guilty, of that he was certain. The torture would have to continue, and the principes seemed well capable. Flamininus had had enough, however.

'Take this piece of shit away,' he ordered. 'Somewhere quiet. Make him talk. I want to know where those letters come from, and what information he has shared with . . . whoever his employer is. Use whatever force you wish.'

'And if he dies, sir?' asked the pliers-wielding princeps.

Hardening his heart, not looking at Pasion, Flamininus shrugged. 'It matters not. If he's still breathing when you're done, kill him. He's no longer of use to me.'

'Yes, sir.' The principes lifted Pasion between them. Head lolling, he gave no indication of having heard his death sentence pronounced.

'Wait.' Flamininus spoke again.

The principes glanced around. 'Sir?' asked one.

'Speak a word of what you heard in here – or whatever that fool may say when you continue your work – to anyone but me and I'll see you both on crosses. Understand?'

'Yes, sir.'

Flamininus was pleased by the naked fear in their faces. 'Dismissed.'

Pasion's feet dragged along the floor as they hauled him away.

Flamininus shoved his secretary from his mind.

An hour later, Flamininus was at table, bathed and relaxed. There had been no word from the principes yet. Before him was a plate of the honeyed pastries he so loved. Made by his magician of a cook, a princeps he would ensure never had to fight again, they were what Flamininus most looked forward to every morning. He'd taken to having them in the middle of the day as well. An unexpected benefit of being a consul, he mused, was that the time didn't matter. If he wanted to eat honeyed pastries in the early afternoon, as it was now, he could do so and no one would say a thing.

His new habit wasn't without price. A surreptitious poke at his midriff revealed a fold more flesh than had been present when he'd arrived in Apollonia some six months before. Flamininus pursed his lips. This wouldn't have happened in Rome – his wife would never have let him eat three pastries each morning. Or four, he admitted to himself. He stared with regret at the platter in front of him. Two is enough, he decided, and I need more exercise. General I might be, but appearances have to be maintained.

'Sir.'

'Yes?' Flamininus was disappointed to see a third sentry rather than one of the principes he had ordered to torture Pasion. The secretary had hidden reserves, he decided. You could never tell with slaves. 'What is it?'

'A herald has arrived, sir. From Philip.'

This Flamininus had not expected. 'From Philip?' he repeated.

'Aye, sir. What would you have me do with him?'

'Keep him waiting. Summon my senior officers.' Flamininus stood, pastries forgotten. 'I'll send word when to bring him in.'

It didn't take long for his legion commanders and staff officers to gather. Flamininus had had his body slave run a polishing cloth over his cuirass; he had also insisted his red sash be retied. Content he looked every part the Roman general – for the herald would report back to Philip – he took up a prominent pose at the head of the long table in his meeting room and summoned the herald.

Philip's messenger proved to be a heavy-set, bearded man in late middle age. In contrast to Flamininus' rich attire, he was clad in a simple chiton, and wore a white Macedonian *kausia* on his head. Seeing Flamininus, he bowed. 'Greetings, consul.' His Latin was accented but understandable.

Flamininus dipped his chin. 'You come from Philip?'

'I do.' The messenger indicated the four stern-faced principes around him. 'Are these necessary?'

Flamininus gestured, and the soldiers stepped back several paces. 'What do they call you?'

'Menander is my name. I am an adviser to the king.'

Flamininus knew that Macedonians liked to recognise no man as their master, but was still irritated by Menander's familiarity. Pettishly, he snapped, 'How is Philip?'

Menander stroked his beard. 'The king is well. He asks after your health also.'

Wrong-footed – he had expected a barbed reply with mention of the king's happiness over Corinth and Argos – Flamininus grimaced. 'I

75

have no complaints. Can I offer you wine?'

'Thank you, but no,' said Menander. 'It is three to four days' ride back to Tempe, more if the weather worsens. When I have your answer to my message, I shall leave with my escort.'

'Speak then. What has Philip to say?'

'The king wishes to meet with you.'

Flamininus' officers muttered between themselves, but he held his counsel. This was the news he'd hoped Menander might carry. Trapped behind Tempe, stripped of most of his territories, what other reason could Philip have for sending a herald? 'Why?' Flamininus asked, probing.

'While the summer has seen some . . . setbacks,' said Menander, 'the king's army, tens of thousands strong, remains undefeated. Akhaia may have broken faith, but Korinth and Argos are yet in Macedonian hands. Akarnania still stands with us.'

'Not for long,' said Flamininus, his tone wry. 'Acarnania is isolated, far from here. It will fall to the first determined attack, and Philip will be powerless to prevent it.'

Menander was unruffled. 'It is true that Akarnania's future lies with the Fates. But there is no denying that if the war continues, the battle for Macedon will be bitter. Thousands of your men will die, even if you win. A peaceful settlement would prevent that undesirable outcome.'

Flamininus ignored the ripple of excitement sweeping his officers. Was it possible, he wondered, that Philip knew what might happen in December, when the elections for the magistracy took place? One of the new consuls could seek to replace him, as Villius had succeeded Galba and he himself had done to Villius. Accept it, thought Flamininus bitterly. One consul *would* want to take his place, would want the chance of military glory over Macedonia.

It wasn't a certainty of course – during the war with Hannibal the Senate had learned that it was better to leave a general in field rather than replace him each year – but his position wasn't guaranteed. Up to this point, Flamininus had relied on his friends and political allies, as well as goodly numbers of bribes, to argue his case in Rome. Now perhaps it was time to investigate the distasteful possibility that Galba might help, for it would also be in his interest to leave Flamininus in command.

'Consul?' asked Menander.

If I reach an agreement with Philip, thought Flamininus, and am ordered back to Rome after the elections, I will return as the man who forced Macedonia's king to the negotiating table. If I am to continue to lead here, I can break any agreement made easily enough, and restart the war. That way, I can smash Philip's army, and bring all of Greece under Rome's control. His mind made up, Flamininus gave Menander a broad smile. 'Where does he wish to meet?'

CHAPTER IX

Nicaea, close to Thermopylae

B ulbus woke the principes long before sunrise with resounding slaps of his vitis off the leather of their tent roof. 'Up!' he cried. 'Up, or I'll make you wish you'd never been born!'

Hiding their resentment, Felix and his comrades clambered out into the dim, predawn light. Bulbus had already moved on to the next tent. A month had passed since the ignominy of their retreat from Corinth. Sadly, Livius had died from blood poisoning during the march north. Felix had grieved the popular optio, as had every man in the century; a memorable night had been spent drinking themselves into oblivion, careless of the pounding heads they would suffer the next day. Even Bulbus had sensed their need to mourn Livius; not a man had been punished for their poor appearance that day.

Rejoining Flamininus near Elatea, the Eighth had dug out a camp in which to spend the winter, but news had come not long after of a conference that was to take place between their general and King Philip. Half the principes – almost five hundred men – and all the triarii had been chosen to escort Flamininus to the meeting at Nicaea. In addition to his military escort, representatives of Rome's allies would accompany the consul.

The previous day, they had marched to within a mile of the chosen spot, Nicaea, a beach on the Malian Gulf. It lay a little way north from the fortress of the same name which guarded the gates of fire, Thermopylae.

Felix and his friends were still stamping about, trying to keep warm, when Callistus, their new optio, appeared. Brutish and evil-tempered, he had been transferred in after Livius' death. Callistus was as fond of his bronze ball-ended staff as any centurion was of his vitis. He strode up and down in front of Felix and the rest, smacking it off the ground for emphasis as he spoke.

'It's a real honour to be chosen to protect the consul.' Thump. 'A rare thing.' Thump. 'Every man of you has to look his best.' Thump. 'Those mongrel Macedonians must *not* outshine the legionaries of Rome. Hear me?'

'Yes, sir!' the principes shouted. They had cleaned their kit and weapons long into the night: whether their efforts had been sufficient would be clear in an hour, when Bulbus would inspect everything.

Still threatening and pounding his staff, Callistus moved on.

Felix exchanged a glance with each of his comrades. Antonius rolled his eyes. Clavus curled his lip. Dordalus, who had discharged himself early from the hospital, shrugged as if to say, 'What can a man do?' and Sparax muttered, 'Motht officerth are bathtards – exthepting you, Felixth, of courthe. It never changeth.'

We were lucky with Pullo and Livius, thought Felix sadly. Matho's optio Paullinus had been a decent sort, too. Now, however, they were stuck with Bulbus and Callistus.

Antonius had sensed his despondency. 'Keep your head down, brother, and your mouth shut. We'll get through, same as always.'

It was sound advice, thought Felix, even if it was unpalatable.

It was after midday when word came of Philip's approach by sea. At last Flamininus gave the order to leave the camp. 'Arriving after Philip shows who's master,' muttered Antonius to Felix as they tramped the gravel road along the coastline.

'Best way to show that would be to slaughter the Macedonian dog the first chance we get,' said Clavus. 'End the war at one stroke, it would.'

Despite the risk of angering the gods by murdering someone during a truce, everyone liked the sound of that. Felix took the opportunity to recount how he had almost hit Philip with a javelin during the clash at Ottolobus, more than a year before. To his annoyance, again no one would believe him. Antonius, grinning at his indignation, refused to back him up.

The subsequent slanging match was still going on – quietly, in case Bulbus or Callistus heard – when Philip's ships were spotted. Five low-in-the-water *lembi* and a ram-armed trireme that had to be the king's lay at anchor a short distance from the beach. Not a soul had come ashore.

'Philip must have heard us talking,' said Dordalus with his usual leer. 'He's scared to leave his ship.'

Dordalus couldn't be too far from the truth, thought Felix, studying the figures on the Macedonian vessels' decks. The movement there told him that they had been seen, but no order brought the ships in to the beach. Pride filled him. Whatever had happened in recent months, Philip was wary of him and his comrades.

The principes halted not long after, and Flamininus soon came riding from his position at their rear. A large party accompanied him: legates, staff officers and scribes, Greek allies, Rhodians and Pergamenes. Bulbus and the other centurions were ready, bringing their men onto the beach behind their commander. Felix was pleased to be deployed on Flamininus' right, quite close by. From his position in the front rank, he had an excellent view of Philip's trireme, which lay little more than threescore paces offshore, but was unable to pick out the king from those aboard.

Sand crunched beneath sandals, and Felix turned his head. His heartbeat quickened. There was Flamininus, resplendent in his finest armour, and with him, similarly well dressed, his legates, staff officers and the representatives of Rome's allies in the war. Two of these last Felix recognised – the sweaty-faced Amynander of Athamania and the hatchet-faced Achaean general Aristaenus – but the others he knew only to be Aetolian, Rhodian and Pergamene.

Gulls sprang skywards as the group neared the water's edge, their mocking cries echoing in the clear sea air.

'Philip! Are you there?' called Flamininus in Greek. 'It is I, Flamininus.'

There was movement on the trireme's deck.

'Greetings, Flamininus.' The figure who had spoken wore a gleaming bronze cuirass; more detail than that was impossible to see.

'Hail, Philip.'

Flamininus said something else, but Felix's poor Greek wasn't enough to let him understand. Surprise filled him as Clavus translated in a whisper, 'He said it would be more convenient to all if Philip came ashore to talk face to face.' The barbed comment made Felix and those who heard the interpretation grin. With Bulbus and Callistus some distance away, Clavus was able to continue translating what each party said.

'I will stay where I am,' said Philip.

'Whom do you fear, then?' called Flamininus, smiling a little at the men around him.

'I fear no one except the immortal gods,' Philip shot back, continuing, 'I have no confidence, however, in the integrity of your companions – in particular that of the Aitolians.'

'In the absence of trust, all men who meet under truce are exposed to the same danger,' challenged Flamininus.

Philip's laughter carried across the water. 'Not so. If treachery is afoot, and blood were shed, it would be a great deal easier for the Aitolians to find another magistrate than it would for the Macedonians to replace me.'

A prickly silence fell, and Felix thought, Philip is no fool.

Antonius nudged Clavus. 'How in Hades are you fluent in Greek?'

'My mother is from Paestum – she grew up speaking Greek. She could never persuade my father to move away from Rome, so she made sure me and my brothers knew her tongue.' Clavus' grin was all stumps of teeth. 'Never had a use for it really, until this campaign.'

'We know who to have with uth nextht time we vithit a brothel, eh?' Sparax winked. 'Maybe Clavuth can get uth a good prithe.'

'Shhh,' hissed Felix, who had seen Flamininus was about to speak.

Again Clavus interpreted from the Greek.

'My demands are simple,' said Flamininus. 'But without them there can be no peace accord.'

Distance made it impossible to see if Philip rolled his eyes, but his tone suggested he might have done. 'Might I see them written down? Having no one to consult, I wish to consider your proposals in my own time.'

Flamininus acted as if he hadn't heard. 'You must withdraw your troops from every Greek city state, and return all the captives and deserters you have taken from Rome's allies in this war. Any parts of Illyria you still control will be surrendered to Rome. Ptolemy of Egypt must be given back the towns you stole from him. And it is only right that you listen to the demands of these allies who stand by my side.'

'I expected no less,' replied Philip, his sarcasm carrying to the shore.

'He's not happy,' whispered Felix, grinning because he had understood these last words. He cocked his head to listen as Attalus of Pergamum's representative, a self-important type, stepped forward, but the speed with which the man spoke meant that once more Clavus had to interpret.

The Pergamene king expected the return of his ships and crews lost at the battle of Chios, Clavus explained, and for the buildings and temples destroyed by Philip's troops to be rebuilt. Next in line was the Rhodian emissary, who insisted that the Peraea, Rhodes' territory on Asia Minor, was handed back. In addition Philip would have to relinquish control of numerous towns, including some on the Hellespont. The Achaean general Aristaenus requested the return of Corinth and Argos.

The two Aetolian representatives were last to speak; this was, Felix suspected, because of the degree of their hostility towards Philip. Former allies with Macedonia, the Aetolians were now its bitterest enemies in Greece.

The first Aetolian repeated many of Flamininus' demands, namely that Philip should withdraw entirely from Greece, and restore to Aetolia the cities and jurisdictions that had formerly been under its control. His colleague weighed in too, accusing Philip of dishonesty in peace negotiations, and deceit and cowardly tactics in warfare. He had burned a greater area of Thessaly during the summer than had all of Thessaly's enemies in the past; the king had also stolen more from Aetolia as an ally than he had as an enemy. Philip had to pay for these many wrongs, one way or another. By the time the second Aetolian had finished speaking, his voice had almost reached a shout.

'Look!' Felix hissed to Antonius. 'Philip's ship is going to come closer to the beach.'

He watched, rapt, as the anchor was drawn up, dripping, from the sea. One bank of oarsmen was sufficient to ease the trireme into the shallows. Philip stood ready in the prow, like a soldier about to leap ashore against his enemies. Felix shot a look at Flamininus, whose face had tightened – he wasn't sure either what the king would do next. The consul had a word with the Aetolian, who smirked.

'The Aetolian wath trying to annoy Philip,' said Sparax. 'And he thuctheeded.'

'Aye,' muttered Felix. Philip was no more than thirty paces from the water's edge now, and his expression was thunderous. He began to speak, but was cut off at once by the first Aetolian.

The Aetolian's words elicited angry cries from the men around

Philip. Two soldiers leaped into the sea and began wading ashore.

Watching centurions barked orders, and the front ranks of principes readied their javelins.

A tiny devil in Felix's head wanted a fight to break out. It would be difficult *and* dangerous to board the trireme, but chances like this did not come often. Capturing or killing Philip would end the war here on this beach.

A savage command from Philip, however, and the hot-headed pair waded back to the trireme, where they were hauled aboard.

After a moment, Flamininus ordered the principes to ground their javelins again. The tension, which had been wire-taut, eased a fraction.

'What did the Aetolian say?' Felix demanded of Clavus.

'He told Philip that he needs to win the war, or to do the bidding of his superiors.'

No wonder those warriors wanted to attack, thought Felix. It made Philip's self-control even more impressive.

With calm restored, the king asked Flamininus to excuse his men's rash behaviour. Pointedly, his words were courteous, but he did not apologise. He then proceeded to belittle the Aetolians in eloquent and amusing fashion, causing Flamininus to laugh at one point; Philip then agreed, out of respect to Rome, to the Pergamene and Rhodian demands. Achaea could have Argos, but he wanted to talk to Flamininus in person about Corinth. Philip made no mention of the Aetolian demands, or for that matter, the Roman ones.

Barely had the king finished when the Achaean and Aetolian emissaries both began to speak. Angered by Philip, neither would give way to the other. Clavus would have struggled to interpret; in this case, there was no need. Resembling two bickering children, the emissaries continued talking at one another rather than to Philip. He stood listening, a mocking smile on his lips.

Flamininus intervened in the end. 'The hour grows late,' he said testily. 'I shall send a copy of my demands out to your vessel. After that, I suggest that we adjourn for the night, and reconvene in the morning.'

'An excellent plan,' said Philip, conveying his amusement in just three words.

The consensus between Felix and his comrades as they marched back to their camp was that despite his weaker position and the foolish behaviour of his soldiers, Philip had emerged from the first bout as the cleverest speaker. Whether that would serve him in any effective way was another thing altogether. When Flamininus came to speak again, there was little doubt among the principes that he would put the king in his place. If Philip refused to go along, the consul would use them – and the rest of the legions – to get his way in the spring. The recent setbacks had been temporary, they told themselves.

Come the spring, Flamininus would lead them to victory.

Later that evening, Felix, Antonius and their three remaining comrades were taking their ease by the fire outside their tent. Wrapped in their cloaks to combat the autumn chill, they passed around a skin of wine and relived what they had witnessed earlier. 'History in the making, that was,' opined Dordalus. 'How often do lowlifes like us witness such events?'

'Speak for yourself being a lowlife,' said Felix, resentful.

'You and your brother were at Zama, sir,' said Dordalus, unperturbed. 'But I'd wager you didn't see Scipio take Hannibal's surrender.'

Uneasy as he always was when his previous career was mentioned, Felix responded sharply. 'Of course I fucking didn't.'

Even as Dordalus apologised, Antonius intervened. 'A shame those two fools didn't come all the way ashore, eh? A volley of javelins would have sorted them out double quick.'

'Aye,' said Clavus, his eyes gleaming. 'And the rest of the Macedonians might have jumped over the side to avenge them. We'd have slaughtered every last one. Won the war for Flamininus, just like that.'

'I'll drink to that idea.' Sparax raised his cup. 'And I'll drink to victory – however it cometh.'

They were still toasting one another and throwing back their wine when Bulbus appeared out of the darkness. It was late – past the time they might expect an officer to check on them – but the principes leaped up as fast as they could, and saluted. 'Sir,' they muttered, quiet and silently resentful. 'Sir.'

'Kit inspection.' Bulbus gestured at the stacked shields and piles of leather-covered kit by their tent.

Felix wasn't drunk, but he'd had enough wine to make him think, *I'm an officer, and this is ridiculous.* Without thinking, he said, 'Now, sir?'

Bulbus was on him like a swooping hawk. His vitis shot up, striking

Felix's chin so hard from underneath that his jaw snapped shut – he was lucky not to bite his tongue. 'What's that?' hissed Bulbus in his ear.

'Nothing, sir.' Gods, thought Felix. The fact that I'm a tesserarius means nothing to the onion-headed prick.

Bulbus hit Felix in the belly with the end of the vitis this time, a painful blow that part winded him. As he straightened, wheezing, Bulbus shoved his face right into Felix's and grated, 'I heard you speak. What. Did. You. Say?'

'"Now, sir?" I said, "Now, sir?"' In all Felix's time in the army, he had never seen a centurion strike another officer. Bulbus was a different breed, he decided.

'And what, precisely, did you mean by that?' The fact that Bulbus whispered made his words far more threatening.

'I suppose I thought it was late for a kit inspection, sir.'

'You thought?' Drops of Bulbus' spittle hit Felix's cheeks. 'You're not paid to think, are you?'

'No, sir.'

'Open your mouth again, and I'll break this and half a dozen others on your back.' Bulbus rammed the end of the vitis right into Felix's face, who had to force himself not to recoil. 'Again, consider yourself lucky not to be stripped to the ranks. You can dig latrines for the next ten days. So can your brother, just because he's your blood. As for the rest of your idiot tentmates, they're sure to have some dirty kit–' Bulbus glared around the fire '–what are you waiting for? Lay it out, close to the flames so I can see.'

Felix's punishment wasn't yet complete either. Bulbus lingered over his equipment and weapons, finding among other things, a few rust spots on his sword blade and a dirty buckle on his baldric. Latrine duties increased to twenty days, he also had five nights' extra sentry duty thrown in, because, a leering Bulbus said, 'I don't like you.'

As Felix lay in his blankets later that night, furious and powerless, he did not even consider Flamininus' and Philip's second meeting.

He had plotted to murder a centurion – Matho – before.

Why not another?

CHAPTER X

Orestis, western Macedon

Freezing rain sheeted down, obscuring the mountains that shaped the valley. The deluge was so heavy that Demetrios had it hard to see a score of paces in any direction. Sodden from the downpour, the ground underfoot more resembled a marsh than a track. His cloak was wringing, and he under it. Four men wide, the narrow column afforded little protection from the cutting wind either. Demetrios had never been so cold in his life. Feeling had long since been lost in his feet, and his legs were mud-coated to the knee. The skin on his hands was chapped and cracked from exposure to wind and water. He had raw, chafing areas where he'd never imagined it possible. The muscles of his right arm and shoulder screamed with tiredness from the effort of carrying the two sections of his new sarissa.

Cold, he thought. I'm cold and wet. And I'm fucking starving.

There was no point complaining. Every man in the speira was in the same situation. During the course of their long march inland, they had heard it all before. Demetrios had whinged. Kimon and Antileon were wreath-winning complainers. The file-closer Zotikos went on a rant at least once a day. Empedokles moaned whenever anyone listened to him. Andriskos' usual good temper had vanished; even Philippos had given in, grumbling that he didn't care if he died, as long as he was warm. Only the file-leader Simonides had said nothing, and that, everyone knew, was because it looked bad for an officer to join in. He wasn't immune of course. Never a talkative type, he now rarely said anything but an irritated aye or no.

'What did we do to deserve this?' It was Empedokles again. 'Some of the king's best soldiers, we're supposed to be. Saw off the Romans over and over again, we did.'

'Shut it,' rumbled Philippos.

Empedokles wasn't listening. 'While the rest of the chiliarchy, who weren't even *at* Elateia, march back to Pella – they're already there, I'd wager, warming their cheesy toes by their fires, or ploughing whores – we are ordered to the furthest shithole part of Macedon there is.'

'And we're not even there yet,' said Andriskos, raising a few chuckles.

'It's not right,' grumbled Empedokles.

'Life's not fair,' said Demetrios, wishing he could smack his enemy in the mouth. Truth was, he wanted to do a lot more than that since Korinth, but the chance hadn't yet come his way. Deep down, however, he wasn't sure he could murder a man in cold blood. Maybe, as Kimon maintained, Empedokles had not intended him to drown. A good hiding would do, Demetrios decided. 'Get on with it,' he snapped.

Empedokles' response – a string of curses – was brought to an abrupt halt by Simonides. 'If you don't shut up, 'Dokles, I swear I'll ram my kopis so far down your throat it will come out your arsehole.'

Startled, Empedokles fell silent.

'Whatever you unhappy bastards might think, there's a good reason *we* are here,' shouted Simonides, his voice competing with the drumming rain. 'The chiliarchy at Korinth was the only unit in the entire army that was still in the field. We weren't that far from the so-called rebellion when news of it arrived. Philokles judged that the entire chiliarchy wouldn't be needed, so the majority were always going to continue their journey to Pella. Our speira was chosen by lot – for the addled heads among you, that means we had a three in four chance of *not* being picked.' He drew in a breath and continued, 'Before I hear anyone whinge that the Fates must have had a hand in seeing that we are the ones here, not anyone else, I have heard it all before. *Enough!*'

The length of Simonides' speech – Demetrios had never heard him say so much – and the savagery with which it was delivered saw calm descend over his men. Those in other files who had heard held their peace too. It wasn't a happy silence – no one could be happy in this sodden version of Tartaros – but a more accepting one. It was, thought Demetrios, as if every man had decided, curse it, let's just march. We'll get there in the end.

There was a village – a mountainous, hard-to-reach region, Orestis didn't have many settlements that could be termed towns – set among some of the western peaks that formed the backbone between Macedon and Illyria. Never a place that had been over-friendly or loyal to the incumbent on the throne in Pella, and a place that had suffered as the Roman legions had marched through it twice in the past year and a half, it was rumoured to be at the heart of the rebellion.

Demetrios' gaze was drawn to a slope-roofed hut set into the hillside a spear throw from the track. A neglected shed, scarce more than a roof and two sides, held a pen of scrawny sheep. From the hut's half-open door, a lad of perhaps twelve summers watched the passing phalangists with an expression of sheer terror. Demetrios felt a pang of guilt. They had to do their duty – put down this uprising before it spread – but the locals here were Macedonian. Not Romans or brutish Illyrians, or even Greeks. They were Macedonian. The same blood as the phalangists ran through their veins; their ancestors had fought for Alexander alongside one another on battlefields from here to India.

A woman's sharp voice came from behind the watching boy, and he vanished. The door slammed shut. Hostile reception and leaking roof aside, thought Demetrios wistfully, it would be warm inside, and drier than he was. Put it from your mind, he told himself. The only shelter you'll have tonight will be a damp, stinking tent, the only food a bowl of cold gruel.

It was hard to believe that he'd ever be warm or have a full belly again.

In that grey, freezing world, absent of sun, it was impossible to judge the passage of time. If the track the phalangists were following had been in better repair, not a morass in which they sank to mid-calf with each step, a man might have been able to judge by the distance they had travelled. Unable to do either, Demetrios guessed that perhaps two hours had dragged by since he'd seen the boy peering from the hut.

The phalangists had climbed steadily since; the rain had been re-placed by snow. On either side, what they could see of the stony slopes were no longer shades of grey and brown: a white blanket covered all. Low over their heads, the clouds were an ominous, dirty yellow. Few people lived here; they had marched by perhaps half a dozen houses, each as miserable and deprived as the next. The only reason to build a village up here, Demetrios decided, was to serve as a defensive strong-hold. Soon the place would be snowed in until the spring, or he was no judge. If the phalangists didn't finish their task fast, they might be trapped here themselves.

No one knew what kind of reception would greet them. Thus far, the 'rebellion' consisted of the locals refusing to pay tax to a group of royal officials a month since. No one had been killed; the taxmen had merely been escorted from the settlement at spear point. It was the message they'd been given, that 'no lackey of Philip had better return here, for fear of his life', which had caused concern in the palace at Pella.

Philippos and the older phalangists reckoned sending the speira here was using a hammer to crack a walnut, and Demetrios could see little reason to disagree. The inhabitants of this valley, hardened yet simple farmers, posed no threat to the kingdom. The people of the lowland towns would pay no heed to the activities of bumpkins in this gods-forsaken corner of Macedon. Philip on the other hand, was furious, pride smarting at the recent losses of Thessaly and Phokis. 'I want the rebellion crushed!' he had reportedly thundered. 'Utterly crushed!'

'That's why we're freezing our balls off in the mountains,' Philippos had said, laughing his great belly laugh. 'And we won't get to warm them again until the king's peace has been restored.'

It didn't feel right requesting help of Ares, the god of war, to help defeat his own people, thought Demetrios. He felt the same ambivalence about Zeus, thunder god and master of the other deities. Almost in the clouds here, they were in Zeus' territory, which meant he might look favourably on the locals. Demetrios opted for the shepherds' favourite, Hermes, messenger of the gods. Let us bring this sorry matter to a swift end, Hermes, he prayed. I'd like to be warm before the year's end, if not sooner.

They climbed. The temperature dropped. A heavy mist fell, obscuring the junction between cloud and hillside and making it seem as if they had climbed to the very skies. At times, Demetrios almost expected to look down and see nothing beneath his feet but empty air. Sourness filled him again that three in every four phalangists in the chiliarchy were back in the army's camp at Pella, but not he and his comrades. The king ordered you to Orestis, he told himself. It's your duty to be here.

A rumble from their left.

'What's that?' Simonides' voice was taut, strained. 'Halt!'

The men in the speira ahead – Demetrios' unit was second in the column – had not heard. They kept marching. Simonides' file was at the front of their speira, and his halting forced everyone else to obey. Heads turned; eyes searched the murk to their left. Visibility was terrible, no more than fifteen paces, affording a glance of snowy, rock-covered ground. No houses. No livestock. No sign of life. Of the slopes above, the phalangists could see nothing at all.

Scrape. Clack. The sound of stone on stone was unmistakable.

'Ambush!' Demetrios spoke before he had time to think.

Empedokles sneered, but Simonides muttered, 'I think the lad's right,' and men gripped their sarissa shafts tight.

'Face left, nice and quiet. Assemble pikes. Shields ready,' said Simonides. 'Pass the word down the line.'

They were almost prepared, standing four deep, when harsh rumbling sounds dragged everyone's attention to the fog-shrouded slopes above. A blur of lichen-covered stone flashed past Demetrios, taking the man to his left with it. One instant he was there, the next he had vanished, gone without so much as a yell. Pushed by unseen attackers, more hurtled from the gloom.

Sarissa discarded as worse than useless, Demetrios dodged a boulder the size of a horse. To his right, Philippos was unhurt, and cursing their attackers at the top of his voice. Demetrios called to Kimon and Antileon, who were behind him, but got no reply. More rocks rumbled out of the semi-darkness, threatening obliteration. A small landslide set off by the larger boulders followed, injuring men a little way to his left. Curses rang out; a man screamed, and was cowed into silence by a furious file-leader.

A short pause. Men checked their weapons. Wiped sweat away. Glanced at each other, relieved to be alive. One or two hotheads advanced a little way up the slope, and were ordered back into position.

'Stay where you are,' barked Simonides. 'Break the line and we become vulnerable.'

We're already fucking vulnerable, Demetrios wanted to shout. Instead he gritted his teeth and stared into the fog, wishing he could see the cowards who were attacking them.

More rumbling noises carried from above.

Philippos shouted, 'Look out, Demetrios!'

Several rocks, each large enough to maim, were heading straight for them. Philippos had seen, he would be fine, thought Demetrios. The comrade to his left was in danger, however. Without thinking, he grabbed the man – mid-lunge, he was horrified to find it was Empedokles – and propelled him several paces clear of the stones.

Sneering at Empedokles' ungrateful reaction – a curse and a shove back at him – Demetrios palmed sweat from his forehead and listened.

Voices muttered above, but no more rocks came. Injured men groaned and swore. Demetrios shot a look behind him. Everything was chaos. Bodies were scattered like discarded dolls in between the rocks that had felled them. He looked next for Philippos, but could not see him. Unease tickled the base of Demetrios' spine. He called Philippos' name.

There was no answer.

Heart pounding, Demetrios shouted, 'Kimon! Antileon!'

A moment's delay, and Kimon replied, 'We're here. You hurt?'

'No. You seen Philippos?'

Before his friends could answer, Simonides' voice cracked like a whip. 'Set down your sarissae. I want shields facing front. Draw swords and form a line. Fast!'

Demetrios obeyed. Philippos was somewhere close by, he told himself. He'd been tending to the wounded, like as not. Slipping out of the neck strap, Demetrios shoved his left forearm into the strap on the inside face of his aspis. Kopis ready in his right fist, he closed up with the nearest men, Empedokles and Andriskos.

Andriskos' usually happy face was pinched with concern. He glanced at Demetrios. 'Have you seen Philippos . . .?'

Demetrios' worries swelled. 'No.'

'Anyone else?' asked Empedokles, without his usual animosity.

Demetrios found his hate for Empedokles subsumed by his desire to find their attackers. 'I don't know.'

'Nor I,' said Andriskos, his expression hard. 'We have to stay sharp, though. Those sheep-humping dusty feet might not be finished with us.'

'Should we advance up the slope?' called Kimon.

Kimon didn't hear Empedokles snort with contempt, but Demetrios did. He had no opportunity to think of a suitably acid rejoinder, because Simonides interjected, 'We stay where we are. Gods know how many of the bastards are up there in the murk.'

They stood and stared into the clouds – that's what they were, thought Demetrios bitterly – for the span of a hundred heartbeats before Simonides was satisfied their attackers had gone. Ordering every second man to stay in line, he directed the rest to see to the injured.

Concern nipping him like a dog worrying a bone, Demetrios set down his sarissa and hurried to find Philippos. Seeing his big friend lying fifteen paces to the rear, his head up, filled him with joy. 'There you are!'

Philippos laid his head back down without answering.

Sudden fear clawing his belly, Demetrios sprinted forward. Philippos didn't open his eyes. He lay there, face a sickly grey, shallow breaths the one indication he was alive. Demetrios' eyes roved down Philippos' body – he seemed unharmed. The only damage appeared to be a massive dent in one side of the lower half of his breastplate. It's nothing, Demetrios decided, even as he wondered why his friend wasn't responding. 'Philippos. Are you hurt?'

A grunt.

'Can you sit up?'

'Maybe, aye, but there's no point. I'm done.'

'You're a little shaken, that's all,' cried Demetrios, setting down his apsis and sword. He knelt and slipped an arm behind Philippos' shoulders. 'Come on. I'll help you up.'

Philippos' eyes opened. He stared at Demetrios. 'I can't feel my legs.'

'Your legs?' Demetrios asked stupidly.

'When I shouted the warning at you, there was a stone I hadn't seen. The bastarding thing hit me when I was half turned. It must've snapped my spine. I'm a dead man.'

Please, no, thought Demetrios. I saved Empedokles and this happened? He flailed for something to say. 'You're mistaken,' he declared in a confident tone. 'Come on.'

Philippos did not resist as Demetrios hauled him into a sitting position. He was too heavy for one man to lift; Demetrios called for help, and Antileon came running. Arms linked around the big man's shoulders, they hauled him into a standing position.

'There,' said Demetrios brightly, turning his face towards Philippos'.

'Look down.' Philippos' tone was flat. Resigned.

Demetrios obeyed. Nausea tickled his gullet. Philippos' toes were dragging in the dirt; his feet were limp and above, his meaty calves hung slack. 'The feeling will come back,' said Demetrios, hating the false note in his voice.

'Course it will,' added Antileon.

'I'm finished,' said Philippos. 'There's no sensation in my legs. I was bursting for a piss just before the ambush, but I can't feel my bladder now. Put me down.'

They sat him down as gently as a small child. Over his head, Demetrios and Antileon exchanged a look of dismay and helplessness. A heartbeat later, Demetrios felt a vice-like grip on his left wrist. He looked down, into Philippos' fierce eyes.

'I'll not be a burden to any of you.'

'You won't,' protested Demetrios, already worried about hauling someone of Philippos' size to the settlement – for a battle – and then back to Pella. It would be a Heraklean task.

'Odds are, I won't survive. Even if I did, I'd be a cripple. Good for nothing but pissing and shitting myself for the rest of my life. That's no kind of existence.' Even one-handed, Philippos was able to pull Demetrios' ear down to his lips. 'I deserve a soldier's death. A blade death.'

Horrified, Demetrios pulled free. 'I can't.'

Antileon, who had been about to ask what Philippos had said, realised. He shook his head at Demetrios, no.

'I ask you as a friend.' Philippos' deep voice had gone husky.

'I can't.' Demetrios' throat closed; he stumbled away. Empedokles, he thought, his heart filled with a savage mixture of shame and hate. Why in Tartaros did I save Empedokles and not my friend?

'Demetrios!'

He ignored Philippos' cry.

There had been no revenge-taking. When a light breeze shifted the mist, revealing the slopes to either side, Simonides had sent men to search for their attackers. They had come back empty-handed an hour later, having seen nothing but a few mountain goats. The locals had vanished like wraiths returning to the underworld. By that time, Stephanos had brought the rest of the speira back and ordered camp set up. Remaining where they were meant the injured could be tended to. The phalangists were on the only road to the settlement; those inside were going nowhere. Let them dwell overnight on the reprisals coming their way, Stephanos had announced to a fierce, cruel cheer.

Morale was low as the phalangists sat about the few sputtering fires they'd managed to light. The cleverly worked ambush had seen a dozen men die, including one of Demetrios' tentmates. Perhaps half that number again had broken limbs; one other had been maimed like Philippos.

Demetrios' bowl of porridge lay untouched. The pitiful blaze at his feet gave off so little heat that Kimon had only been able to half cook their dinner. Spying Antileon's greedy eyes on the porridge, he handed it over.

Antileon spooned in a large mouthful. 'Not hungry?'

'No.'

'Philippos?' muttered Kimon, sensing his reason.

'Aye,' said Demetrios, his heart heavy with grief and a smouldering fury towards Empedokles. Demetrios didn't quite realise it, but the guilt of not having saved Philippos had led him to lay the blame for what had happened at his enemy's feet.

Their eyes moved to the fire by the next tent. Simonides, Andriskos and Empedokles were sitting around Philippos, who had propped himself up on an elbow. Taurion and Skopas, who didn't know Philippos as well, were on the other side of the fire. It was impossible to hear what was being said, but everyone's expression was troubled or unhappy. Philippos seemed angry – something he never was – as well as frustrated.

'He's asking them to end his life,' said Demetrios. 'They don't want to. They're telling him he needs time, that his injuries might come good with rest.'

'They won't.' Antileon, ever the blunt one.

'You don't know that,' said Kimon, the optimist.

'Antileon's right,' snapped Demetrios, his grief morphing into anger. 'I had a dog once that fell from a low cliff and broke its back. I was too small to understand. I begged my father to let me nurse it. Against his better judgement, he agreed. After ten days it was clear, even to an eight-year-old, that it was suffering.' Demetrios could still see the spiritless dog, caked in its own filth, coat staring, eyes sunken. Could hear the dull crack as his father brought down the heavy stone on its head. 'Philippos deserves better than that.'

'I can't draw a blade over a comrade's throat,' said Kimon, his expression tortured.

'Nor I,' said Antileon. Their two other tentmates – quiet types – shook their heads in agreement.

'One of the front-rankers will do it,' said Demetrios, even though it didn't look like it from where he was sitting.

Philippos refused to let his comrades carry him into their tent when the time came to climb into their blankets. 'I have a cloak,' he shouted. 'Leave me be.'

Demetrios, who had lingered outside after his own comrades had retired, waited until Philippos was alone before walking over. 'Join you?'

'Do what you like. I can't stop you.' Philippos didn't look at him.

'Any feeling returned to your legs?'

'Piss off. No. Did you see the boulder that hit me?'

'No. Philippos, I'm sorry.'

'For what?' He sounded more like the old Philippos.

'When you shouted, I thought you'd be all right – you're always all right – so I grabbed the man beside me and heaved him out of the way of the rocks. It was fucking Empedokles.'

Unbelievably, Philippos laughed.

Demetrios stared at him. 'What?'

'My father always said that the Fates were spiteful crones. I've always held different, but this – this proves him right.' Philippos shrugged. 'It's not your fault, Demetrios.'

Demetrios felt no better. Guilt battered him still. He blamed Empedokles still.

An uncomfortable quiet fell, allowing the groans of the injured to remind them that others were also suffering. Most of the poppy juice had already been used as well; it would be a long night, thought Demetrios.

'Poor bastards,' said Philippos. 'At least *I* can't feel anything.'

They were back to this, thought Demetrios with a sinking feeling. 'Did you ask Simonides or Andriskos . . .?'

'I did. They refused. Said it was too early to be talking like that. Taurion and Skopas said the same, even though it's plain as the nose on my face that I'm a cripple.' Philippos waved a hand in frustration. 'Some truths are hard to accept, I suppose.'

'What about Empedokles?'

A scornful look. 'I'm not asking that prick. He wouldn't have the balls anyway.'

Demetrios chewed the inside of his cheek.

'It's got to be you.'

Their eyes met. Demetrios held the gaze with difficulty.

'I'll be covered in bedsores within a few days,' muttered Philippos. 'Don't make me beg.'

Demetrios hadn't cried since his father's death, years before. Tears came now, however, unbidden. He wiped them away savagely. 'I won't.'

'So you'll do it?'

'Aye.'

Philippos smiled, the big grin that Demetrios knew and loved so well. 'Thank you.' He reached out a great paw, and they shook, eyes locked on one another.

Demetrios couldn't bring himself to let go the grip; it was Philippos who did, his smile still somehow there.

'I'll sit up.' Grunting a little, Philippos pushed himself into a sitting position. He held out a bronze-hilted dagger. 'I sharpened it this evening.'

Demetrios hesitated.

'This way, I can go to meet my ancestors with pride. The other way, I—' Philippos hung his head and shoved the dagger forward.

Grief-stricken, Demetrios took it. He moved to kneel beside Philippos. The big man let his cloak slip down his back, and unfastened his chiton on the left side of the neck, exposing his chest. Wordless, he guided Demetrios' hand to the flesh two fingers' breadth to the left of his nipple. Under the ribs, Philippos' heart beat slow and strong.

Battered by horror, Demetrios gritted his teeth.

'You are a fine soldier,' said Philippos. 'A good comrade. The best of friends.'

The acceptance in Philippos' voice and eyes was almost impossible to take. The gods were cruel beyond belief, thought Demetrios. 'So are you,' he whispered, carefully placing the dagger's tip between two ribs. With his left hand, he gripped Philippos' right shoulder, the better to hold him when the blade went in. 'Why did you welcome me that first night, after you'd knocked me out?'

Philippos tensed, and then, incredibly, he chuckled. 'I had to show you some kindness after punching you halfway to Tartaros. When you woke, your eyes were still rolling in your head, remember?'

'That's not true. I could have gone a third bout,' said Demetrios, praying the lie would distract Philippos.

The gods answered.

'Eh? You were—' Philippos' eyes widened as Demetrios slid the dagger into his barrel chest. He took a juddering breath.

Demetrios drew Philippos into an embrace, which forced the sharp-edged iron deeper.

Philippos coughed once, twice. His left hand came up to Demetrios' right, as if he were trying to seize the blade, but instead he patted Demetrios' shoulder – the loving touch of a father to a son – and his arm fell away.

Demetrios held Philippos close as the great heart slowed. He cared nothing for the blood soaking around the blade into his chiton. He cared not for the ache in his back from his awkward posture, or that his face was running with tears, that his body shook with silent sobs. 'Forgive me,' he whispered into Philippos' ear.

No answer came.

Demetrios had never felt so alone.

A day and a half later, standing outside the village they'd been marching towards, Demetrios' guilt and grief had hardened into a burning desire for revenge. Loathsome though he was, Empedokles had not pushed the boulder that had maimed Philippos. The men who'd done that were staring at him from atop the palisade that ringed their miserable settlement. A mixture of youths, men in the prime of life and hunched greybeards, they looked downright terrified. It hadn't been their intention, their wreath-bearing messenger had said not an hour since, to kill. The ambush had only been intended to be a warning. As his men cheered, Stephanos had told the messenger that he could take his lies and shove them up his arse.

'We're coming in,' Stephanos had snarled. 'And when we do, it won't be pretty. For every soldier of mine who died, four of yours will be executed.'

Demetrios had roared his approval too, even as he'd thought that ten lice-ridden mountain men couldn't replace Philippos, or even twenty. Yet it would be something to kill the villagers, he thought fiercely, gripping his kopis. Someone had to pay for the death of his friend. It no longer mattered to Demetrios that the men on the palisade were Macedonian, and from the grim expressions on his comrades' faces, it didn't matter to them either.

Early that morning, they had encircled the village to make sure no one tried to escape. A couple of hours' work had seen a dozen crude ladders fashioned from the timbers of nearby outbuildings. Now they were ready. A few men might be lost scaling the defences, but the phalangists' fury was such that no one doubted they would soon storm their way inside. When Stephanos gave the signal, the entire speira would attack. No quarter was to be given. 'I don't have to tell you why,' Stephanos had said to loud cries of 'Kill them all!'

Demetrios looked down at his kopis, a solid, well-made weapon. He'd only used it a few times in battle, but he hungered to wield it now. To bury it in flesh. To see blood spurt. To hew. To hack. To send men to Tartaros. Gods help anyone that comes within reach, he thought, feeling nothing but hatred for the villagers.

'Ready?' cried Stephanos.

The phalangists hammered their blades off their shields, creating a mighty clamour.

Stephanos raised his arm.

Demetrios tensed, ready to run forward. He'd been chosen to climb one of the ladders; he would run alongside the men carrying it, and the instant it had been leaned against the palisade, he would start ascending. It was a dangerous task; even more so because, in order to climb, he'd have to leave his shield behind.

'Look, sir!' shouted Simonides.

Stephanos stared. His arm fell.

Loud creaking noises announced the opening of the gate into the village. Framed in the entrance was the messenger and a dignified-looking older man – possibly the chieftain. Both were holding wreaths aloft, a sign that they wished to surrender.

Furious, not wanting to be robbed of his vengeance, Demetrios glanced at Stephanos.

Stephanos hawked and spat towards the wreath-bearers. 'Faithless murderers! You think to escape justice?' Turning to his left and right, he asked his men, 'Shall we accept their plea?'

'No!' bayed Demetrios and everyone else.

'Shall we give them what they deserve?' cried Stephanos, his face red with rage, veins bulging in his neck.

The phalangists' answer was a death-promising, blood-curdling roar.

No one heard Stephanos' command to attack a moment later, but when he pointed his kopis at the now petrified-looking pair in the gateway, it was signal enough.

Demetrios and the rest charged forward like hounds slipped from the leash.

CHAPTER XI

The Malian Gulf, close to Nicaea

The king's trireme was beating southward, both banks of oarsmen working in smooth unison to the flautist's measured tune. Close behind, in a long 'V' formation, came five lembi. A low coastline – stone beaches, with farms behind – ran along to starboard. The hilly island of Euboea lay on the ship's port side. Philip stood at the prow, cloak blowing in the breeze, gaze locked on the grey-brown mountains of Lokris and Phokis which filled the horizon before him. There lay the hallowed gates of fire, where Leonidas and his Spartans had won themselves immortal glory. Part of Philip would have given his entire kingdom to have fallen in that battle. Few deaths could be as magnificent.

He was remembering Thermopylae not from vanity, but for the events of the time, and how the Greeks and Macedonians had united against a common enemy. Their alliance had been riven by argument and treachery, but it *had* worked. Soon after the death of Leonidas and his men, a combined force of Greeks had won a glorious naval victory at Salamis; this was quickly followed by another success at Plataea. Not long after, the Persians had left Greece's shores, never to return.

Why can't they see? Rome is no different from Persia, thought Philip. Agelaos of Aitolia knew it – he told everyone at the Nafpaktos conference almost a generation before, for Zeus' sake – but all the short-sighted fools can see is Macedon. Philip let out a quiet sigh. It was fruitless to dwell on the past, and what might have been. The Greeks were not going to unite, and the chances of any joining him in his battle against Flamininus were slim indeed.

'Can I join you, sire?'

Philip turned. 'Of course, Brakhylles.'

Brakhylles of Boeotia was one of his few remaining allies. A short, bald man in early middle age, he was nine years older than the king. He was someone that Philip could easily have been enemies with, because his hard-drinking, strong-minded and combative nature was so similar to the king's own, but the shared experience of going to war together had seen their friendship cemented. Brakhylles could be trusted, of that Philip was sure. That was why he was here.

Brakhylles cast an eye at the sun, which had passed its high point in the sky. 'We must be three hours late, sire.'

Philip shrugged. 'Flamininus wants to talk. He'll still be there. So will his lickspittle allies.' He spat the last word.

'They hang off Flamininus' words as if he were Zeus himself,' said Brakhylles. 'Agreeing with everything he says, laughing at his jokes – apart from your one about the Aitolians, that is.' He chuckled. 'Didn't appreciate being told they weren't Greek, eh, sire?'

'They did not.' It had been one of his better quips, Philip decided. Flamininus had certainly seemed to like it. The animosity that had marked their last meeting over the Aous appeared to have vanished, which, Philip hoped, was to his advantage. Yesterday the consul had also laughed at his humorous offer to send gardeners to restore the precincts of Pergamene temples destroyed by his army. Gods willing, Philip thought, Flamininus would agree to a private meeting today. Without the craven Aitolians, Rhodians, Pergamenes and Akhaians looking on, not to mention the cursed Athenians, he had a greater chance of seeing his offer – under which he would accede to almost all of the demands made the previous day – accepted.

'If Flamininus agrees, sire, the mongrel Greeks will fall into line behind him,' said Brakhylles.

'Yes,' said Philip. 'But we must remain awake to the possibility of treachery. Even when I have an agreement ratified by the Senate in my hands, I will not be totally at ease. In the end, it may still come to a battle.'

'If that happens, I shall be there, sire.'

'I know, Brakhylles,' said Philip with a pleased nod. What was it about short men, he wondered, always looking for a fight? In this case, he was glad, but Brakhylles would pick a quarrel with his shadow given half a chance. He would have to be watched – the day before, he had been about to follow the two headstrong fools into the shallows.

'Beach in sight!' called the lookout.

Philip thought of his visit to the temple at Gonnos, and the prophecy he'd been given there. It was impossible to know if the priest had been telling him what he wanted to hear, as priests so often did, or whether Zeus *had* spoken. To follow the prophecy entirely – in other words, to place all his hopes on a military victory – would be rash. Only a fool put every egg in one basket. Reach a negotiated settlement with Flamininus here, and the war could be brought to an early, bloodless end. Given the size of the Roman army in Phokis and his numerous enemies, that would be a satisfactory result for the moment.

For the moment, thought Philip. In time, things might change. King Nabis of Sparta – as yet, neutral in the conflict between Macedon and Rome – was someone to be won over. Philip's own overtures towards the Seleucid ruler Antiokhos might bear fruit. Even if these possibilities never came to pass, his phalangists *could* defeat the legions given the right ground.

No doubt Flamininus thought he held all the best gaming pieces, thought Philip.

He didn't.

Shingle crunched as the trireme ran up onto the beach. Accompanied by Brakhylles and another general called Kykliadas, Philip leaped down; he was pleased to see Flamininus had come to meet him. His allies scurried behind, jostling one another in their efforts to be ahead of the rest.

'You're late,' said Flamininus in Greek.

Resentful mutters rose from his followers – Aitolians and Akhaians, Rhodians and Pergamenes and Athamanians. 'Typical Macedonian.' 'Arrogance beyond belief.' 'I'd expect nothing less.'

Philip didn't even acknowledge their existence. 'Well met, consul,' he said, half bowing.

'And the same to you.' Flamininus returned the gesture. 'After your *deliberation*, did you reach a decision?' He smiled, but not in a friendly way.

'The demands given to me yesterday were severe and unreasonable,' said Philip. 'I have therefore spent the morning considering them.'

Flamininus' features remained smooth and unperturbed.

Deciding that this meant Flamininus remained well-disposed

towards him, Philip decided to throw the dice. 'I would talk with you alone.'

'The Aetolians and Achaeans have not yet responded to what you said yesterday.' Flamininus cast a look at the emissaries, who uttered indignant ayes.

'I am sure that none of us wish the bickering of yesterday to be repeated,' said Philip in a conciliatory tone. 'Let us walk together, you and I, and come to agreement. Two voices may find a clearer path than many. When we are done, your allies will have their opportunity to see if our plan is acceptable to them.'

'I would be happy to discuss matters,' said Flamininus. Again he glanced at his allies. 'What say you?'

None of the emissaries seemed happy; one of the Aitolians, thought Philip, looked as if he were sucking on a particularly bitter lemon. None had the conviction to protest, however, and so after a moment, Flamininus declared, 'We are agreed then.'

'Which direction shall we walk?' asked Philip. 'West or east?'

'West, if it please you, for Thermopylae lies that way.'

Philip had heard of Flamininus' interest in all things Hellenic, but witnessing it was a revelation. 'You know of the battle?'

'It remains one of the most famous clashes in history. Every educated Roman is taught about Thermopylae.' Flamininus' sigh was wistful. 'What it must have been like to stand there with Leonidas.'

Philip looked at the enthusiasm lighting Flamininus' eyes, and thought, perhaps he's not unlike me. 'I often think the same thing.'

'I am not surprised. Would you have stayed to the end? Died merely so your allies could retreat?'

'I would,' Philip said at once. 'If Leonidas had gone with the troops that retreated, the Persian cavalry would have wreaked a fearful slaughter on the open ground beyond Thermopylae. Someone had to stay, and he would suffer no one else to take it, the most dangerous task. To die that some of your soldiers might live is the mark of a hero.'

'Many would say that if an army loses its leader, defeat is inevitable. If you were to fall, say, Macedonia would not fare well against Rome.' Flamininus cast him a look.

Anger boiled up inside Philip that Flamininus should slide inside his guard with such ease. It was true – his son Perseus was not quite old enough to rule, and none of Philip's generals had his tactical ability or charisma – whereas if he were to strike down the Roman general this very moment, another would be sent to replace him within the span of a few months. He fixed Flamininus with a hard stare. 'Maybe so, yet here I stand, hale and hearty. The Fates have woven me a long life, say the priests, and I believe them. Would *you* have stayed with Leonidas?' Philip's tone was mocking, the implication – that Flamininus was a coward – clear.

'I too would have remained with the Spartans.'

Philip studied Flamininus' face and decided he was telling the truth. Barbarian he might be, but the man has balls. He nodded, and said in a more conciliatory tone, 'Perhaps we could have stood side by side.'

'I think we could. We are not so different, you and I.'

They smiled at one another, and the tension that had sprung up eased a little.

The pair walked for a time, waves from the incoming tide threatening to erase their footprints, leaving no trace of their passage.

He's waiting for me to speak, thought Philip, to give way to his demands. Clever. It was hateful to find himself in such a position – a *king*, for Zeus' sake – and yet here he was. Better it was to have only one witness rather than half a score of gloating hangers-on. In a measured voice, he said, 'Rome shall have the entire coastline of Illyria, and any Roman prisoners or deserters I have taken.'

'These are good tidings,' said Flamininus.

'Attalus,' said Philip, thinking, the flea-bitten dog, 'shall have back his ships and crews. I will return to Ptolemy of Egypt his settlements, and the Peraea to the Rhodians also, but my troops will continue to occupy Iasos and Bargylia. Aitolia can have all the towns named yesterday, save Thebes.'

Although the last city was at risk because of the close proximity of Flamininus' legions, Philip had hopes for it to resist assaults as the Akrokorinth had.

'And Achaea?'

'To Akhaia I shall return Argos *and* Korinth.' Philip made no mention of the Akrokorinth fortress, and hoped that Flamininus assumed he meant to surrender both – he did not.

Flamininus rubbed a finger over his lips, thinking.

A pulse hammered in Philip's throat. He watched the Roman sidelong, unsure if his offer was about to be thrown back in his face, or fresh demands made. He would go to Tartaros before he would ask Flamininus his mind, however. It was a case of strolling on, pretending he hadn't a care in the world.

The silence stretched on for almost a hundred paces – it felt like ten stadia.

'What of the Fetters – Demetrias, Chalcis and the Acrocorinth?'

He's sharp as a blade, thought Philip. Better to come clean. 'They have been Macedonian for generations – I wish to keep them. Without their protection, Macedon is vulnerable to attack from Greece.' There was no immediate reply, and his nerves stretched wire-taut.

'I accept your offer.'

'You do?' Philip almost cried. Smooth-featured, as if he had expected nothing else, he said instead, 'Why?'

Flamininus' expression now contained a mixture of coyness and embarrassment. 'The consular elections are almost upon us. Inevitably, my successor as consul will want to replace me in the field. It's not certain that they will succeed in doing this, but my sources indicate that one of the largest groupings of senators that has supported me in the past is close to supporting another candidate. My command here seems unlikely to continue. You'll understand that I wish to avoid the humiliation of returning to Rome as the general who failed to defeat Macedonia,' said Flamininus with a meaningful look. 'A negotiated settlement suits us both.'

'I see.' Philip's spies had brought him whispers of the moves being made against Flamininus, but until this moment he hadn't known how much weight to give the information. Letters would need to be sent to check whether the Roman was telling the truth. He was pleased by Flamininus' confession, yet wary still of the Aitolians' and Akhaians' enmity. 'And if your allies will not accept your suggestion?' he asked, not seeing how Flamininus could do anything in that case but support them.

'You are an eloquent man – if anyone can persuade them, it's you.'

Philip let out a phhhh of contempt. 'You and I both know that it's unlikely.'

'They must be given their chance to speak, to feel that their demands are being listened to.'

Had there been a sardonic note in Flamininus' voice? Philip wondered. 'I have no argument with that. But if the Aitolians and Akhaians refuse my terms, say, we shall be back where we started.'

'Greeks do not determine the Senate's policies,' said Flamininus with an unmistakable tone of contempt. 'Nor can the importance of our potential agreement be understated – it offers peace instead of war. Failing to consult the Senate before making any decision to reject it would be both rash and inadvisable.'

'Go on,' said Philip, still unsure where this was going.

'In the event of your offer being refused by my allies, therefore, you could ask to send an embassy to Rome, its mission to speak to the Senate. No reasonable man would argue against such a request – I, least of all. My allies would not dare take a different position from mine.' Flamininus' smile was toothy.

'And will the Senate accept the same terms as you have here, with me?' It would be a pointless exercise, thought Philip, if the senators supported the troublesome Aetolians' and Achaeans' demands.

'I can make no guarantees, but a letter from the general in the field–' Flamininus tapped himself on the chest '–recommending that you should be allowed to retain the Fetters will go a long way towards persuading the senators.'

'Very well.' Philip stuck out his hand. 'Let us shake on it, as equals. As men who might have stood together at Thermopylae.'

Flamininus chuckled and took the grip. 'Done.'

In more optimistic mood than he had been for some time, Philip strode towards the trireme and the emissaries waiting by it.

Next morning Philip's good spirits remained, despite the lack of agreement that had persisted at the end of the previous day's negotiations. Returning with Flamininus, things had gone well at first. The Pergamenes had accepted Philip's offer, but matters had soured straight after, with the Rhodians, Aitolians and Akhaians all refusing it. Causes for friction would linger for ever if Philip continued to maintain garrisons in Greece, the Aitolians and Akhaians had repeatedly cried.

So indignant had these emissaries been that he had been a little uncertain how to progress. Glancing at Flamininus, he had interpreted the discreet shake of the Roman's head to mean, do not mention the embassy today: they will argue against that, out of stubbornness and anger. And so Philip had proposed an overnight halt to the talks, a suggestion accepted with reluctance by the Aitolians and Akhaians.

His hunch about Flamininus' head-shake had proved correct; on a pretence of settling a time and place for the next day's meeting, Flamininus had approached him and indicated that a night's rest would cool heads. 'Tomorrow, they will be open to your idea of sending ambassadors to the Senate at Rome,' he had said conspiratorially. 'I will see to it. They will think it a fine plan too.'

With these words in his mind, Philip directed his trireme to the beach at Thronion, a little to the east of Nikaia where they had met for the previous two days. Flamininus and his allies were already there: he could see them.

How pleasing to have reached an arrangement with Flamininus alone, thought Philip. The Aitolian and Akhaian emissaries' only agenda was his humiliation. That he should have to withdraw his troops from towns that had been Macedonian for decades and more was degrading enough, but that he, a king, had to negotiate this agreement with enemies who were his social inferiors was unbearable.

In this regard, Philip decided, he and the Roman general were quite alike. Some of Flamininus' comments the previous day had seemed to indicate that he also found the Aitolians and Akhaians petty and small-minded. It wasn't surprising, thought Philip. Men who served as consuls weren't of royal blood as he was, but they were noblemen, whose families had long, proud lineages. They were leaders, accustomed to getting their own way. It stood to reason that Flamininus would hate having his every move scrutinised by those who followed at his heel.

This, Philip had concluded, was why the Roman general had come to a private agreement with him. The Aitolians' and Akhaians' displeasure at his request to send an embassy to Rome would give Flamininus as much pleasure as it would him.

Philip remained wary. He was still at war with Rome; Flamininus was his enemy. Yet the possibility of a settlement that allowed him to remain king of Macedon, with his pride and his army intact, now seemed possible.

CHAPTER XII

Thronium, east of Nicaea

Sitting at his desk in his tent, Flamininus had to stop himself calling for Pasion. Worm food, buried in an unmarked grave outside Elatea, his secretary would never answer his summons again. Pasion had died without talking, something Flamininus still struggled to comprehend. He had always believed the face and personality given a man by the gods allowed judgement of character, but Pasion, someone he had judged to be entirely lacking courage, had proved him wrong.

The notion that he had been mistaken, that he had unfairly accused Pasion, had entered Flamininus' mind, but as more time went by without another letter from Galba, the more convinced he became that Pasion had been the malevolent ex-consul's spy. It was a pity that the Greek had not given up what he knew, thought Flamininus, but a man couldn't have everything. Although part of him grieved for Pasion, it was satisfying to know that Galba's source of information in his camp had been cut off at the root.

'Potitius!' Flamininus remembered the name at last. 'Get in here!'

A paunchy figure sloped in, a stylus clutched nervously in his ink-stained fingers. Short, chinless and without any discernible personality, he had come recommended from one of Flamininus' senior officers. Potitius licked his fleshy lips. 'Master?'

'Stop that!' Flamininus despised the habit.

Potitius looked like a child caught taking a honey pastry from the kitchen: surprised, guilty, fearful. 'Stop what, master?'

'Licking your lips. It's disgusting.'

'Licking my lips, master?' Potitius repeated, doing just that.

'Yes, like that!' cried Flamininus.

Potitius, aware of what had happened to his predecessor, quailed. 'S-sorry, master.' Then, like a moth that circles a lamp endlessly to its death, he licked his lips again.

Flamininus' cup hurtled through the air, catching Potitius on the side of the face. He reeled back. Wine sprayed everywhere. The cup bounced off the floor, the last of its contents soaking into the thick carpet. Potitius fell to his knees. His bottom lip wobbled; there were tears in his piggy eyes. 'Don't kill me, master, please.'

'Out of my sight!' Flamininus' temper was such that he could have slain the lip-licking idiot, but the idea of having to find yet another secretary was more irritating than he could bear.

Potitius scuttled out like a whipped hound, all hunched back and downward-cast eyes.

'Consul?' From outside, the voice of the Aetolian emissary Euripidas.

'Gods give me patience,' Flamininus grated. 'I am surrounded by fools.' He considered ignoring the call, but the shouts he'd directed at Potitius made it clear he was in the tent. It would appear childish to pretend he wasn't here. Flamininus ground his teeth.

'Consul?'

Never mind decorum, thought Flamininus, presenting yourself to the sentries and asking to see me. Just shout my name, why don't you? Ignorant Greek. 'What is it?'

'I was hoping to have a word before the king arrives.'

Were you indeed? thought Flamininus. 'I see,' he said, managing to sound civil. 'Tell the sentry you can enter.' He smoothed down his tunic, and wiped any traces of wine from his lips. He did not rise from his desk as Euripidas was escorted in.

'Greetings, consul.' Euripidas bowed.

'Greetings.' Flamininus had encountered the grey-bearded Euripidas four years before, when the Aetolian had visited Rome to beg for assistance in his city state's struggle with Philip. Euripidas had been the more serious of the emissaries, his companion Neophron the comedic one. In their recent meetings, Flamininus wasn't sure he liked Euripidas. 'It is early to come calling.'

'Your pardon, consul,' said Euripidas, looking discomfited. 'You are such a busy man that I wasn't sure what hour to see you.'

Flamininus would have preferred not to talk with Euripidas at all, but it was better to keep his allies sweet wherever possible. 'You are here now.'

Euripidas nodded. His eyes dropped to the stool in front of the desk.

Flamininus pretended he hadn't seen. 'Speak.'

Euripidas cleared his throat. 'Yesterday's talks brought us no nearer to agreement with Philip, consul.'

'A pity, is it not?'

'It is.' Euripidas frowned. 'And we Aitolians cannot countenance a settlement that sees Macedonian garrisons remaining in fortresses such as the Fetters, and Thebes. They will ever be a reminder of Philip's ability to mount attacks on us and other city states.' Flamininus made no reply, and Euripidas hurried on, 'Consider how the people of Rome might feel if Carthaginian troops occupied Capua, say. I'd wager a hundred drachmae to one that they wouldn't like it, consul – I would go as far as saying they would hate it.' Euripidas folded his arms.

'I cannot argue with you,' said Flamininus, thinking, it matters nothing to me if Philip's soldiers watch over parts of Aetolia or the Peloponnese. What's important is that I emerge from this war in the best possible situation. He smiled. 'Rest assured, Euripidas, Rome has your best interests at heart.'

'So you will also insist – as you did at the outset of these negotiations – that Philip withdraws his troops from Greece?'

'I will.' What you don't know, thought Flamininus, is that before I 'have a chance' to do that, Philip will suggest sending emissaries to the Senate, and I will agree. By the time his embassy reaches Rome, my continued command will have been approved, gods willing, and the Senate will rebuff them. The war will be recommenced in the spring. If, on the other hand, I am to be relieved of my command here, the price of peace shall be for Philip to keep his fortresses and garrisons in Greece. Either way, I will go down as the general who subjugated Macedonia.

Flamininus smiled at Euripidas, thinking, and you will accept that or suffer the consequences. 'Content?' he asked.

Euripidas seemed surprised to have achieved what he wanted with such ease. 'Yes, consul. Gratitude.'

'If there's anything else . . .?' Flamininus' tone implied there had best not be.

'No, no. Until later, consul.' Muttering his thanks, Euripidas made himself scarce.

There was a third outcome to Flamininus' plotting, in which he lost his command and the Senate *also* rejected Philip's terms for peace. In that case, the war against Macedonia would continue under the command of another general. Flamininus did his best not to think about that possibility.

Before the negotiations with Philip recommenced, he decided, fresh messages must be sent to his most important supporters in the Senate. *No* effort could be spared to ensure that he was reappointed to the command of Macedonia.

'Potitius!'

'I am here, master.' Potitius shuffled in.

'Have you writing materials? A stylus? We have letters to write.'

'A moment, master.' He hurried out.

Flamininus decided to pretend he hadn't seen Potitius licking his lips as he turned. There were only so many tribulations a man could deal with at a time.

Over the course of the next two hours, Flamininus had more visitors; the Achaean emissary was followed by the Rhodian. The former came seeking the same outcome that had brought Euripidas, and the latter an assurance that Philip would relinquish control of the towns of Iasus and Bargylia. Flamininus lied blithely, telling both what they wanted to hear. Fixed on nothing but his career and the growth of his reputation, he felt not a scrap of remorse. Nodding, smiling, he ushered them from his office happier than when they had entered.

At length, a sentry brought word that Philip's trireme had been spotted. Flamininus was ready. Breastplate polished to a mirror-like finish, scarlet general's sash tied just so around it, he donned his favourite helmet, which had a long red-dyed horsehair crest that trailed down his back. Yet again he made to call Pasion. It had been the custom for him to perform the final check ensuring Flamininus looked his best. With a glare at the lip-licking Potitius – he wasn't about to ask that fool – Flamininus stalked from his tent.

Escorted by a century of principes, he walked the short distance to the beach. It had irritated him that Galba had insisted his escort be soldiers from the Eighth, just so he could also be present at the meetings. Wise to this, Flamininus had sent Galba back to Elatea on the pretext of ensuring that all was well there. He wouldn't witness this meeting, thought Flamininus with satisfaction.

Philip's trireme was nearing the shallows; Flamininus' allies waited in a cluster on the sand. He acknowledged their greetings with a dignified inclination of his head, and let them approach his position rather than the other way around. While they muttered among themselves, he watched Philip standing at the prow of his ship. Flamininus wasn't the only one who had dressed for the occasion. Clad in an ornate panoply, wearing a fluted Boeotian helmet, he looked every part the monarch.

Nonetheless, Flamininus decided, Philip didn't have *his* presence. *He* was the one more like Alexander, of that there was no question, and gods willing, that was how history would remember him. If Flamininus closed his eyes, he could see himself standing in a chariot as his triumphal parade moved through the streets of Rome; he could hear the crowd's adulation. 'Remember thou art mortal,' Potitius whispered in his ear.

'Consul.'

Flamininus blinked at the staff officer before him. 'What is it?'

'The king has come ashore, sir.'

'Good.' Flamininus glanced at his allies. 'Ready?'

They paced towards Philip and his companions. Throughout the exchange of greetings and pleasantries, a distinct tension notched the air. Flamininus decided that the faces of the Aetolians and Achaeans were easiest to read: nervous, resentful and expectant. The Rhodian emissary looked combative. Philip seemed tense but determined. Only the Pergamene appeared untroubled. Flamininus himself felt calm. He was in control.

He smiled at the king. 'Would you care to start proceedings?'

Philip nodded. 'I meet you today earnest in my desire for peace, consul.'

Someone snorted. A voice muttered. Flamininus glowered at his allies, who subsided, and then returned his gaze to the king. 'Continue, please.'

'Peace is possible,' said Philip. 'Yet we have struggled to reach agreement these past two days. It is my suggestion, therefore, that we bring matters to a temporary close. I ask to send a party of trusted counsellors to Rome, there to deal with the Senate. Zeus willing, I will gain peace on the terms I have offered here. If not, I will accept whatever conditions the Senate demands.'

Complete uproar descended.

Everyone was shouting: the Aetolians and Achaeans, the Rhodians and Pergamenes and Athamanians. Fists were being waved, insults hurled. One emissary, an Aetolian whose name Flamininus could not recall, even took a few steps towards the king, shouting that he was delaying in order to gather more forces. Philip sneered, which infuriated the Aetolian even further.

'Calm, gentlemen,' Flamininus shouted. 'CALM!'

Shocked – this was the first time he had raised his voice before any of them – the gathering fell silent.

'I was not referring to you, King Philip,' said Flamininus in a gracious tone. 'You are the very picture of calm.'

Philip smiled. 'What think you of my suggestion?'

My suggestion, you mean, thought Flamininus with satisfaction. 'It is a good one.'

'How can you say that?' cried an Aetolian. 'Philip's intention can only be to give himself time to prepare his army.' Loud cries of assent rose from around him, and he continued, 'Clearly, I am not alone in thinking this. We cannot allow him to pull the wool over our eyes like this, consul.'

'Come now,' said Flamininus in a bluff tone. 'If this were summer, I would heed your words, but winter is upon us. To all intents and purposes, the war is over until the spring. Whatever might have been agreed on here would have to be ratified by the Senate anyway, which means there is nothing to lose and everything to gain in granting the king his wish. We have two months, perhaps three, for the possibility of a peace settlement to be explored in Rome.'

It took a while, and assurances from Flamininus that of course his allies could send their own embassies to address the Senate alongside Philip's, but in the end, agreement was reached. A two-month truce was declared.

Flamininus then sprang a final surprise, a move intended to show his allies that his stance towards Philip remained tough, but not one that would alarm the king overmuch. 'Any remaining Macedonian garrisons are to be withdrawn from Phocis and Locris.'

The king's eyes narrowed; this had not been mentioned in their private discussion the day before. It was not a difficult thing to grant, however, because Flamininus already controlled most of this territory. Philip nodded. 'So be it.'

With that, the meeting came to a close. Bidding a courteous farewell to Flamininus but ignoring his allies, Philip returned to his ship. Not entirely happy, but unwilling to argue further with Flamininus, the various emissaries continued talking among themselves.

That went well, thought Flamininus, deciding that a sacrifice to his favourite gods – Jupiter and Mars – would be appropriate. Retain their goodwill, and things would go well in Rome. There remained the unpleasant and costly matter of his secret arrangement with Galba, but ways around that might be found. His spies had been ordered to delve deep into his enemy's background – he would have Potitius pen a barbed reminder of this. Everyone has a weakness, mused Flamininus. A vice. Find the chink in Galba's armour, and their roles would be reversed as neatly as the flip of a coin. Remove him from the equation, Flamininus gloated, and Macedonia and Greece would lie at his feet. The thrill he felt from this was almost sexual.

'Sir?'

Irritation pricked Flamininus. He hadn't summoned Potitius to write the letter to his spies, yet here he was. And yes, curse it, he was licking his lips. Flamininus levelled his coldest stare. 'Lick your lips in front of me again, worm, and I will see the skin flayed from your back. Maybe I'll cut out your tongue after. Understand?'

'Yes, master.' Potitius' face bore an expression of absolute terror.

'Why are you here?' Pettishly, Flamininus decided he no longer wished to dictate letters; a large cup of wine would be preferable – a reward to himself for the proceedings he had just overseen.

'I have this, master.' In Potitius' trembling hand, a rectangular wooden tablet.

'Who's it from?' Perhaps it's news that Macedonia will continue to be in my charge, thought Flamininus with a little flash of excitement. There was no answer, and he glared at Potitius. 'Well?'

'I . . . I don't know, master. One of the sentries gave it to me.'

The shock was as great as if Flamininus had been unexpectedly shoved into the cold pool at a public bath. 'A sentry?'

Potitius nodded, and before he could help himself, licked his lips. A little sob escaped him.

'Hades below!' Flamininus snatched the tablet. He knew without looking that the wax seal would bear no mark. Galba wasn't here, but he could still reach into the heart of Flamininus' camp. Ripping it open, his eyes roved over the short message within.

> *In Rome, the sands are shifting.*
> *The fortunes of your political rivals wax*
> *even as your own wane. Know that*
> *to lose command over Macedonia would*
> *change <u>nothing</u> about our agreement.*
> *Your future – and fate – lies in your own hands.*

The word 'nothing' had been underlined so deep that the wood beneath the layer of wax was exposed.

As weary as if he'd spent an entire day at the gymnasium, Flamininus closed his eyes. He cared nothing for Galba's warning: Pasion filled his mind. In normal circumstances, a slave's life mattered not a whit, but this was different. Pasion, who had given him years of loyal service, had been innocent. Innocent. The knowledge ripped off an internal scab, and the grief and regret that Flamininus had been denying since his secretary's death washed over him. Pasion's confusion and terror as he'd been beaten made sense now: it had sprung from disbelief that his master should treat him so.

Irritated to find a quivering Potitius still before him, Flamininus was about to lash out, but he reined his temper in. He took a couple of deep breaths, and thought of Galba. It was *he* who had caused Flamininus to leap to conclusions about Pasion. It was *he* who should pay. Like that, the decision had been made. Flamininus would quadruple the men seeking information on Galba.

Something would turn up in the end.

It always did.

CHAPTER XIII

Rome

As the city docks hove into view, Felix's delight at their situation began to escape at last. He checked, but Bulbus was nowhere in sight. No doubt he was further down the ship browning his nose with the senior officers, thought Felix, and Callistus was too far away to hear. 'Can you fucking believe it?' he hissed to Antonius, standing beside him at the rail. 'We're here, in Rome!'

'Two and a half years it's been,' said Antonius. 'D'you remember the last time?'

Felix could almost see Dordalus' ears waggle, the man was listening in so hard. It was vital that no one knew of their dishonourable discharge from the legions, so he rolled his eyes sideways, indicating Dordalus to his brother, and said, 'Aye. Of course.'

'It's good to be back, eh?' said Antonius. 'First chance we get, we will raise a cup to Fabius.'

They fell silent, remembering their comrade who had died at Corinth. Their plan of opening a tavern together would never now come to fruition.

'We could set up business anyway,' said Felix. 'Call the place "The Legionary's Rest" in his honour.'

'Fabius would have liked that,' said Antonius.

'I'll supply the girls, sir,' offered Dordalus with his customary leer. 'Sparax and Clavus could stand on the door.'

The brothers exchanged a look. 'I've heard worse ideas,' Felix admitted.

'We'll think about it,' said Antonius. 'Knowing you, Dordalus, all the girls would be diseased, and I suspect Sparax and Clavus would drink us dry.'

Good-natured banter and insults followed. The bond between the five surviving members of the contubernium was strong; a lot had happened in the two months they had served together. First it had been the savage battle at Corinth, then the march back to Phocis, and an unexpected voyage to Italia.

The last had been a bolt from the blue, and had come thanks to Flamininus ordering officers to accompany his allies' embassies to Rome. Such men needed an escort. 'I want fine examples of soldiery,' Flamininus was purported to have said, prompting the commander of the Eighth to volunteer his principes. Felix and his comrades didn't know – or care – how and why, but Bulbus' century had been one of the two chosen.

Long sea journey behind them, they had reached Ostia that morning. Paperwork checked by the port officials, they had been allowed to enter the mouth of the Tiber. It was an easy haul upriver to Rome, and now they were here. Small craft passed close by on either side, fishermen returning from the sea, merchants transporting goods and passengers over the river, lowlifes eyeing up any unguarded goods on the dock. Houses pressed in from left and right. Here and there, faces watched from small windows. The air was thick with the smell of human waste; clouds of gulls screeched overhead. Anticipation was in every face, thought Felix, from the oarsmen who would soon rest, to his fellow principes thinking of a night in the city's hostelries, and the officers whose duties were just beginning.

With a shouted command, the trireme's captain directed the helmsman towards a space between a deep-bellied merchantman and a low-slung patrol vessel. Oar masters shouted, and the port-side oarsmen dug deep, while those to starboard pulled their oars from the water. The prow turned several degrees. The flautists' tune slowed, then stopped. A short series of notes followed; both sets of oarsmen backed water for a couple of heartbeats before lifting their oars free of the river. The ship was gliding now, moving at the same speed as a man strolling with his lover.

Another order, and the port-side oars came rattling in. The trireme was close to the wharf now, less than a javelin throw. Dockers stood with long poles, ready to prevent it smashing into the great carved slabs that formed the quay. The starboard oars made one more gentle dip into the water, angling the approach a fraction, then they too were heaved in. With the last of its momentum, the ship came nudging in, prow scraping off the stone as the first dockers failed to stop it in time.

A shower of threats and curses from the captain saw their fellows leap into action, using their poles to see the trireme come to rest half a spear's length out from the quay. All along the deck, ropes flew from waiting sailors to more dockers. Three and four to each line, they pulled the ship in against the stone with a satisfying thunk. The gangplank had dropped before even half the ropes had been lashed to bollards. A messenger – a member of the officers' staff – leaped down and ran off in the direction of the Senate.

'If you wanted reminding of how important our mission is,' muttered Felix, 'there you have it.' Philip's embassy was to have sailed the day after them; they'd seen no sign of it during their journey, and although that didn't mean it wasn't already here, chances were that they had reached the capital first. The messenger's immediate departure made it clear, however, that Flamininus had given instruction for his officers to meet with the senators as fast as possible.

'Look lively,' roared Bulbus. 'Even you fools will know that swords and javelins are prohibited in Rome – you're to leave them aboard. Shields too. Helmets on, though. Onto the dock, quick as you can. Callistus, have them form up on either side of the gangplank. Move!'

'What about our kit?' Felix asked Antonius as they assembled on the quay.

'We'll have to come back and get it later.' Antonius jerked his head at the ox carts that were already lining up, their drivers seeing the trireme's arrival as a chance for business. 'No one's going to supply those for us, eh?'

'Onion Head will have one,' muttered Clavus. 'Curse him.'

'Bathtard,' added Sparax with considerable venom. Bulbus had taken to mocking his lisp. 'Thparaxth', he called him.

Hobnails clattered onto the quay; Bulbus appeared between them, his gaze raking left and right. Everyone stared into the distance, praying that he would find no fault. There wasn't a man among them without rust spots on his mail shirt – after a sea voyage, it was a fact of life – and few still had all three feathers atop his helmet. Fragile, susceptible not just to knocks but to gusts of wind, they were most unsuited to journeys aboard ship.

To everyone's relief, Bulbus had more on his mind than parade-standard kit. Calling them to attention, he took up a position at the end of the 'tunnel' they had formed. Within a few moments, the senior officers they had accompanied disembarked. Serious-faced, talking between themselves, the three paid no attention to the principes as they strode past.

Felix caught a few words of their conversation. 'Do we know if Flamininus' command in Macedonia is to continue?' asked one. 'The messenger will soon return with news, gods willing,' replied a second. 'If he's to be replaced,' said the third, 'the entire situation . . .'

Felix strained his ears, but missed what was said next.

'First six ranks, about turn,' called Bulbus. 'Form up, four wide. Follow!'

In neat ranks, Felix and his comrades marched off with the first half of the century, in front of the three officers. Commanded by Callistus, the rest formed up similarly at the back. An imposing column, it created its own path through the crowded streets. No one wanted to stand in its way, from the butcher with a sheep carcase on each shoulder to the carpenter and his apprentice carrying lengths of timber to a half-built house. Carts proved more of an obstacle, but even they didn't need much encouragement to pull over to the side of the thoroughfare.

Felix could see people looking, in particular women. He stuck out his chest, smiled at an attractive girl standing in the doorway of an ironmonger's. This was altogether more pleasant than the last time he'd been in Rome, a bruised and beaten ex-doorman. He wasn't the only one getting attention either.

'Been a while thince they've theen men in uniform, eh?' muttered Sparax. 'The women can't keep their eyeth off uth.'

'Legionaries haven't been needed in the city for several years, since Hannibal was contained down in the south. All the better for us, brothers. We won't need any help, Dordalus,' jibed Antonius. Their comrade had been filling their ears with promises of the fine whores he'd find for them.

Dordalus muttered something rude.

The simpering girl was replaced by another further down the street, but Felix was able to talk to neither. Their business was at the Senate; it would be many hours before he'd get off duty.

The knowledge didn't dampen his mood.

Compared to a windy, exposed camp in Phocis, this was Elysium.

*

During his previous time in Rome, Felix had walked by the *Curia*, the seat of Rome's power for nigh on three centuries, on countless occasions. He'd never paid the tall, square building any attention; the matters discussed within had little to do with him, he'd reasoned. Standing outside it now with his comrades as the future of the war against Macedonia was being debated, he longed to enter the hallowed chamber. While that wouldn't happen, the great iron-studded doors remained open, allowing him from his close-by position to listen in on the proceedings.

It was the day after their arrival in Rome. Their night off duty had been quiet – Bulbus had warned them on pain of death not to drink too much – and they had escorted Flamininus' officers back to the Senate a little before midday. Not long after, the various embassies had arrived and entered: Aetolians, Achaeans, Athamanians, Rhodians and Pergamenes. Philip's emissaries had also reached the city, but they were not to be permitted to address the senators until after their enemies. Instead they stood in a glowering group by the *Graecostasis*, where foreign dignitaries waited for their invitation to enter the Curia.

'Their faces would be even sourer if they could hear what's being said about them,' said Felix to Antonius from the corner of his mouth.

Antonius' lips twitched.

Every emissary had spent the first part of his address to the Senate pouring vitriol on Philip. Murderous and untrustworthy, the Aetolians had called him. Faithless and an oath-breaker, said the Achaeans. Craven and lacking any respect towards the gods, the Pergamenes and Rhodians claimed. Mercurial, unpredictable and liable to fits of killing rage, swore the Athamanians.

Felix pricked his ears. The senior consul, Caius Cornelius Cethegus, had been introduced. Thanking the various embassies for their assessment of Philip, Cethegus asked the Greeks among them to describe the Hellenic landscape, that he and his fellows might better understand the implications of Philip having garrisons outside his own kingdom.

A chorus of indignant and descriptive comments followed, about Demetrias in Thessaly, Chalcis in Euboea and the Acrocorinth in Achaea.

Having marched through much of Greece, and seen the strategic importance of the Acrocorinth at first hand, Felix understood the emissaries' outrage at the king's intention to retain the Fetters. They were a means of control, plain and simple.

It seemed the consuls and senators saw this too. After thanking the ambassadors again, Cethegus told his fellows that he had heard enough, and asked, had they?

The roar that met this query carried out into the forum. Passers-by turned to stare, and the Macedonian emissaries gave each other worried looks.

Within moments, Philip's representatives were summoned inside. They had barely stepped over the threshold when Cethegus spoke.

'I have a single question for you,' he shouted. Into the Macedonians' surprise he demanded, 'Will Philip evacuate the so-called "Fetters"? Will he give up the fortresses of Demetrias, Chalcis and the Acrocorinth?'

A stunned silence resulted.

'They haven't the first idea what to say,' whispered a grinning Felix to Antonius.

'Well?' Cethegus' tone was peremptory.

'We have no specific instructions with regard to the Fetters,' came the answer in poor Latin. 'Our understanding was that the Senate would agree to their remaining in Macedonian hands.'

'After the illuminating information provided by our loyal Greek allies, the Senate will do no such thing,' gloated Cethegus.

'W-we cannot accept the loss of the Fetters before consulting with the king,' the Macedonian protested.

'And the Senate will not negotiate a peace without these terms – terms you are unable to offer,' said Cethegus. 'It shall be Flamininus, therefore, who determines whether the war continues or an agreement with Philip can be reached. You may go.'

Delighted, Felix mouthed at Antonius, 'That's it. The war goes on.'

They would yet make their fortune, he decided. Returning to Rome, they would open a tavern called 'The Legionary's Rest'.

'Your round,' said Felix, aiming his cup at Sparax. Wine slopped onto the already soaking table. No one noticed.

Hours had passed since the short shrift given Philip's emissaries at the Curia. Released from their duties, the five comrades had headed for a drinking den close to the forum recommended by Dordalus. The customers within were packed as tight as a mob at a boxing match, but they had worked their way into a corner and by dint of time spent in the place, moved on to take 'ownership' of a rickety table and five stools.

'Your round,' Antonius repeated.

'Ith it?' Sparax's face was the picture of innocence.

'You know it is, curse you,' roared Clavus, giving Sparax an almighty nudge. 'Felix bought the first one, then 'Tonius. I bought the third, Dordalus the fourth. You were last as usual. *We've* done that twice, and now it's your turn again.'

'Three times,' said Dordalus owlishly.

Clavus frowned. 'Eh?'

'It's Sparax's turn, but this will be our fifteenth drink, not our tenth,' said Dordalus, and belched.

Everyone laughed.

'All right, all right,' said Sparax. He clambered, weaving, onto his stool. After a time, he managed to catch the eye of a barman over the heads of the thronged customers. Signalling, he made it clear they needed more wine. 'It'th coming,' he declared, lurching to the floor.

'It'll be a long wait,' said Felix, heaving himself upright. 'Time to break the seal again.'

'I'll come as well,' said Antonius. 'Easier to forge a path with two.'

'Do *not* let any whoreson take our stools,' Felix warned. At once his comrades promised to offer them to the first men who asked. He made an obscene gesture and warned them not piss off their tesserarius. They laughed even harder, which warmed his heart. Promotion had brought changes to his life, most of them good, but he would always be comrades with his tentmates. With Antonius a step behind, Felix shoved his way towards the back door. Beyond, an alley served as the tavern's latrine.

Pissed as Felix was, the smell of sweat and unwashed bodies in the depths of the crowd was thick enough to cut with a blade. Fresh air diminished the reek close to the back door, but as he emerged, the familiar tang of piss and shit filled his nostrils. A pair of oil lamps in niches shed a weak yellow light on the alleyway.

'Take care where you stand,' said Felix. 'Some filthy bastard has emptied his bowels two steps from the threshold.'

'What is it about civilians?' Antonius grumbled. 'Dirty cocksuckers.'

'Latrine duties are a pain, but it helps to have a place for *this*.' Felix waved a hand at the pool of foul-smelling liquid that extended off into the gloom.

'Ha. You two are soldiers.' Jiggling his hips to shake off the last drops, the man who'd spoken turned. Short, in a military-cut tunic and a metalled belt, he had an unkempt beard and a beaten-down look. He looked the pair up and down. 'You must be, or I'm no judge.'

'We're in one of Flamininus' legions, aye. Only here for a few more days before we head back,' said Felix, the wine easing his usual wariness. 'You a legionary as well?'

'I was. Fought the *guggas* for years like everyone, and then I served in Macedonia, under Galba.' He raised his right arm, revealing a stump where the hand should have been. 'I'd be there still if it wasn't for this.'

'Hades, brother,' said Felix, feeling a rush of compassion. 'That's a terrible wound.' Beside him, Antonius made sympathetic noises.

A shrug. 'I'm alive. That's more that can be said for a lot of my comrades.'

'Aye,' said Felix heavily, thinking of Fabius, Peri, Hopalong, Mattheus, and a multitude of others who had died during the war with Hannibal. Easing past the amputee, he tugged up his tunic. Over his shoulder, he continued, 'You were discharged after you'd recovered?'

'It's the legions' way, eh? They patch you up, and if you can't fight again, it's on to the street before you know what's happening. Forget being given any money to keep the wolf from the door either.' His laugh was bitter. 'It's always been the same. Footsloggers like us are beggared, while the commanders do well for themselves.'

'I can't argue with that,' said Antonius, who had joined Felix.

'Is Flamininus any less of a thieving cunt than Galba?' asked the amputee.

Felix caught the man's eye. 'Eh? What d'you mean?'

A knowing look. 'Heard of Celetrum?'

'Aye. We were close by when it fell, but missed the sacking of the town,' said Antonius.

'You two were in Macedonia then too? Why, we're comrades!' The amputee stuck out his left hand. 'Marcus Junius Pennus.'

They shook. 'Felix Cicirrus.'

'Antonius Cicirrus – we're brothers,' said Antonius.

'I'd never have known,' said Pennus, grinning. 'You're like two peas in a pod.'

'We can never see it,' said Felix. 'Come, let us buy you a drink, and you can tell us about Galba.'

Pennus' worn face lit up. 'I won't say no.'

Clapping him on the shoulder, Felix led the way inside.

Sparax's wine had just been delivered when they reached their friends. Introducing Pennus, Felix appropriated a discarded cup from a neighbouring table and insisted it be filled for their new comrade. A toast was made, and then the shouted conversations that had been interrupted by their arrival began again. Felix and Antonius were left with Pennus.

'Tell us about Galba,' urged Felix.

'Aye,' said Antonius. 'We never had much to do with him.'

'Nor did I,' said Pennus, taking a great slurp of wine. 'What legionary does, with a consul?' He raised his cup. 'Here's to us rather than those noses-in-the-air bastards, eh?'

Laughing, the brothers saluted Pennus. They drank.

'I was at Celetrum,' said Pennus. 'A shithole town, it was, like so many in Greece and Macedonia. Nothing special, or so we thought during the attack. Who could have known that it was home to one of Philip's secret treasuries?'

Felix and Antonius stared at one another. 'Not us,' said Felix.

'Aye, which makes you the same as most men in the army,' said Pennus, draining his cup. He nodded in gratitude as Felix quickly re-filled it. 'That's how Galba wanted it.'

'You're making no sense,' said Felix.

Pennus took a drink. 'Me and my century, we were some of the first over the wall, see. You know what it's like when a town falls. Madness. Bodies everywhere. Men running. Buildings on fire. Women screaming.'

'Aye.' Felix would remember Antipatreia to his dying day.

'We were looking for booty, same as everyone. Came upon what looked like a big merchant's house. There were guards outside, which drew our attention. They fought well too, like soldiers. Killed two of my mates – but we soon got the better of 'em. Inside the courtyard, there were more soldiers, so we did for them too. We assumed that they were garrison troops, but when our centurion went inside the main building, he came out with a stupid smile on his face. "Those were Philip's men," he said. "We're rich, boys. Rich as Croesus."' Pennus winked at Felix. 'Turned out the place was where local taxes were stored before being shipped to Pella, and we had attacked Celetrum the day after the year's levies had come in.'

'How does this make Galba a thief?' asked Felix, confused.

A scowl. 'We were sitting around on piles of coins – literally – drinking the scant amount of wine we had and talking about what we'd do with our shares, when a glory-hunting tribune happened to stray into the courtyard. He took one look and set a dozen of his men on the front door, sending at the same time for Galba.' Pennus drained his cup again.

'Here.' Ignoring Sparax's glare, Felix seized the jug and poured until Pennus' cup was overflowing.

'Gratitude.' Pennus wiped his lips with the back of his good arm. 'Galba arrived quicker than a fly lands on fresh manure. We were allowed to keep fifty *denarii* each – counted out by one of his staff officers – and told that the rest of the haul would go towards the war effort.'

Antonius frowned. 'Galba rewarded you. Hardly theft from the Republic, was it?'

'That's not what I'm talking about. I've an old mate who was a scribe in Galba's headquarters, see. It's a boring job, but as he says, better to be at a desk than risking his life in the front line.' Pennus saw their confusion, and said, 'Bear with me. Ten days after Celetrum, me and my mate were sharing a skin of wine, and I told him about the treasury we'd found. He laughed at me and my talk of all the coin. "Come off it," says he. "I had to record the details of everything found in that building. It wasn't that rich a find."' Pennus leaned back against the wall, and eyed the brothers. 'Explain that if you will.'

'Galba secreted away most of the coin,' said Felix, his gaze roving to Antonius, who nodded in agreement, and back to Pennus.

'You got it in one. The clever cunt used his own men, presumably, after we'd been given the heave-ho. My scribe mate – who I'd trust with my life – was given a figure that must have been a quarter of the amount of coin we saw.'

Wine-slowed, the brothers pondered what this meant. Loot taken in battle had to be surrendered to the quartermasters; it was shared out afterwards according to rank. In practice, high-value items like coins and jewellery could vanish into men's purses, but fear of punishment meant that for the most part the rule was obeyed. Theft on this grand scale was a crime, punishable by law.

Felix glanced at Antonius. 'A tribune got caught doing that after Zama, didn't he?'

'Aye. Half a dozen gold and silver vases he took, from one of the temples in Carthage.'

'He was discharged from the army for that, and fined a hundred thousand *asses*,' said Felix to Pennus. 'It sounds as if what Galba did was twenty times worse.'

'A hundred,' spat Pennus. 'A thousand. And nothing will ever come of it because the only witnesses were simple soldiers like you and me.'

'What about your centurion and the other officers?'

Pennus snorted. 'They must have been paid off, because when we went complaining to them as we left Celetrum, they were having none of it. Ten days of forced marches taught us not to mention it again. Not long after, I lost my hand, and that was that. Now I scrabble to find enough to eat every day, while Galba gets appointed as a legate and sent back to Greece.' He pulled a face and drank.

'That's a tale and a half and no mistake,' said Felix. 'Someone like Galba is untouchable – we can't help you there. But we can see you right, can't we, brother?' He gave Antonius a meaningful look.

Pennus pretended not to look as they rummaged in their purses.

'This should put food on the table for a while.' Felix held out several denarii. Antonius offered two more.

Shame flooded Pennus' face. 'I didn't start talking to you so you'd feel sorry for me. I—'

'We know,' said Felix warmly. He placed the coins in Pennus' grimy palm and closed his fingers over them. 'Consider it a loan. You can pay us back after the war.'

'Our tavern will be called "The Legionary's Rest",' said Antonius grandly. 'On the Esquiline, gods willing. You'll always be welcome.'

'We might even have a job for you,' confided Felix.

'Gratitude.' Pennus' voice was tight with emotion.

'Now, let's forget that prick Galba, and get properly pissed,' declared Antonius, pouring them all another cup of wine.

That, Felix decided, was the most sensible thing he'd heard that night.

CHAPTER XIV

Pella

P hilip was on his way to the city's main *palaestra*. Despite spending much of the autumn in Pella, he hadn't spent enough time with his son Perseus. Word had reached him that his son was training with his friends that morning; it was a chance for Philip to escape the palace and with luck, see Perseus as well. With a workman's cloak over his simple chiton, wearing a kausia, the king cut an unremarkable figure. If anyone looked, the two Companions ten paces to his rear were a giveaway to his high status, but on this windy autumn day, with rain threatening, most people were going about their business, heads down, arms keeping cloaks tight.

A thousand tasks awaited Philip at his desk, in his palace and at the army's camp, but he had decided that an hour would not affect his plans for the defence of Macedon, or for that matter, the outcome of the war. Seeing Perseus might also keep his mind from the question that had troubled him since Menander had journeyed to Rome the month before.

Had the Senate accepted his terms for peace?

Philip's stride checked. Rather than the palaestra, perhaps he should go to the docks, there to wait for a sign of Menander's ship. He discounted the notion, and kept walking. It was impossible to know the day or hour of Menander's return; besides, the messengers stationed in the port would hurry to his side with any news.

The palaestra was a long, unremarkable building with a plain stuccoed outside wall. Overshadowed by the facilities at the newer gymnasium, it remained popular with noblemen and their sons thanks to its proximity to the royal palace. A pair of *herms*, stone columns adorned with a phallus at groin level and topped by a bust of Hermes, flanked the doorway. Philip was careful to dip his chin and mutter a prayer as he entered.

The changing area looked the same as when he'd been a young man. Wide benches around the walls with discarded chitons on them; a few more benches in the centre of the tiled floor. Sandals lying here and there. The seven or eight men present were in various states of undress or nudity. Three were stretching; another pair were oiling their bodies in preparation for wrestling or pankration. The rest had their backs to the king and were laughing and throwing insults about who'd lost the most bouts.

With the Companions standing watch outside – Philip's pride would not let them follow him everywhere – he attracted little attention. Passing along a corridor, he glanced into the chambers on either side. Shelves and stacked amphorae marked the oil storage room; in another, a youth lay flat on a table having a massage.

Philip glanced through the next open door. Grain-filled leather bags hung from the ceiling. Men stood close, punching them, one-two, one-two. Others lifted light weights; in a corner, three men took turns kicking and boxing a squat, sand-stuffed hide sack. A trainer paced about, commenting and encouraging. On occasion, he tapped an athlete with his stick, a reminder that he could deliver a beating if he chose.

A couple of men glanced at the figure in the doorway. Recognising the king, they bowed low. Philip gave the briefest sign of recognition and, satisfied his son wasn't present, moved on to the larger rooms. The first, roofed so the large central square of mud remained moist, was full of pairs of wrestling fighters. Grabbing, throwing and attempting to roll one another over their hips, they bobbed and weaved to and fro in a centuries-old dance. Mesmerised, entirely forgetting his concerns, Philip watched two of the nearest men.

Grappling fiercely, the larger managed to gain a hold on his opponent's right thigh with both hands. Lifting it, he dropped his head and pushed forward in an attempt to topple his opponent. Hopping desperately backwards, the second man wrapped his arms around his attacker's bent neck.

The move and countermove were familiar, classic even, and Philip chuckled. Effecting a chokehold on one's opponent while balancing on one leg was exceptionally difficult, but if a man could do it for long enough, victory was certain.

Thump. Down went the hopping wrestler onto his back. The trainer signalled that the bout was over, with victory going to the larger man. Even if the choke-attempting wrestler had managed to keep a grip around his opponent's neck – he hadn't – the contest had been lost thanks to his fall.

Perseus wasn't in this chamber either. Just like him to be at pankration, thought Philip. Easily the most dangerous of sports, pankration was his son's favourite. As he moved away from the doorway, a soft sound – that made by someone in bare feet – made him turn. Silhouetted against the light from the changing room far down the corridor was a figure. Something long dangled from his right hand, and with a sudden rush of fear, Philip thought: a knife! Half-closing his fingers, the better to throw a punch or to grapple with his attacker, he slid his feet forward, into the middle of the corridor.

His combative stance brought the figure up short. 'There's no fighting allowed except in the mud room or on the *skamma*.'

Philip peered, saw that the man was holding a strigil, not a blade. He barked a laugh. 'Apologies, friend. I thought you were one of my mates. We're jumping each other whenever the chance presents itself.' He dropped his gaze and, grateful for the dim light and his kausia, made for the skamma, the sandy-floored room used for wrestling and pankration practice.

Tartaros, thought Philip, it was foolish coming in here without my Companions. If that had been an assassin, I might well have been bleeding out on the floor now. There wasn't any particular reason to think he might be murdered – the last attempt on his life, plotted by his admiral Herakleides and the Aitolians, had been almost a year before, but he had enemies everywhere. The Aitolians hated him enough to try again. Attalos of Pergamum was known to have enemies assassinated. Closer to home, not every nobleman in his court could be trusted.

Reaching the skamma, Philip poked his head around the door jamb. A smile touched his lips at the sight of Perseus, pickaxe in hand, preparing the floor with his friends. Heir to the throne he might be, but in the palaestra he was just another student. A sinewy-muscled, grey-haired trainer watched, expressionless, as the eight youths chopped at the packed sand until it was broken up to his liking. At length, he grunted a command to stop. The youths leaned the pickaxes against the wall, and then, directed by the trainer, formed into pairs. They scooped up handfuls of sand and rubbed it over their bodies, making their skin easier to grip.

'Remember, this is a training session,' warned Sinewy Muscles. 'Light sparring. No full punches. If I see even the hint of an eye gouge, you'll feel my rod across your back.'

'What about a bite, grandfather?' Despite his apparent deference, Perseus' tone wasn't entirely respectful.

'My stick cares not who it hits, majesty,' came the acid rejoinder. 'Biting is also prohibited, as well you know.'

'Yes,' said Perseus, affecting not to notice his friends' titters.

'Down to it then. Olympic champions practise rather than stand around gossiping,' said Sinewy Muscles.

Philip leaned against the door frame where he wouldn't distract the youths. Perseus attacked his opponent with vicious enthusiasm, driving him across the uneven sand with a blistering set of kicks and punches. It was all the other could do to block them. He's overeager, thought Philip.

'Ease off, majesty.' Despite his age, Sinewy Muscle's attention was blade-sharp.

Chest heaving, Perseus stepped back. His gaze flickered over his opponent's shoulder, to Philip. Recognition flared in his eyes; his attention lapsed.

Seizing the chance, his opponent lunged forward, delivering a one-two punch combination to Perseus' belly. Full strength, they would have knocked the wind out of him; even so, they carried enough force to make Perseus wince. 'Apologies, majesty,' said the youth at once.

Perseus lifted his hands in rueful acknowledgement. 'Fairly landed. I didn't react in time.' He threw an annoyed glance at Philip.

Amused – he would have reacted the same way at his son's age – the king elected to leave the young men at it. Perhaps he'd have a massage, and come back after, he thought.

'Sire.' From down the corridor, a voice. 'At last I've found you.'

This must be how Atlas feels, Philip decided, as the familiar weight of responsibility sank onto his shoulders. 'Who's there?'

'Stephanos, sire. Commander of one of your *speirai*.'

I have many speirai, thought Philip. 'Approach.' Stephanos drew near, and he noted the mud spatters on his officer's face, arms, cloak, chiton and legs. It was the mark of a long journey, Philip decided, and the only speira left in the field was the one he'd sent to quell the rebellion in western Macedon. 'You have returned from Orestis.'

'Aye, sire.' Stephanos bowed from the waist. 'Forgive my appearance. I have come straight from the road.'

'Mud never harmed anyone,' said Philip, disliking the uncomfortable feeling in his belly. 'What news?'

Stephanos hesitated, and then said, 'The people of Orestis remain defiant, sire, but I have bloodied their noses.'

Zeus above, thought Philip, can nothing be easy? 'Tell me.'

Stephanos described the muddy, foot-dragging march into the mountains. The lack of food and horrific weather. The ambush and the heavy casualties taken during it. 'It was bad, sire.' Stephanos' eyes clouded. 'Boulders half the size of a house tumbling down at us. Men were crushed to death, maimed. Some of them lost limbs.'

'Blades you expect, eh, but not rocks,' said Philip.

'Aye, sire. I lost brave men. Understandably, the mood of the rest wasn't good. They wanted revenge. When we attacked the main settlement, things got a little out of hand. We killed all the men, and quite a few women as well.'

'They had it coming,' said Philip. Seeing the surprise on Stephanos' face, he added, 'The fools could have paid their taxes, and none of this would have happened.'

Stephanos looked relieved.

'Did the other settlements surrender?'

'No, sire. It was as if what we did made them more determined. I would have attacked each and every one of them, but the weather took a turn for the worse. Snowstorms, gale-force winds – it was as bad as you'd expect in the middle of winter. If I'd stayed, my losses would have been much worse; I made the decision to retreat. I failed you, sire.' Stephanos' voice was resigned. 'I am sorry.'

'If you'd had more men . . .?'

'The conditions would have made the price very high, sire.' Stephanos hesitated.

'Speak your mind. No harm will come to you.'

'They're stuck in their cursed villages until the spring now, sire. Orestis can wait until then.'

This had been Philip's inclination too. There wasn't much else he could do either, he thought wryly. Commending Stephanos for his efforts, he sent the weary officer on his way.

Any plans he'd had for a massage and watching Perseus after vanished at the doorway to the changing room. A messenger Philip recognised came rushing in, the Companions at his back.

He caught sight of Philip. 'Sire!'

Philip thought again of Atlas, and set his jaw. Every eye in the room was on him now, and ears would be pricked too. 'Tell me outside.'

They stepped onto the street, and Philip beckoned the messenger close. 'What news?'

'Menander's ship is docking even as I speak, sire.'

Philip's mouth was drier than it had been during his mad charge on the Dipylon gate at Athens two years prior. 'You're sure?'

'Aye, sire. The royal flag flutters halfway up the mast – it's the arranged signal.'

Gripping the messenger's shoulder, Philip told him he'd done a fine job. 'Back to the port with you. Menander is to attend me in my private quarters at his earliest convenience.'

Delighted by the king's praise, the messenger ran off as if he were in the final of an Olympic footrace.

What would Menander's news be, Philip wondered.

Good or bad?

Overhead, a brilliant blue sky. From over the palace walls, faint shouts of shopkeepers and playing children. Among the bare vines in the centre of his favourite courtyard, Philip was wondering if he would ever be here to see them heavy with grapes. As king, he had been at war almost every year from the first buds of spring to the first crisp, dew-laden days of autumn: his return was always too late to see the harvest. It was a pleasing notion, but a passing fancy nonetheless. Despite the odds facing him, he lived for war. It was what Philip did, what he knew best. The god of war Ares, and his sons Fear and Terror, were old friends.

Footsteps echoed from the corridor that led into the rest of the palace, and Philip's heart gave a little leap, just as it did when he crossed blades with an enemy. He thought, one way or another, everything will soon be clear.

A blind man could have read the news Menander carried from fifty paces. His face was tight, grim. Raising a hand in greeting, he hurried towards the king.

Rome wants war, not peace, thought Philip, folding his face into an expression of welcome. 'Hail, Menander,' he called.

'Sire.' Menander looked careworn, but his smile was genuine. 'I am back.'

'The Senate rejected my terms.'

'Is it that obvious, sire?'

'It is,' said Philip, managing a chuckle. 'Who will take command of Flamininus' legions?'

Looking awkward, Menander pulled his fingers through his beard.

Philip swore. Swore again. 'To think I believed the whoreson. He said that he was sure to be replaced.'

'Flamininus might not have been certain at Nikaia, sire, but he must have suspected. A clear majority of the Senate voted for his reappointment.'

'So your embassy was doomed to failure from the start.'

Menander nodded. 'If there had been any doubt in the Senate, the Aitolians and Akhaians laid it to rest with their descriptions of the Fetters. We were summoned inside soon afterwards. Two steps inside the door, I was asked if you would surrender Chalkis, Demetrias and the Akrokorinth.'

'And you could give no answer, because Flamininus had told me they were to remain mine, which meant that I had given you no instruction.'

'As you say, sire. We were dismissed on the spot. I heard within the hour that the Senate had voted for Flamininus to continue the war. We set sail for Macedon the same day.'

'Faithful Menander.'

Menander's eyes were troubled. 'I failed you, sire.'

'I could have done no better. Zeus himself would have come to grief in that pit of vipers.' Philip clasped Menander's hand. 'The Fates' weave is their own. You cannot change it, nor I.'

Relieved by Philip's acceptance, Menander's expression eased.

'Flamininus wants war, and that is what he shall have,' said Philip, furious at Flamininus' duplicitousness, and at himself for having believed the lie. 'A bitterer struggle shall not have been seen since the Persians invaded, when the soil of Greece was drenched in the blood of its sons and daughters. I will not walk away from the fight.'

'You know I will stand beside you, sire.'

'I do.' Philip's smile was warm. 'You must be weary, but I have need of your counsel.'

'I can sleep when I am dead, sire. What would you have of me?'

'When Argos came over to us, I thought to use it and the Akrokorinth as bargaining chips with Flamininus. With that need gone, I find myself wondering what to do with them. To give up the Akrokorinth seems foolish. It offers the chance to attack Attika and the heart of the Peloponnese should the need arise, as well as the coastline to east and west. Argos is a different matter. Entirely surrounded by enemies, it is bound to fall sooner or later. Joyous as it was for Philokles to steal in and seize control, I can do nothing with the town, yet I do not want the treacherous Akhaians to take it back without a fight. I was thinking that Nabis might be interested.' Enemy to Akhaia, the Spartan king had on occasion worked with Philip. Isolated in the southern Peloponnese, he had yet to become involved in the war against Rome.

'He is a hawk, sire. His gaze ever seeks for easy prey. He would wish to take it without paying any price, if I know him.'

'Yes, but if I entrust Argos to his care on a temporary basis, while also offering my daughters' hands in marriage to his sons, the offer would appeal more. After the war, he shall return it to me.'

'With every respect to your daughters, sire, what is in that deal for Nabis? Perseus shall take the throne of Macedon after you, and his brother after him, should he have no sons. Like as not, Nabis would take Argos and thumb his nose at you after.'

'Which is why I will sweeten the offer. In the event of his having to return Argos, Nabis shall have a large chunk of my remaining territory in Akhaia as compensation.'

Menander tugged an earlobe, thinking. After a moment, he said, 'It is a risky move, sire.'

'Curse it, Menander, I do not trust Nabis either, but what other choice is there? Do nothing, and the Akhaians will weasel their way into Argos before the spring. This way might prove Nabis to be an ally yet.'

'True, sire. Better to have some hope of success than none.'

'Ho now, keep your spirits up,' said Philip, his dark eyes glittering.

'You haven't heard my latest plan. Lay it out in the right fashion, and Flamininus' legions will walk into a fine trap.'

'Tell me, sire.' Menander's voice held a new eagerness.

And so Philip did.

CHAPTER XV

North of Pella

Demetrios squinted at the grey, lowering sky, willing himself to see a sign of improving weather. He soon gave up. Clouds roiled and swelled in great banks, scudding towards him with what seemed gods-sent malevolent purpose. More snow was on the way. Demetrios had thought Pella was chilly, but here in the north–south running Axios valley, there was nothing to stop the wind, which seemed to whistle down from the furthest limits of barbarian Thrake.

The village he was in with his comrades stood on the river's western bank, small buildings and sheds reaching almost to the water's edge. They would have to cross it later, an experience Demetrios was not looking forward to. At least they wouldn't have to face an enemy afterwards, he reflected, as the Romans had done against Hannibal at the Trebia.

There was no battle to win or lose here, however; at least not one with spears and shields. The fight was to win men's hearts, and to make them leave their homes and farms willingly, rather than at kopis-point. Demetrios' gaze ran down the line of men beside him. The entire file was armed and dressed for war, helmets and greaves polished, sarissae aimed at the heavens. Empedokles was beside him, reminding Demetrios afresh of Philippos' death. Grief cut Demetrios again like knives. How he missed the big man, and how good Philippos would have been at securing new recruits.

Demetrios had taken to saying that the Gorgon herself would have been won over by Philippos' huge smile and booming belly laugh, and none of his comrades argued. Truth was, thought Demetrios, it wasn't just him who was suffering. Everyone had been affected by Philippos' death – before they'd left Pella, phalangists from other files had offered their sympathies; even Stephanos had come to speak with Simonides about it.

Demetrios was the only one to carry shame as well as sorrow, however. Ending his friend's life had taken its toll. He struggled to sleep at night; when he did drop off, his rest was fitful and plagued by terrible dreams, most of which featured Philippos. Sometimes he begged to be slain; at others he pleaded with Demetrios to be carried back to Pella, that he might rest and recover. The worst dreams involved Philippos dying in his arms, as he had in the mountains of Orestis, only to come to life moments later. Sunken-eyed, bleeding from his chest, Philippos taunted Demetrios for saving Empedokles, not him. For having murdered him. For not killing him cleanly enough.

Demetrios felt at a complete loss. Kimon and Antileon sympathised, but didn't have much else to offer. They tended to pass him the wineskin if there was one around. Once Demetrios would have refused it; now he was glad to accept. Dionysos' comforting grip, reached after sufficient consumption, dulled the edge of his grief and allowed him to sleep. It stopped him from wanting to kill Empedokles, because right or wrong, Demetrios blamed him for Philippos' death. Slaying Empedokles would solve nothing, he told himself when sober, but nothing made his desire for revenge go away. Nothing except vast quantities of wine.

Demetrios' attention returned to the present. A raggle-taggle of farmers had come to listen to the man leading him and his comrades. Short, stout and florid-faced, Abantidas was one of the king's *epistates* or supervisors. The epitome of a bad government official, he was officious, thin-skinned and fond of his own voice. It was an immense source of frustration to Demetrios and his comrades that Abantidas outranked Simonides; the supercilious prick liked to let every phalangist know it too. Judging by their file-leader's fixed grimace every time they saw him with the epistates, Simonides had as low an opinion of Abantidas as they, but like them, he had orders to follow.

Those orders were to march through a designated area of the kingdom, spreading news of Philip's recent *diagramma*, or royal decree, which had changed the age-old eligibility requirements for conscription into the army. Scores of similar groups – comprising an epistates, secretaries and a file of phalangists, sometimes more – were spreading out through Macedon, doing the same as they. It was a mark of their task's urgency that before their departure, the chosen soldiers and officials had been addressed by the king himself. 'The army needs fresh blood, and plenty of it,' Philip had declared. 'New recruits – thousands of them – must be found the length and breadth of Macedon. I place my trust in you to fulfil this command.'

In each village or settlement, Abantidas repeated the king's message; that was what was about to happen now. Demetrios watched sidelong as Abantidas went through the little ritual he performed just before each of his speeches. Rub his hands together. Frown. Walk up and down a few steps, lips moving through what he'd say. Gesticulate: a fist in the air, a stabbed forefinger, a mimed sarissa thrust. There might be a cough, a clearing of his throat, or even a surreptitious scratch of his balls.

It was comical, but Demetrios had to admit Abantidas was good at his job. Every place they had visited thus far – five, or was it six? – had yielded more than the expected number of recruits.

'I've got tools as need repairing,' said a thickset man. Despite the chill wind, he wore his chiton with one shoulder bare. 'You going to tell us why you're here?'

'I'm a busy man too,' said a greybeard, another one with an exposed shoulder. His calloused, soot-blackened hands marked him as a smith.

'Father will be wondering why I'm not back,' said a stripling whose cheeks had never seen a blade.

Abantidas gave them an irritated look. 'I will address you in my own time.'

'Aye, well, best do it soon, or you'll be talking to the air,' advised the thickset man to a rumble of amusement. A few of those watching shuffled their bare feet, as if to warn Abantidas they too were restive.

Abantidas drew himself up to his full height, which was less than most men. 'It would be advisable to stay where you are,' he said with a sniff.

'Why's that?' demanded a willow-slim man whose chiton was better cut than most of those present. 'We are all freeborn Macedonians here. There's no law I know that can compel us to stand about rather than get on with our business.'

'It isn't that far from Pella, but clearly this backwater doesn't receive much in the way of news,' said Abantidas. 'I am an epistates of the king, come to announce a new diagramma. Philip wants every man in the land to hear his words. In other words, I speak for the king. Is that enough for you?'

138

'It is,' said the willow-slim man, smoothing his features. Even in Macedon, famous for its plain-speaking population, criticising the monarch was unwise.

The crowd settled. Demetrios studied their faces, seeing a mixture of wariness and fear, and in the faces of the young, curiosity and excitement. The latter were the easy ones, often happy to enlist after they'd grasped a sarissa or tried on a helmet and held an aspis. As ever it was the older men, the ones who knew what it meant to go to war, who had perhaps done so before and lost friends, who needed to be won over if possible. One way or another, the newly eligible would be joining the army, but it was better for all if they came of their own free will.

Ready at last, Abantidas raised his arms for quiet. 'Two years ago Rome landed its armies near Apollonia, soon after it invaded western Macedon. The war since has been bitter, as you will all know. There have been considerable setbacks – the defeat at Ottolobus and the loss of Thessaly, for example. The king commands us not to forget the victories won, however, at Pluinna and of recent days, at the fortress of Atrax. There the legions shattered on the phalanx's sarissae!'

It was the phalangists' cue.

'Now!' shouted Simonides.

Aspides already on their forearms, Demetrios and his comrades took a step forward, simultaneously lowering their pikes fifteen degrees.

Gasps rose. Several youths stepped back. A small girl hid her face in her mother's skirt.

Abantidas smiled, and flicked his hands at the crowd. 'Move. Move away, if you don't want to lose an eye – or worse.'

Obediently, the crowd shuffled back.

Demetrios wasn't fond of this part. He felt like the performing bear he'd seen once, trained to dance so its master could earn a coin.

'Rome will never forget its recent defeats,' cried Abantidas. 'Thousands of legionaries were slain by our glorious phalangists – such as these men here!'

'Lower pikes!' roared Simonides, and like that, sixteen sarissae came down to point at the gathered farmers. 'Forward, one step!' said Simonides, and the phalangists obeyed.

Demetrios saw none of the terrified faces in front of him. His vision was filled with the snarling faces of legionaries, his ears with shouts and screams.

'Impressive, is it not?' asked Abantidas in a loud voice.

Heads nodded. Men muttered to one another. A couple of excitable youths shouted, 'Macedon!' A small boy ran out in front of everyone; lowering the stick in his hand, he turned and drove it at the legs of the nearest man, raising a laugh.

'Macedon has need of more brave phalangists,' said Abantidas. 'Rome has not yet learned its lesson. King Philip calls on you to set down your tools, to leave behind your sheep and goats. Join the phalanx here, today!'

A muted cheer rose, and Abantidas frowned. 'I thought to see more enthusiasm here.'

'All the men of fighting age have gone from here, near as,' said the grey-bearded smith to nods of agreement. 'We've all seen more than forty-five summers, or fewer than twenty.'

Abantidas' smile grew sharp as a fox's. 'The king has seen fit to alter the regulations, father.' Into the surprised silence, he continued, 'The obligation of each household to provide one man of fighting age remains, but the age limit has changed. Everyone between the age of fifteen and fifty-five is now eligible.' To the greybeard, he said, 'How many summers have you seen, father?'

'Fifty-six,' came the reply. 'But I'll serve if the king will have me.'

'We can always bend the rules for the right man,' said Abantidas with a greasy smile. 'What about your smithy?'

'My wife can run the business blindfold, and my slaves have craft enough.' The greybeard stood forward from his fellows, as if daring them to join him.

'A fine start,' said Abantidas. 'Who's next? My secretaries are ready to take your details.'

Nine or ten men formed a line behind the greybeard; most were young. Despite the greybeard's courage, Demetrios saw, few of the middle-aged men had volunteered. This wasn't uncommon, and it was where the more unpleasant side to their duties came into play. Once Abantidas' secretaries, seated at the desk nearby, had taken the recruits' names, the epistates would take several phalangists and go through the village door to door. Hard questions would be asked about eligibility, and neighbours brought in to corroborate or refute any seemingly doubtful answers.

Demetrios watched Empedokles trying to make eye contact with those who had not come forward. His enemy was often first to offer himself for the task of seeking out those who had not volunteered at this stage of the proceedings. 'I've a nose for yellow-livers and tent-sulkers,' Empedokles would crow, sometimes throwing an evil look at Demetrios. 'Trembler,' Demetrios would mouth back at him, using the nickname given to a youthful, fearful Empedokles before his first battle, a decade and more before. The tactic always worked, enraging Empedokles just when he could not retaliate, and keeping the flame of their enmity bright – which was Demetrios' exact intention. One way or another, he thought, I'll get you back for living when Philippos did not.

'Don't be shy!' shouted Abantidas. 'Step this way, and do your duty for Macedon!'

To everyone's relief, the vicious northern wind had abated by late afternoon. The handspan of snow that had fallen lay pristine and white on house roofs; on the paths through the fast-darkening village, it had been ground into a thick brown slush. Most people were in their houses, sitting by their fires, or eating their evening meal. With their duties over for the day, the phalangists had headed for the only tavern, a small, run-down building by the Axios. They made up the majority of the customers, some of the eager-faced younger recruits the rest. Abantidas was not present; according to his browbeaten secretaries who *were* there, he regarded himself as too good to share the company of mere foot soldiers.

'Aye, well, let's be grateful for small mercies,' said Demetrios. 'It's bad enough listening to him all day without having our ears bent at night as well.'

'He's doing a vital job,' chided Simonides. 'We need more men to fight the cursed Romans.'

'I know that, but we could have had a more agreeable epistates. Abantidas is a nose-in-the-air, arrogant prick,' said Antileon.

Andriskos joined in. 'Putting up with him for the guts of a month is as bad as being set one of Herakles' twelve labours, I tell you.' He gestured with his cup at the amused faces around the fuggy, dim-lit room. 'Am I not right?'

Derogatory comments about Abantidas rained in, and the laughter rose to the smoke-blackened rafters.

Simonides rolled his eyes and wisely kept his opinion to himself.

The jokes had lightened Demetrios' mood. Happier than he had been since Orestis, he gave in at last to his twinging bladder. Slipping from the bench he was sharing with Kimon and Antileon, he made his way outside. With no latrine in sight, he wandered down to the Axios. There was something very satisfying about watching his piss arc up and down, vanishing into the turbulent water. Job done, he turned and took a step towards the tavern.

'Think you can escape that easy, you little shit?' Empedokles' voice carried through the crisp, chill air.

Demetrios peered into the darkness, making out three figures by a building behind the tavern.

A slap rang out; someone yelped in pain. 'Answer me!' shouted Empedokles.

Demetrios was moving before he knew it. Fast and silent, bent low, he ran towards the commotion. Twenty paces away, he took cover behind a statue to Zeus, the only effigy in the entire village.

Empedokles had two youths pressed up against the mud-brick wall of a house. 'Fifteen summers and older, the king says,' he growled. 'The size of you, you must be closer to twenty. Your father hasn't a tooth in his head, and he's a cripple anyway, which means you have to join up.' He jabbed a finger into the chest of the taller youth once, twice for emphasis.

'A big lad he might be, but he's only fourteen,' said the second youth, the smooth-cheeked one who'd mentioned his father wanting him home. He had enlisted, and been assigned to Simonides' file. The youth edged closer to Empedokles, and said, 'He's not lying!'

'I say he is,' said Empedokles, giving Smooth Cheeks a shove. 'What say we walk down to Abantidas' tent and get you signed up right now?'

The tall youth didn't answer, and Empedokles punched him in the belly. He doubled over, retching, and Empedokles laughed. 'Coward you might be, but you're still going into the army. King Philip needs every man he can get.'

Smooth Cheeks threw himself at Empedokles with a cry of anger.

He didn't have a chance. Empedokles ducked beneath Smooth Cheeks' left-right punch combination and, with a vicious uppercut to his jaw, sent him sprawling to the ground.

Demetrios stormed in, anger buzzing in his head like a swarm of furious wasps, images of Philippos lying in the snow, his legs useless. Empedokles began to turn, but was too slow to stop Demetrios leaping onto his back. Legs encircling Empedokles' midriff, he wrapped his left arm around his enemy's throat and with his stronger right arm, pulled it tight in a chokehold.

Empedokles lurched to one side, pulling desperately at Demetrios' encircled arms. Unable to free himself, he reached up and backwards, fingertips seeking a home in Demetrios' eye sockets. Demetrios twisted his head to the side, saving his eyes and barely preventing Empedokles' nails ripping down his cheek. Even angrier, he squeezed tighter with his thighs, and with his right arm wrenched his left inwards, increasing the pressure on Empedokles' neck.

Empedokles staggered; his arms fell to his sides, and Demetrios thought with savage delight, die, you whoreson. This is what you deserve.

Empedokles made a second, weaker attempt to reach Demetrios' face with his hands. Its failure seemed to sap the last of his strength. One knee buckled, and then he was falling. They landed hard, with Empedokles mostly underneath. His head slammed into the dirt; he went limp almost at once. Demetrios didn't slacken his grip even a fraction: in his mind, until Empedokles was dead, he was capable of anything.

He lay there, left hip smarting from where it had hit the ground, arms tight around Empedokles' throat. Another fifty heartbeats, thought Demetrios, and the bastard will be gone. Philippos will be avenged. The youths can help me bury him.

'You're going to kill him!' Smooth Cheeks was crouching over Demetrios.

Not before time, thought Demetrios. I should have done it a long time ago.

'He was bullying us, that's all.' The other youth was there too. 'He couldn't have made me enlist. My father would have sworn before the gods that I am fourteen – so would half the men in the village.'

There was more in their faces than fear, realised Demetrios, looking up. He could see revulsion too, and that hit him hard. They did not know of the long-standing enmity between him and Empedokles, nor that the malevolent bastard had almost drowned him near Korinth. They did not know that, because he had saved Empedokles,

Philippos had been maimed. Shamed by their reaction, Demetrios slackened his grip. Empedokles' head lolled forward, limp as a rabbit with a broken neck, and Demetrios thought, *Tartaros, he's already dead.*

Pushing Empedokles away so that he could get up, Demetrios rolled his enemy onto his back. Empedokles' face was puce, his lips swollen and engorged with blood. A purple line around his throat marked Demetrios' chokehold.

'Is . . .? Is he gone?' whispered Smooth Cheeks.

Demetrios moistened a couple of fingertips and placed them under Empedokles' nostrils. A heartbeat hammered past, then another. Then, almost imperceptible, a cool feeling on Demetrios' skin – a breath. Disappointment mixed with relief. He eyed the youths. 'A tough one, this bastard. He's alive.'

The fourteen-year-old looked as if he were about to cry. 'Wh-what should we do?'

'I suggest you make yourself scarce,' said Demetrios, climbing to his feet. 'Go and visit a friend in the hills, or another village. Don't come back for several days, until you know we're long gone. And you,' he said, eyeing Smooth Cheeks. 'Say nothing to a soul. If this prick–' here Demetrios poked a toe at Empedokles, who had started coughing '–says a word, threatens you, does anything at all, tell him it was Simonides who attacked him.'

'Our file-leader?' Smooth Cheeks' eyes were wide.

'Aye. Empedokles here was in the wrong, and when he comes to, he'll know that. He also didn't see me. If the prick thinks it was Simonides, he'll have to forget about the whole thing.'

Smooth Cheeks looked confused. 'You don't want him to know it was you?'

Nothing would give me more pleasure, thought Demetrios, but instead he said, 'I do, but this way, scared of Simonides, he'll leave you alone. If he thinks *I* attacked him, he will make *your* life a fucking misery as well as trying to get back at me.' The pair still looked uncertain, and Demetrios added, 'Being a phalangist is hard enough without having an enemy like Empedokles, believe me.'

They came to a decision almost in unison.

'Aye.'

'We'll do as you say.'

'Move. Be gone before he wakes up.' Demetrios urged them into the darkness, away from the stirring Empedokles.

A real opportunity had been missed, he decided as he retraced his steps to the tavern, but it wasn't all bad.

Empedokles lived, but *he* had gained a new ally in the file.

CHAPTER XVI

Corinth

Flamininus winced as his thumbnail tore at an awkward angle. Removing his bleeding fingertip from his mouth, he regarded the damage he'd done with fury. Even at Atrax he hadn't bitten his nails. It was a mark of his nervousness, he admitted to himself. Two months had passed since Philip's embassy had travelled to Rome only to be rebuffed, and Galba and Villius, both fresh-appointed as legates by the Senate, had arrived in Greece. A just-departed messenger had brought the news of their ships docking at Cenchreae; the pair would reach Flamininus' camp north of Corinth before sunset.

Flamininus didn't care about Villius – that fool was malleable – but Galba was a different creature altogether. From this point, Flamininus would no longer be able to focus only on defeating Philip; one eye would always have to be kept on Galba. If he didn't summon the pair here to his tent the moment they entered the main gate, moreover, he would suffer the ignominy of Galba calling on him, which would hand an invisible advantage to his enemy.

'Curse it all,' muttered Flamininus, sucking his smarting thumb.

'You called, master?' Potitius came sloping in from his desk, gaze cast down. It was a newly adopted posture, chosen, Flamininus suspected, to prevent him from seeing Potitius lick his lips.

'I didn't,' snapped Flamininus.

'Sorry, master.' Head still down, Potitius turned to go.

'Wait.'

'Master?'

'I want to see my brother. Send one of the sentries.'

'When, master?'

'Now.' Before facing his enemy Galba, Flamininus wanted to take counsel with his main ally in Greece. Lucius was a wastrel, but he was loyal.

'Yes, master.'

Flamininus could have sworn that as the wretch Potitius scuttled out, he was licking his lips again. His concern about Galba was such, however, that he was able to set his irritation aside. Galba's and Villius' appointments meant that Flamininus would have to relinquish command of two of his legions. Allocating the Eighth to Galba and the Thirteenth to Villius, Flamininus continued to worry what else Galba might demand.

Gods, he raged inwardly, why couldn't my spies in Rome have found something of value about him, something I could use against the cocksucker? They had discovered various interesting details about Galba, it was true – a predilection for dark-skinned whores of both sexes, a tendency to wager large sums on chariot racing – but neither of these would disgrace Galba, less still cause him to be forced from office.

Calm, Flamininus told himself. Stay calm. The Senate reappointed *me* to lead the war against Macedonia, not him. Galba can try to manipulate me, but *I* am in charge here. It is in his interest that I should succeed; that way only lies his chance of yearly receiving the four thousand thousand denarii we agreed in Rome.

Part reassured, part consumed still by worry, Flamininus decided to pray at the stone altar in the antechamber to his bedroom. He held little hope that his household gods would intervene – they were as fickle as the greater deities – but he needed the distraction.

How good it would be, he thought, to have sent a messenger to the commander of the Acrocorinth, advising him of Galba's arrival. A swift mounted attack by enemy cavalry would see Galba sent to the underworld, and no one to blame but the Macedonians. It wasn't worth the risk, Flamininus decided. Any messenger he sent would have to be slain afterwards, and then he'd have the men who'd done that to worry about. If word ever got out that he had arranged the killing of a legate, forced suicide would be the kindest death he could look forward to.

No, thought Flamininus, I shall have to bring down Galba another way.

He hoped that the means to do so presented itself soon.

As ever, Flamininus heard Lucius before he saw him. Possessed of a loud, enthusiastic character, his elder brother liked men to like him. It didn't matter whether they were of his own social class or just ordinary soldiers; he even wanted slaves to like him, thought Flamininus, listening to Lucius' attempt at friendly banter with Potitius. It didn't work, and Flamininus' lips twitched.

In the main, however, Lucius succeeded, which was a cause of much irritation to Flamininus, because *he* didn't possess the same skill. If he admitted it, he was jealous that his brother could pass through life with such amity around him. Men tended to respect Flamininus, or to fear him, but it was rare for them to *like* him.

Nonetheless, he smiled as Lucius entered his office. 'Brother.' As they embraced, he noted wine on Lucius' breath. Flamininus bit his tongue. A rebuke now would sour the meeting, and he wanted Lucius' support against Galba.

'How goes your preparation?' Flamininus asked.

'Well,' said Lucius, taking the stool across the desk from Flamininus. 'The ships are almost provisioned. We shall set sail for Acarnania tomorrow. You say it should be easy to take?'

'Most of it, yes. My information is that the Acarnanian forces are grouped in or near the fortress on Leucas. You may have to storm that.' Leucas was a peninsula in western Acarnania.

Lucius waved a confident, dismissive hand. 'Leave it with me, brother.'

Flamininus nodded, thinking, it was time to bring up Galba. Noting Lucius' eye roving around, he asked, 'Thirsty?'

'You know me too well.' Lucius' smile was rueful. 'I wouldn't say no.'

'Business first,' said Flamininus, his tone crisp.

Lucius made a face, but didn't protest.

'Galba will be here within the hour. Villius too.'

Lucius' expression changed, growing almost furtive. 'Galba?'

'Yes,' replied Flamininus, surprised, and thinking, you must have known he'd been appointed legate, and that he would make his way here soon after.

'Will you meet with him?'

'Of course. They are both legates. I shall have to give each the command of a legion.'

'Galba will want more than that, from what you've told me.' Lucius' attention drifted to the documents on the desk, the jug of wine, the clay beakers and the two expensive, blue-coloured glasses – anywhere but Flamininus' face.

'He will,' said Flamininus, feeling suspicious now, and deciding that his plan to reveal the extent of Galba's hold over him might be best kept to himself for the moment. 'Are you well, brother?'

'Me?' Lucius' eyes shot to Flamininus' and darted away. 'A little rough-headed, perhaps. Too much wine last night – you know how it is.'

'That might work on someone who knows you less well. I'm your brother,' said Flamininus archly. 'Are you also worried about meeting Galba?'

'Me? Why would I be concerned?' replied Lucius a little too rapidly. Without asking, he helped himself to a glass of wine.

'You tell me.' Flamininus' flinty stare bore down on Lucius, the practised look he'd given Pasion and countless others who'd crossed him over the years.

Lucius slurped wine, the wet sound amplifying the silence between them.

Flamininus knew well the power of not speaking. The longer nothing was said, the more uncomfortable Lucius would feel, and the more likely he was to crumble. Face blank, he picked up a letter and pretended to read it.

Lucius lasted another thirty heartbeats. Then, cursing, he said, 'I'm sorry.'

'For what?' snapped Flamininus.

'I should have been stronger.'

Puzzled, aware that Lucius might yet clam up, Flamininus said gently, 'I don't understand, brother.'

'Galba blackmailed me.'

'As he did me, the bastard.' Again Flamininus considered telling Lucius about Galba's extortionate price for his silence; again, he decided to say nothing. He guessed, and asked, 'Was it . . . a man?'

Lucius nodded miserably. 'A slave in a favourite brothel of mine in Rome. Somehow Galba found out I was fond of him. He bought the slave, and then told me he'd have him crucified if I didn't do what he said.'

Flamininus felt the first stirrings of disquiet. 'What did he ask you to do?'

Lucius' face grew anguished. He didn't answer.

'Brother. *What* did you do?'

'I told him I wouldn't do anything to harm you.'

'I'm glad to hear it,' cried Flamininus, thinking, even my brother can't be trusted. 'By the gods, tell me, Lucius!'

'I . . . I sent him word of your campaign against Philip. Where your legions were, and my fleet. The details of the clashes with the enemy, and so on. Just information he would have learned anyway.'

'Yes. Days later, in the carefully worded letters *I* sent to the Senate!'

'I didn't give him the full details of everything. Take the situation in the Aous, for example. I never said how many men you'd lost, nor how you had failed to take any ground for forty days.'

'What am I supposed to do – thank you for that?' roared Flamininus. Potitius chose this moment to enter; seeing him, Flamininus' temper exploded. He hurled the nearest object to hand – a stone ink pot – and caught Potitius in the side of the head. He stumbled and almost fell.

'Get out!' screamed Flamininus, spittle flying from his lips. He could barely see through the red mist that had descended. White-knuckled grip on the edge of the desk, he breathed in and out. In and out. A modicum of control returned; he glared at Lucius, and said, 'What else did you do for him, brother? I warn you, be honest. Lie to me, and by all that's sacred, I will have you dragged out and slain.'

Lucius began to cry. 'I'm sorry, Titus.'

His brother's weakness repulsed Flamininus. 'I don't want a cursed apology. I want the truth.'

'There wasn't much else other than the information I sent to Galba.'

'Lucius!'

More tears. 'Now and again, I had to pass his letters to you.'

Flamininus didn't quite believe his ears. 'Letters.'

'Yes. They would sometimes arrive with official correspondence, at others they'd be delivered by a messenger – a different one each time, never a man I recognised.'

'When did you pass on these letters exactly?' demanded Flamininus.

'The night before we sailed from Brundisium was one occasion. Another was more recently, when I had sailed to meet you at Anticyra.'

'Anticyra,' said Flamininus stupidly.

'Yes.'

Pasion's screams rang in Flamininus' ears; his secretary's terrified face filled his vision.

'Are you well, brother?'

With a start, Flamininus realised that there were tears in his eyes. He fixed Lucius with a furious glare. 'D'you remember Pasion?'

Lucius' brow wrinkled. 'Ah yes – I thought the fool you threw the ink pot at was new. What happened to the last secretary – Pasion, did you say?'

'Pasion, yes. He was Greek,' said Flamininus, even angrier now. A man could be forgiven for not recalling a slave's face, but Pasion had been with him for more than a decade. 'You met him countless times, *brother*.'

'Yes, I recollect him now,' Lucius admitted. 'The worried-looking one. Thoughtless of me to forget him.'

'Curse you to Hades. I thought Pasion was the one bringing me the letters,' said Flamininus, wishing that he could march back time. 'I had him tortured – to death. Now I find out from *you*, from my *brother*, that he was innocent.'

Lucius' throat worked.

Flamininus had never felt guilt over a slave before, but it washed over him now. He forced back tears. It would be unseemly to show such emotion over a mere slave; he also did not want Lucius to see him lose control. He marshalled his anger, focused his rage, and said, voice dripping with contempt, 'After all I've done for you, this is how you repay me?'

'I'm sorry,' whispered Lucius.

'*Sorry?* An innocent man is dead.'

'A slave.' Lucius' hand went to his mouth, but it was too late.

Flamininus came around the desk so fast that Lucius was still gaping when Flamininus' fingers closed around his throat.

'Yes, he was a slave,' snarled Flamininus. 'A slave like the catamite whose arse you were so fond of. That man-whore has sucked half the cocks in Rome, like as not. Yours was just another. Pasion on the other hand was loyal to me. He was conscientious. Discreet.'

Lucius made a little choking sound, and Flamininus realised his brother couldn't breathe. He wasn't resisting, however – he knew who was master. While the idea of suffocating him was pleasing, thought Flamininus, Lucius could still be of use. He did not want to have to appoint a new admiral as well as two legates. He loosened his grip.

Lucius coughed, retched. Tears spilled from his reddened eyes. Snot ran from his nose. 'Forgive me,' he muttered.

'You are an embarrassment.' Flamininus wiped his hands together in distaste.

'Will you tell Galba you know?'

'Of course. He might have power over me, but I will *not* stand for him blackmailing my brother as well.'

'And the slave he bought? The one I care for?'

It was all Flamininus could do not to wrap his hands around Lucius' throat again. Through clenched teeth, he said, 'I will tell him that the man-whore is not to be hurt.'

Lucius' face lit up. 'Will you buy him?'

'No,' said Flamininus, twisting the knife. 'He shall remain Galba's property. For ever. But he shall not be harmed. That is a small price for you to pay, compared to Pasion, who paid with his life.'

Lucius looked unhappy, but had sense enough not to argue.

'One more thing.' Flamininus' voice was light, yet laden with threat.

'Yes?' Lucius could not meet his gaze.

'If I find out that you have been disloyal to me a second time, brother, Pasion's fate will be as nothing to what you will suffer.'

Flamininus' meeting with Galba and Villius didn't last long. Both legates were tired from their journey, he'd declared, after giving them details of their new commands. The pair hadn't protested; no doubt remembering his dismissal by Flamininus at Apollonia the year before, Villius had been quick to make his excuses and leave. Galba lingered, which was no surprise. The moment Villius had gone, he returned to the large table that dominated the chamber where Flamininus met with his senior officers. A gaunt figure in late middle age, Galba wore a toga that was somehow the gleaming white it might be on an important day in the Senate. He planted his fists on the table, shoulders and arms stiff, the action of someone who thinks he is the master over the others present.

'So, here we are.' Galba's eyes moved from Flamininus to Lucius and back again. In an acid tone, he added, 'How pleasant.'

Flamininus took the bull by the horns. 'Lucius is no longer yours to order about.'

Galba's turn to look surprised. 'You know about our little arrangement.'

'I do,' said Flamininus. 'And it's over.'

'Really?' Galba sounded curious. 'There is the small matter of the slave with whom your brother is besotted – who, I should add, belongs to me. The creature is all doe eyes and long, fluttering eyelashes. Quite the beguiler, he is.' Only a blind man could have missed Galba's leer.

Dirty old bastard, thought Flamininus, shooting Lucius a warning glance just in time. He fixed his eyes on Galba. 'The slave is no longer of any consequence. He gives you no hold over Lucius.'

'Does your brother agree?' Galba turned to Lucius, who turned his face away. 'It seems he still cares for the creature.'

'You will keep your lecherous hands off him in future,' said Flamininus. 'You will not harm him either. If you do, rest assured I will hear of it, and you will pay.'

'Listen to him.' Galba's expression had hardened. 'Remember it is I who holds the whip, not you.'

'You will do as I ask in this regard, Galba,' said Flamininus, slow and deliberate, 'because if you do not, I will gut you myself. Here. Now.' He reached over to the stand on which his armour and weapons were arrayed, and drew his sword. Its only concession to wealth was the ivory hilt; otherwise it could have been an ordinary legionary's gladius. Long, tapered, keen-edged, its like had put the fear of the gods into the Macedonians during the summer. Flamininus pointed its tip at Galba, and advanced until only the length of the sword separated them. 'Well?'

Galba's face had drained of colour, but he did not back away. 'Have you gone mad?'

'I have never been saner,' said Flamininus, revealing his teeth. Even from the corner of his eye, he could discern Lucius' amazement. Watch and learn, big brother, he thought.

'The guards—' began Galba.

'Are loyal to me. Only me.' Flamininus moved his arm a little, so the tip of the blade touched Galba's toga, right over the breastbone. 'The slave with whom Lucius is infatuated is to remain unharmed. He is not to be raped to death, or to be tortured or crucified. His life is to be tranquil. Do I make myself clear?'

Galba's expression was murderous, but he nodded. 'I will not forget this.'

'Nor I,' said Flamininus, wishing that it was Pasion he had saved rather than a slave he would never even meet.

'Our agreement—' grated Galba.

'Stands,' Flamininus finished. 'You will receive the first payment when I take a city with a treasury worth talking about. That's not likely to be before the spring, before you start getting ideas.'

'Do not try any tricks,' warned Galba. 'Your brother may be lost to me, but I still have eyes everywhere.'

'Get out.' The sword swung to point at the entrance.

'I leave because we have nothing left to discuss.' Galba stalked to the threshold. Turning there, he said quietly, 'Know that Benjamin is with me.' With that, he was gone.

'Who's Benjamin?' asked Lucius.

'I have no idea.' Despite the confident lie, Flamininus' satisfaction at confronting Galba was seeping away like water through sand. He had won this skirmish, but his enemy had lost none of his strength. Moreover, a killer like Benjamin possessed the skill to creep past the sentries who guarded his tent night and day.

Flamininus converted the involuntary shiver that tickled his spine into a roll of his shoulders and a forward thrust of his sword. 'What I'd have given to run this into the filth.'

A voice in his head shouted:

That might have been the only chance you will ever get, Titus Quinctius Flamininus.

CHAPTER XVII

Near Thebes, Boeotia, late winter 198/197 BC

F elix, Antonius and their comrades were marching along a narrow
road bounded on both sides by hills. Occasional shepherds' huts
perched on the scrubby slopes above, abandoned since the arrival of
the bad weather. Winter still held the land in its grip; farmers and
livestock alike kept to their houses and pens on lower ground. Few
creatures were abroad. Several vultures hung in the grey, cloud-laden
air overhead. A fox watched, beady-eyed, from behind a large boulder.

Almost two thousand legionaries, the Eighth's entire complement of
hastati and principes, were on the move. In the ranks furthest from the
senior officers – currently, that included Felix's – the usual grumbling
about not being in camp like the rest of the army continued. Although
Felix would have preferred to have had his feet close to a warm fire,
or better still, to be wrapped in his blankets having a well-earned nap,
their purpose here today had his interest. It had been like this since
Rome, when he had witnessed the Macedonian embassy being laughed
out of the Senate.

'Thebes is the last place in Greece that's allied to Philip,' Felix said.

'Apart from the Acrocorinth,' observed Antonius to much
amusement.

'You know what I mean,' said Felix, rolling his eyes.

'Do we, sir?' asked Dordalus, now firmly established as one of the
century's jokers.

'Aye, you dogs,' Felix said into their laughter. 'Take Thebes, and
Philip's isolation will be complete – apart from the Acrocorinth, *I
know*, but it alone cannot offer serious threat to our legions. After this,
he will be barricaded behind Tempe.'

'We have to get inthide Thebeth firtht, thir,' said Sparax.

'Which is why Flamininus is a mile ahead of us, accompanied by
only a single maniple,' said Antonius, repeating what they all knew.

'When the Thebans see him approaching with Attalus and the other deputations, they won't fear his small escort.'

Clavus leered. 'He's going to slow his pace, as if to allow time to meet the crowds coming from the city to welcome him. That will allow us to catch up.'

'When the Thebans realise what's happening, it will be too late, gods willing,' said Felix.

And so it proved. Three hours later, the city was in Roman hands. Lulled into a false sense of security, hundreds of Thebans had flocked out to meet Flamininus and Attalus. The throng and the winding road combined had prevented soldiers on the ramparts from seeing the two thousand legionaries massed behind the consul's party. There would have been time for a quick-thinking sentry to slam the gates, but human nature – not quite believing what one was seeing – and indecision had seen that tiny window of opportunity vanish. The instant that the first century – Felix's – was inside the walls, they had fanned out and seized the gatehouse.

Once the entire force had entered, the city was theirs – the garrison was perhaps five hundred men in total, many of whom were not trained soldiers – and a sneering Bulbus had handed back control of the gatehouse to a still-shocked-looking officer of the guard. Making their way to the agora, the largest open space in the city, they joined the rest of their comrades, who were already setting up their tents. Shopkeepers, stallholders and passers-by watched in consternation and muttered in each other's ears, but not one dared protest.

Space had been set aside for Bulbus' century; it was close to Flamininus' tent. Felix was able to see what was going on, outside their general's headquarters at least. There was lots of toing and froing. Flamininus entered – he had been meeting with the city's council, apparently – followed by a large group of staff officers. Not long after, Attalus arrived and was admitted. Various deputations came after; Felix didn't recognise them all, but he could hear them announce themselves to the guards. Achaeans, Aetolians, Athenians. There were even a few Spartans. How quick they are to turn on each other, Felix thought with contempt. The same had happened in Italia during the war with Hannibal, but not to the same extent. A sizeable portion of Rome's allies, as well as its own citizens, had remained loyal even when their territory was overrun by the Carthaginians. How the Greeks must hate Macedonia, Felix decided. He could think of no other reason.

Thump. Something struck him in the head. Men laughed. Felix stilled his thumping heart – for a moment, he had thought they were under attack – and regarded the *harpastum* ball at his feet with a jaundiced eye. Irregular in shape, it was formed from a piece of badly cured, stitched leather packed with feathers. 'Who threw that?' Felix asked, glaring at Clavus, its owner.

Clavus shrugged. 'I did, sir.'

'He did call your name, brother,' said Antonius, smirking. 'We're having a toss around.'

'You were too buthy thpying on Flamininuth' tent to notithe, thir,' said Sparax, to a chorus of chuckling.

Everyone in the contubernium except Felix was standing in a rough circle in the space before their tent. There was no room for a proper game of harpastum, the brutal contest beloved of legionaries; besides, thought Felix; tackling each other with only the agora's paving stones to land on risked injury. A toss around was the next best thing.

'Where's Onion Head?' he asked, his eyes roving the tentlines.

'Gone to talk with the other centurions,' answered Antonius.

'I heard him tell Callistus he'd be an hour at least, sir,' added Dordalus.

Felix glanced around again. 'And the cocksucker?' Bulbus' nickname had soon given rise to Callistus' own. The danger of being overheard by either their optio or centurion only added to the thrill of using them.

'Drinking wine with a couple of other *optiones*, sir.' Clavus jerked a thumb over his shoulder. 'We'll see him coming in plenty of time. Throw the ball.'

Their distance from Flamininus' pavilion meant he couldn't hear anything of importance anyway, Felix thought with disappointment. He bent and picked up the ball.

Clavus gestured. 'To me, sir!'

Felix lobbed it the opposite way, to Antonius.

'Hey!' cried an annoyed Clavus. 'I should have been next.'

No one needed to be told. For the next dozen throws, the ball flew back and forth between Felix, Antonius, Dordalus and Sparax. Left out, Clavus ranted and raged to no avail. In the end, he lost his temper and tackled Antonius to the ground when he had it. That was the cue for Felix to dive in, defending his brother. The ball was quickly forgotten, and the struggle became a wrestling match. Not wishing to miss out, Dordalus and Sparax joined in as well. Headlocks were attempted and avoided, punches delivered to whichever part of a man presented itself. By unspoken consent, no one eye-gouged or bit – such tactics were only used during a real game of harpastum, against one's opponents.

Spying the ball – the prize they were supposed to be fighting for – lying unnoticed a few paces away, Felix managed to worm his way free of the confusion of arms and legs. Picking it up, he thought with amusement that if this had been a real contest, he would have made the easiest score of his army career. 'I have the ball, you fools!' he cried.

Disentangling themselves from one another, his laughing comrades formed a circle again, and the toss around restarted. Clavus' blood was still up; whether this was from Felix's initial refusal to throw to him or the spontaneous wrestling match was unclear. Each time Felix got the ball, Clavus came lunging at him. To annoy his comrade – he was the one who had started it, after all – Felix waited until Clavus was almost on him each time before throwing. In the end, however, he grew cocky. On Clavus' fifth attempt, he got so close that Felix misjudged his throw, hurling it over a surprised Antonius' head and into the open ground beyond their tent.

Bundled earthwards by Clavus, Felix did not see it land. He did hear Antonius mutter, 'Shit.' Freeing himself from Clavus' grip, Felix stood.

'Who threw that fucking ball?' an irate voice shouted.

Felix's eyes met those of Antonius, whose lips framed the word, 'Galba'.

No, thought Felix. Please, Fortuna, don't do this to me.

'I said, "Who threw that fucking ball?"' The voice was coming closer.

'I did,' called Felix. Mouth dry, he stepped out into the space before their tent.

The gaunt figure of Publius Sulpicius Galba, their new legate, stalked into sight. A gaggle of staff officers hurried at his heels. Gripping the harpastum ball in his bony hands, face pinched with fury, Galba came to a halt in front of Felix. 'You did . . . what?' he hissed.

Felix managed to come to attention, salute and cry, 'I did, *sir!*' in the same heartbeat. Fixing his gaze into the distance, he hoped, prayed, that Fortuna had finished laughing at him. 'Begging your pardon, sir. It was an accident.'

'What were you thinking?' Galba bounced the ball off Felix's head. It hurt, as it was meant to.

'I . . . I wasn't thinking, sir. Me and my comrades, we were just fooling about. I overthrew – I'm sorry, sir.'

Galba bounced the ball off his skull again, harder this time. 'Name and rank?'

'Felix Cicirrus, sir. Tesserarius of principes, Eighth Legion.'

'An officer should know better!'

'Aye, sir,' said Felix, embarrassed now as well.

'You must have been in the army for years to be promoted.'

'I'm a veteran of the Hannibalic war, sir. Seven years I spent fighting Hannibal.'

For the first time, there was interest in Galba's fierce eyes. 'Were you at Zama?'

'I was, sir, with my brother.' Felix waved behind him, in Antonius' direction.

Galba's gaze didn't move. 'A bitter day, I'm told.'

'It was a hard fight, aye, sir. We lost a lot of good men.'

'You re-enlisted to fight in this war?'

'Yes, sir. I was here during your term of command. We fought at Antipatreia and Ottolobus.' Never before had Felix so longed to have won an award for bravery, but even after he had slain the elephant at Zama, Matho had been too mean-spirited to see his feat acknowledged. Although it would have risked discovery of his dishonourable discharge, mention of such a thing might have leavened the punishment Galba was thinking up. Felix shoved the useless thought from his mind.

A slight easing of the fierce expression. 'You're a proper veteran.'

Wary, wondering if he might yet win over Galba, Felix ventured, 'I've seen a few things, sir.' Deciding to mention the elephant, he opened his mouth again.

Bounce. The ball hit his head a third time. Catching it, Galba slammed it against Felix's chest, crying, 'A soldier with your experience should know better! And a tesserarius should be even more aware of his position.'

'Aye, sir.' Hades, thought Felix with dread, he's properly angry.

'Where's your optio? Your centurion?' demanded Galba.

It took a few moments for Callistus to arrive, slightly longer until Bulbus had been summoned from his meeting. Embarrassed that they hadn't been present, incensed by Felix's actions, they both had to endure a lecture from Galba about the standards he expected of his troops.

'I may be old, but I've been around. I was consul during the war against the gugga Hannibal, and a second time after, remember!' Every vein in Galba's neck and head was distended; his eyes bulged dangerously. 'I have fought not just one war against the dog Philip, but two!'

And you didn't win either of them, thought Felix.

'*I* am the commander of this cursed legion. I deserve to be shown respect as I go about my business, not struck in the face with a filthy object like this – by an officer, no less.' Galba hurled the ball, and it bounced off a startled Bulbus' mail shirt.

Bulbus managed to catch it, just. 'You are correct of course, sir. My apologies,' he muttered, shooting an evil glance at Felix.

'You were never any good at harpastum, that's clear,' Galba sneered at Bulbus, holding out his hands. He smacked the ball off Callistus' bald dome next, laughing as the optio flushed with shame and humiliation.

Felix would rather have charged a Macedonian phalanx at that moment than suffer the wrath of both his centurion and optio afterwards – and that was before Galba doled out whatever punishment was rolling around his malevolent skull.

In the event, the legate demoted Felix and sentenced him to twenty lashes, and the loss of three months' pay. His comrades were each to receive five lashes and to be fined a month's pay. Callistus was given twenty nights of sentry duty; Bulbus received a brutal dressing-down, much of which consisted of Galba mocking him for having such a useless tesserarius.

Tapping his foot with impatience, Galba then stayed to watch the whippings. Men gathered as a mule cart was fetched; Felix was stripped to his undergarment, and one hand lashed to either side of the back of the wagon. Ordered to administer the beating, Callistus shed his mail shirt to afford himself more ability to swing. Puffs of dust rose as he flicked the whip to and fro along the paving.

Felix could taste bile. Thirty lashes could cripple a man; in the hands of a brute like Callistus, furious at his own punishment, twenty might do the same. Even if the cocksucker went easy on him, his back would be a raw mess by the end. The thoughts made Felix's bowels loosen. He clenched his buttocks, determined not to shame himself even further.

'Get on with it,' ordered Galba.

Felix made the mistake of looking at Bulbus, who drew a finger across his throat. Hades, thought Felix, my life is not going to be worth living from this day forward. Why did I even think of accepting promotion? If I'd still been an ordinary princeps, Bulbus wouldn't be half as angry.

The air whistled. Sweet agony licked across Felix's back, from the right shoulder to the left side of his waist. He managed – just – to hold in his cry.

'One,' said Callistus, changing his stance.

Air moved again. The pain cut a line diagonally opposite to the first. Lips pressed tight, Felix bucked and twisted against his restraints. The leather strips held fast.

'Two.'

The third lash was an almost exact replica of the first. The fourth, a copy of the second. Neat and precise, Callistus whipped Felix's back left and right, left and right. He had bitten his lip and was tasting blood by the seventh lash. By the tenth, he was grunting as the whip made contact with his smarting flesh. He cried out when the twelfth landed, mortified but no longer able to keep silent. Felix lost the tally at fifteen. He didn't hear Callistus count out the last five lashes; hanging limply by his wrists, he felt nothing as he was untied by a distraught Antonius and carried to one side.

Felix awoke to a world of pain. He was lying on his front, clad only in his undergarment; his arms and legs were cold, but his back felt as it were on fire. He opened his eyes, seeing in the dim light panelled leather, blankets, a rolled cloak that served as a pillow. He was in the contubernium's tent. He lifted his head, wincing at the agony even that small movement caused, and looked around. There was no one with him. 'Tonius?' he croaked.

A heartbeat later, the flap was pulled back, revealing his concerned-looking brother. 'I'm here. How are you feeling?'

'As if there isn't an inch of skin left on my back.' Felix could see by Antonius' reaction that his comment wasn't far from the truth. 'It's fucking agony. And you?'

A bitter shrug. 'It hurts.'

Felix tried to get up on his elbows, but the pain mastered him. He sank down, sobbing for breath.

'Stay where you are,' ordered Antonius. 'The surgeon gave me a salve, which I slathered all over you – it and rest are all that can be done for the moment.'

'My duties . . .' Felix could already see Callistus beating him out of the tent, with a leering Bulbus watching.

'Don't worry, brother. You won't be able to do a thing for days – Onion Head and the cocksucker know that.'

Felix sighed into his cloak-pillow. 'Why did Clavus have to keep tackling me?'

'It's probably little consolation, brother, but he is feeling bad about it. We all are. Fact is, we've decided to even out the loss of pay, so each of us is in the same boat. Simply put, that means you'll only lose a month and a half's coin, instead of three.'

Pay was the last thing on Felix's mind, but he managed to mutter his thanks.

'D'you need water? Wine?'

'A sup of water, aye.' He closed his eyes as Antonius hurried outside. Left alone, Felix's mind soon turned to Galba. What a cruel bastard he was. As bad as Bulbus and Callistus, thought Felix, maybe even on a level with Matho.

Matho. How good it had been to see that prick leave this world. Felix was quick to tell himself that the centurion's death, and the fact that his and Antonius' role in it remained undiscovered, had been a gods-given gift. Such things landed in a man's lap perhaps once in his life. The same would not be happening to Callistus and Bulbus; Felix and his comrades must needs endure the torment that the two officers would put them through because of the incident with the harpastum ball.

If Callistus and Bulbus were untouchable, Felix decided, Galba was akin to a god. Nobleman, senator, ex-dictator, ex-consul, now a legate, he ranked among the most important men in the entire Republic. Lay a hand on him, and Felix could expect to die in the worst fashion possible. You're a lowly footslogger again, he thought. Remember that. Galba will have already forgotten you. Do the same thing with him. Move on, and remember always to look before you throw a ball.

Even the smile that brought to Felix's lips hurt.

For some odd reason, he heard the one-armed veteran Pennus' toast again. 'Here's to us rather than those noses-in-the-air bastards, eh?'

Galba was a thief, Felix remembered. He had stolen a fortune from the Republic. Somehow reveal that, and *he* might get his revenge for the savage whipping. Another heartbeat, and his hopes turned to ash. An ordinary legionary like him had no hope of bringing down a legate. He might as well plan to steal the sun from the sky.

Grateful to be alone still, Felix gave in to the pain, and wept.

CHAPTER XVIII

Pella, early spring 197 BC

Philip was pacing about his favourite courtyard. Despite the magnificence of the colonnaded walkway, and the lemon trees and vines that filled its centre, it felt for all the world like a prison. Apart from regular visits to his army's camp, and less common escapes disguised as an ordinary Macedonian, the royal quarters were where he had spent the winter.

Hearing his youngest son Demetrios playing with a laughing Perseus in the next courtyard over, Philip thought, Menander would tell me to enjoy the time with my family while I can. He had done just that after the conference at Nikaia, first seeking out the company of Polykratia, his concubine. He had also tried to make amends with his queen, Penelope, the mother of Demetrios.

The first tactic had soon palled. Polykratia's beauty was long departed. Coupling with her before had been a joy; now it had become a chore. Her unfortunate tendency to bend Philip's ear about Perseus becoming king even as they lay together only soured his desire quicker. His efforts with Penelope had also been doomed to fail. Married by arrangement as was the norm, Philip's union with her had ever been loveless. It was no surprise, he decided, that Perseus, Polykratia's child, had been born a full four years before Penelope's offspring, his legal son Demetrios. A rueful smile flitted across Philip's face. Not that the age gap stopped Penelope from wanting Demetrios to become his legal heir. On that, however, Philip would not budge. His kingdom had never been in greater jeopardy, and it was bad enough considering what might happen if he were killed and Perseus had to take the throne at fifteen, let alone the consequences of an eleven-year-old Demetrios doing so. This was lost on Penelope, who maintained she could help her son to rule. As if his nobles would follow her against Rome, thought Philip. Men need a warrior to lead them in war.

He rolled his eyes. Women. A man couldn't live with them – or without them. The company of men, now that was a different matter. Philip knew where he stood with men. Lacking women's guile for the most part – Herakleides had been a notable exception, Philip remembered darkly – they were simple creatures like himself. Give me good food, fine wine, a battle every so often and a woman to plough at the end of the day, and I'm a happy man, he thought. If only life were so simple.

The company of his children *was* something he would miss once the campaigning season reopened. Perseus would come with him, but Demetrios and his three-year-old sister Apama needs must remain at court. It might be months before he saw them again. An impetuous idea – to steal into the city and buy his younger offspring presents – took Philip. He could already picture their delight, hear their happy cries. Hurrying to his sparsely furnished bedchamber, he changed his fine chiton for the oldest he had, a favourite often worn to war. Finishing his disguise with a simple belt and a kausia, the king left the palace by a long passageway that exited into a back street by way of a locked door.

A dozen steps from the threshold, and Philip noticed a spring in his step. Zeus' beard, but I should do this more often, he thought. It was a complete pretence to imagine he was just a fond father in search of toys for his children, yet it served to lighten his load. Just like that, his worries about Flamininus returned with a vengeance. Cursing, Philip swept them away again. The weather had not grown warm enough for an army to march. He had another ten days, if not more. His plans were set, his soldiers trained, his supplies bought and paid for. His hopes for a reply from Antiokhos had almost died. If the Seleucid emperor hadn't replied by now, chances were he wasn't interested in an alliance. Victory could yet be Philip's, however. The plan he had laid out to Menander was daring, but by no means impossible.

Philip paused to buy fried mutton at a street stall, and decided again that an hour of pretending to be an ordinary Macedonian would harm no one. Handing over an obol in payment, he was amused by the woman stallholder's shock as she realised who he was. Even as she tried to bow – there was no space behind her laden-down stall – he gestured at her, no, she was to remain quiet. With a friendly nod, Philip went on his way.

It was market day, and the streets were packed with farmers from the surrounding districts, and city dwellers and off-duty soldiers keen for fresh produce. The vegetables and grains on offer in the shops were the same as they had been all winter, however: barley, onions, cabbages and leeks. A few green-fingered types, those perhaps who knew every line of Hesiod's *Works and Days*, had refused to sell to the shopkeepers. They sat instead in the agora, offering – for a high price – the fresh herbs they'd laid out on squares of cloth. Red-handed butchers bellowed about the quality of their cuts of mutton and pork, and bakers, always popular, relied on the delicious smells emanating from their ovens to pull in customers.

The scene was no different from what it had ever been, and Philip loved its ordinariness. The war preyed on his mind night and day, but here in Pella, life went on. These people, his subjects, were more interested in filling their bellies than knowing whether it would be he who emerged victorious, or Flamininus. Life had always been so, he suspected. What was to hand, one's everyday situation, as it were, was of greater importance than world-changing events unfolding far from home.

Gods bless them, thought Philip. They know no different. Let a horde of ravening legionaries come rampaging through the streets, and their opinions would soon change. Scowling because of the ease with which his worries had resurfaced, he renewed his search for a toyshop. Finding one at last, a small premises squeezed between a ramshackle builder's yard and a vendor of parchments and ink, he ducked his head and entered.

His humour improved at once. The shop was deeper than it looked from the outside. Counters on either side ran off to the back wall. He spied dozens of wooden dolls, varying in size, some painted, some not. Cloth versions lay alongside, for those with babies rather than children of Apama's age. Clay rattles with pebbles sealed inside had been moulded into animals' heads: lions, bears, wolves. Stone pull-along horses stood in rows, almost as if they were about to race one another. Carved bone and antler figurines represented the gods, or mythical warriors and animals. Dice shaped from sheep tail bones and boxwood served as temptation for old and young. This entire shop was Elysium for a child, Philip decided, wishing that Demetrios and Apama were with him. Inside a heartbeat, he set the notion aside. Apama would have demanded to be carried from the moment he exited the passage-way, and Demetrios could be expected to run off whenever the notion took him.

'Looking for anything in particular, sir?' The voice belonged to a middle-aged, slope-shouldered giant with an amiable face. Emerging from a doorway at the back of the shop, he nodded a greeting.

Here was the most unlikely shopkeeper of a toyshop imaginable, thought Philip. The man looked born to be a phalangist. He wasn't here to recruit, however. He made a friendly gesture, at the same time keeping his chin dipped so the kausia obscured his features. 'I have a three-year-old daughter, and an eleven-year-old boy, who thinks he's as old as his elder brother – of fifteen.'

'Aren't they all like that?' The slope-shouldered man laughed, an odd, high-pitched sound for someone so large. '"He's allowed to do that, father. Why amn't I?"'

It was as if the shopkeeper had overheard Demetrios' very words earlier that morning. Philip chuckled. 'I can remember being the same way.'

'Aye, and me. It has ever been so. Boys, men, they always covet what they cannot have.' The shopkeeper ran a hand over a line of pull-along horses. 'These are very popular. Your daughter would love one, I am sure.'

'She would.' Philip picked one up. Its body shaped from black stone, the horse had four brown wheels. A hole bored through the bottom of each of its front and back legs allowed the insertion of parallel wooden spokes to which the wheels were attached. A thin strip of leather at-tached to a ring on its head allowed the toy to be pulled along the ground. 'Clever,' said the king.

'I make them myself.' There was pride in the shopkeeper's voice.

Philip's tongue ran away with him before he could help it. 'Why aren't you in the army? Toys are secondary to Macedon's needs.'

'I could ask you the same thing, friend.' The enunciation of the last word conveyed many things, but friendship was not one of them.

The challenge was shocking, and yet, Philip thought, entirely under-standable. The man had no idea who he was. His initial reaction was to take off his kausia and thunder that he was the king. That would cow the shopkeeper and possibly provide another recruit for the army, but, he decided, his anonymous excursion would have been ruined. Philip raised a hand in apology.

'True. Each man's business is his own. I'll take the horse.'

Surprised, mollified, the shopkeeper asked, 'Don't you want to know the price?'

'You seem an honest man, not a swindler. Am I right?'

'You are.' The shopkeeper named a sum lower than Philip had been expecting. 'A gift for your son now?'

'Demetrios would like these,' said Philip, pointing to the antler figurines. 'I'll take two different ones for him, and another for my daughter.' Again the price was fair; he handed over the necessary coins. Smiling, because he hadn't even thought to bring a basket, he scooped up his purchases. 'I'll be on my way. Zeus' blessings on you.'

'And on you, friend.' The shopkeeper's tone was genuine.

Philip was at the door when the shopkeeper spoke again.

'Both my sons were phalangists. They fell in the Aous valley last summer. One died to save the other, I'm told, before he too was slain. My daughter helps to run the shop now.'

Never assume, thought Philip, ashamed that he had been so quick to form an opinion. He lifted his gaze to meet the shopkeeper's, and said, 'Your sons sound like fine men. I am sorry for your loss.'

A grateful nod, but still, to Philip's relief, no recognition. 'Many fathers will know my grief before this year is out, sadly. Gods grant that the king defeats the Romans, eh?'

'Let it be so.' Philip's wish had never been more heartfelt. To lose Perseus *and* Demetrios in one fell stroke of Ares' sword was unimaginable. Nor could the shopkeeper be the only father to suffer such a loss; as he said, more would soon experience it. Philip had long known the heavy price of war. A warrior king, he had seen countless men die, in many terrible ways, but seeing the raw, naked grief of someone left behind was new to him. Still certain that the fight against Rome had to be continued – even with the price to be paid – but discomfited and feeling a little guilty, he left.

Again pondering his best options when the time came to march south, he didn't see the man in his path until it was too late. Their heads clashed; Philip dropped the toy horse. Quick as lightning, the man stooped, grabbing it half a heartbeat before it struck the stone paving.

'My apologies.' His Greek was heavily accented. He held out the horse. 'Here.'

'It is I who must say sorry. I walked into you,' said Philip. 'My thanks also for catching the toy. It would have been sure to shatter.'

A wry smile. 'It's for your son or daughter?'

'My daughter. She's three.'

'A nice age.' Something that might have been regret, grief, or perhaps both, flashed across the man's dark-skinned face. Of a similar age to Philip, he was tall, thin, with black hair and green eyes, and wore a tight-fitting red woollen singlet with a central white stripe, and knee-length breeches. With a friendly nod, he took a step away from Philip.

'Wait. By your dress, you're Carthaginian.'

The man's face hardened. 'Aye.'

'What are you doing here?'

Without another word, the man walked away. The crowd swallowed him up at once.

Philip reined in his desire to plunge after him. Pella wasn't that big a place. He would send out an order for any Carthaginians to be detained and questioned. In a friendly way, of course, he thought. Carthage might have been defeated, but it was still a power. There was no point potentially antagonising a people who might once have been his ally.

Curiosity filled him as he retraced his steps to the palace.

What purpose had a Carthaginian in Pella?

An hour later, Philip had forgotten the encounter. Delighted with their gifts, relishing the rare company of their father, Demetrios and Apama would not let him out of their sight. Like all small children since the dawn of time, they were jealous whenever the other got attention. Apama stamped the ground when he knelt down with Demetrios and his figurines, and he was no less jealous, standing stony-faced over Philip and Apama as they pulled the horse along the mosaic.

'It's my turn, father.' Demetrios' voice had the whining tone every parent comes to loathe.

'No!' Apama's bottom lip jutted.

'Not yet,' said Philip to his son. 'I have only just started to play with Apama.'

Demetrios hmphed. A moment later, he edged a foot forward;

another few heartbeats, and the pull-along horse would hit it.

'Demetrios mean!' cried Apama, seeing his intention.

'Move your foot,' said Philip.

Sulkily, Demetrios obeyed.

Delighted by what she saw as Philip's support, Apama stuck out her tongue at her brother.

Angry, Demetrios tipped over the horse.

Apama began to cry.

Deciding that soldiers were easier to lead, Philip did his best to calm the situation. He was glad a moment later when one of his guards, a phalangist, appeared. It was just the excuse he needed. Giving each child an affectionate pat, and promising to visit later, he consigned the pair to the care of their nurses.

Philip beckoned to the phalangist. 'Speak.'

'My file-leader sent me, sire. We're on duty at the main gate. There's a man outside demanding to see you.'

Philip frowned. 'This had better be good.'

The phalangist looked as if he'd rather be anywhere but in front of the king. 'My apologies, sire. The file-leader thought you should know. The man says he's been sent by Hannibal Barca.'

'Hannibal, you say?' said Philip, thinking of the man who'd caught the stone horse.

'A-aye, sire,' said the phalangist, wincing in expectation of a blow.

'Bring him to my private quarters at once!'

The palace's main gate was some distance away; Philip waited with increasing impatience for the phalangist to return. When at last the sound of footsteps announced the imminent arrival of the Carthaginian messenger, it was all the king could do not to go out into the corridor. Decorum was vital, however, so he smoothed his features and took an apparent interest in a bust of his stepfather, Antigonus Doson.

A rap at the door, and Philip cried, 'Enter.'

The original phalangist entered, preceded by his officer. Behind came the man Philip had met; at his back, for security, another phalangist.

Recognising Demetrios – the Demetrios who had saved him from an assassin's blade – Philip's smile of welcome broadened.

'Simonides, sir,' said the file-leader. 'My apologies for intruding.'

Philip waved a hand. 'Approach. Tell me who this man is.'

'Says he's come from Carthage, sire. Says Hannibal sent him with a message.' Simonides held out a rolled parchment. 'This was on him. Along with a knife.' This last was said accusingly.

'Rest easy, Simonides,' said Philip, taking the document. 'Most men carry a knife.'

'Aye, sire.' Simonides' voice still held plenty of suspicion.

Philip's gaze moved to the Carthaginian. 'We meet again.'

Surprise blossomed on the man's face. 'It's you!'

Philip dipped his chin. 'You saved a princess' toy.'

The Carthaginian performed a deep bow. 'I hope she is happy with it, sire.'

'She is.' Philip looked at the seal on the parchment, and his heart gave a little leap. The palm tree and horse were two important symbols of Carthage. 'What do they call you?'

'Hanno, son of Malchus, sire.'

'A common name, Hanno.'

A little smile. 'That's true, sire, hence my mention of Father.'

Philip stared him up and down. 'You are no messenger. I know a soldier when I see one.'

'Your eyes do not deceive you, sire.'

'You fought for Hannibal?'

'I did, sire.' Hanno's chin lifted with pride, revealing a terrible scar on his neck. 'At the Trebia. At Lake Trasimene, Cannae, Syracuse and many of the ones after, in Hispania. I was at Zama too, curse the day.'

Philip prided himself on being able to tell when a man was speaking the truth. He had been wrong before on occasion but in general his gut instinct proved to be correct. This was a brave man, he decided, and he *had* been sent by Hannibal. 'I'm sorry I didn't send more phalangists to Zama.'

'Gratitude, sire. You would have had to have sent thousands, and even then I am not sure we could have carried the day. Scipio is a shrewd bastard, if you'll forgive me. He paid a fortune before the battle to win over the best of the Numidians, giving him an enormous superiority in cavalry. Our elephants hadn't had enough training either, and when his legionaries opened up channels between their units, the wretched creatures charged straight through his army.'

'I heard,' said Philip, shaking his head in sympathy, and thinking, however bad it was to have Flamininus as an enemy, Scipio would be worse. His gaze returned to the parchment. 'This is from Hannibal?'

'I watched him dictate it to a Greek scribe myself, sire.'

Wondering what in all the gods' names the man he had nearly formed an alliance with more than seventeen years before could want of him now, Philip slit the seal with a nail.

> *Greetings, Philip, King of Macedon.*
> *It seems but yesterday that we were to join forces and*
> *fight Rome together. Word reached me some time later*
> *how misfortune led the enemy to intercept your messenger*
> *on the open sea. If he had reached me, the war in Italia*
> *might have taken a different course. The gods can be cruel.*

Zeus, but they can, thought Philip, imagining the victories that might have been won if he had sailed a fleet to join Hannibal the year after fifty thousand legionaries had been slaughtered at Cannae. It was almost too bitter to contemplate. He began to read again.

> *You will know something of the conflict and its later stages;*
> *I will not bore you with the detail. You have my gratitude*
> *for sending troops to join us at Zama. They fought well.*
> *On another day, with better cavalry, I might have prevailed*
> *against Scipio, but it was not to be.*
> *For a time after the battle, the ruling council saw fit to let me*
> *lead my people. Of recent months, however, political*
> *rivals in Carthage, jealous these twenty years of my*
> *achievements, have conspired against me, sending false mes-*
> *sages to Rome about my plans to recommence the war at the*
> *earliest opportunity. Their support grows by the day. It will*
> *not be long before I am forced to flee the city of my birth.*
> *Know that my desire to see Rome vanquished remains un-*
> *dimmed. I wonder if you, King Philip, might see the value in*
> *retaining a general with some history of success against your*
> *bitterest enemy? I remain with respect, Hannibal Barca.*

Under a squiggled signature, Hannibal's scribe had added in spidery script,

Hanno, who bears this message, can be trusted.

Tartaros, thought Philip, letting out a long breath. In all my days, I could never have predicted this. He looked up, finding Hanno's eyes on him. 'Hannibal will have to flee Carthage?'

Hanno's nod was grim. 'It's inevitable. If not now, then soon. The cowards who gloried in his victories for a generation cannot bear to see him lead the city. They would rather ally themselves with Rome than stand with the greatest son of Carthage ever to have lived.'

'Hannibal will be welcome here,' said Philip warmly.

He had never spoken a truer word.

CHAPTER XIX

Dio, Macedon, spring 197 BC

Warm sunshine bathed the land. A light breeze kept the air fresh. Birds trilled their joy at the heavens. It seemed every tree was budding, every plant green with growth. Close to the town of Dio, a great camp sprawled for tens of stadia in every direction. Winter was over, and the king's army had assembled. By far the greatest part of the almost-town was given over to Philip's sixteen thousand phalangists; in the midst of those hundreds of tents, Demetrios strolled with Kimon and Antileon. The three had been here from the time of the first tents going up, a month before. They knew the place like the backs of their hands.

'Those tents belong to the Whites,' said Demetrios with a jerk of his head to the left.

'I know,' said Antileon, with a sly look that both the others knew too well.

'Why are we here?' demanded Demetrios.

Antileon did not answer.

Demetrios and Kimon exchanged a glance. There was no love lost between the two *strategiai* of Philip's phalanx, the white shields and the brazen shields. Even the thousands of new recruits, with no knowledge of the historical rivalry, were aware of it. Beware the lone Brazen phalangist who strayed into the tentlines of the Whites or vice versa. Even three men might come to grief. The same applied if one were to wander at the wrong time into the areas occupied by the king's allies, two thousand each of wild Illyrians and Thracians, and the fifteen hundred mercenaries from every part of Greece and beyond. High standards were expected and maintained in the cavalry, so a man might expect to come to no harm in their tentlines; the same was possibly true of the two thousand peltasts, but Demetrios wouldn't have wagered his life on it.

'Where are we going?' demanded Kimon.

Antileon marched on as if he hadn't heard.

Demetrios could already see Whites watching them. His sense of urgency grew. *They* were obeying the strict order not to carry weapons when off duty, but men running from their tents could easily pick up a blade. 'Tell us, Antileon.'

Again no answer. Demetrios ground his teeth and wondered why Antileon loved to wind people up, most of all his friends.

There was always a degree of hostility between units – since the dawn of time, it had happened in armies – but with the war about to begin again, tensions were running high. Everyone knew that Flamininus' legions would march north any day. Drills and weapons training – ordered by Philip himself – served to dissipate some of the troops' nervous energy, but not all. Barely a morning went by without news of a terrible beating inflicted on a Brazen, a White or a tribesman the previous night. Rumours of men being murdered were rife, and never disproven.

Unless you were with a large group of comrades, Demetrios had concluded, the safe policy was to stay close to one's tent – although with Empedokles nearby, the potential for trouble remained. With their comrades all around and Demetrios, Antileon and Kimon on the lookout for treachery, however, Empedokles could do little except spread spiteful rumours.

This was his latest trick. Demetrios had been badmouthing their commander Stephanos. It was Demetrios who had taken a shit beside Simonides' tent, or the sentry who'd mistakenly called the alarm two nights before. For the most part, men told Empedokles to shut his mouth, but, as Demetrios thought bitterly, if you threw enough dung at a wall, some of it stuck in the end. Perhaps he was imagining it, but it felt as if those in other files – Empedokles was flapping his lips to anyone who would listen – seemed to be less friendly than before. What a pity it was, he thought, that he hadn't killed his enemy by the Axios. In the same instant, Demetrios remembered the shock on the two youths' faces as he'd strangled Empedokles. Better, he decided, to have another friend – as the baby-faced recruit Eumenes had become – than a dead Empedokles.

'Brazen bastards!' called a voice.

'Go back to where you belong!' added another. A third man whistled his disapproval, and Demetrios' attention returned to the present with a jolt. He looked to his left. A group of perhaps ten phalangists – all Whites – was watching. None of their faces were friendly.

Demetrios spun and planted himself in Antileon's path, forcing his burly friend to stop. 'Tell me what you're up to, you dog, or I'm going not a step further.'

'What he said, aye,' muttered Kimon. 'There'll be fighting enough in the coming months without having seven shades of shit beaten out of us for no good reason.'

'Have you no trust in me?' Antileon could put on a hurt expression with the best of them.

'We have, *if* you tell us what in Tartaros you're up to,' said Demetrios.

By way of answer, Antileon tapped the cloth-wrapped bundle under his arm.

Demetrios had been asking him about it since they had left their tent, but Antileon had refused to answer. He glared now at his friend. 'What is it?'

'A sword,' guessed Kimon.

Antileon nodded.

'Yours?' demanded Demetrios.

A shake of the head.

'It's not mine, because I put an edge on that just before we left,' said Kimon, glancing at Demetrios.

'Did you thieve my kopis?' Demetrios lunged at Antileon, who danced out of the way, grinning.

'I didn't,' Antileon answered. 'Can't you guess whose it is?'

'Dionysos' sweaty balls,' said Demetrios. 'You didn't.'

As Antileon smirked, Kimon looked from one to the other, confused.

'Why?' cried Demetrios, by turns delighted at his friend's ingenuity, annoyed that he hadn't thought of it himself, and worried about what would happen when the theft was discovered.

'Taking his sword is nothing compared to what the prick did to you,' said Antileon.

At last Kimon understood. 'You stole Empedokles' kopis? Zeus above, but that will put him in a killing rage. You know it was his father's blade, and before that, his grandfather's?'

'No,' said Antileon. With it, a shrug. 'That would explain why it's been so well looked after.'

Demetrios had noticed how proud Empedokles was of the sword, but hadn't been aware of its history. He gave Antileon a look. 'What are you planning?'

'I was at the end of our section when we were on sentry duty the other night. Not all the Whites are pieces of shit, it turns out. I fell to talking with one, the next man along the perimeter. His kopis had cracked during an overeager training session with a comrade; he was worried that the smiths weren't up to making a good enough replacement.' Again Antileon tapped the cloth-wrapped bundle. 'He'll pay a good price for this, or I'm no judge.'

Part of Demetrios wanted to give Antileon a piece of his mind for interfering in his business. Then he laughed, picturing Empedokles' face when he noticed the theft.

'You think it's funny?' Kimon was regarding him with disbelief.

'*I* do,' said Antileon, chuckling.

'You would. Big oaf,' said Kimon, giving him a shove. 'It's not you who Empedokles wants dead, though.'

''Dokles won't have the vaguest idea of who took it,' said Antileon.

'He'll blame Demetrios regardless,' challenged Kimon. He looked at Demetrios, who was still laughing. 'What's so funny?' cried Kimon.

'It doesn't matter if we sell his sword. The whoreson hates me anyway. He almost killed me once already, remember, that time we went fishing. He also suspects that I attacked him in that village where we were recruiting.'

'But Baby Face told him it was Simonides,' said Kimon.

'His name's Eumenes,' said Demetrios. The lad's permanent expression of wide-eyed wonder and smooth cheeks had earned him the immediate nickname of Baby Face. Naturally, Eumenes hated it, but could do nothing to prevent the men from using it.

'I know,' said Kimon, grinning. 'So Empedokles blames you – rightly, as it happens – for choking him half to death. And now he'll blame you for this.'

Demetrios shrugged, happy to infuriate Empedokles. 'What can the prick do? I can handle myself. People keep an eye on him.'

Simonides had laid down the law to both Demetrios and Empedokles more than once, warning them to leave each other alone. He'd told his men that he would hold every one of them responsible for any blood that might be shed. 'There are enough fucking Romans to kill without sticking blades in our own,' he'd growled, giving Demetrios and Empedokles the evil eye.

'See? Demetrios is happy enough,' said Antileon. 'Come on.'

'I'm still not sure this is wise,' said Kimon, ever the level head. 'If Simonides or another officer hear of this . . .' Execution for theft wasn't common, but a man could have his hand amputated.

'How could they ever find out?' said Demetrios, growing more confident. 'The phalangist who wants to buy it is one of eight thousand Whites. Soon the kopis will be gone for ever. Even if Empedokles were to accuse one of us, it would be his word against ours.'

'Exactly,' said Antileon.

'Smug bastard,' retorted Demetrios, but he was grinning. 'Show it here.' Checking no one was looking, he unrolled enough cloth to examine the weapon. He let out a low whistle. 'Old it may be, but it's a beauty. Even the scabbard is a work of art.'

'I thought of keeping it for myself,' said Antileon, adding drolly, 'but I decided Empedokles would notice.'

'Who would he hate more then,' said Kimon, 'you or Demetrios?'

They all laughed.

Demetrios relished the idea of angering Empedokles, whom he still held part responsible for Philippos' maiming. He wasn't sure that he could murder his enemy in cold blood, but stealing his kopis was more than acceptable.

Hours had passed before they returned to their speira's tentlines. Impressed by the kopis, Antileon's phalangist had made little attempt to haggle; the coins he'd handed over had convinced even Kimon that the theft had been worthwhile. Making their way to one of the many tavern tents outside the camp, the trio had laughed and joked their way through first one, then several jugs of wine. Demetrios had called it a night in the end, reminding his reluctant friends that they had training in the morning. 'Simonides will have something to say if we can't even hold our pikes up,' he'd warned, shaking a not entirely steady finger.

Encased in a warm glow, they weaved through to the Brazen tentlines, grateful for the protection granted by the blackness. Hundreds of points of light stretched away to either side, the fires outside men's tents. Bursts of song mixed with laughter, and from further off the occasional bray of a mule was answered by a horse's whinny.

'Let's have another drop when we get back,' suggested Antileon. He lifted the skin of wine they'd purchased before leaving the tavern tent.

'Bed,' said Kimon, tutting.

Surprised – Kimon was never the one to hold back – Demetrios said, 'Aye. Bed.'

'Killjoys, the pair of you,' said Antileon, but there was little heart to his protest.

Reaching their tent, they saw that Eumenes – Baby Face – was still up. The instant he saw them, he leaped up, his blanket falling unnoticed from his shoulders. With a wary glance at Simonides' tent, he beckoned.

From nowhere, a sick feeling in Demetrios' stomach. 'What is it?'

'Empedokles,' whispered Eumenes. 'He's searching for you.'

The three friends exchanged a look. 'Why?' asked Demetrios in as casual a tone as he could manage with his now-pounding heart.

'His kopis is missing. He says you took it.' Eumenes' eyes were wide.

'Me?'

'Did you?'

'No,' said Demetrios truthfully.

Beside him, Antileon and Kimon rumbled a protest.

'Is he angry?' asked Demetrios.

Eumenes looked a little afraid. 'I've never seen a man so furious. He'd been drinking all night, which maybe didn't help. After he'd been ranting and raving for a time, he grabbed a dagger and went off with Skopas – who's as pissed as him – swearing that this would end tonight one way or another.'

Demetrios' wine-glow was diminishing by the moment. 'Does Simonides know?'

'He's not here. He went to see an old friend in another speira hours ago.'

Tartaros, thought Demetrios, wishing yet again that Philippos hadn't died. In Simonides' absence, his was one of the few voices that Empedokles might listen to. 'Andriskos and Taurion – what about them?'

'They went with Simonides,' said Eumenes.

This is not good, thought Demetrios, seeing his misgiving mirrored in his friends' faces.

'What should we do?' asked Eumenes.

His heart warmed by the word 'we' – the lad could have said 'you' – Demetrios clasped him by the shoulder. 'We shall have to keep guard all night.'

'Aye,' said Antileon, 'and hope he doesn't do anything stupid when he returns.'

'Simonides will sort it out in the morning,' said Demetrios, hoping that this was true.

'Skopas!' Out of the darkness, Empedokles' voice. 'Where are you?'

'I'll be there in a moment,' came the reply. 'Nature calls. Better out than in before bed, eh?'

Before Demetrios could decide whether ducking into his tent was a good idea, Empedokles emerged into the orange glow cast by the fire. His expression went flat and hard at the sight of the three friends. He ignored Eumenes, and said, 'Here you are, you arse-humping dusty feet.'

'Empedokles,' said Kimon, his normal friendly tone absent. Demetrios and Antileon didn't say a word.

'Where's my kopis?' Empedokles came closer.

'How in Hephaistos' name would I know where your cursed sword is?' asked Kimon.

'I'm not talking to you.' Taking several steps nearer, Empedokles levelled his gaze at Demetrios. 'You took it, didn't you?'

'No,' said Demetrios, again telling the truth.

'He didn't,' added Antileon, his features as innocent as a babe's.

Empedokles' eyes moved from Antileon to Kimon to Demetrios and back over them again. His lip curled. 'You're all lying. I can smell it.'

Eumenes found his voice. 'Perhaps it will turn up in the morning.'

Empedokles blinked, as if seeing him for the first time. 'Shut your mouth, Baby Face.'

'Don't call me that,' said Eumenes, colouring.

'Baby Face. Baby Face. Baby Face,' Empedokles repeated. 'I'll call you what I like, *child*. You shouldn't even be here – the scrapings of the barrel, you are. Ten drachmae says you will shit yourself before the Romans get within a hundred paces of our sarissae.'

Eumenes hung his head.

'Leave the lad alone, "Trembler",' cried Demetrios. He smiled as Empedokles' head whipped around at the insult. 'Aye, you didn't tell Eumenes that that was your nickname, I'd wager?'

'I've had enough of you.' Empedokles' gaze was murderous. Drawing his dagger, he paced around the fire.

'Kimon. Fetch my knife.' Heart hammering, Demetrios dropped into a pankration stance, arms out from his body, hands half clenched, half open. 'Antileon, go behind him.'

'You're not going to run?' Empedokles lunged a little too soon. His blade sliced the air a handspan from Demetrios' belly.

Wishing he hadn't drunk so much, aware that a wrong step could see him stand in the fire or trip over a piece of kit, Demetrios shuffled away.

Empedokles used the opportunity to turn on Antileon; with a series of savage thrusts, he drove him back a dozen steps. When Antileon fell over the guy-rope of a neighbouring tent, a laughing Empedokles spun back to Demetrios. 'It's just you and me again, dusty foot,' he sneered.

'Coming,' shouted Kimon. 'Hang on, Demetrios!'

Empedokles realised time was running out. He darted towards Demetrios faster than a drunk man should have been able. Firelight winked off his blade.

Shit, thought Demetrios. He's going to gut me.

Dust scuffed behind Empedokles. He turned. There was a gasp of pain. 'Try to stab me, would you?' cried Empedokles, grappling with someone behind him.

To Demetrios' astonishment, it was Eumenes. Each man had a hold of the other's right hand, attempting to control their blade. It was an unequal contest; despite his drunkenness, Empedokles was far stronger. With graceful ease, the tip of his dagger moved closer to Eumenes' neck.

'Trembler,' Baby Face said.

Empedokles' lips peeled back with fury; his blade ran in deep.

Eumenes cried out.

Blood sprayed as Empedokles tugged back his arm, and Eumenes fell in a heap at his feet.

'That was self-defence.' Empedokles was glaring at Demetrios. 'The whoreson tried to murder me.'

'You didn't have to kill him,' said Demetrios dully.

Kimon's face was white. 'Why didn't you disarm him?'

'Murdering bastard.' From nowhere, Antileon had a kopis in his fist. 'With me, Demetrios? Kimon?'

Empedokles' eyes flickered like those of a cornered rat. 'Skopas!'

At last Skopas blundered into the light. His head twisted this way and that. 'What's going on?'

'Baby Face attacked me with a knife,' said Empedokles mildly. 'I put him down, and these bastards looked set to jump me. I'm glad you got here.'

Skopas looked unhappy at the prospect of fighting two against three. 'Isn't one death enough?' he asked in a falsely hearty tone. 'Simonides is going to tear us new arseholes for it.'

Mention of their file-leader was enough. With a curse, Empedokles wiped his blade clean on Eumenes' chiton. Spitting a final curse at Demetrios and his friends, he disappeared into his tent.

Demetrios exchanged a sorrowful glance with Kimon and Antileon, and hurried over to the unfortunate Eumenes. Skopas slouched by the fire and pulled at his wineskin.

A dark, throbbing anger took Demetrios as he closed Eumenes' staring eyes. Simonides would punish Empedokles, but it was hard to see that he'd get more than punishment duty for the killing. Men had been watching from other fires, had seen Eumenes attack first, and in the minds of most, playing with fire resulted in burns. That wasn't enough for Demetrios. One way or another, he decided, this will end in blood.

Blood.

CHAPTER XX

Phthiotis, on the Thessalian border

In fine humour, Flamininus was riding to meet the latest of his Greek allies to arrive. Two maniples of principes and a turma of cavalry accompanied him, as did a gaggle of staff officers. An unhappy-faced Potitius trailed behind on a mule. Flamininus had given orders for the Greeks to present themselves just outside the vast camp containing his headquarters. Let the subjects come to their master, he thought. The addition of these Greeks would complete his army's muster, a pleasing prospect.

All in all, spring had started well, Flamininus decided. There had been minor setbacks, it was true: troops promised by the Athenians had yet to materialise, and some supplies had not been sourced before the legions had left their overwintering camps near Elatea. His attempt to take another Thebes, here in Phthiotis, had had to be abandoned because news had reached him of Philip's arrival in Thessaly.

Set against these small matters, his wastrel brother Lucius was doing well in Acarnania. From the apologetic tone of his letters, Flamininus judged he was following orders and not much else, which was also satisfying. The stronghold of Leucas had just fallen to Lucius' attack; it but remained for him to seize control of the rest of Acarnania. Closer to home, the Aetolians had proved true to their word; six thousand infantry and four hundred cavalry had joined Flamininus' legions several days before.

And now, he thought, the latest contingents of Greeks will appear. If his messengers' information had been accurate, five hundred Cretan archers, three hundred Apollonian peltasts and twelve hundred Athamanian infantry under the fat fool Amynander were marching in from the south. The reinforcements were welcome: losses sustained the previous summer and detachments left in garrisons all over Greece had combined to deplete Flamininus' legions. They now totalled a shade under eighteen thousand soldiers, meaning the combined Aetolians, Cretans, Apollonians and Athamanians would form a third of his strength, and increase his army's size to some twenty-six thousand men. It wasn't an enormous force – Alexander's had often been more than twice as numerous, as had Scipio's in the recent Hannibalic war – but it was large, and if Flamininus' scouts were to be relied on, it equalled the Macedonian king's.

Flamininus' gaze moved north, towards Thessaly. Philip had assembled his men at Dium some time since. Now he was on the move. Where was he heading? What were his plans? A smile tickled Flamininus' lips. He was nervous, but his excitement was greater. The day he had so longed for these past years was on him. Since starting to climb the slippery-runged ladder of Roman politics, all he had wanted was to be consul, to be the general in charge of an invasion.

Now, in Greece, his dream had become reality.

Shorn of every ally beyond Macedonia's borders, his influence south of that reduced to the Fetters, Philip was on the defensive. The momentum was with him and his legions, thought Flamininus with delight. Ensure the gods were on his side with the right offerings, unfold the campaign with care, taking no risks, choosing where to fight and where not, and victory would be his. Anticipation thrummed through his every vein; it lifted the tiny hairs on his neck and arms. Defeat Philip, he decided, and I shall go down as one of Rome's greatest military leaders. The man whose legions smashed the all-conquering Macedonian phalanx. The division of Greece, the organisation of its city states, who shall rule and who shall not, will fall to me. This land's vast riches shall lie at my feet, and history will remember me as a general and statesman combined, a visionary the like of whom is rarely seen.

An image of Galba flashed into Flamininus' mind before he could help himself. The price for Galba's silence was eye-watering, and would greatly reduce the wealth he had intended to seize for himself. His good mood soured, Flamininus ran through his mind the latest information from his spies in Rome. He gave up within half a dozen heartbeats. Nothing. They had found out nothing – again.

'You're a secretive one, Sulpicius Galba,' he said.

His mount, the only creature to hear, flicked its ears.

'I'll find out your dirty little secret,' said Flamininus, although inside, he wasn't so sure.

Spying his Greek allies massed on flat ground to one side of the road, Flamininus' good humour returned. Apart from Amynander, who knew that Flamininus could speak Greek, they would be surprised and pleased by his command of their language. He would sweet-talk them, as he always did with new supporters, and after inspecting their troops, invite them to a meeting at his headquarters where they could discuss his plans to defeat Philip. Galba would be there, with Villius and the rest, but Flamininus would keep him on a short leash. Even a man with Galba's vitriol would not dare to question him in front of so many others.

Deciding it would be useful to have his ideas written down to use during the meeting, Flamininus called for Potitius. He was sure his secretary managed a furtive lick of his lips in the time it took his mule to catch up, but decided to say nothing. Oddly, Flamininus had grown used to the shambling, lip-licking Potitius. Efficient, possessed of a sharp memory, he could often be found at his desk deep into the night. Flamininus' mounds of paperwork had rarely been smaller during Pasion's reign.

The instant that Potitius was close enough, Flamininus said, 'Remember these points. You're to write them down when we reach the Greeks.'

'Yes, master,' said Potitius. They had done this before.

Flamininus began to hold forth. Now and again he paused, allowing Potitius to repeat what he'd said. Enjoying the sound of his own voice, he didn't notice Potitius clearing his throat. Flamininus' concentration was only broken when his secretary did it twice in quick succession. He glanced over his shoulder, irritated. 'Stop that!'

Potitius licked his lips, and quickly, before Flamininus could react, said, 'Galba, master.'

Flamininus stared at his secretary, puzzled *and* annoyed. 'I said nothing about Galba.'

'No, master.' Potitius pointed. 'There. He is with the Greeks.'

To Flamininus' astonishment, Potitius was right. There was no mistaking the gaunt figure at this distance, some two hundred and fifty paces. He knew at once what his enemy was up to: glad-handing the Greeks, winning their friendship before *he* put in an appearance. The enraged part of Flamininus wanted to force his horse into a gallop;

arriving, he would announce in no uncertain terms that he was in charge of the army, not Galba.

In that eyeballs-pulsing-with-fury moment, Flamininus was grateful for the cold, calm self-control he was able to exert. React as he wanted to, and he would seem the child, Galba the adult. Maddening though it was, he had been outmanoeuvred and out-thought. His best ploy was to get through the situation as fast as possible, thought Flamininus. He could assert his dominance at the meeting later that day.

He focused again on Potitius, who was watching him nervously. Flamininus gave him a brittle smile. 'Well spotted.'

Potitius was so pleased that he forgot to lick his lips.

Closer to the Greeks, Galba's ruse was revealed further. He had come with only a handful of staff officers. The prick will have slipped out of the camp, Flamininus decided. If his enemy had taken the usual legate's retinue of soldiers and cavalry, *he* would have been told about it, if not at once, then as he left himself.

The noise of their approach dragged men's heads around. Straight-backed, staring into the distance, Flamininus paid the assembled Greek soldiers no heed. He rode along their front until he reached the group of officers around Galba. He noted with annoyance that Amynander, the Athamanian commander, was smiling and laughing. That was, until he spotted Flamininus, when his expression changed to that of a child discovered with a hand in the honey jar. 'Welcome, Flamininus,' he cried, his tone conveying quite a different emotion.

'Amynander,' replied Flamininus. 'Galba.'

Galba half smiled, but his expression held no warmth either.

Flamininus derived some satisfaction from how put out Galba looked. 'Eager, aren't you?' he asked.

'I have spent too long kicking my heels in Rome,' said Galba, as urbane as if Flamininus were a colleague or friend. Switching to ac-cented but understandable Greek, he added, 'It has been a pleasure to meet you, Amynander. Allies work better together if they know and respect one another, eh?'

'True,' said Amynander, beaming. He glanced at Flamininus. 'Galba doesn't have quite your fluency, but for a student of only six months, his command of the language is impressive.'

Flamininus could happily have gouged out Galba's eyes, but he re-plied, 'The legate is a man of ability, it seems.' He laid enough emphasis on the second word to make it clear who was the more senior, and relished how Galba's lips pinched in reaction. 'Have you met with the others yet?'

'No,' said Galba stiffly.

Excellent, Flamininus thought. Much as he wanted to, it would look bad to shun Galba in public. So with a polished politician's smile, he said, 'After you have shown me your troops, Amynander, will you introduce us to your fellow commanders?'

Galba could not help himself. 'I have inspected the Athamanians already.'

'You may have done, legate,' said Flamininus, 'but these are *my* soldiers, not yours.'

'As you say.' Galba stared daggers at Flamininus.

'Lead on, Amynander,' said Flamininus, thinking, you're not the only one who can play games, Galba.

Flamininus' satisfaction lasted all of three heartbeats. Urging his horse after Amynander's, his gaze travelled over Galba's staff officers, who were waiting to follow in their wake. In their midst, his expression as haughty as Flamininus remembered, was Galba's slave-cum-assassin, Benjamin. The Judaean had the audacity to nod at Flamininus, which threatened his self-control more than the sight of Galba had a few moments before. To his horror, Flamininus found himself nodding back. He prayed with all his might that Galba hadn't noticed.

'You saw Benjamin. Good.' If Galba had been a cat, he'd have been purring.

In that moment, Flamininus would have given his entire fortune to have a lightning bolt streak from the heavens and incinerate his enemy.

Despite his best efforts, the first round had gone to Galba.

By the time Flamininus had concluded the meeting with his senior officers and the commanders of his Greek allies, his mood had recovered somewhat. With so many others present, all deferring to Flamininus, Galba had not put a foot out of place. The most recent scouts' news, that Philip appeared to be aiming for the town of Pherae, was enough for Flamininus to decide that his army should also do so. Whether battle would be joined in that farm-rich, heavily populated area was uncertain, but closing with the enemy reduced the chances of Philip trying to spring an ambush. Like as not, there would be a period of marching and countermarching, Flamininus had told his officers and commanders. Philip would try to draw the legions into battle on ground of his choosing – the flat, level type – and they would try to do the same to him, on uneven or hilly terrain.

'Stay calm, and the Macedonians will make the first mistake,' Flamininus had said. Enthused and confident, he had no need of the earlier notes he had dictated to Potitius. 'Discipline is vital,' he went on. 'There must be no rash moves, no charges made in response to insults hurled or the like. You attack when I give the order and not an instant before. I will have anyone who disobeys–' here his gaze had lingered on the Greeks in the room '–severely punished.'

His allies cowed, his officers encouraged, and Galba reduced to temporary silence, Flamininus decided it opportune to seek the gods' favour. He had done so on many occasions since arriving in Macedonia, but this was the first time a battle of this magnitude was in the offing.

A holding pen and beside it, a long, rectangular stone altar, had already been built on the parade ground outside the camp walls. Flamininus ordered the herd of bulls he'd bought driven in, and summoned the priests. Arriving with Potitius when all was ready, he was pleased by the crowds of legionaries who had gathered to watch. A number of his senior officers were there, but to his relief, not Galba. Ten and fifteen deep, the soldiers surrounded the wooden pen and the altar, upon which burned a great fire. They muttered in low voices and eyed the priests with a mixture of reverence and fear.

A space had been left for Flamininus close to where the sacrifices would take place. Adopting a respectful expression, he nodded to the most senior priest of the four present, an ancient with long, flowing white hair and no teeth. Flamininus soon decided that while Potitius' lip-licking was annoying, the priest's habit of sucking his gums was much worse. Doing his best to ignore it, Flamininus focused on the proceedings.

Controlled by a head rope, surrounded by eight burly acolytes, the first bull came out of the pen willingly enough, but nearing the priests, it let out an unhappy snort. Stiff-legged, the bull bucked and jumped as it was hauled to the altar.

This does not bode well, thought Flamininus. Others had noticed too; among the soldiers, men were whispering.

The bull bent its head under the stream of water, as it should, and died quickly enough beneath the blade wielded by the youngest priest, an angular-faced man with jet-black hair. Hands shaking, the gum-smacking priest failed to catch the first gouts of blood from its neck, however. It sheeted to the ground instead – a bad omen that no one could miss.

Flamininus wanted to shout his frustration. He'd paid the priests enough beforehand to ensure the ritual went off smoothly. The dotard should have been watching, while his younger colleagues did the necessary. To interrupt now, however, risked much. Flamininus asked Jupiter for forgiveness, and promised that more beasts would follow the first.

Much gum-smacking and head-nodding went on as the bull's steaming, pink-grey intestines were hauled out for inspection. This continued after a younger priest leaned into the abdomen with a blade and freed the liver. Arms coated in blood to the shoulder, he held it out to the ancient for inspection.

Scarce three heartbeats later, the gum-smacker pronounced the organ to be diseased. 'This is an ill sign,' he quavered, fixing his watery eyes on Flamininus. 'The beast went to its death unwillingly. Its blood spilled. Now this. Battle should not be joined under these auspices.'

Shouts and prayers rose from the watching soldiers. 'Jupiter, Greatest and Best, watch over us!' 'Do not be angry, O Jupiter!'

Flamininus nodded gravely, but inside he remained sceptical. While the beast had fought its way to the altar, the spillage of blood had been down to the dotard's shaking hands; from where he was standing, moreover, the liver looked unblemished. The priest was passing off incompetency as prophecy, Flamininus decided. It was time to exert a little pressure.

'Kill another,' he said.

The gum-smacker put a hand to his ear. 'Eh?'

'Tell him to kill another,' Flamininus muttered in Potitius' ear.

Potitius sloped to the priest's side and quietly repeated Flamininus' words. Startled, the gum-smacker sucked in his lips, making the sound that Flamininus loathed. He glanced at his colleagues; after a brief conferral, he grimaced at Flamininus and said, 'Jupiter may not like it.'

He's a charlatan, Flamininus decided, like so many of his kind.

'Sacrifice another, or I shall find a priest who will.' He gestured at the penned bulls.

Sensing that resistance was futile, the gum-smacker gave the order. A second beast was roped and hauled from the pen. A magnificent creature with long, widely spread horns, it fought every step of the way to the altar. The water poured to force its head down only angered it further; a swing of its neck almost caused one of the acolytes to be gutted. Nervous, the knife-wielding priest missed his first stroke, cutting the jugulars but not the arteries beneath. Bellowing, blood streaming from its neck, the bull broke free. Hauled to a stand-still only when half a dozen legionaries joined the rope-wielding acolytes, it stayed on its feet until the priest had hacked at it three more times.

Soon after, Flamininus ground his teeth as the ancient priest smacked his gums with more satisfaction than was warranted and decreed that the bull's blood was impure, and its innards diseased. 'A second bad omen,' he intoned, his gaze moving to the hushed crowd of legionaries. 'Battle should be avoided for the moment.'

Into the chorus of Ahhhhhs, and cries to Jupiter, Flamininus said, loud and clear, 'Kill a third bull.'

The gum-smacker stared, disbelieving. He wiped his watery eyes, and squinted at Flamininus, asking, 'You're sure?'

'I have never been surer,' grated Flamininus, thinking, you will see sense in the end, dotard.

The contest between consul and priest continued for another seven-teen bulls. Almost two hours had passed, and now twenty carcases lay on the ground before the altar, purple-mottled livers and mounds of intestines beside each. The earth was soaked a deep crimson. Rumour had spread, and the crowd of legionaries was twice its original size. Men had climbed onto friends' shoulders to get a view of the dramatic events unfolding.

With each successive bull's death, the gum-smacker had prophesied ill portents. Growing bolder, he'd even risked saying that Flamininus would be defeated, that his legions would be driven from the field by the Macedonian phalanx.

Nothing would sway Flamininus. 'Kill another,' he repeated again and again. And again.

There were four bulls left in the pen.

Exhausted, standing over the twentieth carcase, the gum-smacker stared at Flamininus.

Who stared back. 'Another,' he said.

The acolytes were moving before the browbeaten gum-smacker had even given the command.

The twenty-first bull was smaller than many of its predecessors, but it could have been sculpted by Myron himself. Narrow, straight horns and intelligent eyes. Broad chest. Lean flanks. Hindquarters muscled just so. Seemingly blind to the slaughterhouse that was the ground outside the pen, it walked out, slow and confident, oblivious to the acolytes around it.

There was no protest as it was led towards the gum-smacker and his knife-wielding colleague. Down went its head beneath the stream of water. It did not flinch as the blade came in either, and the spray of red fell straight into the bowl beneath.

'The blood is pure,' cried the ancient priest to a reverent sigh from the crowd.

Of course it is, thought Flamininus. As was the blood of all the others.

Tension notched the air as the bull's abdomen was opened, and its intestines examined. Cheers broke out as the gum-smacker announced he could find no signs of disease. In the liver, he saw good portents – the chance of victory over Philip, the phalanx defeated and driven from the field. More cheering.

Across the bulls' carcases, the ancient priest and Flamininus locked eyes.

The priest was first to look away.

I *will* defeat you, Philip, thought Flamininus.

Jupiter himself has said so.

CHAPTER XXI

Kynoskephalae, central Thessaly, summer 197 BC

P hilip eyed the clouds, which had lifted a fraction. The peaks were
still obscured, but at least the rain had stopped, and the thunder
and lightning. He was standing in the foothills of the Kynoskephalae
or 'Dogs' Heads' mountains, known this way because of their shape.
The army's camp of the previous night was less than twenty stadia to his
rear. Around the king, as far as the eye could see, soldiers were marking
out avenues, pitching tents and digging rudimentary defences. Equipment and weapons lay stacked in piles according to the unit working
beside them. Men knelt by sputtering fires ordered by officers wise to
the fact that everyone would need a hot meal later.

It was the third day since Philip had marched west from Pherai.
He didn't dwell on the events there. The skirmish between scouting
cavalry from both sides had been won by Flamininus' Aitolian cavalry, but mattered little, for a full-scale confrontation in and around
Pherai itself had not been something Philip wanted; nor, he suspected,
had Flamininus. It was a pity, however, that the Roman general had
seen through Philip's withdrawal to the west. His hope had been that
Flamininus, seeking battle, would march through the gap in the hills
there. He, Philip, would have let the legions emerge onto the Thessalian
plain before sweeping in to trap the Romans on flat ground and cut
Flamininus' supply route in one fell stroke. A battle would have been
inevitable soon after, and thanks to the terrain, his phalanx would have
emerged victorious.

Flamininus, shrewd, had deduced his plan and rather than advance
through the pass at Pherai, the Roman general had led his army in the
same direction as Philip's – westward. With a range of hills between
the two forces, they had marched roughly parallel, but blind to each
other's progress much of the time. It was at this juncture that the king's
peltasts had come into their own. Sending them up to the heights, that

they might keep eyes on the legions, he received reports several times each day on Flamininus' progress.

Philip's wish was to get far enough ahead of his enemy so that his army could move south, crossing the legions' path to reach flat ground at Pharsalos, a suitable place for battle. Things had been going well in that regard until that morning, when Zeus had unleashed a thunderstorm. Philip eyed the lowering clouds again, and tried not to feel angry. The gods did as they pleased, and raging against them was unwise, not least in the midst of a fluid contest with Flamininus. Ordering camp to be broken, Philip and his officers had agreed that the thunder and lightning, the heavy rain, would soon pass. It was summertime after all.

Philip tried and failed not to feel sour. Summer it might be, but the torrents had grown so heavy that streams of water had run down the hillsides. Under his soldiers' heavy tread, the tracks had turned to ankle-deep, sucking mud. Well before midday, Philip had had to call a halt. Camp the night here, he had decided, and they could renew their march the following day. He would not have lost ground to the legions either, because Flamininus would have been equally affected by the bad weather. Not long after the army had halted, Zeus had seen fit to stop the rain. Philip's more reckless side had wanted to order the march continued, but common sense had prevailed. With the thunder god in capricious mood, prudence was wise.

Seeing Menander approaching, Philip raised a hand. With Menander was the king's old friend Athenagoras, Leon, who led the Macedonian cavalry, and Herakleides of Gyrton, commander of his Thessalian cavalry – and no relation to the Tarentine of the same name. Absent were Nikanor, who had led half the phalanx out to seek supplies, and the Illyrian chieftains, who, along with their men and the peltasts, were ranging over the surrounding hilltops to ensure the enemy could not launch a surprise attack.

'Well met,' said Philip, clasping each officer's hand in turn. 'How are your men?'

'Wet, sire,' replied Athenagoras in a droll tone. 'Hungry.'

The two knew each other so well that Philip only rolled his eyes as the others laughed.

'Impatient, sire,' said Leon. 'The Companions want to fight the Romans, as you do. This weather frustrates them.'

'Tell your men I will visit their tentlines later,' said Philip, smiling. The Companions were his favourite troops; fronting a charge with them made a man feel akin to a god. He would get no opportunity to lead the Companions against Flamininus, sadly. So much depended on his phalanx besting the legions that Philip would suffer no one else to lead it. Nikanor helped him to command it only because of its size. Each was in charge of eight thousand phalangists: Philip the Brazens, Nikanor the Whites.

'The king! I seek the king!' The voice carried down the hillside.

'That sounds important,' said Menander, pulling his fingers through his beard.

Philip brushed away the cup of wine offered him by a slave – the cup he had ordered only moments before. His eyes roved to and fro, seeking sight of whoever it was that had shouted. As a trio of mud-spattered figures emerged from the jumble of men and tents nearest the slopes to their right, he tensed. Great Zeus, he prayed. Watch over me now.

'Where is the king?' The three were peltasts, the light infantry beloved of Macedonian kings since Alexander's time. Barefoot, clad in short tunics, and armed with crescent *pelte* shields and throwing spears, they were crack troops, good at scouting, skirmishing and protecting the phalanx's flanks.

Philip stood forth. 'Here!' he called.

The peltasts skidded to a halt. Heads bowed, they each dropped to a knee. 'Sire,' they said.

Philip took in their appearance at a glance. Heaving chests. Mud-coated tunics. Rip marks on their arms and legs from brambles. 'Stand,' he ordered. 'Do you need water? Wine?'

The peltasts exchanged a look. 'Aye, sire,' said the oldest. 'Gratitude. We bring news—'

Philip cut him off. 'It can wait until your thirst has been quenched. I judge you have run all the way from the peaks.'

'We have, sire.' Silence fell as slaves handed the peltasts water skins.

'Speak,' Philip commanded when they were done.

'Conditions on the tops are dreadful, sire, with clouds so low that a man struggles to see his hand in front of his face. When the enemy appeared not long since, they seemed to come out of nowhere.' The peltast made a face.

'Gave you quite a shock, I'd wager,' said Philip.

'Aye, sire. They were as surprised as we were.'

'Infantry only?'

'For the most part, sire, but there was cavalry as well. Scouts, we reckoned.'

'It appears that Flamininus is not to be put off by bad weather,' Philip observed drily. He wasn't that surprised. 'Continue.'

'Our officers had us form up close, sire, and we launched a couple of volleys into the space where we thought the enemy might be.' The peltast leered. 'The screams told us we'd made a good guess of their position. We couldn't keep throwing, however, for fear of using all our spears and not being able to retrieve them. Sending word to the Illyrians and the Thracians, our officers had us advance at the walk. The enemy did the same, and a vicious battle soon broke out. It was hard to know friend from foe, sire, but we held our line. It was still holding when the commander ordered us to bring you the news. We came as fast as we could.'

'You did well,' said Philip, giving him the warm smile that his troops so loved. 'Rest a little, and then return to your comrades. I am to be kept informed as often as it is practical to send men down the slope. Go.'

Muttering their thanks, the peltasts made themselves scarce.

'Well,' said the king, turning to his generals. 'This day grows a little more interesting.'

Philip and his officers were still discussing the dramatic news when a second trio of messengers arrived, bringing fresh word from the fight. Aided by the Illyrians, the peltasts had driven the Romans from the hilltops. Conditions remained poor, but the cloud had thinned, and the improved visibility was aiding their efforts in throwing back the enemy.

Much encouraged, Philip congratulated the messengers and sent them, too, on their way. 'That'll teach Flamininus to tangle with my light infantry,' he declared, calling for the wine he'd refused not long before. His mind set at ease, but aware that other enemy scouts might be abroad, he ordered word sent to Nikanor. 'His eight thousand phalangists would have little trouble dealing with some light infantry and cavalry,' he joked, 'but forewarned is forearmed, as they say.'

An hour went by. Rain showers came and went. A light breeze

sprang up, giving hope that the cloud would lift entirely, but it died before the mist-shrouded peaks – and the battle waging there – were revealed. A third set of messengers arrived then, carrying less welcome news. Reinforcements sent by Flamininus had come to the aid of the beleaguered Romans. A large infantry and cavalry force, it had pushed up the slopes, and in bitter fighting, dislodged Philip's troops from several peaks. The majority of his men were even now withdrawing to the highest summits.

'What are your orders, sire?' asked the peltast – the selfsame who'd brought the initial message.

Deep in thought, Philip didn't answer at once. This is a dangerous situation, he thought. Glancing at his officers, he said, 'In the poor visibility, retreating, the troops might panic and rout. If that happens . . .'

'The Romans could wreak heavy casualties, sire,' said Menander grimly.

Several heads nodded.

Without his peltasts and tribesmen, thought Philip, he lacked protection for the flanks of the phalanx. He could not afford these potential losses, and by his generals' faces, they knew it too. Mind made up, he said, 'Leon, Herakleides – gather your riders. Athenagoras, you are to accompany them with all the mercenaries. Bolster the peltasts' positions, and if you can, retake the peaks lost. No more than that. Keep me informed.'

In the time that followed, Philip found it impossible to concern himself with the mundanities of seeing the camp constructed. Enough cloud had lifted for the struggle on the hilltops to be visible; when the breeze shifted, shouts and the clash of weapons were faintly audible. The king stood with a hand raised to his eyes, watching with grim intent. He wanted to cheer as the figures of horsemen appeared – his Companions and the Thessalians, surely – and drove the enemy from their positions close to the assailed peltasts and tribesmen. Athenagoras and the mercenaries arrived a short time after; regrouping with the troops atop the peaks, they formed a long line and followed the route taken by the cavalry. Dipping down into draws and defiles almost at once, they were lost from sight.

Philip cursed. He'd have given a talent of gold to have had wings in that moment, to soar above his men and spy out the enemy for them.

Instead he was confined to the camp, able only to wait for fresh news. Stay calm, he thought. There is plenty that can be done. Beckoning to his bodyguards, he ordered the phalangists to be ready to march out.

It would not come to a full battle, the king decided – Flamininus wouldn't want to commit his entire army to a fight in such treacherous conditions any more than he did – but if it came to it, his men needed to be prepared.

So did he.

Entering his tent, Philip began dressing himself for war.

He was almost fully armed when, through the clamour that hung over the camp, he heard fresh shouting of his name. Great Zeus, Philip prayed, let Flamininus see the wisdom of breaking off an engagement he cannot win without risking everything. Let that be the news I am about to hear.

Donning his favourite red-crested helmet, the one with ram's horns, he tugged down his scabbard so the baldric slung from his right shoulder went taut, and strode from the tent. Menander was waiting for him; the messengers were in sight, sprinting towards Philip's tent. King and nobleman exchanged a grim smile.

The peltast – again the same man who'd brought the first news – began shouting when he was still some distance off. 'The enemy is in full retreat, sire!'

Philip, pleased, said, 'Flamininus is playing cautious, as we must.'

'Wise counsel, sire,' said Menander.

Philip raised a hand in salute as the peltast approached with his two companions. 'You are a born runner. Who else could go up and down the slopes as you have this morning?'

'Been doing it since I was a lad, sire,' said the peltast with a proud grin. 'Our farm is at the bottom of a valley, and the grazing at the top.'

'You bear good news, I'd wager.'

The peltast's smile grew broader. 'Aye, sire. The mercenaries and your cavalry arrived at just the right moment. Even now, the enemy is in full flight from the hilltops. The pursuit is tough, up and down, through bushes and long grass, but your men are harrying the foe. Their casualties grow heavy.'

Philip eyed Menander, who said, 'Pleasing news, sire, yet it is not what you ordered. They were to regain the peaks and no more.'

'Men are ever the same,' said Philip, thinking the situation had a certain inevitability to it. 'Blood rushes to their heads when the enemy breaks. Like hunting hounds, few soldiers can resist the chase. Yet such a fluid battle can be easily turned on its head.'

Menander looked worried.

'I have no wish to send the phalanx onto such precipitous slopes.' Philip eyed the peltast, and was irritated by his poorly concealed consternation. Perhaps the fool thinks I am scared to fight, Philip thought. Let him think on. 'Return to your officers. Tell them to contain the pursuit of the enemy at all costs. The cavalry must also be told—' Philip stopped. By the time the peltast ascended to the heights again, it would be too late. Summoning the captain of his bodyguards, he ordered several riders to carry his commands to the cavalry on the hills above.

The peltast and his mud-spattered companions were still standing there when he turned back. Philip was about to dismiss them, but was interrupted by a cry from the slopes close to the camp.

'The king! Where is the king?'

Again Philip wished that he had wings, the better to see what was going on. 'Wait,' he ordered the peltasts. 'Fresh news?' he asked Menander.

'I'd reckon so, sire.'

Their guess proved correct. Moments later, a pair of Companions hove into view, urging their horses through the throng with loud cries.

Despite himself, Philip felt a little thrill of fear. Given the uneven terrain and the fractured nature of the fast-moving clash, it was possible that the enemy had turned on his men and reversed the situation. He had been king for long enough, however, to show none of his concern. Calm-faced, he waited for the Companions to approach.

The two riders, one younger, the other a junior officer, were grinning all over their faces. 'Sire,' they cried in unison, giving him parade-quality salutes. Throwing his reins to his subordinate, the officer slipped from his horse's back and dropped to a knee before the king.

'Rise,' said Philip. 'You come from the hills?'

'Aye, sire.' The officer pointed south. 'The fighting draws near to the enemy camp.'

Pricked by concern, Philip asked, 'Is all well?'

A firm nod. 'Yes, sire. Your troops continue to advance. The cursed Aitolian cavalry are giving a good account of themselves, however.

Their efforts have slowed their comrades' retreat a little.'

'What are your commander's thoughts?' Philip pinned the Companion with his gaze. Much hinged on the answer he received.

'Tell the king, he said, that the enemy's formation is shattered. The ground is littered with discarded shields and spears. Riderless horses gallop hither and thither, and the slopes echo with cries of fear and orders to retreat. Press home the attack, sire, and there will scarcely be an enemy scout left alive by the day's end.'

'What of the legions?' demanded Philip.

'At the time I left, sire, our lead riders had seen no sign of their having left the enemy camp.' The officer grinned. 'Aye, sire, we have pressed that far forward.'

It will take a while to deploy the phalanx, thought Philip. By the time it reached the peaks, should he give that order, Flamininus will have had opportunity to field some or all of his army.

Philip chewed the inside of his cheek. He could feel the weight not just of Menander's and the peltasts' stares, but that of every man within earshot. It was a heavy, uncomfortable feeling, one he was well used to – but never had so much depended on his decision. From what he knew of Flamininus, the Roman general was not a man to sit on his hands while significant numbers of his troops were being chased towards his camp. On the other side of the hills, Philip decided, legionaries were already being mobilised. Act now, and he could ensure his troops retained the upper hand – and if things continued to go his way, he could deliver a hammer blow that would drive the legions from the field.

'Flamininus *will* react to this, so let us push what troops he has in the field right back to their camp, before the legions can deploy.'

Menander looked alarmed. 'You only have half your phalanx, sire. Nikanor—'

'The Whites are not far away, and I shall send word to them this instant,' interrupted Philip. He lowered his voice, that the others present might not hear. 'We are caught between a rock and a hard place, old friend. I do not like this place, or the timing, but not to act risks more than to seize this opportunity with both hands. Victory *can* be ours.' Loudly, he said to the Companions, 'Ride to Nikanor with all speed. Tell him that a fine chance to beat the Romans is within our grasp. He is to return in haste, and to follow our trail. Go!'

The men around Philip looked delighted by his words, which had been his intention. Ordering the trumpets sounded, he directed Menander to lead the thousand men who would defend the camp. Taking the reins of his Thessalian stallion from a waiting groom, he mounted.

'Zeus and Ares be with you, sire,' cried Menander.

Philip raised a hand. Zeus was watching, he decided, that was certain. Storm clouds yet hung over the hills, and the air continued to tremble with an occasional rumble of thunder. Thus far, Zeus had favoured him, helping his light troops and cavalry to drive the enemy off the hilltops, towards their camp. To pull back now, thought Philip, would be akin to throwing the gift back in the god's face, whereas to advance showed Zeus his determination. 'Remain steadfast,' the priest at Gonnos had said. He had added, 'Keep your face to the enemy.'

Philip felt the hairs on his neck prickle. Sometimes the priests *did* speak with the voice of the god, and recalling those words, here, now, gave him a new confidence that to attack would see him win. Would see Flamininus defeated.

CHAPTER XXII

Kynoskephalae

The files of trudging phalangists blackened the slopes like so many ants climbing a tree. The tension in the air was so strong Demetrios fancied he could reach out and touch it. The sweat on his brow wasn't just from the exertion of ascending the hills at pace either. His unease was mirrored in the pinched faces, the hunched shoulders to either side. He could hear it echoed in the unnatural silence. Soldiers generally sang, or talked in low voices as they marched. Here they only cursed as they stumbled on the uneven ground, or knocked their disassembled but still cumbersome sarissae off the man in front.

The low mood wasn't surprising, Demetrios decided. After a difficult journey through the rain and mud that morning, they had halted to build a camp. Weary from digging, wet to the bone, the phalangists had paid little heed to the news of the fight on the hilltops. Toil ended, bellies growling with hunger, he and the others in his file had scoured the lower slopes for any fuel not soaked through by the downpour. Succeeding at last in lighting a fire, they had just managed to half-cook their barley porridge by the time of the trumpets' shrill summons.

Hungry and damp, sweaty and irritable, they had slung their aspides over their backs and shouldered their sarissae. Men had muttered to each other, disbelieving, that the king couldn't be about to make them fight on a hillside. Could he? The question continued to roll around Demetrios' skull, and nothing he did would make it go away.

'How much further?' Skopas had become the file's main complainer after Empedokles.

'Can you see the top of the slope?' Empedokles this time. Clang went the two parts of his sarissae off Demetrios' helmet. Taurion could not move position after Philippos' death, being the quarter-file leader, so it had fallen to Demetrios to move forward into fourth place, right behind Empedokles, who had taken the big man's position in the file. Their close proximity meant that an argument was never far away.

'Cut that out!' cried Demetrios. But for the risk of causing Simonides or Andriskos to stumble, he would have tried to trip Empedokles.

'Not my fault if you're too blind to see it,' came the surly answer.

'Shut your mouth, Empedokles,' thundered Andriskos. 'We'll get there when we get there, and not before.'

Unprepared to challenge Andriskos, Empedokles muttered something under his breath.

Up they trudged, leg muscles burning, nailed sandals skidding off rocks or catching on protruding roots. The clouds loomed overhead, obscuring the peaks, but now and again clearing to reveal their destination. Gone were the fast-moving figures that had fought to and fro just a short time before: their own light troops and cavalry, and the enemy's scouts and horsemen. It felt as if they were heading into the unknown, thought Demetrios, yet a furious battle was being waged – if not on the far side of the slope they were climbing, then on the one beyond.

He cast a look behind, to the camp at the foot of the steep slope. 'I can see Nikanor's men,' he cried, relieved. 'They're not that far behind.'

'Mayhap the king will pause at the top to allow them to catch up,' said Andriskos. 'If it comes to a battle, 'twould be better for both halves of the phalanx to be there.'

Demetrios thought of the oft-repeated wisdom that the phalanx was ill-suited to fighting on uneven ground, but it seemed disloyal, even cowardly, to mention it. He concentrated instead on trying not to lose his footing.

'I can see the top!' cried Simonides. 'Not far now, brothers.'

The same realisation was spreading through the ranks, as other fileleaders saw too. A loud sound went up from the phalangists – it wasn't quite a cheer, Demetrios decided, but it wasn't far off – and like that, the gloom of the ascent began to depart.

At last a breeze sprang up, scattering the banked cloud that had hung over the hills like a smothering grey shroud. Areas of sky, startlingly blue, appeared. There was even a hint of sunshine.

Demetrios' mood lifted several degrees.

Zeus' anger – the thunder and heavy rain – had passed. Now the greatest god, beloved of Macedonians, was looking down, willing them to victory over the Romans.

When a Companion cavalryman appeared atop the slope and with hand cupped to his mouth, roared that they should hurry, for the enemy was retreating, the last of Demetrios' worries were replaced by hard certainty.

The day would be theirs.

The top of the slope proved to be the first of two. Cursing, the phalangists had to trudge down into a dip before climbing another small peak. Demetrios would remember the sight that met them there for the rest of his days. The moderate downward incline before him was dotted with sun-browned grass and scrubby bushes. Bodies lay here and there, men and horses, Macedonian, Greek and Roman. There were wounded too, soldiers lying in their own blood, wailing for their mothers, or hauling themselves along in a vain attempt to flee the battlefield. Drawn by some sixth sense, vultures were already floating on the warm, humid air overhead.

About five stadia below, two massive rectangular shapes marked the ditches and defences of Flamininus' twin camps. The bottom part of the slope and the ground before the enemy camp was thronged: this was where most of the fighting was going on. Demetrios strained his eyes, trying to make sense of the confusion.

It was soon clear that the Macedonian light infantry, mercenaries and Companions no longer retained the upper hand. During their headlong charge, any sense of formation had been lost; their 'line' was a mixture of all types of troops, which meant a cohesive attack – or defence – was impossible. Cavalry charged and broke away, wheeled and repeated their attack. Groups of peltasts and mercenaries hurled spears and swarmed forward in quick, vicious assaults, before also withdrawing to regather and return to the fray.

The Roman line on the other hand was solid and well-formed. Legionaries were formidable foes at the best of times – Demetrios knew this from bitter experience – and well capable of holding their own against light infantry and cavalry. A shield wall and ready swords were working against the former, while a shield wall with protruding javelins kept the latter at bay. Positioned high above the struggle, it was

203

easy to see how the Macedonians could prevail – that was, thought Demetrios, unless they were reinforced.

'See there.' Simonides was pointing to their left, a short distance away from the fighting.

Demetrios swore. He had missed the other half of Flamininus' army, as yet not engaged with any Macedonian forces. Upwards of ten thousand men strong, it stood drawn up in neat lines, ready to climb the slopes towards where Nikanor and his Whites phalanx would eventually emerge. 'They've got elephants,' said Demetrios, offering a heartfelt prayer of thanks to Zeus that they would not have to face the terrifying, grey leviathans.

'Aye,' said Simonides grimly. 'Ten, no, twelve of the things. Who's glad not to be in the Whites today, eh?'

Mutters of assent from those who could see.

More and more phalangists had arrived now. Looking over his shoulder, Demetrios reckoned the majority of the Brazens were present. They had marched in the usual open order and double depth. If there was to be a fight, the officers would have the rearmost files break away and move forward to form speira by speira. The phalangists were well trained; the process wouldn't take long.

'You think the king will send us down there?' asked Demetrios.

'He doesn't have much choice, lad,' said Andriskos. 'Here come the mercenaries and the light infantry. They've had enough.'

'The Companions have too,' said Demetrios in dismay, spotting not just the figures of men heading back up the slope, but threes and fours of horsemen.

'Flamininus will send his legions after them,' said Simonides with certainty. 'If the king doesn't react – by ordering us forward – we will soon have to retreat too. No matter how we tried, it would all go to shit when those poor bastards reach us. You were at the Aous, lad. Remember what happens when men panic.'

'Aye.' Demetrios could picture the battle in the Aous valley as if it were yesterday. They had held back the Romans with ease for half the campaigning season, using their artillery to deadly effect, and after that, their well-prepared fortifications. They'd have been there still, thought Demetrios, if Flamininus hadn't found a way around the Macedonian position. Attacked from front and rear, the king's army had broken. Only a desperate defence by part of the phalanx had prevented a complete slaughter. Here the situation would be even worse: with no narrow valley walls to confine the fight, the phalangists risked being flanked. Although he had little chance of seeing past the serried ranks to his left, Demetrios craned his neck. 'Where's Nikanor?'

'Maybe we should wait for him,' said Empedokles, joining the conversation.

It wasn't a bad idea, thought Demetrios. As long as the light infantry and mercenaries formed up on their flanks, sixteen thousand phalangists should be able to hold their position, even if it was at the top of a hill.

Cheering broke out, drawing his attention. The king had arrived – there he was astride his stallion, some hundred paces off to their left. A gaggle of officers and Companions was with him. Philip was already gesticulating towards the fighting below. It was clear he wasn't happy. A finger stabbed at the Roman right wing, with its elephants, and back to the Macedonian left, where Nikanor should have been. The king pointed down the slope again, and shouted something.

Demetrios looked, and didn't like what he saw either. What had been a partial withdrawal by the Macedonian troops had become a full-scale retreat. It wasn't a rout yet, he thought with relief. The likely reason for that was *their* presence atop the peaks. Get to the phalangists, the fleeing men were reasoning, and they would be safe. Simonides and Andriskos were right. To pull back now would allow the hordes of legionaries advancing up the slope to wreak havoc.

Philip barked a series of orders at his officers. One questioned him; he was savagely rebuked. Pairs of the officers began riding along the front of the phalanx, calling orders. Along with everyone else, Demetrios pricked his ears to hear.

'The files are to remain double depth. I repeat, double depth. Assemble your sarissae and form up in battle order. When the light infantry and mercenaries return, they will move to our flanks. The moment they are in place, we shall advance. Wait for the signal.'

Repeating the commands over and again, the officers rode on along the face of the phalanx.

'You heard,' cried Simonides. 'Assemble your sarissae!'

Although Demetrios had practised the move scores of times since joining the speira, it was still a difficult task to complete. Planting the butt spike into the earth, he held the bottom half of the shaft vertically upright with his left hand. Using his right, he fed the top half of the spear upwards, heaving it a little way through his fingers at a time until he could see the brass threads that formed its end. Wrist aching from the effort of holding the lengthy piece of wood and metal aloft, he positioned the threads over the socket at the top of the bottom half. Praying that the meeting was 'true', he lowered one into the other and gently twisted to his right. His luck was in – thread met counterthread, and the two halves screwed together as neatly as if he'd had them laid flat on the ground.

A savage oath. Empedokles was wrestling with his sarissa; from the slight angle at the joint, it was clear he hadn't brought the two parts together straight. 'Need a hand?' asked Demetrios sweetly.

'Piss off,' snarled Empedokles over his shoulder.

'Like a new recruit, you are,' said Demetrios, relishing the chance to insult his venomous comrade. 'Just as well the enemy's nowhere near, eh?'

Empedokles could only mutter curses as he unscrewed the top half from the bottom and started again.

There were more important things at hand, thought Demetrios, returning his gaze to the slopes. His heart thumped. The first of the Companions were less than a spear throw away. Their mounts' flanks were lathered in sweat, and although none of the riders seemed panicked, they were grim-faced to a man. A good number were wounded. Not far behind came the strongest and fittest of the light infantry and mercenaries. Scattered all the way down to the Roman camp were hundreds of their comrades, so many that Demetrios, taking heart, decided that the casualties they'd suffered couldn't have been too heavy.

Philip rose to the occasion, riding to and fro, shouting encouragement to the weary troops who came clambering, red-faced, up the slope. Brave men, he called them. Valiant soldiers who had driven the enemy from the hills and sent them scurrying to the safety of their camp. Heroes, whose efforts would long be remembered. It wasn't the king who started the chant of 'MA-CE-DON!' but he waved his arm in encouragement the moment he heard. 'MA-CE-DON!' roared Demetrios, stamping his foot to the rhythm.

He had never before heard so many thousands of voices singing in unison. The chant soared up to the clouds, and reverberated out and down to the Romans who were ascending. Their advance checked

– only for a few heartbeats, but it was enough to redouble the vocal efforts of every Macedonian soldier. So loud the cheering became that Demetrios judged Nikanor's men would hear it. Heartened, some of the retreating light infantry turned around and launched a brief attack on the enemy. Hurling spears and insults, even baring their arses at the legionaries, they received a cheer of their own from the nearest phalangists.

A hundred heartbeats went by.

'Here they come,' said Simonides, his voice as steady as if he'd been observing a flock of sheep. 'Not be long now.'

Only a small section of the Roman front line had been affected by the light infantry's rally; it lagged a little behind, but the rest of the enemy troops had climbed to within a stadion of the peak. Demetrios' mouth was dry. Philip had been waiting until all his retreating troops reached him; leave it any longer, and the Romans would be upon them. Their current advantage of height would have been lost, for nothing.

'Aspides in position,' ordered Simonides, file-leaders echoing his call through the massed phalangists. 'Front five ranks, prepare to lower pikes on my command. Other ranks, keep your sarissae aimed at the sky. Ready!'

'Zeus Soter, watch over me,' Demetrios prayed. 'Ares, guide my spear.' He could hear similar requests all around. Throats cleared; men spat. Feet shuffled on the short grass. Someone muttered, 'I've got to have a piss,' and a wag replied, 'Aim at the ground, you dog, not my legs.' 'Go on, spray his legs,' cried another, and men laughed.

'It's madness to attack down a slope like this,' said Empedokles.

Simonides twisted, his face furious, but Demetrios had already leaned forward. 'Be quiet, you fool!' he hissed. 'Do you want men to feel afraid? Do you want us to lose?'

Astonished, Empedokles just stared at him.

'We're here, and there's nothing to be done about it. The king is about to order us to advance,' Demetrios continued, his tone hard enough to cut stone. 'Pretend you've got some spine at least, Empedokles. Do your fucking duty. That's all anyone asks.'

Empedokles went to say something, then thought better of it

'Philippos would be proud of you, lad,' said Andriskos over his shoulder.

Demetrios thought his heart would explode with pride and grief. He'd have given a lifetime's pay to have had the big man back with him at that moment. Watch over me, brother, he prayed. Watch over all of us.

'There's the flag,' said Simonides.

Demetrios watched the soldier standing beside the king, a white rectangle of fabric held aloft in his right hand. Trumpeters stood ready, instruments at their lips. Philip looked left, right, assessing his phalanx, and nodded once. The flag dropped earthwards, and the trumpets sounded.

'Forward!' yelled Simonides. 'Nice and steady.'

Down they went, five steps and then ten. Calf-high grass rippled past the first men's legs, and was tramped flat by those following. Uneven, hummocky, the ground made it easy to stumble, but Simonides and the other file-leaders kept their pace slow. Men who tripped – such as Empedokles, inevitably – had time to right themselves.

'Hold the line. Stay together!' came a shout from off to their right. 'Hold the line!'

They had to descend as one unit, thought Demetrios, or the front of the phalanx would not be complete when they reached the enemy. *That* would offer the Romans a chance to break their formation at the outset, and that meant disaster.

'MA-CE-DON,' bellowed Andriskos, lingering over each syllable.

It was as if the entire phalanx had been waiting for his summons. 'MA-CE-DON!' roared thousands of voices.

An answering shout of 'ROMA!' came back at them, but it was reedy and unconvincing.

Twenty-five steps they descended, in good order. Fifty.

'Less than half a stadion,' said Simonides calmly.

Demetrios could make out individual Romans now. Groups of velites, youths as young as Eumenes, capered about in front of the legionaries. Unencumbered by armour, carrying small shields and bundles of spears, they screamed obscenities at the Macedonians and each other to bolster their nerves. One, brawnier than most, heaved a spear into the air. Strong though he was, the slope was against him, and it thumped into the grass fifty paces in front of the phalanx. Demetrios had to smile; the abuse the *veles* received from his own kind was as loud as the phalangists' jeers.

'Front five ranks, lower pikes!' ordered Simonides. 'Next eleven, angle yours downwards.'

Demetrios obeyed. Taurion's sarissa came down past his right shoulder. All Demetrios could see now was Empedokles' and Andriskos' shoulders and beyond him, part of Simonides', and five long cornelwood shafts. If he looked left or right, he could see the same bristling wall of sarissae. Above his head, he knew a forest of pikes – those of the eleven rear-rankers in each file – would protect them from enemy javelins.

There had been a momentary pause as the sarissae were lowered. Orders rang out from file-leaders, including Simonides, and the advance resumed. Unprepared to face the phalangists, the velites threw ragged volleys of spears and took to their heels. The ill-aimed shafts clattered into the upward-pointing mass of sarissae; shorn of any penetrative power, they tumbled down among Demetrios and his comrades. An isolated cry, an even rarer scream, indicated casualties were light.

The hastati were next to the attack. Men of similar age to Demetrios, they came on in a great mass. At twenty-five paces, much closer than normal, they flung their javelins. Again, few phalangists were injured.

Although Demetrios could see little of his enemies' faces – obscured as they were by helmets and high-held shields – the hastati weren't happy. Here and there he could see gaps in the front rank, and when the shouted order to advance was given, they moved forward with real reluctance.

'Pick your targets,' roared Simonides. 'Keep your aspides up.'

Demetrios aimed the tip of his sarissa at a *hastatus* straight in front, a man who'd seen fit to paint a large phallus – for luck, probably – on the top half of his shield. 'The one with the cock is mine,' he said, and Andriskos chuckled.

Incensed by their men's hesitancy, centurions up and down the line roared orders. At last the hastati obeyed, covering the final dozen paces at a shuffling run. Forced to halt again by the dense line of sarissae, they were easy prey.

'Now!' shouted Simonides.

So eager was Demetrios that he missed the wielder of the phallus shield. His sarissa scraped off the side of the hastatus' helmet, knocking him sideways, and slid into the open, horrified mouth of the man in the next rank. Given extra momentum by the slope, the blade lodged in the top of the Roman's spine. Choking on his own blood, he fell away, fortunately dislodging the sarissa tip. Demetrios tugged back a handspan, and aimed his pike at the phallus-shield hastatus. The man ducked down; instead of his life, he lost only one of the three black feathers atop his helmet.

Demetrios cursed, and drew back his sarissa again. He waited. The two remaining feathers on the hastatus' helmet jiggled. He's wondering what to do, thought Demetrios. All I must do is remain patient. Time slowed. Andriskos cursed as his sarissa stuck in a shield. Simonides slew a hastatus with a short, precise thrust to the cheek. Behind Demetrios, Skopas was grumbling, and Taurion was telling him to concentrate on the enemy, not his fucking blisters. The black feathers moved again, and Demetrios cocked his right arm. Up came the helmet a couple of fingers' width, just enough for the hastatus to peep over the rim of his shield. Demetrios' sarissa took him between the eyes, crunching through bone to slice his brain in two.

Grunting with effort, Demetrios freed his blade. The hastatus dropped, and wasn't immediately replaced. There was no one else within reach, which allowed Demetrios, panting, to glance to either side. The impact had brought the phalangists' line to a halt, but the same had happened to the hastati. Here and there, individuals had tried the tactic used at Atrax. Breaking formation, the hastati turned side on and slid their way between the sarissa shafts, each of which, thanks to the five ranks of men holding them, did not protrude the same distance from the phalanx. Succeed in getting past the fifth, and a man could charge the lines of aspides. Reach them, and the deadly gladius could be brought into play.

To Demetrios' relief, he could see only one hastatus who had even come close to the phalangists' shields, and a quick-thinking file-leader soon dispatched him with his kopis.

As ever, Simonides had his finger on the pulse of the situation. A muttered word with the file-leaders to either side, and he shouted, 'Forward, one step!'

Tramp. Down the slope they went, sarissae aimed at the hastati.

Officers further away who hadn't heard gave the same order, and the entire section of the phalanx as far as the eye could see advanced a pace. Despite their centurions' protests, the hastati retreated a little.

'Forward, one step!' repeated Simonides and a host of other file-leaders.

This time, the sarissae found homes in flesh. Screams. Choked cries. The soft thump of bodies hitting the ground. More yelled orders from centurions.

'Stab!' The long cornel-wood shaft in Simonides' right hand shot forward.

Demetrios and every man in the first five ranks thrust their sarissae at the enemy. More hastati died. More hastati suffered life-changing wounds. The rest retreated two steps, and then a couple more.

On it went, a bizarre dance led by the Macedonians and reacted to, poorly, by the Romans. Faster and faster they withdrew down the hill. It was a testament to the discipline of the hastati that they continued to face the phalangists, and human nature that the phalangists' speed picked up.

'SLOWLY,' ordered Simonides, seeing what might happen. 'SLOWLY, curse you!'

Without warning, Andriskos stopped dead. Demetrios, unable to prevent himself, came to rest with his shield in the centre of Empedokles' back. Andriskos was pushed forward, but managed to hold his position. Alive to the potential for a mass collision and with it, dozens of men falling over, Demetrios dug his heels into the earth just as Taurion's aspis hit. Demetrios staggered, and leaned forward again into Empedokles.

Between them, they managed not to fall on their faces. Other phalangists weren't so lucky. A distance to their left, two file-leaders were knocked to their knees by the men behind. Down went the five forward-pointing sarissae, and like that, a quick-witted centurion broke formation, screaming for his men to follow. Four did, and together the little group covered the length of the sarissae – all that separated Roman from Macedonian – in the space of a few heartbeats.

'Pikes ready!' cried Simonides.

Hearts pounding, Demetrios and his fellows brought their spear tips up to face the enemy not a moment too soon. The hastati who had been about to charge them thought better of it. Insults and jeers rained down on them, but every Macedonian's eyes were on the gap in the front rank of the phalanx, and the mad centurion who had attacked it.

A savage fight was in full swing, with more hastati seeing the chance to reverse their retreat.

The half-file leaders behind the gap saved the day by ordering the men behind to lower their sarissae. Presented with a fresh array of spears, the hastati faltered and stopped. It was a fatal error. Forward came the rear-rankers into the 'hole', a step at a time. Two of the five hastati died. A third took a grievous wound to the shoulder trying to help his comrade, whose cheek had been opened by a skidding sarissa tip. The centurion was killed as he turned, shouting at the hangers-back to come to his aid. Two men left alive, one barely able to walk, the other pumping blood from his face, could not prosecute an attack. The pair of surviving hastati shuffled backwards, desperate to avoid the flesh-hungry sarissae, and the phalangists let them go.

It was a credit to the Roman centurions and their junior officers that, in the following mayhem of phalanx pushing downhill, and legionaries dying in droves, they contrived to have the principes move forward to take the place of the hastati. Mail shirts or not, greater experience or no, the principes did no better against the phalangists and their sarissae.

Backwards the Romans went, down the slope at a fast walk, with the phalanx in slow but inexorable pursuit. Morale was rising among the phalangists with every step. The enemy seemed to have no answer to their overwhelming advance. Reach the flat ground, Demetrios decided, and they would smash the legionaries apart.

Victory was at hand.

CHAPTER XXIII

Cynoscephalae

Felix hadn't been happy about Galba being their new legate since the unfortunate episode with the harpastum ball. Months later, at the foot of the Cynoscephalae hills, his back healed but forever scarred, he liked his commander just as little. With the battle opening on the left flank, and Galba's legion deployed on the right, Felix had a chance to think. He suspected there was enmity between Flamininus and Galba.

Felix's interest had been aroused during the meeting between Flamininus and his senior officers – conducted a short time before, close to the principes' position. Galba had clearly been unhappy about having to stand and watch Flamininus' troops face the phalanx. Fists had been punched into palms. A lot of finger pointing had gone on, until Flamininus, incensed, had shouted so loudly that everyone within a hundred paces had heard, 'I am the commander of this army, Galba. You will follow my orders!'

Felix had never seen the like of it. Nor had anyone else. The basis for the quarrel was unclear too, and provided the principes with much to talk about as they watched the legions of the left wing advance up the hillside after the retreating Macedonians. The arrival of the phalanx at the top of the slope a short time before had stilled their conversations, however, and sent a ripple of concern through the ranks. There had been a horrible inevitability to the failure of first the velites' attack on the phalanx and then that of the hastati.

'Rather them than us, eh?' Felix muttered to Antonius.

'We'll have to clear up the situation soon enough if they don't break and run,' replied his brother in a resigned tone. 'That, or the second half of Philip's army will finish scratching its collective arse and appear at the top of the hill in front of us.'

'It'th alwayth uth,' said Sparax, as if it were they and not the left flank who were fighting. 'Elatea. Corinth. Now thith shithole.'

'We can't complain too much,' said Felix. 'Nicaea was an easy number. And we got sent to Rome. Not many here can say that.'

Sparax, who liked always to have something to grumble about, muttered under his breath.

'Complaining again, Thparaxth?' Bulbus had stolen up unseen.

'No, thir,' said Sparax tonelessly.

'Thir?' Bulbus let out a loud sigh. 'How many times have I told you, Thparaxth, it's "sir". Try it.'

'Thir.'

Bulbus' chuckle held a combination of amusement, condescension and downright cruelty. 'No, no, no. "Sir." Say it!'

The muscles of Sparax's jaw twitched. 'Thir.'

Bulbus' vitis swung sideways. Sparax's helmet cheekpiece took the brunt of the blow, so an infuriated Bulbus hammered the stick down from above. Once, twice, thrice, he struck, so hard that Sparax's head must have been ringing. The black feathers had been torn away; it surprised Felix not at all that Bulbus next accused Sparax of presenting himself for battle in an improper fashion. 'What kind of soldier are you?' the centurion screamed.

'A bad one, thir.' Sparax's eyes burned with humiliation and impotent fury as Bulbus mocked his lisp again, standing back a few paces so that more men could hear.

'How the gods must laugh, sending a fool such as this to trouble me!' Bulbus waxed lyrical about Sparax's faults – none of which were true. A few principes in other centuries laughed, but none in Bulbus' own. This seemed to anger him further, and from his new position, he launched into another attempt to make Sparax say 'sir'.

Sparax's fist clenched on his sword hilt. 'I'll fucking kill him,' he hissed.

'Stay where you are,' warned Felix from the side of his mouth. 'You'll end up dead.'

'I'll kill him,' said Sparax again.

Aware that Bulbus would see, but unprepared to let his comrade die for no reason, Felix seized Sparax's meaty bicep and muttered, 'Lay a hand on an officer, worse still murder him, and you *will* die in the most painful way possible. Is that what you want?'

Sparax's maddened gaze swivelled to Felix. A heartbeat passed. Reason returned, and Sparax shook his head, no.

'Eyes front!' Bulbus' voice was very close.

As Felix and Sparax obeyed, their centurion stalked to stand before them. 'Finished gossiping?'

Answer or no answer, thought Felix, it didn't matter. Bulbus would punish them regardless. He fixed his gaze on the hillside before them and said, 'Yes, sir.'

'Yeth, thir,' echoed Sparax.

'Good.' Bulbus' tone was light, almost friendly. 'Step forward, both of you. Three paces.'

As they obeyed, Bulbus launched an attack with his vitis. He aimed for exposed flesh: their arms, legs and necks, wielding his stick with a vicious intensity that soon had Felix struggling not to fall down. To do that risked further punishment; by locking his knees he managed to stay upright. Sparax was bigger and stronger than he, but caught by a stinging blow to the side of one knee, he staggered and almost fell. A crowing Bulbus beat him back into a vertical position with a flurry of blows to his right arm and shoulder.

'What *are* you doing, centurion?' demanded a voice.

Bulbus' vitis froze in mid-swing. He turned, looked, came to attention. 'Punishing two of my men, sir.'

'I can see that.' The voice was dry and unamused. 'Why?'

Felix's eyes moved; Galba, the prick, was there on his horse, and Flamininus was with him, along with the usual retinue of staff officers. Galba it was that had spoken. Flamininus looked on, disapproval writ large on his face.

Wrong-footed, Bulbus floundered. 'They . . . They had dirty kit, sir.'

You lying, onion-headed cunt, thought Felix, burning to scream out the real reason.

Before Galba could reply, Flamininus said, 'Is that really important, centurion, with a battle going on?'

A light flush marked Bulbus' cheeks. 'Err, perhaps not, sir.'

'We've met before. What do they call you again? Bulb-Bulb . . . I can't remember.' Flamininus' voice was deadpan.

Felix could have cheered. Flamininus' comment had to have been deliberate. Stifled snorts and chuckles rose from all around, which added to Felix's mirth. All their centurion could do was splutter, 'Bulbus, sir. It's Bulbus.'

Flamininus rode on without another word.

'Prepare your men,' said Galba to Bulbus. 'The general is here to take command of this flank. Scouts report that the second half of Philip's army – a force similar in size to the phalanx already on the field – is about to arrive.'

'Above us, sir?' asked Bulbus.

'Even so.' Galba's eyes raked the principes. 'Do your duty for Rome, all of you.' He rode away, following Flamininus towards the elephants.

Urging Felix and Sparax back into line, Bulbus launched into a monologue about the crushing defeat he expected them to inflict on the enemy. He wandered off along the front of the century, and Felix risked saying something.

'How in Hades are we supposed to do what the legions on the left flank can't?' he whispered to Antonius.

'Maybe the elephants will help.'

'Philip sent men to Zama,' countered Felix grimly. 'He'll know about the "corridors" we used there. Who's to say the bastards won't try the same tactic?'

'If they succeed, that'll leave us against the phalangists,' said Antonius.

'That's my point.' Felix couldn't take his eyes off the phalanx to their left, which had now pushed the legionaries all the way down the slope. It showed no sign of slowing. Sooner or later, the Roman left would break.

When Galba ordered the advance, thought Felix with a sinking feeling, the same would surely happen to them.

Time dragged by. Flamininus had the dozen elephants move up the slope a little in readiness. The velites gathered a short distance behind. In acknowledgement of the difficulty of the fight that would face them, he ordered the hastati and principes to intersperse themselves equally along the front line. Expressionless, he rode up and down in front of his troops, his gaze never moving from the hills above.

'He's making me nervous,' whispered Antonius to Felix.

'He wants it to be over, just like us,' said Felix. 'Lucky for him, though, he won't have to risk his life. The same applies to Galba, the bastard.'

'Forget about Galba.' Antonius' opinion never varied. 'It'd be easier to hit the sun with a javelin than hurt him.'

'I know, I know.' Try as he might, Felix could not forgive or forget the whipping he'd suffered. And all because Galba was hit in the face with a harpastum ball, thought Felix, the familiar bitterness thrumming through him. I'd like to see *him* in an actual match, even when he was fit for it.

Further fantasies about what he would like to do to Galba were put from Felix's mind by a shout from Flamininus. 'There they are,' the general waved an impatient hand at the nearest staff officer. 'The elephants are to advance. Quickly!'

Felix stared up the slope. His guts twisted. Although a full line hadn't yet formed, hundreds of figures were already visible. More appeared with every thumping beat of his heart. The sun, escaping from behind a cloud, lit up the hilltop, its rays bouncing off myriad spear tips.

Trumpets signalled, and Bulbus shouted that the legions were to follow the elephants and velites. Assuming his place at the very right of the front rank, close to the next unit, formed of hastati, he continued to relay the orders that came down the line.

'Shields up. Shoulder javelins. Forward, at the walk.'

Fortunately, Bulbus' position was far enough away from Felix and his comrades that they were able to talk between themselves as they marched.

'Never thought I'd find mythelf walking *up* a fucking mountain to a battle,' said Sparax to a general rumble of amusement.

'Nor me,' said Felix. 'Never thought I'd have an onion head for a centurion either.'

This caused so much hilarity that Bulbus, unsuspecting, barked out, 'Silence in the ranks!'

Before long, everyone's attention was on the enemy, which had now reached the hilltop in great numbers. Oddly, the phalanx didn't seem to be forming. Instead a column of phalangists perhaps fifty wide was tramping down the slope towards the elephants and the massed legions.

'What are they playing at?' said Felix, perplexed.

'Maybe it's a tactic to defeat the elephants,' suggested Antonius.

Unease gnawed at Felix. Philip was no Scipio, but that wasn't to say he couldn't pull off a devious trick of some kind. Sudden understanding dawned then, and he laughed. 'I know,' he cried. 'They think the battle is won. The fools can't be bothered to form up until they're closer.'

'Are they still in marching formation?' Antonius' tone was incredulous.

'I think so, aye,' replied Felix.

It seemed Flamininus also considered the time ripe for an attack. Not twenty heartbeats later, the trumpets sounded the charge. Then a rider came cantering along the front of the line, urging them all to hurry. 'The general says if we hit them now, they'll break like a falling dish. Up! Up!'

'You heard him,' roared Bulbus. 'Get *up* there!'

They charged. The steep incline soon made Felix's leg muscles scream. His shield felt as heavy as the wicker one used by new recruits, and his javelin bounced about on his right shoulder, every so often clanging off his helmet. Sweat poured down his face. Stabs of pain from the inside of his upper right arm were a vicious reminder of how his sword hilt pinched the skin. There was no possibility of rest. To left and right, hundreds of his comrades were pushing themselves as hard as he was. They were in this together, for better or worse, and a tiny, mad part of Felix was exhilarated by that. If he died, it would be in the midst of his brothers.

Messengers had also been sent to the elephant handlers. With flapping ears, the great beasts lumbered up the slope ahead of the velites and legionaries. Perhaps twenty paces separated each elephant from the next – plenty of room, Felix thought nervously, for determined men to advance through and attack the legionaries. If the phalangists stayed in a narrow formation, there was every chance too that the elephants would charge past most of them. No match for heavy infantry, the velites would break away and retreat, leaving the legionaries to a fight every bit as brutal as that being waged on the left flank.

Felix prayed that he would live through the carnage. That Antonius and his other comrades also would. Over the years, he'd lost too many friends to Hades. These dark memories brought back creeping, superstitious images of the twenty bulls that had died before the soothsayer had professed the omens to be good. Plenty of men had opined since that Flamininus had been foolish to tempt the gods so. That he had been arrogant to insist the sacrifices continue until he heard what he wanted. Felix's guts churned. If the rumour-mongers were right, Jupiter was angry, and they were about to be slaughtered.

Head down, concentrating on pumping his legs up the slope rather than his fear, Felix didn't take notice of the cries from above.

'Look!' panted Antonius.

Felix obeyed. The elephants had come to within two hundred paces of the still-unformed phalangists. Rather than halt and present their sarissae, or move into a special formation, the Macedonians stopped in their tracks. Felix noticed with a thrill of excitement that not a man among them had even assembled his sarissa, that the shouts he could hear were those of alarm.

'The fools,' Felix said, not quite believing what his eyes were telling him.

Screaming insults, as was their wont, the velites swarmed forward in a great, disorganised mass. No one reacted in the Macedonian ranks. Emboldened, the velites closed to within fifty paces and hurled their spears. They didn't cause many casualties – throwing uphill was too difficult – but here and there, a phalangist screamed.

Bulbus had seen the Macedonians' disorganisation by now. So had every centurion worth his salt. With loud shouts of encouragement, they urged their men to new efforts.

At last the enemy officers sprang into action. Commands rang out, and the front-ranking phalangists began assembling their sarissae.

New fear coursed through Felix. A single line of pikes held by brave men would stop the elephants' charge. This success would stiffen the phalangists' resolve, and a bitter fight would follow. It was still within the realm of possibility that the phalanx here could drive him and his comrades back down the slope.

At that moment, a lone phalangist took matters into his own hands. Holding his sarissa at the right angle to threaten an elephant's face and eyes, he marched away from his fellows, towards the lead elephant, a curve-tusked cow. She bugled a challenge, a terrifying sound that made Felix think of Zama.

Rather than stay where he was and plant the butt of his sarissa in the ground, the phalangist kept approaching the elephant. It was his undoing. Unbalancing on a loose stone, he tripped forward, dropping his pike. The elephant's reaction was frighteningly quick. Even as he clambered to his knees, scrabbling for his sarissa, she came thundering in, a grey wall of muscle, bone and tusk. The phalangist was still trying to bring up his pike when the elephant's trunk wrapped around his middle and swept him into the air. His despairing wail made every man within earshot, Macedonian and Roman, wince.

Thousands of mesmerised eyes watched in horror as the elephant delicately laid the phalangist on the ground, placed a trapping foot on his chest and then, with a flick of her trunk, plucked off his head. A spurt of crimson issued from the remnants of his neck. With what almost seemed to be distaste, the elephant dropped his head in the grass. It rolled and bounced a dozen paces downhill, before coming to rest against a grassy hummock.

After a stunned silence perhaps two heartbeats long, panicked shouts broke out among the phalangists. The assembly of sarissae was forgotten, the desire to fight vanished. Like a flock of birds that changes its direction of flight without communication, the entire body of Macedonian troops wheeled and fled for their lives. A few brave men tried to stand their ground, and were knocked down and trampled for their troubles.

An inanimate roar went up from the hastati and principes both.

Felix could *smell* victory; he could see it in his comrades' sweating faces. The battle was already won, on this flank at least.

What would happen on the other was in the hands of the gods.

Terrified first by the elephants, and unable to form up, the fleeing phalangists were easy prey for Flamininus' legionaries. Slaughter followed. Even the velites, never ones to involve themselves in face-to-face fighting, joined in the fray. Felix and his comrades, their energy renewed by the ease with which the enemy had broken, were in the thick of it too. Up the slope they drove the Macedonians, hacking and killing. Chaos reigned; all sense of the Roman front line dissolved. It became a case of sticking with your century, your comrades. Side by side, swords at the ready, the principes hunted the enemy with grim purpose. In places, the phalangists rallied and formed little squares, but, outnumbered and demoralised, they were soon overwhelmed.

No man could keep charging uphill and fighting, though, especially on a day muggy with summer heat. Here and there, centurions began ordering their soldiers to halt. Even Bulbus could see the sense in it, and in the end, he did the same. 'Catch your breath,' he ordered, his usually ruddy face a deeper flush of red. 'Have a drink.'

Felix was glad he'd been abstemious earlier; his water bag was more than two-thirds full. Limiting himself to a few mouthfuls – a man didn't want a full belly during a battle – he risked taking off his helmet to wring out his arming cap. It was a delight to feel the breeze on his sweat-soaked hair, but he donned his helmet again. Twenty paces away, Bulbus was lambasting an unfortunate who'd been foolish enough to sheathe his sword instead of stabbing it into the ground.

'Pick up your shields,' shouted Bulbus. 'Other units are moving. We can't be left behind.'

Felix rolled his eyes at Antonius, but Bulbus was right. No one wanted to be stuck at the back. If the enemy camp was overrun – a distinct possibility – they would miss out on whatever booty was to be found. Hefting his shield, Felix threw an idle glance to the left, where the Macedonian phalanx had shoved the Roman left flank down the hill. The battle was still going badly for his side; the legionaries continued to hold their line, but their position was much lower down the slope than it had been when Felix and his comrades had been ordered to charge. Felix's field of vision was filled by the phalanx. He stared. Pulled his gaze up and down the slope. Could see no sign of the light infantry or cavalry that usually guarded the phalangists' vulnerable left side. The rear of the phalanx was also unprotected. A third of a mile lay between his position and the Macedonians, he thought, or perhaps half. It wasn't that far.

'Brother!' Antonius' voice, low and urgent.

Felix was still turning, a broad grin smeared all over his face, when Bulbus' sword tip shot in to touch his throat. He froze. There was blood all down the blade, and beyond it, Bulbus' eyes were full of malice.

'Deaf, are you?' asked Bulbus. 'That why you're not ready?'

'No, sir.'

Bulbus pushed a little, so the sword point pressed into Felix's flesh. 'I don't like you. Never have.'

The feeling's mutual, thought Felix.

'I knew you'd be no good as a tesserarius from the moment I set eyes on you. The incident with the harpastum ball proved it. This is further evidence, as if I needed it.' Bulbus leered. 'There's no Flamininus here. No Galba. No one to stop me sliding this in all the way.'

Behind Bulbus, Sparax loomed, sword at the ready.

Don't do it, Felix pleaded with his eyes. Bulbus is only bluffing – even a prick like him wouldn't murder me for no reason. 'I wouldn't, sir,' he said loudly.

221

Bulbus' lip curled. 'Why not?'

'The battle on our left flank is there to be won, sir.'

'Eh?' Bulbus' eyes were slits. 'Explain. Fast.'

Felix jerked a thumb behind him. 'The entire flank of the phalanx over there is exposed, sir. So is the rear.'

Bulbus looked. Whistled in disbelief.

'Hit them with a couple of thousand men, sir—'

Bulbus pushed his sword in a little more, drawing blood. 'Trying to tell me my job?'

'No, sir,' said Felix, thinking, if I hadn't said anything, you onion-headed cunt, you'd never have seen it.

Sparax padded back to his position, unseen.

At last, Bulbus lowered his arm. Calling Callistus to him, he ordered the optio to remain where he was with the century. 'I'm going to find the nearest tribune,' he said. His eyes flickered over Felix, but there was no recognition, no gratitude. Just contempt.

'You should have let me kill the bathtard,' said Sparax when it was safe.

It was hard to argue, thought Felix, yet if Bulbus managed to bend the ear of a senior enough officer, the result would have been worth letting their malevolent centurion live.

News of Felix's revelation spread fast. An air of excitement and anticipation fell as they waited. Even if nothing came of it, the principes were happy to prolong their rest. Above them the Macedonians were still running and dying, and the vast majority of the Roman right flank continued in vengeful pursuit. After a time – Felix couldn't be sure how long – trumpets brought sections of the principes and hastati to a halt. Messengers galloped to and fro along the ragged line, issuing orders. Slowly, under the direction of shouting centurions, the maniples re-formed. Then they turned and began marching downhill, towards Felix and his comrades.

'Bulbus found that tribune,' declared Antonius.

'He must have,' said Felix, proud to have been the one to notice the opportunity, and already resentful that Bulbus would give him no acknowledgement whatsoever.

A young, determined-looking tribune came riding back with a wheezing Bulbus trailing in his wake. 'I hope twenty maniples is enough,' the tribune said, staring at the phalanx.

Felix couldn't help himself. 'Course it is, sir!' His comrades cheered.

Bulbus stared daggers at him, but the tribune smiled. 'That's the spirit. Well, there's no point hanging about.' Quickly, efficiently, he had the maniples split into two groups of ten. He would command the group that swung around to take the Macedonians in the rear, and a smug-faced Bulbus would lead the rest to hit the side of the phalanx. 'We'll meet somewhere in the middle,' he said.

'Yes, sir!' Bulbus was beaming.

Felix had never hated his centurion more than he had in that moment, but he had no time to brood. There was no trumpet fanfare, but they were off a dozen heartbeats later, traversing the slope at a fast walk. To run, the tribune had declared, would make little difference in the time of their arrival, and would result in men breaking their ankles.

A swelling sense of excitement filled Felix, who was in the front rank with Antonius and his comrades. Fifty paces they went, and he hadn't seen a single head in the Macedonian ranks notice them. Wrapped up in their struggle with the legionaries on the left flank, ears filled with the screams and cries of the dead and dying, the phalangists had eyes only for what was in front. A hundred paces, and still Felix and his comrades were invisible. He glanced to either side. Thanks to the different pace of the maniples, and the slope, their line had grown ragged. Bulbus' century was out in front, leading the way. Their centurion made no attempt to slow them down, and, eager not to be left behind, the maniples to either side increased their pace.

Two hundred paces, Felix counted. Perhaps twice that distance still separated them from the Macedonians. Not a man in the phalanx had noticed their approach. Even if they did, Felix decided, they wouldn't be able to rip themselves free of their formation in enough numbers to form a decent line before the principes struck.

Incredibly, they had closed to within three hundred paces before any Macedonians saw them. Shouts of dismay rose, but nothing immediately happened to the enemy formation.

Ha, thought Felix. The ordinary rankers in the phalanx who have seen are in the same situation as me. Their officers think they're worthless, and won't listen. Gods willing, they won't until it's too late.

More heads turned among the phalangists now, and something like a shudder passed through the ranks.

'CHARGE!' screamed Bulbus. 'Fast as you can!'

Felix and his comrades ran. Two hundred and fifty paces remained between them and the Macedonians, who were still shouting and roaring at one another in confusion. Three, maybe four men that he could see had stepped out of rank and aimed their sarissae at the principes. Plenty of astonished and frightened faces were looking in their direction, but as is so often the case when things happen at great speed, their reaction time was slow. Two hundred paces. Now a dozen men had formed a rough line against the incoming principes, but there were huge gaps between them. Several phalangists were already skulking back up the hill – retreating.

'ROMA!' shouted Felix. 'ROMA!'

At a hundred and fifty paces, the front of the phalanx must have suddenly shoved the legionaries facing them backwards, for the frontmost ranks gave a great heave, and walked forward ten steps. The phalangists who were trying to react to the principes' attack didn't see it coming. Some managed to tramp forward; others resisted, and were knocked off balance by the men behind who were following the leaders. Down went several, their sarissae knocking into the ones around them, or hitting other phalangists on the head. Curses rose. Officers shouted contradictory orders – to break formation, to march forward. Few men were joining the phalangists facing the principes, and they wavered.

Felix had never run for so long in kit. His lungs were on fire, his legs were screaming for a rest. Sweat stung his eyes, almost blinded him. Only the death-grip he had on his lead-heavy shield prevented it from falling to the ground. His drawn sword was like an extension of his arm. Reaching the enemy was all that mattered. Fourscore paces, Felix told himself. Seventy. Sixty. He had no breath left to shout a war cry.

By fifty paces, the phalangists who had broken away to face the Romans were looking terrified. In the section nearest Felix, they now numbered perhaps two dozen, but they were mostly one deep. Men were manoeuvring out of line behind them, but the unwieldy sarissae were tricky to bring around and down into place.

'Slow down!' Bulbus' voice. 'Halt!'

Felix obeyed gladly. Chest heaving, in, out, in, out, he looked at the Macedonians thirty paces away.

'Catch your breath,' ordered Bulbus. 'Who's got a javelin?'

Ten or more voices answered, 'Aye.'

'Throw them,' said Bulbus. 'Now!'

The men with javelins stepped forward. Glancing at each other, they hurled a decent volley. At such close range, with so many Macedonians grouped together, they couldn't miss, and thanks to the disorganisation of the phalanx nearest them, the usual protection offered by the sarissae wasn't there. Judging by the cries of pain and gaps that appeared in the ranks, most javelins had found a target.

'Ready?' asked Bulbus.

The principes forgot what a hateful bastard he was, and shouted, 'Yes, sir!'

'Form a line, six deep. Shields together. Swords ready.' Bulbus loped around the side of the century.

'Where's he going?' hissed Antonius. At times like this, a centurion needed to lead from the front.

Felix shot a look. 'He's in the rear rank, at the opposite end to the cocksucker.'

'You wouldn't have caught Pullo doing that,' said Antonius sourly. 'Nor Matho, the bastard.'

'Onion Head ith a fucking coward,' growled Sparax.

'Aye,' said Felix, who had wondered the very same thing since the assault on the Acrocorinth, when Bulbus had stayed at the bottom of the breach.

Seeing Felix and the rest slow down and halt, other units had done the same, and formed up on either side. Bulbus exchanged a few words with the optio of the century next to him; Callistus did the same with a man in the unit to his left. The instant that was done, Bulbus ordered the charge.

They had been halted less than fifty heartbeats.

Felix trotted forward, shield and blade at the ready. He remembered Atrax, where the phalanx had proved victorious. Where Pullo and many of his comrades had died. He shoved the dark memories away, and focused on the phalangists, who were only a little better organised than before. A golden opportunity still awaited, thought Felix. 'We're coming for you,' he shouted in his bad Greek. 'WE'RE COMING!'

It might have been his imagination, but a man in a green-with-age Phrygian helmet visibly quailed. Felix's heart leaped.

Reaching the ends of the sarissae – which were still few in number – the principes split up and darted into the gaps between the shafts. Felix led the way into one such 'corridor', Antonius and Dordalus on his heels. Sparax, Clavus and a princeps from another tent group came barrelling into one on his right.

Felix could see the terror in the faces of the closest phalangists long before he was within blade reach. Left arms fitted snugly into shield grips, left and right hands both gripping their sarissae, they were defenceless at close range. Each man was armed with a curved kopis sword, but needed a free hand to be able to draw it. Speed was vital, thought Felix. Using his large shield as a battering ram, he slammed into two aspides at once. Lacking the support of comrades behind, the phalangists both staggered back. Felix's blade licked between them, once. Moved a fraction to the side. Twice. Both men were dead before they'd even realised.

Felix stepped over their bodies and found no one facing him. Sparax was through as well, with Clavus and the other princeps. Ten paces to their front was the undefended side of the phalanx. Gods, Felix thought exultantly. We're going to slaughter them.

A disbelieving laugh came from behind. 'Is that it?' asked Antonius. 'We've broken through?'

'Aye,' said Felix. 'We have. Ready?'

Too late, he saw the phalangist, a man several ranks into the phalanx who'd somehow managed to turn around. The sarissa came down the last few degrees, and thrust. Felix had time only to move his head a fraction. The blade shot past his ear.

Antonius made an odd, coughing sound. Thump went his shield on the ground.

Horror swamped Felix. He twisted.

Antonius hung like a rag doll from the sarissa, which had skewered him through the throat. There was bloody froth on his lips. He stared at Felix, unable to speak, his gaze pleading. Then the light in his eyes flickered and died; he slumped, dragging the sarissa earthwards.

A madness took Felix, a desire to kill like he'd never felt. He turned to face the phalangists, the nearest of whom were regarding him with naked terror. In an oddly calm voice, he said, 'Clavus, Sparax. You there? Dordalus?'

'Aye,' came the grim replies.

They charged, Felix in the lead.

Uncaring if he lived or died.

CHAPTER XXIV

Cynoscephalae

Flamininus reined in his horse at the top of the slope. He was tired from the effort of the climb, but *its* neck was lathered in sweat; below the bottom of the saddle blanket, he could feel the same moisture against his legs. He gave it an affectionate pat. 'Good boy. Well done.'

'Quite a sight, sir, eh?' The voice belonged to one of his staff officers, an overkeen, boyish-faced type who was always there when Flamininus wanted him, and also when he didn't.

Flamininus looked. As far as the eye could see, thousands of Macedonian soldiers were retreating. Not long after the enemy left flank had broken, the right had done the same, thanks, he'd been told, to a keen-eyed tribune. Flamininus was intrigued, and decided he would get to the bottom of that later. Now though, he enjoyed watching the phalangists run. Shields discarded, weapons flung away, in many cases even helmets taken off the better to flee, they had entirely given up the fight. Howling like hungry wolves, his legionaries chased after. 'We've done well,' said Flamininus, permitting himself a little smile. Galba, he thought, you couldn't manage this. I am the better general. Even though my success will make you wealthy, you must hate it.

'It's rather uncontrolled, sir. Have you any orders, sir?' asked the staff officer.

The thought of Galba's anger gave Flamininus such pleasure that he didn't bother biting the eager fool's head off. 'What's your name?'

'Longinus, sir. Cassius Longinus.'

'Do you think, Longinus, that sending orders after that mob—' Flamininus gestured at the chaos that was the top of the Cynoscephalae hills '—will be of any use whatsoever?'

Longinus stared; he coloured. 'No, sir.'

'Quite. I can't even *see* the elephants. They are miles away, like as not. Their job is done, so it doesn't matter – they will stop when tired. As for the men, well, the centurions are in control after a fashion, but there will be no commanding the legionaries until the bloodlust has been sated. Do you remember a little while ago when one of our allies – Amynander, I think it was – sent word that the phalangists holding their pikes up in the air were trying to surrender?' Flamininus had been intrigued by the ranks of Macedonians standing with their lethal sarissae pointing at the blue sky.

'Yes, sir,' said Longinus, looking a little distasteful. 'The men didn't realise what the phalangists were trying to do. They killed them.'

'Exactly so. Know, Longinus, that men turn into wild beasts when the scent of blood fills their nostrils. Roman legionaries resist the urge for longer than most in battle – you can thank our discipline for that – but in the end, they too succumb.' Flamininus waved a hand at the hilltops again. 'Like the elephants, they will stop when fatigue overtakes the desire to kill.'

'Yes, sir.' Longinus' face was crestfallen.

Flamininus didn't care; his goodwill was shrinking. 'War is not all triumphs and parades, glory and honour. It's about death and dying, plain and simple.'

'Yes, sir.' Longinus looked grateful when Flamininus waved a hand in dismissal.

'Potitius!' Flamininus had insisted his secretary accompany him on the field. On the few occasions during the advance up the hill that Flamininus had paused for a drink, it had amused him how scared Potitius had seemed. 'Where are you? I want you to write something down.' His advice to Longinus, he decided, had been excellent. It needed to be recorded, so his wisdom wasn't forgotten.

By the time the sun was setting, it was clear that Flamininus' victory had been total. Many thousands of Philip's soldiers lay dead in the hills; several thousand more had been taken prisoner. The king's camp had been overrun, annoyingly by the Aetolians, while Philip fled with what men he could gather towards the town of Gonnus. Roman and Greek casualties totalled just over a thousand dead and perhaps twice that number of injured: light losses considering the battle's outcome.

Delighted, Flamininus ordered his senior officers and the commanders of his Greek allies to attend him in his great pavilion. After the meeting, he would address the army. The heavy clouds of earlier had cleared some time prior; the ground had mostly dried off, and the temperatures were pleasant. It was a beautiful summer's evening, and Flamininus ordered the sides of the great tent rolled up to let in the balmy air.

The first to arrive was a group of tribunes, who came in saluting and looking embarrassed. Remembering when he too had been over-awed by his senior officers, Flamininus bade them welcome. A click of his fingers brought hovering slaves in with cups of wine on trays. The rest weren't long after, his legates with Galba among them, the proud-looking Aetolians, a sweating Amynander and his Athamanians, the Apollonians and rough-looking Cretans.

When all those present had been served, Flamininus raised his glass – a sign that he was a man of taste and wealth, for glassware was rare and expensive – and a hush fell.

'Today was a good day. Today, the once-great Macedonia was humbled – by Rome.' Flamininus cast an eye at the Greeks. 'Never again shall the Macedonian king dominate your lives, tell you what to do. Never again shall your lands be overlooked by his fortresses. You are free!' He raised his glass high.

As everyone in the room did the same, the Greeks nodded and smiled at one another, and Flamininus thought, free from Philip, but not from Rome, you fools.

'To liberty,' said Flamininus, and drank. Spotting Galba's eye on him, he felt a dart of fury. His own freedom was as false as the Greeks'. The sale into slavery of the prisoners taken after the battle would raise a large amount, and Galba would expect a first payment from it. On and on it would go, for years. Flamininus continued to rack his brain at every opportunity, seeking a weakness that would allow him to black-mail Galba, or to bring him down. Nothing ever came to mind; his spies could discover little of use either.

'Each and every one of you played his part today,' said Flamininus. Apart from you, he thought, giving Galba a hard stare. Your actions bordered on insubordination. 'So did our troops. Today the phalanx proved no match for the might of the legions. Let us drink to them!' Flamininus noted Phaeneas, leader of the Aetolians, pursing his lips. He wasn't surprised, therefore, that the Aetolian spoke when the clapping died away.

'You made no mention of the Aitolians, Flamininus.'

Rankled by Phaeneas' familiarity – the prick seemed to think they were equals, thought Flamininus – he replied casually, 'The Aetolians?'

Phaeneas frowned. 'There are over six thousand of us in your army, as well you know. The cavalry in particular proved themselves today, on the hilltops before the battle proper started.'

'They also proved excellent at scavenging the enemy camp before any Roman troops arrived.' Flamininus' tone was acid. He'd had several reports from officers of men who'd been denied what they regarded as theirs.

'Aitolian cavalry reached the Macedonian encampment first,' protested Phaeneas.

'That does not mean they can keep all of the booty, nor even the best of it!' Everyone's eyes bore down on Flamininus, who, uncaring, continued loudly, 'I am in charge here. Under the terms of the treaty you made with the Senate, any goods and chattels taken in war are to go to Rome – that would include the contents of the enemy camp, as well you know. If you are to receive a share, it will be my decision how that share is calculated. Am I not right?'

Phaeneas knew that no one was about to come to his aid. He glowered, and muttered, 'Yes.'

'Another thing,' said Flamininus. 'Address me as general, or sir.'

Encouraged by the slightly alarmed glances the other Greeks were giving one another, Phaeneas cried, 'Do we not stand as allies, on an equal footing?'

'Sir,' said Flamininus.

'Sir.' Phaeneas spoke with gritted teeth.

'We do not,' declared Flamininus. 'More than two-thirds of the army is Roman. The same is true of the ships in our fleet. Need I say more?'

Phaeneas shook his head.

Down, you dog, thought Flamininus. He made a mental note to watch the Aetolian closely: the man would continue to cause trouble, of that there was no doubt.

Sensing that his speech was over, those present began to talk among themselves.

'That was well done,' said a voice in Flamininus' ear.

Annoyed and discomfited that Galba should creep up on him

unawares, suspicious to be complimented, Flamininus kept his composure. 'You think?'

'I do.' Galba clinked his cup off Flamininus' glass. 'To your victory.'

His suspicion deepening with every heartbeat, Flamininus dipped his chin. They both drank.

'We Romans deserve the lion's share of the booty, and the Aetolian needed to know that,' said Galba.

Here it is, thought Flamininus, before answering stiffly, 'There hasn't been time to calculate its worth yet.'

'No hurry.' Galba's smile was like that of one of the sharks occasionally hauled up in fishermen's nets: wide-lipped and full of teeth. 'I do expect a share, however. A decent share. It's an expensive business, war.'

'You shall have your cut,' said Flamininus, longing to punch Galba's teeth down his throat. 'I am a man of my word.'

'Of course you are.' With a bow so tiny it could only be taken as mocking, Galba walked away.

Flamininus' pleasure at his victory had been utterly soured. He threw back the entire glass of wine and held it out to a slave for a refill. Downing more than half of that, he advanced with purpose on the tribunes, who were standing to one side of their superiors and the Greek allies. 'Which of you led the attack on the side and rear of Philip's phalanx?' Flamininus asked.

A square-jawed man with an open, determined face saluted. 'I did, sir.'

'Fine work,' said Flamininus in a warm tone. 'You will be rewarded handsomely. A place in my triumphal parade shall also be yours.'

The tribune's grin could have split his face. 'Thank you, sir!'

'Keep it up, and you'll be legate before long.'

'I will, sir.'

'Your position during the battle – behind your men – meant that you couldn't have seen the opportunity first, though,' Flamininus observed.

The tribune looked deflated.

'Fear not. You ordered and led the charge. The glory is yours. Who was the man to bring the enemy's weakness to your attention, however?'

'A centurion of principes, sir. Bulbus, I think his name was.'

No, thought Flamininus, almost laughing out loud, but it had to be.

The chance of two centurions in his army with such an unfortunate name was slight. 'Bring him to me.'

'Sir!' The tribune vanished.

Flamininus' on-the-spot judgement of Bulbus at Elatea, months before, had been that the man was too full of himself. Seeing him punishing two men today had done nothing to change his mind. It *was* possible that he had been overhasty, he decided. The outcome of the battle would have been a great deal more uncertain if Bulbus had not acted. A soldier who could spot such an important opportunity merited recognition, and possibly promotion.

Flamininus moved among the tribunes, commending those he knew to have proved themselves on the field. In reality, he would have lost not a wink of sleep if many of them had died – as long as he'd won the battle, of course – but it looked better to seem to care.

'Here he is, sir.' The square-jawed tribune was back.

Flamininus turned. Bulbus *was* the centurion from Elatea; the man who'd thought it more important to beat two soldiers for a minor in-fraction than to focus on a battle vital to Rome's cause. He was also, Flamininus reminded himself, a sharp-minded, incisive leader whose action had allowed *him* to win a famous victory.

Both men saluted.

'May I present Gaius Atilius Bulbus, sir, centurion of principes, Eighth Legion,' said the tribune.

Nervous, Bulbus saluted again.

'Ah, we met earlier,' said Flamininus, amused by the trace of panic in Bulbus' eyes. 'Have you punished the two men since?'

'No, sir. I decided they'd learned their lesson. They also fought well today.'

'Wine?' asked Flamininus.

'Thank you, sir.' Bulbus' strained expression eased a little.

'A fine victory today, was it not?' Flamininus raised his glass towards Bulbus, who had accepted a cup from a slave.

'It was, sir. Attacking the enemy left flank with the elephants was a masterstroke.'

Flamininus was used to this type of fawning, but he liked it all the same. He inclined his head. 'I'm told you had a part to play in the rolling up of Philip's phalanx.'

Something flickered in Bulbus' eyes. 'I have that honour, sir.'

233

'It was well done.' All Flamininus' attention was on Bulbus now. The man's reaction wasn't quite right. Embarrassment would have been understandable. So too would awkwardness or diffidence. But this . . . this smacked of fear. Flamininus stared at Bulbus. Within a few heartbeats, the centurion's gaze dropped. Gods, thought Flamininus, *he* didn't see the exposed flank of the phalanx. One of his men did.

'Where do you stand in a fight?' he demanded.

Bulbus, confused, said, 'Sir?'

'Most centurions stand at the rightmost position of the front rank, or in the same position in one of the ranks behind. Don't they?'

'They do, sir.' Bulbus had the grace to flush. 'I tend to stand in the middle or at the back.'

'By my judgement then, you wouldn't have had a view of the phalanx – it was to our left as we climbed the slope. Only the men in the leftmost part of your century would have seen it.' Flamininus stared at Bulbus, whose eyes again fell away. It was possible that the centurion had noticed the phalanx's weakness when he'd been checking on his men during a brief water halt, he thought. If that had been what happened, however, he had no reason to look away. Bulbus had stolen another man's glory. Flamininus felt sure of it.

'I—' began Bulbus.

'Careful,' warned Flamininus.

'One of my men saw it, sir,' admitted Bulbus.

'Ah,' said Flamininus, thinking in triumph, I knew it. Wise to the nerves men feel during a long pause, he said nothing more.

'After commending him, I myself made my way to the tribune here.' Bulbus gestured. 'He took charge from that point, sir.'

What Bulbus had done was not wrong. It was the way of the world for officers to take credit for their men's actions, for senior officers to do the same to their juniors, and indeed, thought Flamininus, for generals to appropriate the glory won by their commanders. A clever man, however, one who didn't want to make enemies, made sure that their subordinate was suitably rewarded. Flamininus was full sure that Bulbus, beater of men during a battle, was not one of those.

'What other reward do you plan to give him?' Flamininus' tone was full of crisp authority. 'A purse of coin? A promotion perhaps?'

'I . . . I hadn't decided yet, sir.'

I bet you hadn't, thought Flamininus, deciding that Bulbus was

234

that rare beast, a centurion with little spine and leadership ability, who ruled his men through fear and intimidation. Bulbus didn't deserve promotion for what he'd done. Spying Galba closing in, his expression vulture-keen, Flamininus abruptly changed his mind. Galba knew Bulbus for what he was – he'd been the one to intervene during the beating earlier. It would piss him off to see Bulbus rewarded. Even a small opportunity to get at his enemy gave Flamininus satisfaction.

'Galba,' he said, loud enough for everyone to hear. 'This is the brave centurion who first brought word of the phalanx's weakness to the tribune here.'

'I know him, sir,' said Galba, his gaze cold enough to freeze water.

'He is to be promoted to centurion of triarii with immediate effect,' said Flamininus, smiling at Bulbus' incredulity and savouring Galba's impotent fury.

Galba looked as if he'd trodden on a caltrop. 'Of course, sir.'

'The soldier must also be rewarded. What's his name?'

'Felix Cicirrus, sir,' replied Bulbus.

'Like the clown?'

'Even so, sir,' said Bulbus. 'He's a veteran of Zama.'

'I like the sound of him. Fetch him at once,' said Flamininus.

It took some time to find Felix. Basking in the adulation of his officers and to a far lesser extent, his Greek allies, Flamininus drank a good quantity of wine. Encased in a warm glow, his enmity with Galba pushed to the back of his mind, he pictured the scene of his triumphal parade in Rome. It wouldn't be for some time – Philip had to negotiate for peace, and the Greek city states were yet to be brought fully to heel – but that meant Flamininus could make plans to ensure it was the grandest seen since the Republic's founding three centuries before. It would lay down in the most public fashion, he decided, that his incredible victory at Cynoscephalae and the subjugation of Greece afterwards made him one of the greatest Romans to have lived.

'Sir?'

Flamininus' eyes came into focus again. Bulbus was back; a sturdy, black-haired princeps stood a few paces behind. 'Bulbus.' Flamininus lingered over the word, and the princeps hastily bent his head. He *does* have the nickname 'Onion Head', thought Flamininus. He jerked his chin at Felix, and said, 'This is the man who saw?'

'Aye, sir.' Bulbus stepped to one side and with a motion of his arm, indicated Felix should approach.

Felix stamped up and came to attention. 'Sir!'

'Name and rank,' said Flamininus.

'Princeps Felix Cicirrus, sir, of the Eighth Legion. Also veteran of the Hannibalic war, sir.'

'You were at Zama, I hear,' said Flamininus.

'I was, sir. Me and my brother Antonius.'

'He's also in the Eighth?'

'Was, sir.' Felix's voice was heavy with grief. 'He fell today.'

'I'm sorry to hear that,' said Flamininus sombrely. 'Did he die well?'

'Aye, sir. He was there when we hit the side of the phalanx.' The corner of one of Felix's eyes twitched.

'He will be a sore loss to the army. Had he a wife? Family?'

'No, sir. Just me.'

'You have my sympathies.'

'Sir.'

Flamininus didn't especially care about Felix's brother dying, but he let a few slow heartbeats go by to make it seem he did, and then he said, 'I am told you were the one to spot the vulnerability of the phalanx.' He was aware that Galba had approached, but pretended not to notice. 'Tell me what happened.'

Those nearby heard his words, and a silence fell. Abashed, Felix hesitated, but after an encouraging gesture from Flamininus, told his story. Apart from Bulbus, no one realised that he omitted the centurion's attack on him just before his revelation.

When Felix finished, Flamininus gave him a nod of approval. He eyed the ring of watching faces. 'He did well, eh?' Into the chorus of agreement, Flamininus asked Bulbus, 'Is your optio experienced?'

'Callistus? Yes, sir,' replied Bulbus. 'Nigh on twenty years he's served.'

'Take him with you to the triarii,' Flamininus ordered the delighted Bulbus. To Felix, he said, 'Congratulations, optio.'

Felix's mouth opened. Closed. He said, wonderingly, 'Me, an optio, sir?'

'But, sir . . .' Bulbus interrupted. Realising what he'd done, he faltered. 'Galba demoted him only recently.'

Flamininus glared at Bulbus, then turned to Galba. 'What happened?'

His mouth pinched, Galba related the incident with the harpastum ball.

Relishing that he could rub Galba's nose in it, Flamininus exclaimed, 'That must have been a genuine mistake.' His eyes moved to Felix.

'It was, sir. I would never have wanted to hurt the legate, sir.'

Galba made a strangled noise.

'Let us put it in the past, eh?' declared Flamininus. 'Your actions today are of far greater consequence. It's fair to say that Rome needs soldiers like you. My promotion stands.'

Embarrassed but proud, Felix saluted. 'Thank you, sir.'

Promising Felix a suitable donative, Flamininus dismissed the princeps and his centurion. Galba faded into the background, scowling but powerless. Flamininus exulted in his enemy's annoyance. While it was Flamininus' right to interfere as he had, both men knew that it hadn't been done to reward Bulbus, Callistus and Felix, but to piss off Galba. And, thought Flamininus, noting his enemy's furious expression – Galba was usually good at appearing not to care – he had succeeded in royal style.

He held out his glass. 'More wine!'

CHAPTER XXV

Gonnos

The sky was a deep shade of blue, and fading to black. Bats shot to and fro overhead. Some distance off, an owl called, and was answered by its mate. It was the evening of the day after Kynoskephalae. Philip's camp, such as it was, sprawled around the walls of Gonnos, and into the nearby woods. Thousands of soldiers had already reached the place; more continued to straggle even as the light leached from the western horizon. Thanks to the warm temperature – the fine weather had returned – it didn't matter that no one had a tent. Water could be had from the nearby River Peneios, but food was in short supply. Philip had entered Gonnos earlier and met with the town's leaders. Paying for all the supplies they could spare with his own money, he had ordered it distributed among his soldiers.

The king had not eaten himself; he had no appetite. Supping from a skin of watered-down wine, he had been walking through the camp for hours. In a sweat-stained chiton, armed only with a dagger, he looked no different from anyone else. His unexpected arrival at men's fires was greeted with almost pathetic gratitude, over and over. Never had Philip felt the burden of kingship more. Somehow, he smiled. Joked. Offered mouthfuls of his own wine. Gripped the shoulders of men who'd lost comrades. Promised that back in Macedon, they would all be fed and watered like lords.

No one asked what the future held, and he did not offer an opinion.

In between the fires, when he was alone, Philip's face grew solemn. After a hard ride north from the carnage at Kynoskephalae, he had passed the night at the so-called Tower of Alexander. Grieving for his dead soldiers and humiliated by the defeat, he had barely slept. Another day's riding had seen him and his companions reach Gonnos, where he had prayed to Zeus what seemed a lifetime before. Even though the temple was close by, Philip had no desire to pay another visit. The

238

thunder god had spoken in the loudest fashion at Kynoskephalae. He was displeased with Philip; he had abandoned Macedon and its people. No one knew, the king least of all, if his favour would return.

'Sire, is that you?' The figure was backlit by the flames behind him.

Philip stepped closer. His face creased with genuine pleasure. 'Berisades!'

Lankier than ever, toothless, his tunic caked in blood, Berisades bowed. 'Sire.'

Philip seized the peltast's hand. 'It's good to see you.'

'And you, sire.' Berisades bobbed his head.

Philip pointed to the bloodstains. 'You're unhurt?'

Berisades snorted. 'That's not my blood, sire. This is.' He stuck out his left leg, which was wrapped from knee to ankle in a rough linen bandage, and grumbled, 'I'm getting slow. Ten years ago, I never would have taken such a wound. It bled like a bastard, begging your pardon, sire.'

'Is the cut clean? Has a surgeon seen it?'

'Clean enough, sire. I sluiced it with wine. A waste, really.'

'And the surgeon?'

'The treatment area is overrun, sire. There are many men waiting with far worse injuries than mine.'

'It should still be looked at.'

'I'll live, sire.' Berisades' grin was crooked. 'When you are as grey-haired as me, you get a sense of when the Fates are wielding their shears close by. There are more interesting threads to cut at the moment, sadly.'

Clasping Berisades' hand again, and deciding he would send his own surgeon to check on the peltast, Philip took his leave. It was time to return to the makeshift hospital, which consisted of a clearing among the trees a short distance from the rest of the camp. To reach it, he picked his way through the remnants of a speira of Brazens, telling them how proud he was, and apologising for their poor quarters that night. A few men responded, but there was no hiding the forced tone to their laughter.

Philip's grim mood settled on him like a cloak the instant he had left the phalangists behind. In his mind's eye, he ran through the day of the battle. Marching at dawn, their purpose to cross the Roman army's path unseen, and reach Pharsalos. The thunder and torrential rain that had made progress impossible. Choosing a site for a camp only a few stadia from the one they had just left. How he had sent scouts up into the hills. The all-enveloping cloud cover that made it impossible for anyone to see far beyond the length of their own arm.

I would have done nothing different until then, he thought. It had also been the right decision to send reinforcements to his scouts' aid. Where he had gone wrong, Philip decided, was perhaps to have committed his half of the phalanx to the fight before Nikanor's troops had arrived. If he had stayed at the top of the slope and let his light infantry retreat towards him, he could have held the enemy long enough until the rest of his phalangists had arrived.

Even if Nikanor's men had been ready to fight, the king admitted to himself, they might not have stood before the cursed elephants. But then again they might – Scipio's legionaries had at Zama. The day might have been so different if he'd prepared his troops better, he thought bitterly.

Through the familiar churring of cicadas, loud here among the trees, he made out a new, less pleasant sound. Men's cries. Moans. Every now and then, a scream. Mixed in, he heard reassuring voices, surely those of the surgeons and their helpers. Skirting around a large cypress tree, Philip entered the clearing. Torches burned some distance off, but in between, darkness reigned. The neat lines of wounded and maimed and dying men needed no light. He could smell piss, shit and stale sweat, and over all of them, the copper tang of blood.

Philip almost turned around and walked away. He had been here earlier, and the experience had been harrowing. Stay, he told himself. Your men bled and died for you – you owe them this. He took a deep breath – through his mouth – and let it out again.

'Mother.' The voice belonged to a soldier not ten paces away. 'Mother.' No one answered. No one came.

By the man's armour – a fine bronze breastplate – Philip judged him to be a phalangist. The thick bandage around his upper right thigh was almost completely soaked through with blood. Tartaros, thought Philip. How he had made it here from Kynoskephalae beggared belief. Whatever blade had sliced into his leg had cut the artery. The wound was too high up for amputation to be an option; the surgeon must have put on the dressing as tight as possible, and hoped for the best. Judging by the dark stain under the phalangist's leg, his future was bleak.

'Mother.'

'She's not here,' said Philip in a gentle voice. He knelt and took the man's hand, which was clammy with sweat.

'Father?' The phalangist sounded confused.

'No,' said Philip, tugging from his belt the strip of cloth he used to wipe his own brow. He dabbed it against the phalangist's forehead. 'Try to rest.'

'Where's Mother?'

'It's late. She's gone to bed,' lied Philip. 'Your father too.'

The phalangist's eyelids fluttered, but they didn't open. After a moment, he whispered, 'Who are you?'

There was no point revealing his identity, thought Philip. The man was too far along the road to the underworld. 'I'm a friend,' he said. 'Just a friend who came to sit with you.'

This seemed to satisfy the phalangist, who drifted into a deep sleep.

Philip's heart was heavy. The slumber would be the wounded man's last. If the end came before dawn, it would be a blessing. The army could wait for no man, and Flamininus' legions would not be long arriving.

The phalangist didn't stir as Philip eased his fingers free and stood.

The king moved on, giving a couple of mouthfuls of wine to a Thracian missing half an arm. Unable to converse – neither spoke the other's tongue – Philip didn't linger. More patient than he'd ever been with his children, he sat and talked with scores of the injured. Held their hands. Shared his wine, and fetched water from the wooden buckets close to the surgeons' work area. Wiped away their tears. Waited with several, as they slipped, rattling-breathed, into oblivion. Some recognised him, most didn't. Philip didn't care either way. He wasn't here as king, but to honour his soldiers. Deeply moved by the final request of a Companion to tell his parents he loved them, and thinking of his own children, Philip lingered by the cavalryman's cooling body.

It was hard not to conclude that his soldiers' deaths had been for nothing. Flamininus had won. More than that, he had inflicted a crushing defeat on Philip. The greater part of his army was gone. How many men were dead or dying on the battlefield, prisoners of the Romans, or following on behind the soldiers who had made it to Gonnos, he had no idea. And yet all was not lost, Philip told himself. He remained the king of Macedon; for numerous reasons, it would not serve Flamininus to see him deposed.

'Sire.'

Philip lifted his head. A shape loomed over him, a bearded man in a once-cream, now dark-red chiton. His arms were bloodied to the elbows, and in one hand, he held a large knife. 'You're a surgeon,' said the king, stating the obvious.

'Yes, sire. The stretcher-bearers told me you were here a little while ago. It's good of you to come.'

'It is my duty,' said Philip, meaning it.

'You have my respect, sire, and your men's love.' The surgeon touched his tunic over his heart.

Moisture pricked Philip's eyes. He was grateful for the dim light. Committing the Companion's name and the village he was from to memory, he climbed to his feet. 'How goes it?'

'I do what I can, sire, and when that isn't enough, I give them poppy juice or wine. Mostly the latter.' Suddenly, the surgeon looked beaten down, weary beyond his years. 'Some will survive. Many will not. Only Asklepios can tell.' He shook himself, and smiled. 'I'm not here to complain, sire, but to bring you news. Your son is here.'

Philip stared. 'Perseus?'

'One and the same, sire. They say that apples don't fall far from the tree, and so it is with the prince, the gods bless him. He's over there, ministering to the soldiers, just as you have been.'

Philip felt a combination of anger, that his son should leave Pella against his orders, and pride, that Perseus was growing into a man who made his own decisions. 'Take me to him.'

'If you'll follow me, sire.' The surgeon led Philip around the edge of the operating area. Stopping a distance from a figure kneeling by an injured soldier, he pointed. 'That's him.'

'Is there no one with him? No bodyguards?'

'There don't appear to be, sire, but no one would harm him. They love him, as they do you.'

Glad, Philip smiled. Perseus is as mule-headed as me, he thought, thinking of his own habit of stealing out of the palace without his guards. Muttering his thanks, he dismissed the surgeon and waited until Perseus had risen to his feet.

'Perseus.'

His son's head turned. 'Father?'

'Yes.' All his anger gone, Philip opened his arms. They embraced fiercely, then came apart to grin at one another. 'What in Tartaros are you doing here?' the king asked. 'I told you to stay in Pella.'

'It was so hard, Father, waiting every day for news. I stayed as long as I could. I arrived here only to find out that I left too late, that I missed the battle . . .' Perseus' face fell.

'The gods be thanked you weren't there,' said Philip, trying not to think of Perseus caught up in the slaughter.

'Was it terrible?'

'It was.'

Perseus' eyes searched Philip's; he gestured at the injured soldiers around them and said quietly, 'It must have been.'

'I will tell you what happened, but not now. Walk with me to my tent,' said Philip.

'But the men—'

'Will still be here in the morning. Those that won't, well, we can't comfort them all.'

His expression sombre, Perseus nodded.

Across the clearing they went, past stretcher-bearers carrying the dead away. Close to a surgeon who was sawing a semi-conscious man's leg off. Past a trio of phalangists crouched around a comrade, praying.

Philip felt a deep relief to be leaving behind the wails and moans, the blood and death, if only for a time. Felt a quiet joy at seeing his son, young and strong and alive. He threw an arm around Perseus' shoulders and squeezed. 'I'm glad you came,' he said.

Joined by thousands of survivors at Gonnos over the next few days, Philip made his way to Tempe unhindered by the Romans. Trusted soldiers were sent to Larisa; there all royal documents were destroyed so they did not fall into Flamininus' hands. Rather than pursue the Macedonians, the Roman general had marched on the centrally placed town.

Another three days went by, and the emissaries Philip had sent south returned. After hearing their news, the king summoned his generals. Now he waited for them in his tent. Perseus was there: before sending him back to Pella, Philip had decided to let his heir see first-hand what it was like to rule in times of war. The defeat at Kynoskephalae meant that there was no certainty Perseus would rule after him, but Philip was hopeful.

Pacing about like a caged beast, Perseus managed to keep silent for quite a time. In the end, however, he could restrain himself no longer. 'What did the emissaries say, Father?'

Philip shook his head. 'You'll find out when everyone is here, not before.'

'It's not fair. I am your son and heir!'

'That you are,' said Philip, offering a prayer to Zeus, whom he hoped was over his anger towards him, to ensure that Perseus *did* take the throne. 'But you are still a boy. If men twice and thrice your age have to wait to hear, so should you.'

Perseus scowled and walked off to the far end of the 'chamber', which was formed by leather partitions. There tables had been set with wine and food. He made a great show of pouring a cup of wine, and drinking it, without offering any to his father.

Well it is for him to have such small concerns as who hears what and when, thought Philip. He heard voices outside; a moment later, the sentries asked who had come calling upon the king.

Before long, Menander and Nikanor had been ushered in. They were followed by Athenagoras and the handful of surviving Thracian and Illyrian chieftains. Leon and Herakleides, Philip's cavalry commanders, had both died at Kynoscephalae; their replacements Demosthenes and Kykliadas were present instead.

'I have called you here to take counsel,' said Philip when everyone had a cup of wine. He was amused to find Perseus by his side; the boy could sulk, but he didn't want to miss out either.

Heads nodded. Chins dipped. 'Sire,' they rumbled.

'Your son is here, sire,' said Menander, looking pleased but surprised.

'I couldn't bear being in the palace any longer,' said Perseus. 'I wanted to be with Father. With the army.'

A weighty silence fell.

Embarrassed, Perseus took a step back, behind Philip.

'The messengers I sent to Larisa have returned,' said the king. 'They carry good news. Flamininus has granted me permission to bury our dead at Kynoskephalae. He has also agreed to meet and discuss making peace.' Philip's eyes roved the chamber, gauging his generals' reactions. Menander looked relieved. So too did Demosthenes and Kykliadas. Nikanor, who had been badly injured in the battle, seemed defiant. Philip wasn't surprised; he had lost many, many men. The anger playing over the tribal chieftains' faces was also understandable. No doubt they wanted revenge for their heavy losses. Athenagoras was harder to read; it had ever been so.

No one ventured an opinion.

'Well?' asked the king. 'Have you lost your tongues?'

'Peace?' cried Perseus, stepping forward again. 'Thousands of your men lie dead at the Dogs' Heads, Father, and you talk of peace?' The tribal chieftains growled in approval, and encouraged, Perseus continued, 'Surely we must defend the pass here at Tempe? If the Romans are to enter Macedon, they will pay for every stadion in blood.' Chest heaving, he gave Philip a bold stare.

'Are you finished?' asked Philip.

Someone chuckled, and Perseus flushed. 'I . . . Yes, Father.'

The boy had just shown his inexperience to the generals, thought Philip, but he had also shown his fighting spirit, which counted for a lot. Cutting him down to size would be counterproductive. 'My army is half the size it was at Kynoskephalae, Perseus. The Romans' losses were a tiny fraction of ours. Tempe, moreover, is far harder to defend than the passes in western Macedon. Flamininus could flank us within days. To give battle again would be foolish for all these reasons. Bitter as it is to admit, defeat would be inevitable.' Philip transferred his gaze to the others present. 'Knowing that, I refuse to let thousands more men die needlessly. Too many have already gone to Tartaros.'

Reluctant nods, even from Perseus. Looks of relief. A couple of muttered prayers.

'You think the same as I then,' said Philip, addressing everyone.

More nods. Some 'Ayes'. Silence from two of the Illyrians.

'Flamininus does not have all the gaming pieces,' said Philip. 'It suits him to leave me on the throne of Macedon. He is no fool. Even the Romans know of the savage tribes of Thrace and Dardania–' he paused to throw an ironic look at the Thracians present '–and their regular incursions into our lands. He will also be aware of Antiokhos' designs on Greece and Macedon. What better buffer against Antiokhos could Rome have but me and my still-substantial army? That is not the only reason he will come to the negotiating table either. My spies–' here the king smiled at Perseus' surprise '–tell me there is discord in Flamininus' camp. The Aitolians in particular are unhappy that he continues to make decisions without consulting them or the other Greeks. They also resent his allowing us to bury our dead at Kynoskephalae, but their biggest concern is that he will agree that I should continue as king.'

'What of Flamininus, sire?' asked Menander.

'He is furious with the Aitolians. Not only did they plunder our camp before any of his soldiers, but they are spreading word of how *they* won the battle. If Flamininus hadn't realised it before, it will be clear now that once the legions leave, the Aitolians intend to be the dominant power in Greece.' Philip was pleased by the angry mutters this revelation produced.

'If you give Flamininus what he wants, Father, and he agrees you should remain king, will that not leave you exposed to Antiokhos?' Perseus' tone was perplexed.

'Not if we utilise the discord between the Aitolians and Flamininus by becoming Rome's ally,' said Philip into a chorus of shocked gasps. He smiled. 'Think about it. Fight on against the legions, and we will lose. Make a bitter peace with Flamininus, and our treatment will be harsh indeed. Aitolia's chances of becoming the main power in Greece will also increase. Come to an amenable agreement with Flamininus, however, and immediately offer our assistance against Antiokhos . . . Do you see my intent?'

'The legions could stand alongside the phalanx?' Athenagoras shook his head.

'It sounds mad,' said Menander. 'But it makes sense.'

Philip glanced at the others. 'Nikanor?'

A heavy sigh. 'Like Athenagoras says, sire, it doesn't seem right.'

'The men who fell at Kynoskephalae will never be forgotten,' said Philip, discerning the reason behind his general's reticence. 'But if we aren't to see them joined in the underworld by thousands more of their comrades, this is the future we need to consider.'

Their eyes met.

After a moment, Nikanor nodded.

'That leaves you,' said Philip, eyeing the Thracians and Illyrians. 'What say you brave men?'

'We hate Romans,' said one of the Thracians, nodding at his companions' growls. 'Too many us . . . die at Dogs' Heads. But we not want . . . die more. If make peace with Romans, men live.'

Philip studied the faces of the chieftain's companions, as well as those of the Illyrians. They would go along with him for the moment, he decided. Whether they would continue to serve in his army or slip away in the dead of night remained to be seen, but that had ever been the nature of such mercenaries.

'We agree then,' he said.

'Father . . .' began Perseus bullishly.

Philip's gaze bore down on his son. 'Enough. I let you stay that you might learn, not question my authority.'

Perseus looked down. 'Yes, Father.'

'Just because we seek peace with Flamininus does not mean that other issues should be forgotten,' said Philip. 'The garrison of the Akrokorinth must be strengthened. Opportunists like Nabis of Sparta or the Akhaians might see Kynoskephalae as an opportunity to strike. I shall send a chiliarchy south, by ship. Gods willing, the men will have little to do but compare their battle scars, but if Nabis or the Akhaians should come knocking, they will get a nasty surprise.'

'Can I go, Father?'

'To the Akrokorinth? Out of the question.'

'Why not?' demanded Perseus. 'If there's to be no fighting here, my best chance is in the south.'

'Your bravery is commendable,' said Philip. 'But you are my heir. It's too dangerous.'

'Father—'

'I will not hear of it.'

Perseus scowled. 'Yes, Father.'

His mind caught up with deciding what he would say to Flamininus, Philip missed the crafty expression on his son's face.

CHAPTER XXVI

Off the coast of Magnesia, between Macedon and Euboea

F ishing smacks dotted the brilliant blue sea, seeking shoals of mackerel and bream. Clouds of gulls banked and dived overhead, screeching like lost souls. Beating a path through the fishing boats was a large squadron of *liburnians*. Demetrios was at the stern of one, arms resting on the wooden rail. His eyes moved from Mount Pelion, which dominated the western skyline, to the other ships in their fleet. Most of Philip's navy this was, according to the captain, and not a trireme in sight.

Demetrios sighed. Beaten on land, a weak power at sea. What future did Macedon have? Resignation battered him. His friends were dead. Kimon and Antileon were gone. He closed his eyes and let the grief and shame batter him, as it had night and day since Kynoskephalae. Rear-rankers, they should have survived. It ought to have been he who fell, but in the madness and confusion of the shock Roman attack on the phalanx's side, countless men had died who under normal circumstances would not have.

The shouts to his left had first made Demetrios aware that something was wrong. Focused on the brutal effort of driving the Romans off the hill, as the Brazens had been doing for some time, he paid no heed. As the clamour grew louder, and the cries more frantic, it had become impossible to ignore. Some of the level-headed file-leaders, among them Simonides, had called a halt to try and determine what was going on. Consumed by their desire to defeat the enemy, many other files had ploughed on, breaking up the phalanx. As Demetrios would realise later, this had aided the Roman attack.

Blind to what was going on to their left, unable to send men through the massed ranks of their fellows to find out, or around their front for fear of the Romans, Simonides' file had been as helpless as a ship with a broken steering oar. The enemy had been quick to see their opportunity. Cheering broke out among the lines of battered, bloodied legionaries facing Simonides' file, and then incredibly, the Romans had begun to advance.

'Will we ever return to Macedon?' asked a voice.

Demetrios found that he'd been joined by Simonides. His file-leader's face, always solemn, had a new grimness to it since Kynoskephalae.

'Why – do you think we'll die at the Akrokorinth?' Demetrios was indifferent to Simonides' answer.

'There's a good chance.' Simonides spat over the rail.

Demetrios stared down at the foam-flecked water, and wondered how long it would take to drown if he let himself fall in. Not long, he decided. It was tempting. He had never been so miserable, never cared less about the following day, let alone the one after that.

'Don't,' said Simonides. 'Too many good men from the file are gone. I don't need to lose you too.'

Shocked to have his mind read, Demetrios glanced at his file-leader.

'It's hard for you, I know. Philippos was like a father to you, and Kimon and Antileon were friends, not just your tentmates. To lose all three is cruel.'

'I should have saved Kimon and Antileon.'

'How? How could you have? Hell was unleashed on that hillside. No one knew who was where. Like me, you were swept this way and that. When you saw a chance of retreating, you took it. Linger, and you would have died.'

'I know, but—'

'Kimon and Antileon had as good a chance as anyone to get away. It was their bad luck they didn't, and your good fortune that you did.'

Demetrios nodded. Simonides was right, but it was hard to accept.

'The war's not over, not yet. The king wants us to hold the Akrokorinth for him, and that's what we will have to do. Grief doesn't make our duties vanish – that's what he said, remember? You are a soldier still, like the rest of us. Would you have me and Andriskos and the others fight without you?'

'No,' said Demetrios, hating the moisture pricking his eyes. 'Of course not.' He caught sight of Empedokles further along the deck. 'It's just . . .'

Simonides' gaze followed his. 'Aye. Him. Truth be told, I'd rather have lost that prick than men like Philippos . . . or your friends, but the Fates will do as they please.'

They will, thought Demetrios sadly.

'So you'll stay?' Simonides' tone was gentle.

'I will.' Demetrios took great comfort from Simonides' clasp of his shoulder before the file-leader walked away. He had him and Andriskos, thought Demetrios. That would have to be enough.

The liburnian had taken on as many phalangists as could be fitted on the deck. The remnants of four files – almost forty men – were crammed together like salted fish in a barrel. One of the first aboard, Demetrios had secured a spot right at the base of the raised platform at the stern. It meant he would have a neighbour on only one side, rather than being squeezed between two. Returning from his talk with Simonides, he was angered to see that his place had been filched. A slight figure sat where his blanket had been, head covered by the hood of his cloak.

Curious too, for the sun's heat meant that everyone had stripped to their chitons or even less, Demetrios picked a path over men's legs and the shafts of disassembled sarissae. Half a dozen paces away, he said, 'Friend.'

No response.

Demetrios raised his voice. 'Friend.'

The phalangist who'd taken the same spot as Demetrios but on the other side of the deck looked up. 'Aye?'

'Not you. Him.' Demetrios jerked his chin at the huddled figure.

'He's not much for talking, that one.' With an amiable nod, the phalangist got up and eased past Demetrios.

He's going to move, thought Demetrios, or pay the consequences. Standing over the interloper, he said, 'That place is taken.'

No answer.

Irritated, Demetrios gave the figure a none-too-gentle nudge with his heavy, studded sandal. 'Hey! I'm talking to you.'

'Leave me be.'

If the voice hadn't been so light in tone, and Empedokles hadn't been playing dice with Skopas a dozen paces away, Demetrios would have wondered if his enemy had thrown on a cloak and sat here to annoy him. Regardless of who it was, his patience was fraying thin.

'There are two ways this is going to end, and both involve you moving, *friend*. One will be a great deal more painful for you than the other. Which is it going to be?'

'I'm not looking for trouble.'

'You've got a funny way of going about things,' challenged Demetrios. Infuriated by the interloper's refusal to look at him, he reached down and tried to tug back the hood. He met fierce resistance – the man was holding it in both hands.

Curious now – there was more to this than having his spot taken – Demetrios let go. Quick as a flash, he knelt down. He caught a glimpse of a young, sharp-eyed face before the interloper turned his head towards the planking of the platform beside them. This was no man, but a boy, thought Demetrios. A stowaway. Squatting on his haunches, he said, 'It's safe to take down your hood. We're well at sea now. The captain's not going to turn back because of one extra passenger.'

The boy did not move.

The last of Demetrios' tolerance vanished. Using both his hands, he ripped back the hood. Two handspans apart, he and the boy stared at each other. Shock bathed Demetrios. He'd seen Perseus enough times to recognise him, especially this close. 'Forgive me—'

'Shhh,' hissed Perseus before he could say 'sire'. The hood whipped back up again.

Demetrios risked a casual glance along the deck. It was a huge relief that no one was paying attention. 'I'm sorry, sire,' he whispered. 'I had no idea it was you.'

'That was the general idea,' came the sarcastic reply.

Seeing Perseus' intent, Demetrios chuckled. Like most, he'd heard of the king's son's arrival in their camp at Tempe. 'I'm guessing you wanted to travel with us to the Akrokorinth, sire, but the king refused, so you sneaked on board.'

'Yes. I missed Kynoskephalae by two days. Two! The Akrokorinth is my best chance of fighting in a battle before the war is over.'

'You might be disappointed, sire. The Akrokorinth is impregnable, or so they say. Could be all we have to do is patrol the walls until peace has been made.'

'Better that than return to Pella, which is what Father ordered me to do.'

Their lives were worlds apart, Demetrios decided, but he and the heir to the throne weren't so different. Putting from his mind what might happen to him if he aided Perseus, he said, 'I'll help you, sire.'

From under the hood, a look of fierce excitement. 'You will? Why?'

'I was an oarsman on one of your father's merchant ships a few years back, sire, but all I'd ever wanted was to be a phalangist. It seemed impossible, but one day someone gave me a chance. I'm a front-ranker now.'

Perseus' right hand thrust forward. 'Give me your word.'

'I swear it before all the gods.' They shook.

'Found yourself a pillow biter?' called a familiar voice.

Tartaros, thought Demetrios. If you knew who you were insulting, you'd soil your undergarment. Out loud, he said, 'Piss off, Empedokles.'

'Very cosy the two of you look,' sneered Empedokles. 'A nice secluded spot too, compared to the rest of us. I can imagine what you'll get up to come nightfall.'

Angry not just for himself, but for the gravity of the insult to Perseus, Demetrios bunched his fists. Before he could rise, Perseus muttered, 'Leave it. If you fight him, an officer will get involved. Then I'll be forced to reveal my face.'

Demetrios didn't like it, but Perseus was right. He sank back down.

Empedokles hurled a couple more insults, which Demetrios and Perseus ignored. In the end, warned by men who were sick of his vitriolic monologue, he went back to his blanket.

'Who's that prick?' asked Perseus.

'One of my comrades, sire.'

'He doesn't like you much.'

Demetrios grinned. 'He took against me the first time we met, sire, and it's been like that since. Almost drowned me once.'

'Tell me,' said Perseus with the enthusiasm of a small boy.

If someone had told Demetrios a few hours earlier that he was to spend some of the voyage explaining his enmity with Empedokles to the crown prince, he would have laughed in their face. Yet here he was. Demetrios took a deep breath and began. For reasons he couldn't quite explain, he even related how he'd almost left Empedokles to the mercy of the cutpurses in Pella.

'And it all came from the night around the campfire, when you came to ask Simonides if he'd take you on as a recruit?' asked Perseus when he was done.

'Yes, sire. I'd never set eyes on him before.'

'He's a prick and a half, and no mistake. I'm surprised you haven't stuck a blade in him before now.'

Astonished to hear such a thing from the heir to the throne, Demetrios admitted, 'I've thought about it many a time, sire.'

'Better man you for not having done so.' Now Perseus almost sounded like the king, and Demetrios bobbed his head in deference.

Their conversation was brought to an end by the return of the phalangist Demetrios had briefly spoken to when he'd first challenged Perseus.

At once Perseus lay down and turned his face to the planking. 'Wake me when it's dark,' he whispered.

'Aye,' said Demetrios, as if the prince were just an ordinary comrade.

His first test came not long after when Andriskos, whose place lay next to his, came back. He pointed at Perseus. 'Who's that? Why's he taken your place?'

'He's from another file,' lied Demetrios. 'The poor sod has a fever – he wandered here by mistake. I didn't have the heart to shift him.'

'You're too soft-hearted,' said Andriskos, but there was no heat to his voice.

While the men opposite might not suspect anything, thought Demetrios, he wouldn't be able to keep the wool pulled over Andriskos' eyes forever. When his friend found out, he had to hope that Andriskos would agree not to tell Simonides or the ship's captain. If Perseus remained undetected until they had made landfall on Euboea, the chance of his remaining with the speira was good. Their commander Stephanos and his superior, the chiliarch, would not be happy about the prince's presence, but by that point there would be little he could do without delaying or jeopardising their mission.

Demetrios tried not to think about what Stephanos or worse still, the king, might do to him when his role in Perseus' escapade was revealed.

In the event, the rest of the voyage passed without much incident. Amused by Perseus' daring, Andriskos was easy to swear to silence. Laid low by a bad belly, Empedokles gave them no trouble. Not until they were marching across Euboea two days later was Perseus' lack of a sarissa commented on, but so many men had lost theirs at Kynoskephalae that it was simple to explain away. Matters came to a head in camp that night when Demetrios' surviving tentmates, both quiet types usually, quite reasonably demanded to know the identity of the stranger in their tent. Their raised voices brought Simonides, who took one look at Perseus, swore, and called for Stephanos. His oaths were louder and even more colourful. Mid-rant, he realised what he was doing and apologised, red-faced, to Perseus.

The prince grinned. 'I've heard it all before, from Father.'

Stephanos turned on Demetrios. 'What kind of fool are you not to tell me when there was still a chance of returning to Macedon? You'll pay for this.'

'Do not punish him,' cried Perseus. 'What was he to do when the crown prince had told him not to tell a soul?'

Helpless before Perseus' authority, Stephanos could only glower at Demetrios and hurry the prince to his own tent.

The instant they had gone, Simonides cuffed Demetrios round the head, as a father would a wayward son. 'What in Tartaros were you thinking?' he bellowed.

'I felt sorry for him, sir,' said Demetrios. 'He reminded me of myself when I wanted to join the phalanx.'

Simonides gave him a jaundiced look. 'Need I remind you of the difference between you dying as a phalangist and the crown prince doing the same?'

Put as baldly as that, it sank home. Demetrios muttered, 'No, sir.'

To his surprise, Simonides shrugged. 'He's a stubborn one, Perseus – like his father. If he'd failed to come south with us, he would have found another way. Who knows? We might be grateful for him yet.'

Several days went by. Seventy-five stadia to the west of Korinth, a camp sprawled on the near bank of the River Nemea. A poor earthen rampart surrounded it; so did a ditch, although this was scarcely waist-deep in places. To the north, where the river flowed, lay the narrow ribbon of the Gulf of Korinth. Sikyon lay to the west, and beyond it, Pallene. South and south-east were the towns of Phlios, Kleonai and Argos. Just visible in the heat haze to the east loomed the Akrokorinth.

Demetrios was one of the sentries on the western wall of the camp, overlooking the ford across the Nemea. Despite the boredom of such duty, he was enjoying being outside the fortress. Eight months before, there had only been the secretive journey to reach the Akrokorinth, and then the fight to defend it.

'Hot, eh?' Dust puffed up from the earth walkway as Andriskos stamped over.

'It'd be worse marching through that,' said Demetrios, indicating the brown, sun-baked fields. It was the height of summer now, and temperatures at midday were searing.

'True. It's fortunate that Androsthenes knows not to use us as scavengers, eh?' Andriskos slipped his helmet back on his head so he could wipe away sweat.

Androsthenes was the commander of the Akrokorinth, and the man who Philokles had made wait until he'd fed and watered his weary men eight months before. While Demetrios and the other phalangists protected the camp, Androsthenes was ranging the countryside around Pallene with a column of light infantry and cavalry. Two similar columns were doing the same in the area of Phlios and Kleonai. Late each afternoon, the raiding parties returned with whatever they had appropriated: flocks of sheep and goats; farmers' wagons laden down with vegetables and fruit; and if the gods were smiling, amphorae of oil or wine.

The mission had set out the day after the chiliarchy's arrival at the Akrokorinth. With his garrison's numbers now in excess of six thousand soldiers, Androsthenes needed vast amounts of supplies. Leaving only a skeleton force to protect the fortress – 'Who would attack it anyway?' crowed men who'd served there for years – he had led his confident troops onto the Peloponnese.

It wasn't quite what Demetrios had expected, but he wasn't complaining. After the unexpected loss of so many comrades at Kynoskephalae, it was a relief to stand on guard watching over empty fields. Perseus, who came to talk with Demetrios now and again, didn't agree – allowed after much argument to accompany the force rather than stay in the Akrokorinth, he was confined to the camp. To the prince's disgust, a pair of sentries had been set on his tent to prevent him from creeping out with a patrol. 'At this rate,' he complained to Demetrios, 'I will get back to Pella without having unsheathed my blade.' Demetrios had thus far forborne from telling the excitable Perseus that that outcome would probably please Philip a great deal.

Andriskos said, 'Not a bad duty, this.'

'After what we've been through, that–' Demetrios indicated the farmland before the camp '–seems like the Elysian Fields.'

'Elysium would be greener, surely,' said Andriskos. 'Rather than a cracked-earth brown.'

'We need a gentle breeze too,' answered Demetrios, grinning. 'But who's complaining?'

'Not I.'

Demetrios took a slug from his water bag, which tasted of oiled leather, and made a face. An idea struck. 'Let's ask Simonides if we can go down to the river.'

Andriskos' face lit up. 'That's a fine idea.'

Both knew that as well as slaking their thirst, they would go waist-deep in the water to cool down.

Simonides granted their request easily enough. In the two days the phalangists had been guarding the camp walls, not a single thing of note had happened. According to Androsthenes, the enemy – the Akhaians under Nikostratos – had been nowhere to be seen for many days. 'They'll be skulking close to their own borders,' Androsthenes declared. 'Just as the cowards always do when they know we're abroad.'

Empedokles was patrolling the section of rampart next to Andriskos. The moment he realised that the pair were to be allowed down to the river, he began to whinge. 'It's favouritism, plain and simple.'

'Shut it,' growled Andriskos. 'Simonides isn't like that, and you know it. When we get back, he'll let you and one other go as well, or I'm no judge.'

Empedokles subsided briefly, but they could hear him grumbling still as they walked through the 'gate', which was nothing more than an overshoot of the walls on both sides, creating a 'tunnelled' entrance. 'Don't take too long,' he called.

Andriskos didn't answer.

Without looking back, Demetrios made an obscene gesture over his shoulder, and for the thousandth time, wished that Empedokles had died instead of Kimon and Antileon. Give me the right opportunity, Zeus, he thought, and I'll slip a blade into the bastard.

They set down their shields by the river's edge. The water was even more refreshing than Demetrios had imagined. More sedate than at its origin in the mountains to the south, it was warm from the sun's heat at the surface, yet deliciously cool beneath. Wading in to his thighs, uncaring of his already soaking chiton, Demetrios longed to shed his bronze corslet and dive in.

'Should we strip off? Just for a moment,' he said to Andriskos.

'Better not.'

Demetrios wavered. Andriskos would not report him to Simonides, but if something happened . . . 'Curse it all, a quick dip won't matter,' he said, reaching for the first buckle on the side of his breastplate.

'Demetrios,' said Andriskos.

Something in his friend's tone stilled Demetrios' fingers. He looked up. Perhaps eight stadia away on the other side of the Nemea, a dust cloud announced the imminent arrival of a body of men. His heart gave a nervous little jump. Like as not, it was Androsthenes or one of the other columns, but until they came closer, that couldn't be determined with absolute accuracy.

'Fill your skin.' Andriskos' tone was brisk.

Demetrios didn't need telling twice. No soldier, least of all a phalangist without his sarissa, wanted to be caught in the open.

Water dripping from their armour, they waded ashore to their shields, casting frequent glances at the approaching troops. By the time they were halfway to the camp gate, there was still no indication whether they were friend or foe. At length, however, a sharp-eyed sentry cried, 'It's Androsthenes!'

'That was a little uncomfortable,' said Demetrios. They were close enough to the gate now to get inside before the column arrived – just.

'Aye. I wouldn't have wanted to have been any further from the wall.'

Their guard down, neither paid attention to the sentry's cry from the eastern wall, opposite the one outside which they stood.

It rang out again – the sentry's words weren't clear, but his tone was high-pitched. Demetrios saw men atop the rampart near them turning to peer across the camp.

Another sentry took up the cry, and a third, and suddenly their message was clear. 'Enemy! Enemy in sight!'

Demetrios and Andriskos broke into a run, full water skins and aspides slapping off their backs. Reaching the walkway, they joined Simonides and Empedokles.

'What can you see?' demanded Andriskos.

'Nothing but dust,' came Empedokles' sour reply.

Demetrios raised a hand to shield his eyes, and peered over the jumble of tents to the east wall. Right enough, all he could make out was a line of sentries, most of whom were gesticulating or pointing into the distance, where a telltale dust trail marked the passage of men.

'What are the enemy doing to our east?' asked Demetrios, disquieted, because that way lay their path to the Akrokorinth and safety. 'Aren't they supposed to be to the west, towards Akhaia?'

'Aye,' said Andriskos dourly. 'So Androsthenes maintained.'

'Androsthenes.' Simonides could pack a lot of contempt into one word. 'He'll have some explaining to do when this is over. Assemble your sarissae, brothers.' He shrugged at their surprised looks. 'You never know.'

Stephanos and the other commanders were of the same mind. Androsthenes' column had barely entered the camp when an order was issued to the entire chiliarchy to prepare themselves for battle. The speirai began to gather file by file in the space between its tents and the west wall. Atop the rampart, Demetrios and the other sentries were ready.

A short time passed as Androsthenes and a swarm of his officers, among them the chiliarch and commanders of light infantry and cavalry, went to stand on the east wall. More arms were pointed. From the loud voices carrying through the still, hot air, not everyone was in agreement. The argument was in full flow when Demetrios happened to glance over his shoulder, across the Nemea.

'Shit,' he said. 'Simonides.'

The file-leader's expression grew even grimmer as he too saw the long lines of dust smearing the sky from north to south. 'Those are too large to be made by just our men. They're being pursued by the enemy, or I'm a Greek.'

This raised a chuckle – Simonides was fiercely Macedonian, as they all were – but it soon died away. The enemy was on two sides of the camp now, east and west.

Not one to panic, Simonides sent word to Androsthenes.

The situation was turning dangerous, thought Demetrios unhappily. He eyed Andriskos and Simonides, and asked, 'What will he do?'

'If the fool . . .' Simonides lowered his voice and continued 'If the fool had made sure the ditch was dug properly, we could have stayed put and thumbed our noses at the bastards. As it is, we have little choice but to march out and fight.'

Demetrios peered over the rampart. The sections constructed by the four speirai were deep and steeply angled, creating a serious obstacle for any attackers, but where other units had worked, and forming most of the defences, it was woefully inadequate. His anger flared. 'Why didn't Androsthenes order them to do it better?'

'The arrogant fool didn't think it was necessary,' growled Simonides. 'Let's hope his overconfidence doesn't cost us dear.'

Upon finding no resistance before the east gate, the enemy force – more than two thousand cavalry and infantry – swept around the camp and over the River Nemea, disappearing into the countryside. It was safe to assume, said Simonides, that their leaders hoped to be the anvil upon which one or both of Androsthenes' raiding parties were crushed. The hammer would be their Akhaian comrades who were, it seemed likely, in vigorous pursuit of the raiding parties.

Hoping to prevent a massacre, Androsthenes emptied the camp. Assembling on the bank of the Nemea in a long line and facing west-ward, with the speira of phalangists in the centre, his troops waited with increasing nervousness for their comrades and the enemy to return.

Time dragged. The sun beat down, strong as ever despite the waning day. Insects swarmed low over the river. Fish jumped to catch them, and dropped back into the water with disconcerting plashes. Dust clouds over the hills and farmland hid what was happening from sight. At length, faint sounds were audible: shouts, the ring of weapons, hoof beats. Gradually, they grew louder.

Thanks to the chiliarch's insistence – the phalangists had heard him remonstrating with Androsthenes – there were a couple of hundred light infantry on both sides of the speira. Demetrios was relieved to have Thracians on his flank – the right – rather than the Illyrians, who looked to be a shifty, ill-disciplined rabble. Beyond the infantry were as much of Androsthenes' cavalry as had come back with him, about four hundred riders split between the two wings. Demetrios had spotted a grinning Perseus with Androsthenes. The prince was about to have his wish granted.

Whether their numbers would be enough to win, no one could be sure, because they were blind to the enemy's strength, and to the state of their retreating comrades. Everyone knew it, no one liked it, and the muttered conversations among the phalangists focused on this one topic and nothing else.

Well-disciplined, however, and mostly veterans, the phalangists' lines remained solid. Demetrios wished he could say the same of the Thracians. Even as the pounding of hooves announced the arrival of what everyone hoped would be some of their own cavalry, the tribesmen's ranks wavered. The gods only knew what the Illyrians were doing on the left flank.

Out of the dust clouds on the other side of the river burst a confusion of horses and riders. Not Androsthenes' cavalry or those of the Akhaian Nikostratos, but a mixture of the two, locked in a running battle.

Stephanos didn't wait for the chiliarch's order. 'Front five, lower pikes!' he shouted.

Down came the sarissae, forming an impenetrable, bristling wall that no one, man or beast, would want to attack. All along the phalangists' front it happened, smooth as falling rain.

Demetrios had a good view from his position in the file. Worryingly, the fight was going the Akhaians' way; in fact the Korinthian cavalry seemed to be holding their own nowhere. Already no more than a disorganised mob, they were riding for their lives, pursued by the enemy like so many sheep with wolves on their heels. Spears flashed, men fell from their mounts. Swords rose and fell, and men screamed. Anyone who turned to fight was enveloped by a wave of Akhaians.

Cries of alarm rose from the Thracians to the right of the speira.

'Hold your line, curse you!' shouted Simonides. 'Horses won't charge over a river at a well-formed line of troops.'

If the Thracians heard, they didn't understand. By the time the wheeling mass of horses and riders had spilled down to the river's edge, any semblance of order in the allied tribesmen's ranks had vanished. Frightened voices argued with one another. Chieftains shouted in vain to restore calm. The foolhardy lobbed their spears over the Nemea at the approaching riders, uncaring that they might hit friend instead of foe.

Demetrios peered over his shoulder; he could see a few Thracians at the back already slinking away. His guts did a neat roll. Continue like this, and the fight would develop into a second Kynoskephalae.

Demetrios' eyes swivelled again to the front. It was hard to see amid the dust and the whirling, galloping confusion of fighting cavalry, but here and there, he spotted men on foot approaching. Without helmets, carrying shields and spears, they were Akhaian light infantry, and well capable of tackling the Illyrians or the Thracians.

'Steady, curse you,' shouted Simonides, again aiming his words at the Thracians.

Demetrios doubted that any tribesmen heard; he could hope only that the chiliarchy's solidity gave them courage. His wish came partly true. About half the Thracians stood their ground, but the rest began to withdraw. Just then, rather than wait until the confusion of Korinthian and Akhaian horsemen had inevitably swept along the far bank, or over the Nemea and around the lines of infantry, Androsthenes ordered his riders to advance. Whether he thought to turn the tide of the cavalry clash, or was trying to move forward to engage the Akhaian infantry, Demetrios had no idea, but he liked it as little as the Thracians' cowardice.

The tactic was a disaster.

Straight after fording the river, Androsthenes' riders were swallowed up by the enormous mass of horsemen. A great tide of beasts and men, it moved off to the right, revealing massed lines of Akhaians – the infantry Demetrios had seen approaching.

'Where are the foot soldiers who were with our cavalry?' asked Empedokles.

'Not here,' grated Simonides.

Scattered to the four winds, like as not, thought Demetrios, concern gnawing his guts.

'More Thracians are abandoning their positions, sir,' said Andriskos.

Unease rippled through the ranks.

Stephanos noticed. 'The phalanx does not break and run!' he bellowed. 'MA-CE-DON!'

Even as Demetrios repeated the cry, he thought, this is going to be bad.

Really bad.

For perhaps an hour, with almost all of their comrades fled from the field, the phalangists held their own against overwhelming enemy numbers. Their flanks defended by small numbers of the bravest Illyrians and Thracians, they broke charge after Akhaian charge. Mounds

261

of dead and dying littered the ground in front of the deadly-bladed sarissae. They lay in the red-watered shallows on their fronts, and on their backs, staring at the sky.

The Akhaian general Nikostratos, who had come to direct his troops, learned from his mistakes. After a time, he directed his men's attacks on the phalangists' flanks. Whittled down to a couple of score warriors, the Illyrians broke. Discarding their shields, they ran for the perceived safety of the fort. Rather than press home his advantage, Nikostratos next sent soldiers against the right flank of the chiliarchy – Demetrios' side. The last Thracians, brave men all, held on longer than anyone should have in such brutal circumstances, but in the end, the few survivors were also routed. The entire chiliarchy now had no one to defend its flanks.

In good order, the Akhaian infantry near Demetrios re-formed. Runners moved between the phalangists' left and right, no doubt preparing the enemy on both sides for a joint attack.

'We're on our own,' said Andriskos in a calm voice. 'It's only a matter of time. On my order, we retreat.'

Men began to pray. Some chanted the Paean. A few cursed, but no one broke ranks. Not a single man.

Demetrios had never been prouder to be a phalangist. An odd peace descended over him. It would have been wiser to stay an oarsman, he thought, or to have taken his pay from his time on the ships and returned to the hills of his childhood. As a shepherd, he could have escaped a slaughter like this or Kynoskephalae. But then, he thought, he wouldn't have had Andriskos' solid shape in front of him, and before him, Simonides. Empedokles was also in front of him, it was true, but even he could not change Demetrios' certainty that this was where he wanted to be. The phalanx had given him everything. Comradeship. Pride. Brave, dear friends. Philippos. Kimon. Antileon. They were gone, but Simonides and Andriskos were not.

Better to die with them than never to have been part of the file, Demetrios decided.

'On my command,' cried Stephanos, voice cracking with the effort. 'Walk back ten steps. Slow and easy, and we can reach the camp. Retreat!'

They had gone perhaps five paces when the enemy charged.

*

Shame lashed Demetrios as he ran. His sarissa was gone, left behind on the banks of the Nemea. He still had his aspis, and his scabbarded kopis yet bounced off his left hip. Beside him, Andriskos had his shield and sword too, but most of the wild-eyed men around them – their own comrades – were unarmed. The camp, abandoned before they had even reached it, was a long way to their rear, but the howls and whooping cries of the enemy were a good deal closer. Their only hope was reaching the Akrokorinth, and that, thought Demetrios, didn't seem at all likely.

'Where's Simonides?' he panted at Andriskos. The same question he'd wanted to ask since their file-leader had told them to run.

'I don't know.'

Demetrios wanted to suggest that they look for him, but to do that was a death sentence, and from Andriskos' grim tone, he thought the same. There was no sign of Empedokles either, not that Demetrios would have searched for him. Seeking Perseus was a different matter, but to do that would be even madder. Demetrios told himself that on a horse, the prince had a greater chance of surviving.

He almost believed it.

They ran.

Stitch in his side, mouth drier than desert sand, Demetrios ran.

Leaping over the bodies of the injured, pretending not to see those who'd merely turned an ankle, Demetrios ran.

Up a low incline, through thickets of holm oaks and cork oaks, brambles whipping at his face, Demetrios ran.

'Stop.'

Demetrios ran.

'Demetrios!'

Andriskos' voice penetrated his tunnel vision. Demetrios slowed, chest moving in and out like a smith's bellows, and halted. Andriskos, already ten paces behind, gestured to their rear. 'The Akhaians have given up,' he said. 'Rest. Drink some water. We'll go on in a bit.'

'Aye.' They had survived, thought Demetrios grimly, but it seemed they were the only men in their file to have done so.

What future lay in store for them, he did not know, nor at that moment did he care.

CHAPTER XXVII

Near Gonnus

The moon had not yet risen over Flamininus' camp. Overhead the sky glittered with thousands of stars. Low down on the western horizon, Venus burned white-yellow. Home to more than fifteen thousand men, the encampment covered a vast area. The usual rectangular shape, it was surrounded by a double ditch; spiked branches decorated the ramparts. No such defences surrounded the camp of Flamininus' Greek allies, which lay alongside. It was not their habit, and he had more to do than insist they copy his troops.

Chaotic, Felix thought. That's the word for it. He was on his own, and heading towards the confusion of Greek tents and horse lines. A notion had taken him to go for a walk, and he needed to get out of the Roman camp. Wandering on his own into the allied encampment was far from wise, but he didn't care. Antonius' death was weighing heavily on him, and he needed some solitude. There had never been any privacy in the cheek-by-jowl existence Felix shared with his comrades, and now that he was an optio, men sought him out at every turn. It was a relief to leave the principes behind for a time; his new centurion, a man by the name of Falto, had been content with Felix's report that all was well with the men.

Until his promotion straight after Cynoscephalae, Falto had been a senior centurion of hastati. Granite-hard, the recipient of multiple awards for valour, he seemed tough but fair. He was certainly no Matho or Bulbus, and he appeared to think his new optio was performing his role adequately. More than that, Felix had decided, he could not ask. Time would tell if Falto really was a good centurion.

Antonius would have liked him too, Felix decided. Instantly, his grief returned, raw, stinging, and laced with shame. Why hadn't he seen the phalangist before the sarissa thrust? Felix asked himself the unanswerable question scores of times every day. When he slept, which wasn't often, he sometimes dreamed of hacking at the pike's shaft, leaving the phalangist with a splintered stump and his brother hale and unharmed behind him. At other times, he relived the horror of seeing the sarissa pithing Antonius through the throat. Sometimes Ingenuus, the comrade he'd stamped to death, joined his brother. Staring one-eyed in terror at Felix, he wailed as the hobnails came down.

Returning exhausted and red-eyed to reality was a torture that repeated itself most mornings.

'I wish it had been me, 'Tonius,' Felix muttered. 'I'm sorry.'

A fierce desire to drink himself into oblivion swept Felix, but he held it at bay. He had got pissed a few times since the battle, but the pounding head and the concern that Falto might notice was poor recompense for the few hours' relief it granted. It was pointless, Felix concluded, to become an optio only to throw the promotion away through poor performance. What had happened to him as tesserarius must not happen again. His new rank provided him with a reason to go on. To get through each day.

He might make centurion in the end, Felix thought. If someone didn't denounce him for illegally re-enlisting, that was. Antonius would have made a better centurion anyway, Felix decided. He could picture his brother, handsome and proud in his transverse-crested helmet. Fresh sorrow battered him. Antonius had died a humble princeps, without even an award for bravery to his name, let alone an officer's rank. He lay now in a simple grave near Cynoscephalae, alongside hundreds of others.

With no stonemasons to hand, and the army ready to move within a day of the battle, a grieving Felix had only been able to pile stones over his brother's grave, and at its head place a simple piece of wood upon which he had carved Antonius' name. It troubled him that the marker would not last long, or might be dislodged. If that happened, Antonius' last place of rest would be lost for ever. Whenever the opportunity allowed, Felix had sworn to himself, he would pay for a tombstone and haul it by cart to Cynoscephalae. For that reason alone, he hoped the impending negotiations brought peace soon, and that the rest of the bastard Greeks accepted that Rome was their new master. Not until then would there be any hope of asking for leave.

Great Jupiter, let my brother's marker still be there when I return, Felix prayed. It's a small thing to ask.

Wrapped in misery, grieving for Antonius, Felix hadn't been paying attention to where his feet were taking him; looking around, he had not the slightest idea where in the Greek camp he was. Lines of tethered horses to his left told him there were cavalrymen nearby, but that wasn't much use – all their allies but the Cretans had horsemen.

There was nothing for it, he decided, but to ask for directions. Feeling wary – just because the Greeks fought with Rome didn't mean they were friendly – Felix walked towards a group of soldiers sitting around a large fire. More than twenty strong, they were sitting on the bare earth or on their cloaks. At least half were singing to the tune of a lyre being picked by a bearded man of about Felix's age. Cups of wine were being passed hand to hand. A lot of men were flicking wine at their neighbours, laughing uproariously if they got an angry reaction.

Absorbed with their own merriment, no one noticed him approach. He stood at the edge of the circle, feeling a little foolish, and wondering whether he should cough or interrupt one of the conversations.

It was the man with the lyre who saw him. He stopped playing, at which the singers protested. The lyre player jerked his head in Felix's direction, and the singers fell silent. Seeing their reaction, other men's heads turned. The hum of voices died away. Now everyone was staring, and few, if any, expressions were welcoming.

Felix made a conscious effort not to let his fingers drift to his dagger, the only weapon he had. 'Greetings,' he said in Greek to the lyre player.

'You're Roman.'

There had been no humour in the statement, but Felix smiled anyway, and joked, 'Aye. There are quite a lot of us just over there.' He jerked a thumb in what he hoped was the direction of the legions' camp.

The lyre player raised an eyebrow and pointed the opposite way. 'That'll be where you find your encampment.'

Embarrassed, wishing he wasn't on his own, Felix muttered, 'My thanks.'

'We don't get many of your kind round here,' said a broad-shouldered man whose biceps were almost as big as Felix's thighs. 'You must be lost.'

Felix considered lying, but it was clear he had gone astray, so he smiled again, and said, 'I am. Wasn't looking where I was going.'

The comments that met his remark, Felix didn't understand, but the ribald laughter that came after had an unpleasant timbre. Nodding his gratitude at the lyre player, he said, 'I'll be on my way. Goodnight.'

'Aren't you going to thank us first?' asked Broad Shoulders.

'I already thanked your friend,' said Felix, indicating the lyre player.

'Not for the directions. For the victory at Kynoskephalae.'

Felix stared, disbelieving.

'It was we Aitolians who won the battle for you.' Broad Shoulders glanced around the fire as his comrades muttered their agreement, and then back at Felix. 'Without our cavalry, the first skirmishes would have been entirely lost. If that had happened, the battle would have taken a different course altogether.'

'That's not to say that the Macedonians would have won,' replied Felix, his pride stinging. He'd heard how the Aetolians were taking the credit for Cynoscephalae, but hadn't experienced it first-hand. 'Besides, it was the legions' – men like me and my brother, he wanted to shout – 'who broke the phalanx.' You and all your friends couldn't have done that, he nearly added.

'You're a typical nose-in-the-air barbarian,' growled Big Shoulders, cracking his knuckles. 'Never happy to give credit where credit's due.'

'If the rumours are true, his general Flamininus will leave that dog Philip on the throne,' said another man.

'Ha!' A third voice joined in from across the fire. 'He'll let the Macedonian bastard keep the Fetters too, despite his promise to see them delivered into Greek hands.'

Many Aetolian faces were now downright hostile. Linger, Felix decided, and he risked a beating. 'My thanks,' he called to the lyre player, and turned on his heel. He didn't run – pride wouldn't let him – but he walked fast. Although it would show he was nervous, Felix couldn't help glancing over his shoulder at twenty-five paces. To his dismay, Broad Shoulders was staring after him. Several others had got to their feet.

Felix wanted to take to his heels, but like a cat with its prey, that was more likely to make the Aetolians give chase. He could think of only one thing to do. An opening appeared on his right, a gap between lines of tents. He took it, breaking into a loping run. A short distance in, he turned left, and soon after that, right and left. Then he stopped to listen.

From close by, the low mutter of men in their blankets. The crackle as a new piece of wood was added to a fire. Further off, voices raised in song. Right beside him, from a tent, a loud, rippling fart. Soon after, a chorus of indignant protests, and the laughter of the unrepentant farter.

Felix began to relax.

'Where's the barbarian gone?' The man was some distance off.

The hairs on Felix's arms prickled. The 'barbarian' could only mean him. Inching between two tents, he crouched and knelt. With no fires near, the only light came from the stars. To find him here, he decided, the Aetolians would need gods-gifted eyesight.

His ploy was a good one. Little by little, the man who'd called 'barbarian' moved further away, his position marked by regular shouts. One of his companions came close to Felix – no more than a tent length – padding slow and careful, and stopping every few paces to listen. Felix froze, hardly breathing, staring at the ground for fear the whites of his eyes would betray him. To his overwhelming relief, after what seemed an eternity, the man moved on.

Not ten heartbeats later, Felix's nostrils were assailed by the foulest odour he'd smelt since coming across the rotting carcase of a boar that had been in the sun for days. The farter, he thought. Of all places, I had to kneel down beside the fucking farter. As complaints from the man's comrades erupted, Felix risked getting to his feet. Breathing through an open mouth, the better not to smell the revolting miasma, he edged to the gap between this line of tents and the next, and peered up and down. Pleased to see no one at all, he came to the maddening conclusion that, for the second time that night, he was lost.

His situation was so ridiculous that Felix grinned. Antonius would laugh at him now, he decided.

What to do? he wondered. Asking directions was not something to repeat, given his last experience. Judging that if he found a larger 'avenue' – even the Greeks had those – he could find their camp's centre, and from there work his way back out again, he began searching for something approaching that description.

Fortuna had helped him to escape the Aetolians, but she was in no mood to offer her aid again. Up and down he scouted, left and right, for scores of paces in every direction. Finding what appeared to be a main 'road', Felix followed that for a time only to reach a dead end. Frustrated with the incompetent Greeks, he stopped to calm himself.

Lose his temper, and he would draw attention of the wrong kind.

'Jupiter, was that a turd I just stepped in?' The voice spoke in Latin, and dripped with disdain. 'Have the Greeks never heard of a latrine trench?'

Felix couldn't believe it. He wasn't the only Roman abroad in the allies' camp. Peering into the darkness, he made out a pair of figures in the next 'avenue' over. One tall and stoop-shouldered, the other lithe and slight of build.

'Smells like it, master.' The second voice had an accent – no Latin native speaker, this. 'Hold onto my shoulder. I have a rag to clean it.'

Felix crept closer, along the length of the tent that separated him from the two men, until he could have reached around the corner of the canvas and touched them.

'Stop!' The first voice was used to command. 'You've got some of it on my toes.'

'Sorry, master.'

'Leave it. We need light, and a bowl of water. It can wait until we return to the camp. The meeting is more important. Lead on, Benjamin.'

'Yes, master.'

Felix's curiosity reached a new level. He vaguely recognised the first voice, but he couldn't place it. A meeting at this late hour was most odd, he decided. Anyone honest would arrange such a thing in day-light. Deciding to find out what he could, Felix waited until the pair had almost been lost in the gloom before stealing after them. The area where he thought the shit might be, he gave a wide berth. Cat-soft on his feet, still watching for signs of the Aetolians who'd come after him as well as other soldiers, Felix reached a larger way, and from there continued towards what seemed to be the centre of the Greek allies' camp. Now and again, he had to pass men who were still out and about. Drunk for the most part, arm in arm and often singing, they paid him little heed. When one called a greeting, Felix merely grunted in reply and walked on.

A wink of light ahead, perhaps fifty paces, made him pause. Stand-ing close beside a tent so he wasn't profiled in the open space of the 'avenue', Felix stared. Another glitter, and understanding sank in. He was looking at a sentry, and the winks were caused by the reflection of light from a nearby fire on the man's helmet each time he turned his head. A moment later, and a soft challenge was issued. The pair he was following approached. Soft words were spoken in reply, and the sentry lifted the tent flap for the two to pass inside.

The danger had increased severalfold – there could easily be more than one sentry – but he could not hold himself back. Stealing between the tents to his right, he worked his way towards the structure that his quarry had entered. This turned out to be a large pavilion, and Felix decided that it must belong to a senior officer or leader. A distance of twenty paces separated it from the nearest tents, which made approaching it dangerous, but he could spy no sentries down the side, or at the back. Concluding that the guard he had seen at the front was alone, Felix tiptoed closer.

The murmur of voices was audible from within the pavilion. Creeping along the side to the point he judged was closest, Felix placed his ear against the leather. He struggled to make sense of what he was hearing, realising then that the men inside were speaking in Greek. Frustration lashed Felix. His Greek vocabulary was limited, rich only in curses and words like 'wine', 'grain' and 'sheep' – things he'd taken by force from farmers during the campaign in Thessaly. He listened in again, and was pleased to make out the words 'Aetolia', 'Flamininus' and 'Philip'.

Now Felix felt real concern. The Roman – whoever he was – was up to no good. There could be few other reasons for meeting an Aetolian leader in the dead of night. Desperate to hear more, that he might find out enough to tell Falto or perhaps someone more senior, Felix pricked his ears again. He had no luck. The conversation within continued, but in such low tones that he could only make out an occasional Greek word. He would find out nothing here, Felix decided. Discovering the Roman's identity, however, would prove more useful, and that might be done by trailing the tall figure and his slave back to the camp.

A tiny sound behind him – perhaps the gentle scuff of a sandal in the dirt – sounded an alarm in Felix's head. He ducked, and the hand that would have seized him round the neck in a chokehold caught nothing more than air. Spinning to his right, away from the tent, Felix scrabbled for his dagger.

His assailant was on him in a heartbeat, a blade already in his right hand.

The man said something in Greek, drawing his weapon from left to right in a motion that, had it connected, would have sent Felix's guts spilling everywhere.

This was the Roman's slave, Benjamin, thought Felix.

'Who are you?' The question came first in Greek, and was repeated in Latin.

Felix didn't answer. He shot a look behind him in case Benjamin had companions, but could see no one. I'm not running, Felix thought. How good could a slave be with a blade?

As it happened, expert. Only Felix's military training and years of combat experience prevented him dying in the next few moments. Benjamin used his dagger with fearsome skill; Felix soon had a shallow cut to his left arm, and a rent in his tunic, and was lucky not to have suffered worse. Doing little more than keeping the slave at bay, he realised that Benjamin was herding him towards the avenue that opened close to the tent where his master was meeting with the Aetolians. Once they were in the open, the sentry would see them; then he'd have two enemies to deal with.

Felix threw a handful of dirt at Benjamin's face, but the slave twisted his head to the side before it landed. He feinted one way and then another, tried a combination of kicks as well as thrusts with his dagger. They came to nothing, while *he* suffered another gash, this time on one cheek. Felix had a sick feeling in his belly. He was being toyed with, like a cat plays with a mouse.

Time to flee, thought Felix. His pride stung at the idea of running from a slave, but better that than a needless death. Each time he withdrew a few steps, Benjamin matched his pace – if he turned and ran now, the slave would simply stab him in the back. Running out of ideas, Felix launched another desperate attack. It failed, and he managed not to take another wound, but all he'd bought was a few heartbeats' grace. Benjamin closed in again, blade slicing the air, and Felix retreated.

Real fear bubbled up his throat. This is it, he thought. I'm dead.

Ten steps behind Benjamin, someone undid the tent flap and stepped outside.

Felix saw; Benjamin only heard. The slave's head whipped around, and back to Felix, and he redoubled his onslaught.

A voice cried a challenge in Greek.

Somehow Felix parried Benjamin's first thrust. He aimed his left fist at Benjamin's head, at the same time whipping his knife towards the slave's belly. Benjamin blocked the punch with frightening ease, while his left hand seized Felix's right wrist in a vice-like grip. Try as he might, Felix could not break free. Nor, incredibly, did he have the strength to thrust his blade into Benjamin. Grabbing hold of the slave's right arm, Felix was also struggling to prevent himself being stabbed. Face to face, hot breath mingling, they grappled. Felix tried a leg sweep, and failed. Benjamin did the same to him, and almost succeeded.

The slave's blade inched closer to Felix's neck.

Another demand. The Greek voice, angry now, was right behind Benjamin.

'Help,' cried Felix in Greek. 'Help!'

Fortuna smiled.

The Greek soldier seized Benjamin by the shoulder, saying something like 'fighting not allowed'.

Benjamin snarled a warning. He and Felix continued to struggle.

'He . . . try . . . kill me,' said Felix in mangled Greek. 'Help!'

'Stop,' demanded the soldier, tightening his grip.

Spinning like a dancer, Benjamin buried his blade in the unfortunate man's throat.

Aware that this was his only chance – Benjamin had had to let go of his wrist to turn – Felix leaned forward and stabbed the slave in the back, under the ribcage.

Benjamin staggered; the soldier he'd knifed dropped like a sack of grain. Benjamin began to twist, his face screwed up in a rictus of pain and fury.

Terrified, aware that the wound he'd inflicted wasn't immediately fatal, Felix lunged forward and stuck Benjamin twice more, wherever the blade went in. The slave still had enough strength to continue turning and slice his dagger at Felix, but already weakened, his aim was poor. Felix took a step closer and raked his sandal down the front of Benjamin's left shin. The pain caused by the hobnails – as well as his wounds – made the slave stagger.

Felix punched him in the face, and as he reeled, stabbed him in the guts.

Mouth working, still trying to reach Felix with his blade, Benjamin went down at last.

Men were coming out of the same tent that the dying soldier had emerged from. Voices carried from further afield.

Felix wasn't out of danger, that much was clear. Benjamin's attack, sanctioned no doubt by his master, meant that whoever the Roman was meeting in the pavilion would also have an interest in seeing him dead.

Felix took to his heels and ran.

Finding out what was going on was not worth losing his life.

CHAPTER XXVIII

Tempe, on the Macedonian border

Flamininus brushed the crumbs from his lips. Rising from his breakfast table, he looked with regret at the three honey pastries remaining. One didn't seem enough, but a discreet pat of his noticeably slimmer midriff reminded him that abstemiousness paid off. That and being at war, he thought with amusement. During the marching and countermarching against Philip in the lead-up to Cynoscephalae, there hadn't been time for his cook to prepare such delicacies each and every morning. Flatbread and wine are sufficient at times like that, thought Flamininus. Just as they are for my men.

When the histories of this glorious campaign were written, as he would ensure they were, much would be made of his willingness to share the hardships endured by his soldiers. This would allow comparison to Alexander, with whom Flamininus had always wanted to be compared. As the conqueror of Macedonia, and its king who styled himself after Alexander, it could be suggested that he, Flamininus, was in fact superior to Alexander. The grounds for this were tenuous – he had not marched halfway across the world for eight years, defeating every army in his path – but the average citizen of Rome didn't know that.

Yes, Flamininus decided, I shall have placards displayed during my triumphal march declaring me greater than Alexander. He summoned Potitius. Best to have such a gem written down, lest he forget it due to the burdens of his workload.

He spotted the sly lick of the lips as Potitius entered, but chose to ignore it. His slave had grown better at hiding his revolting habit, and that would do. So many things were going Flamininus' way that he was willing to let some things slip by without comment. Although the prospect of a conference with his Greek allies later was tiresome, he would see to it that they knew their place. The next day, he was to meet

Philip to discuss peace. Any progress made would be on *his* terms: the Macedonian king was in no position to argue. With his army shattered, driven back into his own kingdom, he was almost a spent force.

Not quite spent, thought Flamininus, and that is good. For each obstacle crossed, there is always another that presents itself. His mind turned to the Seleucid emperor Antiochus; according to the reports, he was sailing a large fleet up the coast of Asia Minor. Despite the agreements given to Roman emissaries more than two years before, his gaze would surely turn westward next, to Macedonia and Greece. Leave Philip on his throne, Flamininus had decided, and Rome would have a buffer against the Seleucid threat.

Irritation pricked him. This reality, this *need* to be prepared for an invasion by Antiochus, was something the Aetolians could not see, did not understand. Their role at Cynoscephalae had gone to their heads. The previous night one of Flamininus' spies had repeated for him a poem by the Messenian poet Alcaeus; apparently it was doing the round of his allies' camp. While clearly designed to annoy Philip, it praised the Romans *after* the Aetolians.

The cursed Aetolians were behind it, Flamininus decided with mounting anger. It was they who must have sent word to Alcaeus. How else could word of Cynoscephalae have reached Messenia on the Peloponnese, a poem be written, and it come all the way back to Thessaly? The battle had taken place less than a month before. The Aetolians' position would have to be made brutally clear, he decided, his fury bubbling like a pot left too long on the fire; the imminent meeting with his allies was as good a time and place as any. Flamininus was reminded again of Alexander the Great, once asked how he controlled the Greeks. 'By putting off nothing that ought to be done today until tomorrow,' came the answer.

I shall act as Alexander would have, thought Flamininus. As I so often do.

Not long after, his Greek allies began to arrive at his command tent. Following Flamininus' orders, they were ushered inside by staff officers to the partitioned chamber where meetings were held. Unaware that the senior Roman commanders would not arrive for more than an hour, they were offered wine and left to wait. Importantly, the wine was undiluted, which the Greeks would not be used to. Potitius came and went, his slave presence unnoticed by the guests, each time telling Flamininus what he'd seen.

By the time the wine-bearing servants had been around the room with a fourth top-up, Flamininus was in place. There was no chance of his eavesdropping in the allies' respective parts of the camp, and Potitius could not linger too close without being obvious, yet by positioning himself in the right place, Flamininus could listen in with ease. This was a fine opportunity to learn his allies' minds, if Fortuna was kind and the wine did its job. Wearing only a belted tunic and in his bare feet, Flamininus padded to a quiet antechamber and stood – guided by a pointing Potitius – not half a dozen paces from where most of the Greeks had gathered. Only tent leather separated them.

Flamininus nodded, and motioned to the scribe to leave. Potitius licked his lips, and to Flamininus' surprise, it didn't matter. 'You did well,' he mouthed. 'Go.'

With a sickly expression – no doubt unsure why his master wasn't angered by his lip-licking – Potitius retreated.

Flamininus began to listen with all his might.

'Not bad wine, eh?' Amynander's jovial tone. 'I'd wager it could be from Athamania.'

'You would say that.' An acerbic voice – one of the Cretans. 'Give you a row of unmarked wines from all over Greece, and you couldn't differentiate one from the other.'

'Apart from the Kretan varieties, that is, because everyone knows they taste like donkey piss!' said Phaeneas.

Amid the roars of amusement that followed, Flamininus felt sure the Cretan was looking daggers at Phaeneas. He would not care, for Aetolia had always been a greater power than Crete; its six thousand plus troops in Flamininus' army made the Cretans' five hundred seem insignificant.

Phaeneas was arrogant, but not a complete fool. Into the dying laughter, he said, 'Your pardon, friend. I made a joke, to lighten the mood. There are some excellent wines from your island, I know, and some awful ones from Aitolia.'

The Cretan muttered something that Flamininus couldn't make out, but seemed mollified.

'When's he going to appear?' By his accent, this was one of the Apollonians.

'In his own good time,' said Amynander, ever the placatory one.

Phaeneas snorted; Flamininus was irritated to hear others do the same.

'Flamininus thinks he's so much better than us. Typical Roman, eh,' said Phaeneas. 'The arrogant bastard lets us wait here while his slaves buff his armour and polish his sandals one more time.'

'The wine is good, though,' said Amynander. 'And there's plenty of it.'

'D'you think he's heard the poem?' asked Phaeneas with a hint of a chuckle.

'I doubt it,' growled the Cretan. 'He wouldn't lower himself to be seen in our part of the camp, and I daresay he talks to no other Greeks than us.'

Little do you know, thought Flamininus with a smirk. My spies are everywhere. He pricked his ears as Phaeneas began to speak, voice pitched low in an attempt to be heard only by those near to him. Thankfully for Flamininus, the wine had done its work, and his words came out as a loud stage whisper.

> *'Naked and tombless see, O passer-by,*
> *The thirty thousand men of Thessaly,*
> *Slain by the Aetolians and the Latin band,*
> *That came with Titus from Italia's land:*
> *Alas for mighty Macedon! that day,*
> *Swift as a roe, king Philip fled away.'*

More laughter.

Flamininus' satisfaction at having spies among his allies soured faster than cream left in the sun. The indignity of being referred to by his first name – a discourtesy from anyone except family and close friends – was bad enough, but it stung worse than a dozen bee stings to know that up and down Greece, men were hearing that the Aetolians had won Cynoscephalae, not him. Flamininus had to hold in a shout of anger. He willed himself to be calm. Make a single sound, and as inebriated as they were, his allies might hear. That would not do, for when he cut the Aetolians down to size, he wanted them to suspect nothing. Their shock would be equalled only by his delight.

He listened on for a time, but heard little more that was new. It was amusing to listen to Alexander, another Aetolian, bitching about Flamininus' message to Philip after Cynoscephalae. 'He bade the king to be of good cheer. Good cheer, while Flamininus upbraided *us* for sacking the enemy camp,' Alexander cried, his tone as wine-fuelled as that of Phaeneas.

'He's being so friendly towards Philip it wouldn't surprise me if the Macedonian has bribed him,' sneered Phaeneas. 'Far away in Rome, the Senate would never know. Easy to see how it could happen, eh?'

Flamininus glared at the leather separating him from his allies as a chorus of indignant ayes followed. He had taken bribes before, during the war with Hannibal and after, his justification that a man needed wealth to help climb the political ladder. It irked, however, to be accused of it by a Greek, not least because in this instance the accusation wasn't true. Deciding that he had heard enough, that the uninvited Galba might put in an appearance and need to be ejected, he turned on his heel. A voice broke into song in the adjacent chamber, and Flamininus' pace picked up. The wine was taking more of an effect than he had wagered. The law needed to be laid down before any of his erstwhile allies became so emboldened that they refused to accept his demands.

Flamininus paused until one of his staff officers had silenced the rabble – it had not taken long to don his general's attire, but the assembled Greeks already sounded like the inhabitants of a tavern long after closing time – before he entered. His gaze raked the room, noting his allies' flushed faces and exaggerated gestures. More than one had telltale stains on his chiton, either from spillages or the annoying Greek tendency to flick wine at one another rather than a statue, as tradition dictated.

'You grace us with your presence, general.' Phaeneas' bow was so deep he almost fell over.

Flamininus pretended he hadn't seen. He threw a tight smile at the watching faces, and said, 'I trust your thirst has been quenched?'

Polite noises. Mumbled yeses. A gushing sentence from Amynander about the quality of the wine.

'To business then. Philip has arrived at Tempe. We meet him in the morn,' said Flamininus. 'It goes without saying that the peace terms must be established beforehand. Amynander, I would have your thoughts first.'

Amynander beamed to be picked first; Phaeneas and Alexander looked as if they'd both taken a bite of rancid meat. The Cretans grumbled to one another, as Cretans did; the Apollonians held their counsel.

Amynander, obsequious since Flamininus' humbling of him at Gomphi the previous year, asked that Athamania, ever possible prey to a stronger Macedon, not be left at Philip's mercy once the legions withdrew. More than that, he said with a fawning look at Flamininus, he would not ask. Rome should decide the Macedonian king's fate.

Alexander stood forth before Amynander had finished, and asked, 'May I speak next?'

Unsurprised, for the Aetolian's cheeks were flushed darker than most men's, Flamininus indicated he had no objection. Let the Aetolians make their play first, he thought. My countermove will be stronger for it.

'We thank you, Flamininus, for asking us all here to discuss the terms under which peace will be negotiated. It is well that our opinions continue to be of interest.' Alexander's eyes slid to Phaeneas, who nodded in approval.

The first barb, thought Flamininus, more amused than irritated. Now for the second.

'Make terms with Philip, and you will not secure peace for Rome or freedom for we Greeks,' Alexander declared. 'To keep your promises to us, and the agreement we made with the Senate, you must either depose Philip or see him slain.' A tiny smile twitched his lips as several men said none too quietly, 'Let it be the latter.' Alexander caught Flamininus' gaze, and a bullish look crept onto his face. 'Finish Philip now, when he is weak, and it will be easy. Hold back, and Philip *will* rise again. He *will* make war on Greece and Rome again.' He paused and then said loftily, 'To think otherwise is deluded.'

There was a ripple of concern among the least drunk of the allies.

Flamininus made no immediate reply. His eyes roved the room. Even your colleague thinks you go too far, Alexander, he thought, watching Phaeneas purse his lips. Flamininus let the silence drag on, enjoying the rising tension.

Prompted by a sharp jab in the ribs from Phaeneas, a now self-conscious Alexander asked, 'What say you, Flamininus?'

'Strange it is that your views on this matter should entirely change, Alexander and Phaeneas. In all our meetings before Cynoscephalae, you Aetolians were content that Philip should be defeated and forced into a peace settlement. There was no mention of deposing him, still less of regicide.' Flamininus had pitched his voice somewhere between surprised and disappointed. Now he adopted an explanatory tone, such as a teacher might use when explaining something to his pupils. 'We Romans have long-established customs when it comes to sparing those defeated in war. Think of the clemency granted to Hannibal and Carthage just a few years ago. In all the meetings I have had with Philip, his vacating the throne was never discussed. Not once. Are we now to go back on what was an implicit agreement for him to remain the king of Macedonia?'

The awkward question hung in the air.

Flamininus watched his allies. An island people, less affected by Philip than anyone else, the Cretans looked reluctant to argue. The Apollonian leader didn't seem happy, but given his lowly position compared to the Aetolians, was looking to them for guidance. Ignoring their fellow Greeks, Alexander and Phaeneas had bent their heads together.

'Of course not, Flamininus,' said Amynander, glancing to either side for support.

No one else spoke.

Flamininus' patience was wearing thin. It was time to lay down his authority. 'Well?' he snapped.

The Cretans took a sudden interest in fiddling with their belts. The Apollonian stared at the floor. Alexander's uneasy expression revealed that his wine-courage was fast dissipating. Phaeneas opened his mouth to speak.

Flamininus cut him off before he could say a word. 'One should confront an armed enemy with hostility, but when that foe is defeated, the victor with the greatest character – the greatest quality – is he who remains humane. You are not beasts, to rend and tear Philip limb from limb now that he is helpless – are you?' Before either of the shocked Aetolians could reply, he continued, 'You might think Philip a threat to Greece, but if he and his army were eliminated, your situation would grow dire indeed. It—'

'Leave Philip on the throne, and he will soon start another war with the Greeks,' cried Phaeneas.

'Enough of your blustering,' thundered Flamininus. He took

enormous satisfaction from Phaeneas' shocked – and welcome – silence. 'As I was saying, it is thanks to the kings of Macedonia that the savage tribes on its outer borders are held at bay. Think of the Thracians, Illyrians, and after them, Gauls, who could pour into Macedonia and Greece. Do not tear down a state, I warn you, and leave yourselves exposed to others more powerful and dangerous.' A few heads nodded, and neither Aetolian tried to interrupt again. They're listening, thought Flamininus, and realising that I am the master here, and they are the servants. Not wanting to alienate the Aetolians entirely – there was no need – he threw them a bone. 'Do not worry about Philip. So many conditions shall be placed upon him that he will be in no position to start a war.'

Content that his allies were accepting of his intentions – Flamininus cared not if they were unhappy – he brought proceedings to a close.

The two sides met the next morning at the opening to the Tempe pass, the king appearing with a party of noblemen and an escort of cavalry. Already present, Flamininus had with him Galba and the other legion commanders, his Greek allies and ten maniples of principes and triarii. Let Philip be insulted by the size of his escort if he so chose, Flamininus had decided. The victor sets the tone.

The king gave no sign of anything except pleasure at seeing Flamininus again, greeting him like a long-lost friend. It was an act, thought the general, but a well-played one. Philip was no fool – it was entirely possible that he knew of the acrimony between Flamininus and the Aetolians – so by making overtures of friendship to Rome, he was strengthening his position compared to his enemies the Aetolians. Catching Philip's sly look at Phaeneas as the talks began, Flamininus' opinion hardened. Good, he thought. If the king wishes to stand with Rome, so be it. The bulwark he can provide against Antiochus will do nicely.

Flamininus was unsurprised when Philip agreed to the terms he had laid down at their last meeting, and also the demands of their Greek allies. Nor was he surprised when Phaeneas leaped in at once, crying, 'So, Philip, are you returning to Aitolia Pharsalos, Phthian Thebes and the host of other towns you stole?'

'That was my intention,' said the king in an even tone.

Phaeneas turned in triumph to Alexander, and Flamininus said sharply, 'You may have none save Thebes. Because it was taken in war, I may bestow the city upon whomever I wish.'

'But the others were members of the Aitolian league! They were stolen by Macedon,' protested Phaeneas, with vigorous agreement from Alexander. 'The treaty with Rome granted that while you should have the goods taken in war, Aitolia would receive the towns taken.'

Flamininus said, chidingly, 'That detail was in the *first* treaty between our peoples, made fourteen years ago, an agreement which you annulled by making terms with Philip five years later.' The fact that Aetolia had sued for peace because of Rome's reluctance to help it was irrelevant. Relishing that the Aetolians could not protest this for fear of offence, Flamininus went on, 'Even if that treaty remained in place, you would not be entitled to those Thessalian towns. Having surrendered to the legions, they are under the protection of Rome, and under it they shall remain.'

Furious but powerless, Phaeneas and Alexander could do nothing but nod in agreement.

They had been shown their place and forced to sit in it, thought Flamininus. As would Philip, when the rest of the terms of the peace treaty were laid on him. To the king's credit, however, he did not bat an eye when Flamininus demanded an immediate indemnity of two hundred talents – an enormous sum – and the handing over of hostages as a gesture of good faith. Only when Flamininus made it clear that one of Philip's sons had to be included did the king's calm exterior falter.

'A son, you say?' Philip's tone was low and unhappy.

'Even so,' said Flamininus, noting the Aetolians' cruel smiles. Gods, how they hate Philip, he thought.

'I have but two, and Perseus is my heir.'

'He must stay behind then,' said Flamininus.

'Demetrios is eleven years old. A child.'

'He will be well cared for.'

'Swear it.' There was iron in Philip's voice now.

'Before Jupiter Maximus, Greatest and Best, I swear your son will be well looked after,' said Flamininus, meaning it. He did not make war on children. 'Demetrios shall be returned to you when it is evident you pose no threat to Greece or Rome.' He didn't need to add that the Senate would decide when that might be. A year. Five. More. Philip had no choice but to agree, thought Flamininus, feeling a little sorry for his former enemy.

'Very well,' said Philip, for the first time looking like a man defeated. Making his excuses, he left.

Flamininus had no time to savour his commanding performance. With the speed of a striking snake, Galba was by his side. 'Your coffers will soon be full,' he said, eyes glittering.

'Philip's coin belongs to the Senate. To Rome,' Flamininus protested.

Galba made a contemptuous noise. 'So says the law. Since when has that ever stopped a victorious general from helping himself?' Most commanders salted away a healthy portion of their war booty, and as long as they weren't too rapacious, any perceived shortfalls were overlooked by the Senate.

'Scipio took not a single *shekel* from Carthage after Zama.' This was true – much had been made of it in Rome – but Flamininus knew he was fighting a losing battle. He and Galba had made an agreement, and unless he wanted his name dragged through the mud and worse, it would have to be honoured. 'How much do you want?' he asked weakly.

'Autumn is around the corner, and you have paid me nothing this year. I can see no reason not to take the entire yearly amount.'

Flamininus could see no sign of Benjamin, of whom he was terrified, and with a sudden burst of courage thought, kill the bastard now and be rid of him at a stroke. Explaining away the death by his hand of a legate would be difficult to say the least, but it might be done. Flamininus set aside the impulsive idea with reluctance. Let the mind control one's actions, not the heart, he told himself.

'Well?'

'You shall have the money,' said Flamininus, feeling weary as a man after a hard day's toil in the sun. The sum – four thousand thousand denarii – would likely mean losing his entire 'share' of Philip's indemnity, but Galba would have been paid off until the following year. With the threat of Benjamin also removed for a time, the price suddenly became acceptable. Curiosity pricked Flamininus. 'Where is the Judaean?'

'As if you don't know,' hissed Galba.

Flamininus had no idea what his enemy was talking about, but an opportunity like this couldn't be passed up. With a derisory snort, he said as if he *did* know, 'You seem upset.'

'Know that what happened to Benjamin changes nothing,' said Galba in a tone sharp enough to cut flesh. 'I have a mind to increase the monies you owe me.'

Benjamin had been injured somehow, Flamininus thought. Perhaps he was even dead. Emboldened by this unexpected revelation, Flamininus said quietly, 'Do that, and I will see to it that *you* meet with an unhappy accident. Greece is a dangerous place, you know, even for a legate.'

'As it is for a general,' Galba shot back, but his usual venom was lacking. Rather than make another threat, he said, 'The coin is to be delivered within the hour of its arrival from Philip.'

Flamininus nodded. Good temper restored by Galba's backing down, he summoned Potitius as his enemy stalked from the tent. Every spy in his camp would have a new task by sunset. Find out what had happened to the Judaean, and the chink in Galba's armour he had just seen might be widened.

Do that, and his enemy might be brought down.

CHAPTER XXIX

Northern Macedonia

Spying a messenger riding in his direction along the side of the marching troops, Philip prepared himself for news. He was in his usual position, a third of the way along the column. Six thousand phalangists, the cream of the survivors from Kynoskephalae, and five hundred Companions accompanied him. They were four hundred stadia north of Pella, and nearing the border. Less than half a month had passed since the humiliation of Philip's meeting with Flamininus and the curs he called allies, when he'd accepted – rather than be forced to – the Roman general's terms. There had been no time to lick his wounds, so to speak, nor even to drown his sorrows. An hour after the king's return from Tempe, news had reached him of a Dardanian invasion.

'Barbarians,' said Philip to no one in particular. The Dardanians' opportunism was to be expected, but it remained infuriating. 'I'll teach the goat-humping filth a lesson they won't forget.'

Hearing, one of his staff officers grinned and said, 'We'll send them all to Tartaros, sire!'

Philip gave him a nod.

The messenger's news was predictable. Rather than wait for the king's arrival, the Dardanians were in full retreat from the remains of the town of Stobi. As ever with tribal incursions, he would have to give chase. The development changed Philip's intent not an iota; if anything, it sharpened his hunger. He could no longer hurt Flamininus or the Romans, nor even the gods-cursed Aitolians, but the Dardanians were a different matter. They would feel the full extent of his wrath, if it was the last thing he did. His only constraint was time. Crushing the invaders had to be done fast, or like the dogs that steal in to bite the tail end of a wild boar while their fellows are at its head, other enemies would strike at Macedon.

Thoughts of his foes reminded Philip of the Akrokorinth, and his mood darkened. 'Perseus,' he called.

His son, with the column, but still in disgrace, urged his horse forward from among the Companion cavalrymen he'd been keeping company. 'Father?'

Philip shot a sideways look at Perseus. By all accounts, the boy had done only a little fighting amid the slaughter at the Nemean Beck, yet he seemed older. Broader in the shoulder. There was a confidence in his posture when he thought Philip wasn't watching. He's almost a man, decided the king with pride, but he still needs to be reprimanded for disobeying me. Occupied first with meeting Flamininus and then preparing his army to march north, Philip had thus far had no opportunity to deal with his wayward son, fresh-arrived by sea with some phalangists who had also survived. Barking at Perseus that he should find a horse and some weapons and join the column, Philip had ignored him on the journey – until now.

'It was stupid what you did,' the king began.

'I know, Father. I—'

'Silence!'

Flushing, Perseus stitched his lip.

'It's bad enough to have lost almost the entire garrison of the Akrokorinth,' thundered Philip. 'If you had been slain as well, Demetrios would be my heir. Demetrios, eleven years old, who even now is being taken to Italia as a hostage. I would have no heir in Macedon. No heir!'

'I'm sorry, Father.' Perseus' face was full of remorse. 'I wasn't thinking.'

'No, you weren't!' He glared until Perseus' gaze fell away. 'You're a typical bloody fifteen-year-old,' Philip went on. 'Ears that don't hear. Eyes that don't see what's in front of them. A mind that can't link even the most obvious of things. It's a wonder you survived the Nemean Beck, when so many brave soldiers died.'

Perseus' shoulders drooped lower, and Philip felt a pang of sympathy. He had interrogated the officers who'd lived; they reported to a man that Perseus had followed orders, and fought well. He'd slain at least one of the enemy, perhaps more, and he had not lost his head when the rout began. He had also survived, and made his way back to the Akrokorinth. What his son had done was colossally foolish, thought Philip, but he was here. Alive. Wiser. Older. It was important to recognise that, lest the lad's spirit and initiative be crushed. 'Come,' he said gruffly. 'Tell me what happened – from the start. How in Zeus' name did you squirrel your way onto a ship when I'd given express orders that that should not happen?'

At last Perseus' eyes met his father's. 'You suspected I'd try to go with the phalangists?'

'Believe it or not, boy, I was like you once. Rash. Impulsive. So tell me!' Philip listened with amusement as an encouraged Perseus launched into his tale.

He'd crept onto one of the ships in the dark of night, avoiding the lone sentry, and hidden in the hold until dawn. A rare rain shower had helped then; as the vessel was loaded, no one had given a second glance to another labourer with his cloak hood up. Once at sea, the danger of being found had soared, but the Fates had woven a bright thread when the phalangist whose secluded spot Perseus had stolen had agreed to help.

'You'd like him, Father. He's called Demetrios too, like my brother.' Perseus' face fell at the mention of his younger sibling. 'Poor Demetrios.'

'He's tough. And his tutor will look after him,' said Philip, asking the gods to watch over his little son, half a world away in Rome. 'Wait. A phalangist by the name of Demetrios, you say?'

'Yes, Father. He spoke highly of you. Said you'd saved his life once. He didn't die at the Nemean Beck either. I've seen him in the column since we left Pella.'

'Hera's tits,' said Philip, smiling. 'I know who you mean. Demetrios is a fine soldier. It's good to know that he survived the recent battles. Did he mention the occasion *he* stopped an assassin's blade meant for me?'

Eyes wide, Perseus shook his head.

'Herakleides and the Aitolians were behind it.' Philip's mind filled with images of his former admiral, pleading for his life.

'Demetrios didn't mention it.'

He's modest too, thought Philip, making a mental note to have the phalangist brought to him. 'What did Demetrios do?'

'He and a close comrade kept my presence on the ship secret until it was too late to return to Macedon. I didn't see him much after we reached the Akrokorinth – Androsthenes treated me like a glass ornament that might break.' Perseus filled the last few words with disgust.

'Well he might,' said Philip, his lips twitching. 'My heir, in his fortress unannounced and without permission, with enemies all around. What possessed him to let you out with his forces before the Nemean Beck?'

Perseus snorted. 'I told him if he didn't agree, I'd see he was demoted and sent to command a fort on the Thrakian border for the rest of his life.'

Philip chuckled, and thought, that surgeon at Gonnos was right. The apples don't fall far from the tree. He listened as Perseus related the surprise Akhaian attacks, Androsthenes' scrambled response, and how everything that could have gone wrong did.

'What would you have done differently?' asked Philip.

Perseus looked startled, but answered without hesitation. 'I would have had scouts around the camp, not just nearby, but some distance away as well. Androsthenes posted none, and the first we knew of the Akhaians was just before they arrived. Perhaps I'd have sent smaller raiding parties out too – half the army was missing when we formed up on the riverbank – we'd have had a greater chance with more men.'

'Well thought out,' said Philip, who had come to similar conclusions. 'Most important of all, never underestimate your enemy. Androsthenes was a capable officer, but prone to think too much of himself. With his superiority in numbers over the Akhaians, I'd wager he never even gave consideration to being attacked. Too late now, eh?' Androsthenes had not returned to the Akrokorinth; he was presumed dead.

'Yes.' Perseus hesitated, then asked, 'Did *you* underestimate Flamininus, Father?'

The dressing-down had not dented Perseus' confidence too much, thought Philip. Good. 'Far from it. I was sucked into a battle I did not want at Kynoskephalae.' Although the defeat was still raw, it felt rewarding to lay out to his son – his son, so nearly a man now – the unfolding of the events at the Dogs' Heads, and why he had acted as he did. 'Doing nothing was not an option. To have sat on my hands would have risked Flamininus sending his army to assail our ill-defended camp,' said Philip. 'If I could go back and change anything, it would be to have held my part of the phalanx on the hilltop and waited for Nikanor to join us. The light infantry could have retreated to our position and formed on the flanks. Gods willing, there might have been time to do that. If we had then marched down at the legions in one great mass, they would have fled the field, elephants or no.'

Perseus sighed. 'So many men died.'

Philip leaned over and clapped his son on the shoulder. 'And it stings me daily that we have not yet been back to bury them. You did well to visit some of the injured at Gonnos. But enough of defeat and death. What's done is done. Flamininus won, but he needs me to remain as king. Our chance to rise may yet come again. For now let us set our minds to the task before us – finding the oath-breaking Dardanian whoresons who dared to attack Macedon.'

Delighted by this, the first time Philip had ever really included him in his military planning, Perseus grinned like the little boy he no longer was, and listened as his father began to speak.

A glistening snake twisted through the landscape, a mighty waterway running from the mountains on the northern horizon towards the coast of Macedon half a thousand stadia to the south-east. Under the hot sun, a heron flapped slowly by. Swallows dipped and dived overhead, catching insects.

'There they are.' Philip pointed at the large, wooded island in the middle of the fast-flowing River Axios. A palisaded camp dominated the hill on the island's centre. Glints atop the wall marked the presence of sentries. Down by the river's edge, the shapes of small craft could be made out. Perhaps four stadia from the bank upon which Philip and his army stood, it cut a peaceful scene.

Perseus, who had spent every hour with his father since their heart-to-heart talk two days prior, spat into the water, and growled, 'We have no boats. Can we build them?'

So eager for the fight, thought Philip, remembering again his youth. 'To fashion enough for the men we need – five hundred, more preferably a thousand – would take too long.'

'But the Dardanians cannot be allowed to get away with what they've done.'

'You studied Alexander and his campaigns, did you not?'

'Yes.' Perseus thought for a moment; a smile burst onto his face. 'The Triballians!'

'The coin I spent on the finest tutors in Greece wasn't all wasted then,' said Philip wryly. 'Indeed, the Triballians. When Alexander first defeated them, they retreated to an island stronghold on the Istros. Do you remember what he did next?'

'He ordered his men to stuff their tents with chaff, and sew them together to make rafts. Crossing the river by night with their horses, they attacked at dawn. The Triballians fled to the far shore in absolute panic.'

'How did Alexander know to do that? Was it something he thought of himself?'

Perseus frowned; he tapped a fingernail against his teeth, thinking. After a moment, he said, 'Was it Xenophon who wrote about it?'

'Indeed it was,' said Philip, pleased.

'Shall we build rafts too, Father?' Perseus' expression was as keen as a hawk's.

We, thought Philip. He wants to fight. My heart says no, but my head tells me to let him take part. He's a strong swimmer. We'll have the element of surprise, and he needs combat experience. Besides, there's no such thing as a 'safe' battle. He caught Perseus' eye, and said, 'I must stay ashore and direct matters, curse my luck. *You*, on the other hand . . .'

'Thank you, Father!'

'You will not command. That position shall fall to Stephanos, and you will follow his orders to the letter.' The speira commander who'd led a force to Orestis, survived Kynoskephalae and somehow, the Nemean Beck as well, was as solid an officer as Philip knew.

'Whatever you say, Father.' If Perseus had been a dog, his tail would have been wagging fit to fall off. 'When shall we attack?'

'Steady. The sun is falling in the sky, and the Dardanians are going nowhere. They think themselves out of reach. Constructing the rafts will take most of a day, I imagine. Dawn the day after tomorrow will be soon enough.'

Perseus looked so disappointed that Philip had to suppress a smile.

Philip had ordered his table and stool carried outside and positioned by the river. It was too hot and humid to talk with his officers in his tent. Lamps burning scented oil kept the biting flies at bay. Apart from his ever-present scribe, Philip was alone for the first time in hours; grateful for the respite, he wiped his brow with the back of a hand and sat on the iron stool, staring out at the island. It was late. He was tired, but all the arrangements were in place. There remained one thing to do. Hearing footsteps, he thought, and here it comes.

'Sire.' A sentry's voice.

'Yes?' Philip didn't turn his head.

'I bring the phalangist Demetrios.'

'Leave him with me.'

Footsteps moved off into the camp as the sentry obeyed.

'Demetrios,' said Philip, still not looking around.

'I am here, sire.' A flutter in the words revealed his nervousness.

Amused, knowing exactly why, Philip asked in a hard voice, 'Wondering why I summoned you?'

'Is it to do with your son, sire?'

'It is.' Philip rose and turned. Demetrios, he saw, had filled out even more. There was a solidity to him that hadn't been there on the occasion of their first meeting, and a sadness too, behind the eyes. Keeping his own face granite-like, Philip said, 'You helped him when he stowed away on the ship bound for the Akrokorinth.'

'Yes, sire.' Demetrios looked unsettled.

'Did you know that I had forbidden him to go?' Philip's stare bore down on Demetrios.

'I did, sire.'

'You must have known that to do so risked execution. What kind of fool are you?'

'You saved my life a few years ago at Chalkedon, if you remember, sire, when I was but an oarsman. If my file-leader hadn't seen something in me soon after, I'd still be on the benches. Perseus wanted to fight, like I did. I thought he deserved a chance. That's why I helped him.'

'And if he had died at the Nemean Beck?' demanded Philip.

Surprising him, Demetrios countered, 'But he didn't, sire. He acquitted himself well, or so I'm told, and came back the better man.'

They looked at each other for a moment, and then the king said, 'I can't deny what you say. For that, you have my thanks. Know that if he had come to any harm, however, I would have seen the skin flayed from your back.' Philip was a little surprised to detect no fear in Demetrios' eyes. 'Are you not glad to escape punishment?'

'Death holds no terror for me, sire. In some ways, it would come as a release.'

Guessing the reason, Philip said, 'You lost friends at Kynoskephalae.'

'Aye, sire, too many.' Unleashed, raw grief oozed from Demetrios' voice. 'Some I should have saved.'

'Did you deliberately abandon them?'

'Of course not!' Demetrios pulled himself up. 'Forgive my tone, sire.'

Seeing Demetrios so deeply affected, Philip waved a forgiving hand. 'If you could have helped your comrades, you would.'

'I would have *died* for them, sire.'

'But in the panic and the madness you were separated.' Demetrios nodded, his eyes yet full of sorrow, and the king continued, 'That is what happened to almost every soldier who survived. It was unpreventable – no man living could do anything other than try to save himself. You are *not* to blame for your comrades' deaths. The Fates decide whose thread to cut, and when.'

Demetrios' chin firmed. 'Can I ask you a question, sire?'

Curious, Philip said, 'Aye.'

'Why have we not been back to the Dogs' Heads to bury our comrades, sire? Flamininus gave you permission.'

The man has balls, Philip decided. This was a question only a few of his officers had dared to ask. Yet, thought the king, it must be one that troubled his entire army. If anyone deserved to hear an explanation, it was Demetrios, who had proved his loyalty so many times.

'Since Kynoskephalae, men the length and breadth of Greece have been laughing at me. Returning to the battlefield so soon after, not least because Flamininus allowed me, would make me appear even weaker. That is something I cannot allow to happen. The Aitolians, like vultures, are circling. Their only wish now is to have Flamininus depose me, so they can dominate Greece.' His voice grew fierce. 'I will not let that happen.' Softening his gaze, Philip said, 'They shall be laid to rest when the opportunity comes.'

'Very well, sire.' There was something approaching acceptance in Demetrios' eyes.

'I have need of you tonight. Are you still willing to do your duty for Macedon?' Philip probed.

'I am, sire.' Demetrios stood up straight. 'Whatever you command, I am ready.'

'Perseus is to take part in the attack on the island. He's not in charge – your commander Stephanos has that honour – but he will be in the fighting. I want you to stay by his side, keep him safe if you can.' Philip studied Demetrios' face, and was glad to see an eagerness that had not been there appear. 'I will not threaten you with punishment should you fail. I ask only that you do your best.'

'No man shall lay a hand on him while I live, sire,' Demetrios swore.

'You may go,' Philip said quietly. Worry gnawed his guts as he watched Demetrios disappear into the twilight. It didn't matter what he'd asked of the young phalangist. If the Fates willed that Perseus should die in the night attack, that is what would happen.

Kynoskephalae had been a hammer blow, thought Philip. His son Demetrios being made a hostage had felt as if he'd lost a limb.

The thought of Perseus dying was almost too much to bear.

CHAPTER XXX

The first rosy fingers of light crept up the eastern horizon. A breeze rippled the shallows; out in the centre of the river, the water swirled lazily, flurries of white a warning of its true speed. A fox patrolled the water's edge, searching for food. Corncrakes rasped from the rushes a little way downstream. On the patches of grass amid the low trees and scrubby bushes, rabbits grazed. The world was coming to life, thought Demetrios. The island upon which the Dardanians had encamped was visible only as a line of trees – Stephanos had taken his men upstream, opposite its northern end. There, the king said, they would not be seen during their attempt to cross. Certainly there had been no signs or sounds of men keeping watch during the long, cool hours of darkness.

Nonetheless, Demetrios had been awake for a long time; he suspected the majority had been. Wrapped in his cloak, the hood shadowing his face, he was lying by the shore beside his comrades. Empedokles, worse luck, was on his left. Simonides, Andriskos and Perseus were to his right, Stephanos a pace beyond that. Three speirai composed the attack force – weakened from the recent battles, they numbered about five hundred men. Threescore Companions had been delegated to cross with them; their horses' bulk would protect the phalangists from the worst of the current.

'Time to move,' whispered Stephanos. 'Spread the word. Into the river with the rafts, quiet as you can. Cross quickly and silently. On the island, stay low and wait for the order to move. Go.'

Simonides was on his feet, beckoning to the Companions who had been staying back among the trees on this side.

'Ready, sire?' Demetrios asked Perseus.

'Yes.' Perseus looked as excited as a boy who'd been handed his first blade.

'Good.' Demetrios caught Empedokles sneering, but his enemy was careful not to let Perseus see. Ever since the taunts he'd thrown on the ship, Empedokles had been careful to keep out of the prince's way. For his part, Perseus had not made anything of it. 'He did not know who I was,' he'd said. Demetrios had nodded and hidden his disappointment.

Six men to a raft, each an irregular shape of cobbled-together, chaff-filled leather, with a pile of aspides roped in place on top, they waded up to their thighs in the water. Already the current was buffeting, trying to sweep them off their feet. Demetrios was glad when the Companions began leading their horses out into the river. Everyone knew what to do. Stephanos, the second speira commander and the Companions' officers had been through it the night before. As soon as the horses were in place a little way upstream from the rafts, and the phalangists had indicated their readiness, the Companions urged their mounts out into midstream.

The phalangists followed, each man holding onto his raft with one hand and paddling with the other. Despite the protection granted by the horses, the current was powerful enough to sweep them along at a good pace. Aware they would drown with ease because of their bronze armour, they held onto the roughly made raft with white-knuckled grips. Calm-headed, Simonides coordinated their efforts, so his men kicked and paddled at the same time. There was brief amusement at one point as they collided with another raft, and a real moment of horror when a phalangist nearby, panicking because he could not swim, slipped from the grasp of his comrades and sank to his death.

Demetrios hated the crossing, but he managed to divert his fear by keeping a watchful eye on Perseus, who appeared to enjoy every moment of it, and relishing the sheer terror on Empedokles' face. As they waded, dripping, onto the sandy beach that fringed the island, Perseus' grin grew even broader. The first men ashore had already crept off to check there were no enemy sentries close by. With the raft dragged out of the way of those following behind, and their aspides untied, Demetrios and his comrades squatted down and waited for the rest to arrive.

On the bank they had left behind, some way downstream, Philip was hunched down, watching the island. The dice had been rolled; there was little he could do other than pray. He tried to push away the gnawing concern that he should have held off the assault until more rafts were built. Enough, he told himself. Stephanos and his fellow speira commander are good leaders, and their phalangists are some of my best troops. Five hundred men should be enough. That didn't mean disaster couldn't strike, of course. The Fates weave as they will, thought Philip, and wield their shears with reckless abandon when the mood takes them. Some of the rafts might sink. An alert sentry, an uncontrollable sneeze from one of Stephanos' men, and the Dardanians, some fifteen hundred strong, would rise from their blankets to slaughter the phalangists, and Perseus.

Philip cursed himself for not also sending the reserve rafts – a score he'd held back – and more troops. They were of no real use on this bank; if he admitted it, they were a comfort rather than anything else. If Stephanos had the alarm sounded, any soldiers Philip could send over on the rafts would in all probability arrive too late, and be insufficient to make a real difference.

Philip closed his eyes. Calmly, choosing his words with care, he prayed for a second time to the god of the Axios. Every waterway had its own deity, and so the night before, Philip had sacrificed a sheep to gain the god's favour. It was time to make another request. Let my men have crossed over your waters safely, he asked. Six fine bulls shall be yours if they have. Next he asked Zeus, greatest of the gods, and Herakles, the hero god, for their help. Half a dozen bulls each you shall receive, promised Philip, and half a dozen more if my son comes through unscathed.

'Sire.' The word was whispered, but pitched to carry.

Startled, Philip found a phalangist kneeling by his side, and behind him, a weary-faced man he didn't recognise, coated in dust from head to foot. A messenger, thought the king, and he's been travelling all night.

'What is it?' demanded Philip.

'This man bears a letter from Menander in Pella, sire.' The phalangist motioned the messenger forward.

Taking the rolled-up parchment he was proffered, Philip commended the messenger for his efforts and sent him off to be fed and given wine. Alone again – the sentries knew better than to come close – he peered at the island. Still no one stirred. Still no cries of alarm, or ring of battle. Fifteen paces out, a fish leaped into the air, and disappeared in a spray of water. Philip repeated to himself that all was well, that Stephanos and his men were moving into position, readying their attack. He eyed the letter in his hand, which felt heavy as a piece of lead.

Cracking Menander's seal, he unrolled it.

'The fools don't appear to have left any sentries in this direction at all,' said Stephanos, pitching his voice low to the dozen men he'd delegated to lead the phalangists – Simonides, Demetrios, Andriskos, Empedokles, a few others from their file, and naturally, Perseus. 'That isn't to say there aren't any, so stay alert,' he warned. 'If you spot one, halt your comrades. Halt the rest of us. Find out if he's alone. Deal with him, or them. Do it well, or we shall all be in Tartaros ere midday.' He pulled his smile, which resembled a grimace more, and waved them forward.

Simonides went first, with Andriskos and Demetrios behind. Perseus came next – annoying Empedokles, who could do nothing to protest – and after them came the rest. They walked crouched down, aspides facing front and swords drawn; the unwieldy sarissae had been left in the main camp. Low-hanging branches whipped at their faces; dry grass rustled at their feet. A small creature skittered away through the undergrowth.

Demetrios could see little but Simonides' back and the evergreen bushes that were replacing the holm oaks fringing the shore. Every time his file-leader stopped, Demetrios did too, a pulse pounding in his throat. After a pause, sometimes for three heartbeats, at others a good deal longer, Simonides would signal it was clear to continue. Demetrios would let out a hissing breath, and glance back at Perseus, who, youthful and inexperienced, waved an impatient hand to get going.

In this fashion, they covered perhaps five hundred paces. Demetrios was starting to think they would make it to the Dardanian camp unseen when, without warning, Simonides stopped dead. So did Andriskos. Demetrios managed to pull up, just, but Perseus walked into him. An unmistakably metallic chime was the result, as their breastplates made contact.

They all froze.

No alarm was raised. No voice shouted a challenge.

After what seemed a lifetime, Simonides threw a furious glance over his shoulder. Demetrios made an apologetic face; Perseus went crimson with embarrassment.

Simonides mouthed, 'One man. Fifty paces.' He raised an eyebrow at Demetrios, who nodded yes, he would come with him. Setting down aspis and sword, he drew his dagger and moved past Andriskos to the file-leader's side. Simonides placed his lips against Demetrios' ear, and said, 'Straight ahead. He's sitting with his back against a tree. He must be asleep. That noise would have alerted a deaf man.'

Demetrios studied the ground in front. They were on an animal trail. Bushes. Fallen branches. A sprawl of brambles. He spotted the sandals first, then, his gaze moving, the legs, and last, one arm and the torso of a man. The sentry's head was hidden by the tree trunk against which he was lying. Demetrios eyed Simonides and whispered, 'Is he on his own?'

Simonides shrugged an 'I don't know', then mouthed, 'Come on.'

Demetrios indicated to Andriskos, Perseus and behind them, a sour-faced Empedokles, that they should wait. Then, treading light as he could, he padded after Simonides. Despite his best efforts, a twig cracked underfoot at twenty paces. They both stood still, scarcely breathing, but there was no response. Full sure that Dionysos must be watching over them – Demetrios could think of no other reason than overconsumption of wine keeping the sentry asleep – he threw up a prayer of thanks.

They went on again, even slower. The air was cool, yet sweat was running off Demetrios. When Simonides paused again, he quickly wiped the hilt of his dagger on his chiton to make sure his grip remained firm when the time came.

Simonides' left hand came up. He stabbed a finger to their left, and signalled 'one'.

A second sentry, thought Demetrios in alarm. He peered over Simonides' shoulder. The warrior his file-leader had seen was lying on his back, snoring. A jug lay on its side by his uncurled right hand, proof that he and the other man had been drinking. 'I go left, you go right?' Demetrios mouthed at Simonides.

Simonides nodded his assent; abruptly a ferocious scowl twisted his face.

Demetrios twisted. To his disbelief, not ten paces away was Perseus.

Both Simonides and Demetrios made savage gestures that Perseus should remain where he was – that was the only thing he could do if the entire enterprise was not to be jeopardised – and split up, each padding towards their target.

The Dardanian on his back was about Demetrios' age. Long-haired, bearded like most of his kind, he wore a rough-spun tunic and simple leather sandals. His relaxed, peaceful face didn't look cruel or murderous. He and his kind sacked Stobi, Demetrios told himself; they raped women and slaughtered children. Nonetheless, he hesitated over the prone Dardanian.

In that moment, several things happened. A meaty sound, that of a blade sinking deep into flesh, came from Simonides' direction, and was followed in close succession by two more. The warrior at Demetrios' feet opened his eyes – they instantly filled with horror. From somewhere else altogether, but still close, came the unmistakable noise of a fart.

A third sentry, thought Demetrios in utter panic. Dropping to the ground, he clamped a hand over his victim's mouth and slit his throat. Blood spattered Demetrios' face and neck; the warrior's eyes widened in shock. His feet drummed the earth; his hands made a feeble attempt to stem the torrent issuing from his throat. It was all in vain – the wound was mortal and Demetrios was already up and turning. Expecting to see the third warrior running for his life, bellowing at the top of his voice, he saw instead a Dardanian with a dagger buried deep in his chest, sinking to his knees. With a bubbling cough, the man fell onto his face and lay still.

Demetrios turned to find Perseus walking towards him. 'You threw your dagger?' he asked in disbelief.

'I did,' said Perseus proudly. 'I was too far from him to do anything else.'

'I told you to stay behind, sire.' Simonides finished wiping his blade on the tunic of the warrior at his feet, and gave Perseus an exasperated look.

'If I had, you'd have been chasing after the third man, as he screamed the alarm. Tell me I'm wrong,' said Perseus, grinning as he retrieved his dagger.

Simonides swore. 'All right, sire. It was well done, but you can't keep on disobeying orders. It's a quick route to Tartaros, come a real battle.

I don't want to be the one who has to tell the king you got killed doing something rash.'

Perseus' face grew serious. 'I won't do it again unless I have to. Sometimes there's no thinking – you just have to act. You know what I mean, surely?'

Shaking his head, Simonides said, 'Aye, sire.' To Demetrios he muttered, 'He's his father's son and no mistake.'

And he has the makings of a fine soldier and leader, thought Demetrios.

I could follow a man like him.

The contents of Menander's letter were as bad as Philip had expected. The Akarnanian stronghold of Leukas had fallen to the Romans around the same time as Kynoskephalae; news of the king's defeat had caused the rest of the Akarnanians to surrender. It was no surprise, thought Philip with resignation. Isolated on the south-western coast of Greece, small in population, Akarnania had ever been at risk from his enemies. He could only be thankful to its people for staying loyal for so long.

Philip read on, and his mood darkened. For some time his territories on Asia Minor had been under attack by the Rhodians and a force of Akhaians, but the enemy's initial successes had been countered by his generals there. Now, wrote Menander, this threat had been superseded by the Seleucid emperor Antiokhos, whose large fleet was sailing up the western coastline of Asia Minor, attacking and taking every settlement and town of any size. Soon his ships would reach the Hellespont. With no real opposition, it seemed probable that he would gain control of the vital waterway before the harvest.

The glorious heyday of Philip's campaigning in Asia Minor, when he had marched and sailed its coast at will for two summers, was long gone. It had been more than a year since he'd had even the possibility of sending aid to his commanders there. Antiokhos' move had a feeling of inevitability, therefore, but Menander's neat writing and his precise descriptions of Philip's losses rammed home grim reality like a hammer blow. There would be no peace with Antiokhos, no mutual treaty against the Romans.

Menander made no mention of Hannibal, in whom Philip had also placed some hope. The Carthaginian had lost interest in an alliance, decided the king. It was hard to draw any other conclusion, given the lack of communication since his encounter with the soldier Hanno. The only other power he might call on for aid was Egypt, but its Ptolemaic ruling family was weak and in disarray. The chance of it sending soldiers or ships was as likely as Zeus coming down from Olympos to destroy the Romans. Weary from lack of sleep, wearied more by the unending setbacks sent his way, Philip closed his eyes. Can it get any worse? he wondered.

Perseus! he thought.

Philip's eyelids jerked open. Dry-mouthed, he studied the island. Atop the Dardanian palisade, he could see no sign of life. On the shore below, nothing moved save the tribesmen's boats, tugged to and fro by the current. His gaze travelled back to the trees that fringed the hill upon which the Dardanian encampment was built. Nothing.

Philip's worries, held at bay overnight, fuelled now by the bad news in Menander's letter, threatened to surge out of control. Something was wrong, he decided. Some of the rafts – most of them, maybe – had sunk. Men had drowned. Even if Perseus had survived, he was trying to save himself, or other men, rather than attack the Dardanians. I should never have sent him, thought Philip. The attack could have been delayed until more rafts, or even boats, were built. I am a fool. An arrogant fool.

A short time had passed since the three sentries had been slain; the phalangists' advance since had been uneventful. Demetrios and his comrades crouched down, sheltered by the last of the trees that skirted the hill upon which the Dardanians had camped. Silence reigned over the enemy positions; not a sentry was to be seen. Less than a hundred paces of open ground lay between the phalangists and the first tents.

'Ready?' hissed Stephanos, who had been off to confer with the commanders of the other speirai – the three units had spread out to encircle the hill.

Demetrios and the rest gave him eager nods.

'Guard the prince with your lives,' he said, ignoring Perseus' glower. 'And wait for the signal.' A trumpet would have been the best way to alert all three speirai, but that risked the Dardanians hearing. A bird call, one often heard at dawn, was to be used instead. Stephanos moved off, checking for a last time that everyone knew what was expected of them.

Demetrios' stomach was tight, as it always was before a fight. He would have given five years' pay – more – for his dead friends to have been present. The giant Philippos, with his friendly face and infectious belly laugh. Kimon, ever interested and curious, and Antileon, loyal and argumentative. Sadness lashed him that he had only Andriskos and Simonides, and the whoreson Empedokles. There was the file-closer Zotikos, of course, and a few others, but they weren't friends like those who had gone to the underworld. Perseus was here, Demetrios reminded himself, but the prince would only ever be a temporary comrade.

'I'd give anything to have my kopis right now.' Somehow Empedokles had wormed his way in alongside Demetrios. 'Remember that, eh, filth?'

Demetrios' reply was furious. 'How like you, to mention a piece of kit rather than our fallen comrades. What about Philippos? Kimon or Antileon? Wouldn't it better to have them with us than a stupid sword?'

'That goes without saying,' said Empedokles, but his eyes told a different story.

Incensed by the obvious lie, Demetrios threw caution to the wind. 'Want to know what happened to your fucking kopis?'

Empedokles' expression grew ravenous, like a man who hadn't eaten for days. 'Tell me.'

'We sold it,' said Demetrios with savage relish. 'To a White.'

'To a fucking White?'

'Aye, and after what's happened of recent days, you shouldn't care. Our friends and comrades, the defeat at Kynoskephalae, that's what matters. Winning this battle, seeing the king stays on the throne, and that Perseus follows him, that's what matters. Not a cursed sword.' He looked at Empedokles and saw that he was wasting his breath.

'You'll pay for that kopis yet,' warned Empedokles, rage throbbing in his voice.

Demetrios was beyond caring. He made an obscene gesture and turned his face away, blocking his ears to Empedokles' threats and insults. Back turned, Demetrios missed the look of pure hatred his enemy threw at him.

The signal to attack, soon after, was a welcome release. Demetrios was glad too that Simonides, seeing their disagreement, had ordered

Empedokles to move to a different position. Demetrios wasn't scared of his enemy – if it came to a fight, he would have taken pleasure in ending their feud – but it was a distraction always having to look over his shoulder.

Their approach couldn't have gone better. It soon became clear that the three sentries' drunkenness had been a small-scale version of what had gone on throughout the entire Dardanian camp. Warriors sprawled not just in tents, but around the embers of their fires, and everywhere in between. Easy prey for the phalangists, who came stealing in unnoticed, they were slaughtered like lambs in a butcher's pen.

Demetrios stuck to Perseus' side, Philip's command foremost in his head. It didn't surprise him that the prince refused to kill sleeping men, or those who were trying to arm themselves. Warning Perseus about the danger made no difference; he insisted on confronting those few warriors with weapons in their hands. They were easy foes for the most part, bleary-eyed, their reactions slowed by hangovers. No one could deny their bravery, however. Isolated, disorientated, they made no attempt to surrender. Perseus cut down one, then a second and a third. Demetrios and Andriskos provided protection, killing or warning off any Dardanians who tried to join in.

The fourth proved the prince's first real opponent. A bare-chested warrior with thick silver rings on both his wrists, he charged at Perseus like the Minotaur beneath the palace at Knossos. Unprepared for the ferocity of the attack, Perseus fell back several steps, and almost tripped over the body of another Dardanian. Demetrios waded in, slashing at Silver Rings' head, giving Perseus time to recover.

'I didn't need that!' shouted Perseus, placing himself between Demetrios and Silver Rings.

'The king ordered me to protect you, sire,' said Demetrios, his eyes fixed on Silver Rings, who with a roar, had launched himself afresh at Perseus. 'I can't stand by and let you be hewn in two.'

With a neat feint at Silver Rings' face, which made him jerk his head back, Perseus spitted him through the belly. He avoided a mighty thrust from the still-strong Dardanian, tugged out his blade and in the same movement, ran it in hilt-deep into Silver Rings' chest. Cool as a veteran, Perseus said, 'That wasn't ever going to happen.'

Seeing movement behind the prince, Demetrios raised his sword.

Darting past a surprised Perseus, he met the spear of another Darda-nian with his aspis. Wood splintered; the shield cracked, but did not fall apart. Demetrios reached forward as the warrior tried desperately to free his spear tip, and half-cut the man's head from his neck. Con-cerned for the prince, he spun to find a smiling Perseus regarding him. Silver Rings lay dead at his feet; there were no other Dardanians close by.

'We seem to have won,' said Perseus.

The prince was right, thought Demetrios. Few Dardanians remained fighting. Those who were still alive were either trying to surrender, busy dying, or screaming their agony at the blue sky. A smile twitched its way over Demetrios' face. 'The king will be pleased,' he said.

Philip glanced again at the treeline. This time, he was startled to see the figures of men, running, crouched low, scaling the hill. His heart leaped. The rafts *had* made it across – Stephanos wouldn't order an attack unless he had enough men. Rapt, his fists clenched, he watched as the phalangists neared the first Dardanian tents, without any sen-tries' shouts. Philip felt sick. This was the most dangerous time, when the brave men who were leading the attack could be undone by a wide-awake guard.

He heard nothing but the lap of waves off the shore.

The silence didn't last. Perhaps thirty heartbeats later, he heard a sti-fled cry. Then another. There was no immediate response, and Philip's heart leaped. The longer peace reigned over the enemy positions, the greater chance of success Perseus and his phalangists had.

Uproar broke out on the island, but gradually. Shouts. Cries. Shrieks. The clash of arms. A roar of 'Macedon!' Not long after that, the dom-inant sound – almost the only sound – was that of screams. The long, drawn-out trumpet blast from the ramparts was merely confirmation that the Dardanians had been defeated.

When a raft crossed with the news that the Dardanians had been crushed, that Perseus had led the attack and that there had been less than twenty Macedonian casualties, Philip could have cheered. After a moment, he did cheer. Falling to his knees by the water's edge, he gave loud thanks to the river god, Herakles and Zeus.

Their future remained uncertain, but there was hope.

CHAPTER XXXI

Elatea, early spring 196 BC

Flamininus was in his tent outside the small town of Elatea. He still felt a little uncomfortable siting his winter quarters here; it was hard not to think daily of the innocent Pasion, and his horrific, pain-filled last moments. It had been a terrible mistake, Flamininus would think, and Lucius had paid for his treachery, but Elatea's perfect location was more important. Partway between the important cities of Athens and Corinth, close to Thessaly, Flamininus was well situated to react should trouble arise anywhere in Greece. Several supply routes offered themselves: the Corinthian and Ambracian Gulfs, and the coastline of Boeotia and Locris.

Best of all, Galba could be kept busy and at arm's length by ensuring that his legion had to patrol the territory around Elatea. It was frustrating that Flamininus' spies continued to come up with nothing that would give him a hold over his enemy, but persistence tended to yield results, and so his orders to his agents here and in Rome remained the same. Keep digging. Grease more palms with coin. Cajole. Threaten. Blackmail if needs be. Flamininus didn't know when something juicy would turn up, but he had faith that the gods would reward him before he'd had to pay Galba all his money. In that regard, time was on Flamininus' side. Oddly, given that it had happened in his own camp, he had been unable to discover Benjamin's whereabouts, or the reason for his disappearance, but the Judaean was no longer with Galba, and that sufficed. Flamininus had slept easier at night since.

Annoyingly, he was far enough from Aetolia for the treacherous bastards to continue plotting and scheming. As ever, Flamininus had spies in place there, and the news they sent was disquieting. Far from accept his decision to leave Philip in control of Macedonia, the Aetolian council and generals were trying to destabilise the situation at every turn. Hardly a ten-day period went by without something coming to light:

an assassination of a Macedonian noble here, a supposed attack on Greek territory by 'Macedonian' troops there. A sizeable portion of his energy was expended in keeping the war from breaking out for a second time.

Flamininus' own hands weren't clean either. His mind roved back to the winter, some three months prior, when the Boeotians had come to him requesting the return of their general Brachylles and his men – all of whom had been serving in Philip's army. Sure that those in power in Boeotia would punish Brachylles, and eager to win favour among them – thereby bringing another city state into Rome's fold, useful against the threat of Antiochus – Flamininus had brought to bear his influence. To his surprise, Brachylles had only been home for a few days when the Boeotians elected him as leader; to Flamininus' rage, they had then sent thanks not to him, but to Philip!

The humiliation could not go unanswered. With the help of an Aetolian general – who had the means to get close to Brachylles – Flamininus had conspired with the Boeotians to have the recently returned general meet a grisly end. He had not anticipated the backlash – the murder of leading pro-Roman Boeotians had followed, and soon after, more than five hundred Roman troops were slaughtered in an uprising – but this bloody result had allowed Flamininus to march in with his legions and restore order at the point of the gladius. A somewhat uncomfortable peace now lay over Boeotia, which was another good reason he was camped nearby, thought Flamininus.

Potitius coughed and entered. There was no lip-licking. Incredibly, his scribe appeared to have broken his revolting habit.

Flamininus looked up, eager-faced. 'Have they arrived?'

'I don't know, master.'

Disappointed, Flamininus held out his hand for the bundle of documents in Potitius' hands. The victor at Cynoscephalae or not, conqueror of Greece or not, there was no escaping the drudgery of paperwork. 'What are these? Please tell me there are no letters of outrage from Aetolia or Achaea.'

'None of those, master.'

Flamininus wasn't sure whether he was pleased or not. 'It's the usual soul-sapping material then?'

'Yes, master. Approvals for supplies for the army – grain, timber, leather and wine, and so on. A request for a particular medicine from one of the surgeons. Reports from various units that require your signature before being sent to Rome. A letter from a tribune who wants to go home to attend his dying father.' Potitius seemed about to continue, but with a roll of his eyes, Flamininus interrupted.

'Yes, yes. You have read them all?'

'I have, master.'

'Do they seem in order?'

The tip of Potitius' tongue traced a line from one side of his mouth to the other. 'Err, yes, master.'

'Good.' Flamininus sat at his desk, and without reading a single line of the first document, dipped a stylus in the ink pot and signed it. Handing it to an astonished Potitius, he scrawled a signature on the second and passed it over too. He had just written his name for the third time when Potitius asked, his voice trembling a little, 'Aren't you going to look over them, master?'

'The one from the tribune I should, I suppose – where is that?' Flamininus let Potitius search through the pile. Taking the letter, he read it fast. 'This one you must reply to. The tribune's request is denied. The war might be over, but too much remains to be done to allow him a jaunt back to Italia.' It's also because *I* cannot yet return, Flamininus thought with a spurt of viciousness. 'Let him pen a letter to his father, bidding him farewell. As for the rest, well, my signature should be sufficient.' He cast an eye at Potitius. 'You're sure all the requests seem in order?'

'As sure as I can be, master, but I—'

'If you are happy, that's good enough,' said Flamininus. 'Unless there's a mistake. Then I will hold you accountable.'

'In that case, master, I would like to read several out to you for approval.' Horrified by his forthrightness, Potitius licked his lips and then, terrified by *that*, stared at his ink-stained hands.

Flamininus checked his temper. The lip-licking was so rare now he could let that pass, but he wasn't used to a slave standing up to him. He decided that Potitius had balked because he suspected what had befallen Pasion, and was worried that he would meet the same fate. Rumours must be rife between his personal slaves, Flamininus decided. He could overlook this one infraction.

'Very well, but be quick.' Leaning on the stylus, Flamininus signed another document as he listened to Potitius.

Despite Flamininus' intention to cut short the time spent dealing with official paperwork, he was still at his desk an hour later. When a messenger arrived with the news he'd been waiting for – the arrival of commissioners sent by the Senate – Flamininus could take no more. 'The rest can be dealt with tomorrow,' he told a dismayed Potitius. 'Attend me in the meeting room. Bring writing materials.'

Making a quick detour to his private quarters, there to change into full panoply – a victorious general must look the part, Flamininus had always believed – he was in place to receive the commissioners, just arrived by horse from Anticyra, where their ship had docked. Content that the room looked presentable – clean carpet, comfortable seats, polished lamps, and on a lion-legged table, rare, blue glass tumblers and a silver jug of the best Caecuban – he smoothed down his hair and ordered the visitors brought in.

'I bid you welcome,' Flamininus cried as the ten commissioners filed in. It pleased him that the two already in place, his legates Villius and Galba, were at the back. Villius was of little concern, but Galba was ever a worry; at the rear, he would have it harder to make a scene. Of the eight others, half were known to Flamininus. Lucius Terentius, a short, self-important type, was the leader. Publius Lentulus, a quiet, well-spoken man, was the deepest thinker. Lucius Stertinius and Gnaeus Cornelius were typical of many senators: solid, dependable and without an original thought between them.

'How was your journey?' Flamininus' tone was solicitous. 'You must be tired – in need of a bath.' His words were a courtesy, and everyone knew it. The news carried by the commissioners needed to be delivered at once.

'I thank you, Flamininus,' said Terentius. 'I think I speak for us all in saying that we must speak with you before taking our ease.'

'You shall have wine at least,' said Flamininus expansively, waving forward the waiting slaves.

No one protested, and when everyone had a cup in his hand, and had saluted one another – Flamininus made sure to ignore Galba – he dipped his chin at Terentius, and asked, 'Is Philip to be granted the peace he asked for?'

'He is.'

Flamininus smiled. 'Marcus Claudius Marcellus did not succeed then.' Intelligence from his spies had carried to him word of the new consul-elect's efforts to prevent the peace accord being agreed by the Senate and the Centuriate, the people's assembly.

Terentius' eyebrows rose that Flamininus should already know this. 'He did not. It was clear that his reasons were wholly personal, and not in the interests of Rome or its people.' Terentius acknowledged his fellows' murmurs of approval and continued, 'The first clause states that every Greek city state, whether here or in Asia Minor, is to have its independence and its own laws. The second, that Philip's troops shall be withdrawn from all cities and states beyond the borders of Macedonia, and surrendered into Roman control before the Isthmian Games. A subclause to this makes an exception for the following—' here Terentius named a list of settlements in Asia Minor '—which are to have their Macedonian garrisons withdrawn, leaving them free.'

Flamininus could hear the Aetolians' protests already. How was it, they whined, that towns in Greece were to come under Roman control while those further away were set free? Let them grumble, he decided. Although the move would antagonise the Aetolians, it was being made in order to deny Antiochus, the new threat, easy-to-attack targets in Greece. It wasn't just that of course – Flamininus had grown to dislike the Aetolian leaders so much that it was pleasing to spite them.

'All prisoners of war and deserters in Philip's hands are to be handed over to us,' Terentius went on. 'He is to surrender all his warships, save five lembi and his royal galley. Henceforth, his army is not to exceed five thousand men in number – nor is he permitted to own any elephants. Under no circumstances is he to wage war outside Macedonia without the permission of the Senate. Reparations of one thousand talents are to be paid, half now, the rest in ten yearly instalments. More hostages are to be sent. His son Demetrius is to remain in Rome at the Senate's pleasure.' Terentius concluded with a few more details, a short list of towns and islands that were to be given over variously to the Pergamenes, Rhodians and Athenians.

'My thanks,' said Flamininus, pleased. 'Philip will accept the terms, I have no doubt. Since his defeat at Cynoscephalae, he has acceded to every demand made of him. Receiving what they asked for, I imagine that almost all the Greek city states will also agree. Aetolia alone will provide the sticking point.'

'Because of the Fetters,' said Terentius.

'Just so,' agreed Flamininus. 'Did the Senate make a special case for these fortresses as I requested?'

'Yes. We are to leave them in the control of whoever is deemed most likely to keep them safe from Antiochus.'

'There is only one answer to that,' said Flamininus with a snort. 'Although it would not hurt, I suppose, if we were to give the city of Corinth to the Achaeans.'

'The Aetolians will be angered if Rome assumes control of the Fetters,' said Galba, eyeing the other commissioners. Several nodded, and he added, 'I am not alone in thinking this.'

Incensed by his enemy's intervention, Flamininus snapped, 'To Hades with the Aetolians! They will accept the treaty, or suffer the consequences.'

'Roman garrisons in these fortresses will be a far greater deterrent to Antiochus than a Greek rabble,' ventured Terentius. 'We must remain focused on what is most important. Now, is that pleasing the Greeks, or preventing an invasion by the Seleucids? Search your hearts, fellow commissioners, and tell me that Flamininus is not right.'

After a period of muttering to each other, and with apologetic glances at Galba, his supporters agreed that Terentius – and therefore Flamininus – were right.

'And so it is settled.' Flamininus saluted Terentius with his glass, and thought, he is a useful ally. 'We shall inform the Greeks tomorrow. For now, let us drink each other's health.' Catching Galba's eyes on him, Flamininus thought, except for yours, you snake.

He spent the next while circulating the room, thanking the commissioners for their support, and listening to tales of their voyage from Rome, and the political situation at home. An expert flatterer, Flamininus nodded and smiled at the right moments, and chuckled at every joke. He repeated the promises he'd made to several commissioners in times past, when their backing had been crucial, and came to agreement with two others that they would vote again with him should the need arise.

Convinced that the entire group bar Galba was on his side, Flamininus made time to press the flesh with Terentius, someone who liked to be known as incorruptible. Prickly, arrogant and fond of his own voice, he reminded Flamininus of himself. Except of course, thought Flamininus, he is not the general who conquered Macedonia. The man who brought a king to his knees, figuratively. Happy that he was by far the greater individual, but giving the opposite impression, Flamininus supped his wine and let Terentius prate on about the importance of the task set him by the Senate. Asking an occasional question to give the pretence that he cared – Terentius might prove useful as he had just now – Flamininus barely heard the raised voices outside. He didn't notice Galba sidle from view.

More shouts.

Flamininus' attention was wandering. He couldn't work out what was going on at his tent's entrance – where the commotion appeared to be coming from – and when he realised that Galba was no longer present, he determined to go outside. His enemy might contrive to have him miss hearing some important news.

'How dare you appear before me in such a state?' Galba's voice thundered through the tent leather.

'. . . do you think?' asked Terentius.

Flamininus had not heard the first half of the question. 'I'm sure you're right,' he said to Terentius. Worried by the surprise on the other's face, he hoped that he had not said anything too stupid. Promising to conclude the conversation at the earliest opportunity, he made his excuses and left.

Galba was barking questions at someone, but in a low voice. The answers he was getting were also indiscernible.

Flamininus picked up his pace. Hurrying through the antechamber before the entrance, with no time to enjoy the display of incredible Greek statuary that had recently come into his possession, he slowed to a walk, emerging the picture of serenity.

Silence fell. Eleven faces turned to regard him. Eight unhappy-looking sentries. The saluting, embarrassed officer they had presumably found to deal with the problem before Galba had come on the scene. Galba, incandescent with fury, because of the eleventh figure, thought Flamininus, or because he had appeared. Perhaps both. And finally an optio, holding a wineskin, whose face he recognised for some reason. Drunk, swaying at attention before Galba, the optio seemed delighted to see Flamininus. 'Sir!' he cried.

'Silence, filth!' Spittle sprayed from Galba's lips.

'What's going on?' demanded Flamininus.

The sentries knew better than to speak. Terrified of Flamininus, the officer began to answer, but a savage glare from Galba silenced him.

'It's nothing to concern yourself with, sir,' said Galba. 'Everything is under control.'

'I'll be the judge of that,' said Flamininus, relishing the pricks of colour that sprang to Galba's cheeks. 'Explain.'

'This excuse for an optio came demanding an audience with you, sir. He's as drunk as Bacchus. He wouldn't listen to the sentries here, or their officer. I heard the argument and came to investigate. Turns out the prick is in my legion. I even know him. Believe it or not, he hit me in the face with a harpastum ball once.'

'*That's* where I recognise him from,' cried Flamininus, staring at the optio. 'You're the princeps I promoted at Cynoscephalae. The one who alerted Bulbus to the enemy's exposed flank.'

'Aye, that's me, sir,' said the optio in a pleased voice.

'You've got a clown's name. What was it again?'

'Cicirrus, sir. Felix Cicirrus.'

Happy to overlook the optio's behaviour because of his valour, and assuming that the man had come to thank him for his promotion or some such, Flamininus turned his attention back to Galba. 'He's had a drop too much to drink, and why wouldn't he? His brother fell at Cynoscephalae.' Studying Galba, Flamininus didn't see Felix's mouth open and close. He continued, 'The optio hasn't struck anyone, has he, or refused to obey a direct order?'

Galba threw an unhappy glance at the sentries' officer, who shook his head. 'He didn't try to force his way in, sir, when I barred his way. The fool just stood there, shouting that he wanted to see you.'

Galba's gaze returned to Flamininus, and he muttered, 'It appears not, sir.'

'There we are. Punishment is merited, but not too severe.' Flamininus held Galba's gaze until the legate nodded, then he said in a bright tone, 'Good. I will leave you to it.'

Delighted to have humiliated Galba, if only a little, Flamininus turned his back and went back inside.

He missed the imploring look the optio threw after him.

CHAPTER XXXII

It was midday, and despite the fresh spring breeze, the sun was hot. Felix was standing to attention in front of Falto's tent, his position since dawn. Dark patches of sweat marked the armpits of his tunic; trickles of it ran from under his lambswool arming cap. He had a throbbing headache, thanks in no small part to the wine he'd drunk, but also because of his helmet, which appeared to have doubled in weight. It was a small mercy, he decided, that Falto had allowed him to rest his shield on the ground some time before. The muscles of his left forearm still ached from the first hour of holding it in the ready-for-combat position. Felix dreaded to imagine what else Falto had in store.

His centurion had not been best pleased to have Felix dragged in front of him by an officer – the same who'd been on guard outside Flamininus' tent – of a different unit. Falto had listened in stony silence as Felix's sorry tale was told, and had nodded grim assent that he should be punished, but not overly so. Cuffing Felix round the head, Falto had roared to get out of his sight and to present himself again at dawn.

And here he had been for five, maybe six hours.

Alone for the most part, Felix had had plenty of time to consider his situation. In an effort not to think about what Falto might do to him, he had thought about the events since Cynoscephalae, eight months before. The demands of being an optio kept him busy from sunrise to sunset. It was a fulfilling existence, and for the most part, prevented him from brooding about Antonius' death. Evenings afforded a little free time, but not wishing to sink into wine-soaked moroseness, Felix often sought out Falto, trying to learn from someone with experience of the command ladder. They weren't friends yet, but Felix could see – until this episode – how it might have happened. Only a fool could doubt that his foolish behaviour outside Galba's tent would have set that prospect back several steps, if not driven it into the realms of impossibility.

A potential friendship with Falto paled beside the opportunity he'd lost the night before, however. The thought of it dragged Felix's spirits to a new low. The plan had seemed simple, easy even, after a skin of wine. He would approach Flamininus, Felix had owlishly reasoned, and thank him vociferously for his promotion. Once the general remembered who he was – the optio with the clown's name who had turned the tide of battle at Cynoscephalae – Flamininus could not fail to grant his humble request to find and bury his brother's bones.

I was a fool, Felix thought. A stupid, grieving drunk fool. Even if Galba hadn't intervened, there was no surety that Flamininus would have agreed to his appeal. Felix had himself to blame twice over – first for approaching Flamininus' tent when pissed, second for giving up to Galba the reason he was there. Yet it was hard to see how the situation could have played out any differently, for the malicious legate had seemed to sense that he had an ulterior motive for appearing outside Flamininus' tent. Galba had threatened not just to punish Felix, but to have his former comrades flogged if he didn't reveal everything.

Tears of rage pricked Felix's eyes as he remembered Galba laughing at his wish to give Antonius a decent burial. Not two heartbeats before Flamininus had emerged, Galba had hissed, 'After what you did to me with the harpastum ball, I will see that you get no leave – none.' A malicious smile. 'At least until the legion is sent back to Italia, whenever that is. Years, I expect.'

Scraped raw again, Felix's sorrow grew so acute that he almost cried out. The chances of finding Antonius' grave were already slim. Galba's pronouncement ensured that if he ever managed to make his way back to Cynoscephalae, those chances would be close to impossible. Antonius' remains would moulder into dust with the thousands of others who had died there, and never be found.

Felix's heart ached at the thought of it. I will not forget you, brother, he decided. One way or another, I will come back to honour your shade.

His mind soon turned to Galba, and thoughts of revenge. As before, when Felix had lain in his tent, pain-racked after the flogging, he remembered Pennus' tale. How in Celetrum, Galba had stolen a fortune that should have been surrendered to the Senate. Before, Felix had discounted the idea of ever bringing the tale to someone who might be able to act on it, but now his choices seemed clear. Flamininus and Galba did not like each other, of that he was certain. It was even possible they were enemies.

Rather than ask Flamininus for a period of leave, therefore, he should tell the general about Celetrum. Backed up by the word of Pennus and his comrades, Flamininus could use the information to bring down Galba. That thought warmed Felix's heart. Galba wouldn't be executed for the crime – the harsh reality was that high-born Romans did not receive the punishment ordinary legionaries did for stealing a thousandth of the amount – but his political career might be brought to a juddering halt. For a schemer like Galba, Felix decided, that would be akin to death.

'Uncomfortable?' barked Falto, emerging from his tent. 'You look it.'

'I'm fine, sir,' lied Felix.

Vitis tapping off a greave, the habit of so many centurions, Falto paced to and fro in front of Felix, and then, in another terrifying habit beloved of centurions, he walked behind him.

Felix didn't dare move a muscle. Falto might launch an attack with his vitis, or whisper in his ear, a host of other unpleasant things – but if he, Felix, stirred, he would *definitely* feel the vine stick. So, dry-mouthed, stiff-backed, he stared at Falto's tent.

'A good soldier, you seem to be.' Falto's breath was hot in his ear. 'The men speak highly of you, as do other officers. You fought well at the Dogs' Heads, and by all accounts, were one of the reasons we broke the enemy's phalanx. Quite an accomplishment. Some even say that you killed an elephant at Zama. I haven't been able to corroborate it, mind. My inclination is that it's just a tall story you like to hear men talking about.'

He's been asking questions, thought Felix. The old fear that he would be discovered flared anew in his pounding heart. After several years in the Eighth, with Matho the only incident that might have seen him and Antonius executed, Felix had of late worried less about having illegally re-enlisted. Falto's curiosity represented a real danger. Tell the truth, Felix thought, and the centurion might be interested enough to keep digging. So many soldiers had stayed in the army since the victory over Hannibal that there had to be a man, or men, in Flamininus' host who knew what had happened to the two brothers. Better to lie, Felix decided. Falto would think him a rumour-spreading fool, but that was better than the fustuarium.

'Well?' Falto's vitis drove into the small of his back, hurting despite his mail shirt. 'Are you a liar as well as a wineskin?'

Stung, Felix blurted, 'I'm not, sir. The story about the elephant is true.'

Falto whipped around to stand in front of him, very close, almost eyeball to eyeball. The odour of onions, olives and cheese was strong: it was what Falto had eaten for breakfast, sitting at a table in front of Felix. Slow and deliberate, Falto said, 'You. Killed. An. Elephant?'

What have I done? Felix asked himself in utter panic. Antonius would never have been so stupid. 'I did, sir.'

'Tell me.'

Hades, thought Felix. I'm a dead man. He had to obey, though, or Falto's scrutiny would become more intense – and painful. There was still a tiny chance he might get away with it. Avoiding mention of units or his legion, Felix described the battle of Zama, including his near-death experience of bringing down the elephant.

Falto stepped back a little to listen, but his stare moved not a hair's breadth from Felix. Not until the story had finished – Felix was careful to end it with the defeat of the Carthaginians, not later – did he even stir. 'That's quite a tale.'

'It is, sir.' Felix held Falto's gaze. He'd told the truth – it was import-ant his demeanour gave the impression he'd done so too.

'I was there.'

'Aye, sir?' Felix tried to look interested even as his heart sank. This was a topic dear to Falto's heart.

'You were too, from the things you described.'

'Sir.' Felix dropped his gaze, praying that Falto would just beat him, or give him a punishment duty. Anything but continue this interrogation.

'Your centurion must have been proud of you.'

Felix flailed for an answer about Matho that wasn't an obscenity. 'He was . . . an awkward sort, sir. Not much given to praise.'

Surprise writ large on his face, Falto asked, 'You got *nothing* in the way of reward?'

'No, sir.'

'You must be glad he's no longer your centurion,' said Falto with feeling.

Gods above and below, he's going to ask Matho's name next, Felix screamed in his head. 'You could say that, sir.'

Falto's snort was amused, but the look he turned on Felix was as stone-hard as ever. 'I reward my men for their bravery, I'll have you know, but I also punish them when they break the rules. Or do something incredibly stupid, as you did last night.' He leaned in again, close enough to be uncomfortable. 'What were you doing, drunk, demanding to see the general? Has the loss of your brother scrambled your wits?'

'I've not gone mad, sir.'

'Give me a reason, anything not to make you wish you'd never been whelped. It's one thing for a legionary to do what you did, and quite another for an optio.' Contempt dripped from Falto's voice.

'I wanted to ask for some leave, sir.'

'Eh?' Falto's expression blackened. '*Eh?*'

Before he could react further, Felix said, 'As you know, sir, my brother Antonius died at Cynoscephalae. I buried him after, but the only marker I could put up was made of wood. I want to take a proper tombstone there, and set it up over his grave. That's been my plan, sir, gods willing. I thought perhaps the general might see his way to granting my request.'

'There are proper channels to get such things done,' growled Falto. 'You request leave from me. If I approve, the request moves up the chain of command, and so on. *You* know that.'

'I do, sir,' said Felix humbly. 'It was the wine, and the fact that I met the general after Cynoscephalae, when he promoted me. I wanted to ask him direct.'

'You think Flamininus is a friend of yours?'

'No, sir,' said Felix, thinking, but he would love to hear what I know about Galba.

'You're a fool,' said Falto, but there was less heat in his voice than before.

Felix wondered if he could even detect a note of sympathy. 'Yes, sir. I should have come to you instead. I'm sorry, sir.' He put on his most mournful, apologetic face, and prayed.

Falto looked at him long and hard.

Felix prayed even harder.

Half a dozen heartbeats tripped by.

'We've all done something stupid when we're drunk. Hades, I have. The loss of your brother must be grievous hard to live with, but it's hard to come up with a prank as ill-advised as yours yesterday.' Falto's vitis shot up to rest under Felix's nose. He moved it up, forcing Felix to raise his head until he was looking Falto in the eyes. 'One serious mistake is all I allow my men and my officers. One. Make another, and first I'll beat you senseless with this—' the vitis wiggled '—and then I will strip you to the ranks. You'll be on sentry duty every night for six months after that, as well as having your pay docked for a year. Do I make myself clear?'

'Yes, sir,' muttered Felix, feeling a mixture of relief and terror.

'Go on. Clear off.' The vitis pointed left, towards Felix's tent.

Deciding that Falto was as fine a centurion as Pullo, Felix obeyed.

Felix considered his options for several hours. Keep his head down, and his nose clean, and his foolishness outside Flamininus' tent would soon be forgotten – Falto's behaviour had made that clear. Even the threat from Galba would abate. Malevolent though he was, the legate would have more important things on his mind than seeking out a lowly optio for further humiliation. Ordinary life, such as it was, would resume. Felix would be granted leave in the end – even Galba couldn't prevent that – but it might not be, as the legate had threatened, for years. The war was over, yet there had been no indication when the legions might return to Italia. Once Felix's leave came through, or he was demobilised, he would be free to return to Greece and seek his brother's grave.

Or, thought Felix, he could make another attempt to speak with Flamininus.

Unlike his first choice, this option was laden with risk.

The general had been in a good mood the previous evening; Falto had gone easy on him that morning too. Repeat the same foolishness for a second time, and Flamininus was likely to have him flogged within an arse hair of his life. He'd be stripped to the ranks and moved to another century. And that was before Falto got to him.

This grim reality moved Felix not an inch. Revenge on Galba had become more important than anything – except ensuring that

Antonius' grave was suitably honoured. If he could see that both happened, Felix was prepared to lay down his life.

After all, what else had he to live for?

Not long after, Felix had made his way to Flamininus' pavilion. Memories of the night before were bright in his mind, and for the first time, Felix wavered.

The gods were watching.

A braying laugh carried through the air, and Felix saw Galba stalking away from Flamininus' tent, deep in conversation with a staff officer. Felix's hatred quickened. He could not walk away now. Would not.

Free of the wine-haze that had obscured his judgement the night before, he decided that attempting to bluff his way in was doomed to fail. Without an official message in his hand, a low-ranking optio such as he would not get past the sentries, no matter how silver his tongue. Better to wait out of sight, until Flamininus emerged. Steal up beside him, and he would have a chance – the briefest of chances – to bend the general's ear.

Lingering in the vicinity wasn't without risk, however. The only men who stood about here were sentries or officers in conversation, and Felix clearly wasn't either of those. Everyone else was either coming or going, passing along the two main avenues: units marching off to the training ground outside the walls, or back from an early patrol; messengers on horses and on foot; officers going about their business. These last were the most likely to see a lone soldier without any apparent purpose, and challenge him.

Felix tried walking around the enormous block made up of Flamininus' command pavilion and the almost as large tent that formed his private quarters, but that meant Flamininus might emerge while he was out of sight. Better to brave the risks, he decided, than miss his opportunity. Dry-mouthed, unease crawling all over his back, he took up a position a little way down one of the main avenues, diagonally opposite the entrance to the pavilion.

No one passed for a little while. Felix considered his options, deciding that to gain Flamininus' attention, he had to mention Galba at once. Any other method risked the wrath of Flamininus, or that of the plentiful staff officers who trailed in his wake. The heavy tread of hobnailed sandals carried down the avenue, and Felix lifted his head.

A maniple of hastati marched by, the soldiers' eyes facing forward. Luckily for Felix, the centurions, who were at the back, were deep in conversation and did not see him. A messenger rode towards the main gate; preoccupied with his mission, he paid Felix no heed.

This can't go on, thought Felix. Flamininus might not appear for hours; someone *will* question my presence before that. Loath to give up, for the gods only knew if he would ever find himself in the general's presence again, he decided to stay put for another five hundred heartbeats.

With a count of fourscore left, he saw Falto coming up the avenue towards him.

Acid washed the back of Felix's throat. Fortuna, you're an old bitch, he thought. Ducking his head, he turned and walked away from his centurion. Reach the intersection, the main crossroads in the camp, and he could make a quick left. From there, he could dart down into one of the smaller avenues, and if the goddess of fortune wasn't in an entirely spiteful mood, make good his escape. Preoccupied with not being seen by Falto – whose reaction could only be imagined – Felix fixed his gaze on the ground.

With an almighty thud, his head struck someone in the chest. There was an exclamation of surprise and annoyance. Startled, Felix looked up. To his utter horror, he had walked into none other than Flamininus. The general looked most unimpressed, but he also seemed preoccupied, which was perhaps why he didn't appear to have yet recognised Felix.

'A thousand apologies, sir,' said Felix, panicking. 'I wasn't looking where I was going.'

'That much is clear.' Frowning, Flamininus used a fold of his cloak to burnish the spot where Felix's hair had left a mark on his breastplate. 'Remove this man from my path,' he said to an outraged-looking staff officer. 'And punish him.'

Felix had the whisker of a chance before all was lost. Quickly, he said, 'I was coming to see you, sir.'

Already three strides on, Flamininus let out a derisory snort.

Dodging the grasp of the approaching staff officer, Felix kept up with the general. 'I have information you may find of interest, sir.'

'Gods above and below, get this fool away from me!' cried Flamininus.

Again Felix evaded the staff officer's grasp. 'It's about Galba, sir. I know something about Galba.' The staff officer grabbed him by the arm, and Felix did not resist. Strike an officer, and he would guarantee his own death. His spirits fell into the abyss as he was manhandled away. He had failed. Worse, Falto had seen him. Furious-faced, his centurion was watching the proceedings.

'Hold.'

The staff officer stopped.

Felix met Flamininus' stare. In it, he saw his death. I was wrong, he thought. Gods, how wrong I was. Flamininus has no interest in Galba.

Flamininus stalked back to Felix. Recognition bloomed in his fierce eyes. 'It's you. The clown. From Cynoscephalae – and last night.'

Felix had an overwhelming urge to piss. 'Yes, sir.'

'Galba, you say?'

Felix was so scared it took a moment to mutter, 'Yes, sir.'

'Release him,' ordered Flamininus. To Felix, he said quietly, 'Not a word until we are in private. Follow.'

Such was Felix's terror – there was no saying that Flamininus would believe him – that he missed Falto's face, and its expression of complete disbelief. Leaving behind the equally bemused staff officers, he and Flamininus walked not to the command pavilion, but the general's own tent. Past the saluting sentries they went, into the grand antechamber, where Felix presumed Flamininus received visitors. Eyes wide, for the place was better decorated than the wealthiest man's house he'd ever been in, he followed the general deep into the tent.

In a simple, carpeted chamber furnished with a desk, stools, iron lamp stands and a magnificent bust of Hercules wrapped in a lion skin, Flamininus stopped. He sat down, but gave no indication that Felix could do the same.

A worried-looking slave hurried in, carrying a stylus and writing tablet. 'Do you need me, master?'

'No. Leave, Potitius.'

'Master.' With a surreptitious lick of his lips, the slave absented himself.

Flamininus threw a glare after the slave, and fixing his eyes on Felix, said, 'You spoke of Galba.'

'I did, sir.'

Flamininus' gaze bore down on him, flint-hard. 'Why would I want to know whatever trifling detail you claim to know?'

Hades, thought Felix. The disagreement I saw between him and Galba has long since been repaired. Now they get along well. He had to answer, however, so he muttered, 'At Cynoscephalae, I saw you and Galba arguing, sir.'

Flamininus let out an amused snort. 'I had forgotten about that. Nothing like a public argument to get tongues wagging. No doubt you're hoping for some coin?'

Horrified, for he hadn't thought how Flamininus might question his motives, Felix replied, 'No, sir! I don't want a single *as.*'

'Every man has his price,' said Flamininus with a disbelieving look. He clicked his fingers. 'I'm a busy man. Get on with it.'

Felix nodded, as nervous as when Matho had ordered the fustuarium. Without mentioning that he had met Pennus at an inn, drunk, Felix repeated every detail of the maimed ex-legionary's story. With growing interest, Flamininus listened, interrupting only to confirm that the town's name had been Celetrum. When Felix was done, Flamininus said nothing for a time. Felix's worry that he would end up being flogged again resurged. Miserable, wondering if he should have kept his head down, he resigned himself to Galba escaping justice for ever.

'I made it my business to be familiar with every aspect of the war with Macedonia before assuming command,' said Flamininus. 'Celetrum was a small town. Official records detail that the monies recovered there amounted to a middling sum – certainly not the fortune you allude to.' Again his gaze pinned Felix. 'Did you think this veteran, this *Pennus*, was telling the truth?'

'I'd stake my life on it, sir. He was so bitter. Maimed, destitute, he has no future, while Galba's star continues to rise. Pennus would do anything, pay any price, to see justice done. To see Galba punished.'

'And he has comrades still living, who were also at Celetrum?'

'That's what he said, sir.'

'Do you know where Pennus lives?'

'Aye, sir. Me and my brother, we helped him home from the inn.' Felix felt a momentary panic. Mention of the inn would lead Flamininus to correctly assume that they'd been drinking heavily, and that might lead him to doubt not just Felix's story, but that of Pennus as well.

Flamininus' eyes gleamed; he barely seemed to notice. 'I have you now, Galba,' he whispered. 'Oh Jupiter, I have you now.'

Felix thought, Flamininus *does* hate Galba. Better still, he believes me.

'If things are indeed as you have related, optio, you shall be rewarded in royal style.' For the first time, Flamininus' tone was warm. 'You will travel to Rome and meet with my men. Find Pennus, and as many of his comrades as possible. Take a statement from every man. Of course some may still be in the legions here – you can seek them out upon your return.'

'It will be my honour, sir,' said Felix, thinking with savage glee, Galba won't see the punch coming until he sees the floor coming up to meet him.

Flamininus twisted around and unlocked a metal-bound chest. Its top creaked as he heaved it open. Coins chinked. He turned back to Felix and dropped a leather purse on the desk. 'That's for your trouble.'

'Thank you, sir.' Felix bobbed his head. The purse's size and the weighty thud told him there was a sizeable sum within – several years' pay, he'd wager – but he made no move to pick it up.

Flamininus' expression clouded; his mouth twisted. 'Always they want more. You shall have the same again, optio, but only if your information about Galba proves to be true.'

'It's not that, sir,' said Felix, pushing the purse towards Flamininus. 'You are more than generous, but I didn't do this for coin. All I ask, sir, is that I might take a tombstone to Cynoscephalae for my brother.'

Flamininus stared at him.

'That's all I want, sir, on my brother's life.' Felix had never meant anything more.

'He asks not for money or advancement, but for time to honour his brother,' said Flamininus softly, looking surprised. He nodded. 'You shall have your leave, optio, as soon as this matter is laid to rest. For now, you have my gratitude. You may go.'

Delighted, Felix saluted and turned on his heel.

'One last thing.'

'Sir?'

'Not a word to anyone. On pain of death.' Flamininus' face had lost any trace of amity.

Felix thought of Falto, and said, 'My centurion tore strips off me for last night, sir, and he saw us meet outside. He'll have questions for me.'

'I'll see to it he leaves you alone.'

'Thank you, sir.'

Flamininus waved a hand in dismissal.

Felix's heart pulsed with a new-found joy as he exited the tent. He had done it.

Galba would get his comeuppance, and Antonius would have his tombstone.

CHAPTER XXXIII

Pella

Demetrios was stretching in front of his tent. It was still early, but the army's camp was already busy. Half the size it had been thanks to the losses at Kynoskephalae, the tents still stretched for many stadia in every direction. Military routine continued – Philip had seen to that – and so the trumpets sounded each dawn. On the open ground between the camp and Pella, officers would soon be drilling their phalangists, and cavalrymen would practise their skills on straw targets. Men would be sent to fell trees for firewood, and to the river for water.

Demetrios' mood was lighter than it had been. The victory at the Axios had been much needed; his burgeoning friendship with Perseus was also a distraction from his grief. This last was the reason for his stretching; he had arranged to meet the prince at the city's palaestra. Although he'd told Andriskos not to tell anyone he was to train at pankration with Perseus, his hope had proved fruitless. Demetrios had endured a merciless ribbing from his comrades; it had gone on until after they'd retired for the night and had continued without pause since they had risen.

'You ready?' It was Andriskos' turn to cook; he was sitting on a large stone by the fire, tending baking flatbreads. 'Remember to lose the first bout. It wouldn't do to beat Perseus at the outset.'

'I'd throw the second as well,' added Simonides, who was running a whetstone up and down the blade of his kopis.

'And the third.' Andriskos chortled.

'I wouldn't try to win at all,' added Taurion to a chorus of laughter.

Demetrios rolled his eyes and went back to stretching. Although the joking was a little annoying, it was done with love. He did the same to the others if he got an opportunity. It was one of the ways to show each other they cared. They few were the survivors of Kynoskephalae, and the bond holding them together was as strong as that of family.

A moment later, his skin twitched, the way it does when a man realises someone is staring, and he turned his head. Skopas, and beside him, Empedokles, had been listening from their position outside the next tent. Skopas had the wit to look away, but Empedokles ran a lascivious tongue around his lips and with the forefinger of his left hand, shoved it into the ring made by the thumb and first finger of his right.

Angered, Demetrios mouthed a curse in reply. Then, to piss Empedokles off further, he lifted his own kopis and grinned. The fury contorting his enemy's face was easily worth the irritation Demetrios felt at the implication that he and Perseus were lovers. Turning his back on Empedokles, he pondered his upcoming bout at the palaestra. Demetrios wouldn't have admitted it to a soul, but his friends' jokes had struck close to the mark. If Perseus had any ability, and his invitation suggested he did, how could he, Demetrios, dare to try and beat the prince? His pride stirred. It wasn't in his nature to throw even a friendly bout of pankration, and yet, he told himself, not to do so might well bring down the wrath of the king's son.

Pride or not, that was not something Demetrios was prepared to risk.

Cursing, Demetrios ran down the narrow lane, dodging past a donkey-drawn cart laden with bricks. Never having used either the city's gymnasium or the older palaestra, he had assumed that Perseus would prefer the newer of the two. Finding out that young nobles preferred the palaestra because of its closeness to the palace, he'd had to run the entire way from the gymnasium. Although it wasn't far – six or seven stadia – the streets were thronged. Demetrios didn't know Pella well enough to risk taking a short cut through the back alleys, so he'd had to make his way, swearing, through the crowds.

Reaching the door of the palaestra in a lather of sweat, he remembered to mutter a prayer to Hermes – honoured by stone herms on either side of the door – before he entered. The room beyond, for getting undressed, was busy. Upwards of a dozen naked young men were oiling their muscles and bantering with one another. A sandal flew past Demetrios, hitting the wall behind him. The youth it had been meant for laughed and hurled one of his own in reply.

Already self-conscious – by their accents, these were nobles

– Demetrios took another step or two, and then stopped. He didn't know where to go.

A youth with curly black hair and full lips sitting on a nearby bench noticed. 'Ho!' he cried. 'We have a new visitor.' As the hubbub died away, he smiled in a not entirely pleasant way at Demetrios. 'I've never seen you here before, friend.'

'No. This is my first time.' Demetrios wondered about lying, saying that usually he went to the gymnasium, but it would be easy to catch him out as he'd never been there either, so he said nothing more. His eyes found the doorway at the back of the room – that must lead into the exercise areas, he decided.

'From the city, are you?' The question came from another youth, one with longer hair than was fashionable, and a sneering expression.

Tartaros, thought Demetrios. This could end in a fight. He could have walked through the inner door, but he first wanted to be sure Perseus was here. 'I'm not,' he said politely. 'Is the prince within?'

'Hear him!' said Curly Hair. 'The prince, he says.'

'Come to meet Perseus, have you?' The youth with long hair cast his eyes around his friends, who chuckled dutifully.

Whether this preening lot regarded themselves as better than military service, Demetrios didn't know, but he didn't recognise a single man among them from the army. They were also cut from different cloth than the Companion cavalry he'd encountered. For the most part, those were plain-speaking types who gave as good as they got, and who took men as they found them.

'I asked you a question.' The youth's tone had turned hostile.

'I am here to meet the prince, aye,' said Demetrios, peering about in vain for an attendant who might answer his query. Better to avoid confrontation and seek out Perseus himself, he decided, making for the inner doorway.

Curly Hair leaped up to block his path. 'I say you're a liar.' He jabbed Demetrios in the chest with a finger. 'And a dusty footed liar at that.'

Demetrios had had enough. Quick as a striking snake, he grabbed Curly Hair's head with both hands and pulled down with all his strength. Even as Curly Hair's hands flailed at his in an effort to break the grip, the youth staggered forward onto one foot, his left. Slipping his hands down to Curly Hair's armpits to gain better purchase, Demetrios tripped him over his outstretched right leg. Curly Hair landed hard on the floor, yelping in surprise and pain.

Demetrios stepped past. He turned, filling the doorway, and gave the whimpering Curly Hair and his friends, who had swarmed towards them, a hard stare. 'I did not start this, but by Hades I will finish it.'

'I've twisted my ankle.' Curly Hair's voice was petulant.

'You'll hurt more than that if I have to come at you again,' said Demetrios, eyeing the rest and wondering how many he could down before they overcame him.

'Ho now, what's going on?' boomed a voice.

Demetrios found himself being shoved aside. A bandy-legged, shaven-headed instructor old enough to be his grandfather stepped over Curly Hair and into the changing room. 'Trust you to be at the heart of this,' he cried, pointing his stick at several youths. Sheepish grins replaced their murderous expressions, and the trainer wheeled to face Demetrios and Curly Hair.

'Fights take place in the mud room or on the skamma – nowhere else. Every halfwit knows that,' he growled.

'He threw *me* – I hadn't done anything,' said Curly Hair with a spiteful look at Demetrios.

The instructor's attention moved to Demetrios. 'Who are you?'

'I'm a phalangist in the Brazen Shields—'

'Meaning no disrespect, but you should be in the gymnasium,' the instructor interrupted. 'This place is for the nobles, as you can see.'

'I'm here to train with Perseus,' said Demetrios, colouring.

The instructor's face changed. 'The prince?'

'Aye. Meet him here,' he said. 'I'm late, so he may already be inside.'

'That he is. He mentioned something about a phalangist joining him, now you mention it.' The instructor glared at the youths. 'Shame on you lot.' To Curly Hair, he said, 'Lucky this man didn't break your ankle, eh?' And to Demetrios, 'If you'll come with me.' He stumped past, into the corridor.

It would have given Demetrios considerable pleasure to mock Curly Hair and his cronies; he decided that the shock and fear on their faces – the realisation that he *did* know Perseus, and might tell the prince what they had done – would suffice. Turning his back, he followed the instructor.

'A wrestler, are you?' This was thrown over the trainer's shoulder.

'I can wrestle.'

'You must be all right. The prick you threw is no slouch.'

It pleased Demetrios to know that the instructor didn't like Curly Hair either. 'He wasn't expecting me to attack.'

A short laugh. 'Aye, you can't beat surprise, eh? Wins the fight often enough. Here we are.' The instructor stopped at the fourth doorway and said, 'You'll find the prince inside.'

Aware that he was still dressed, Demetrios ducked his head and entered. His eyes had adjusted to the corridor's poor light, so he had no trouble making out the grappling figures on the scuffed-up sand inside. Three pairs, evenly matched from the look of it, danced and weaved around each other, kicking, punching and blocking. Perseus was fighting a blocky-chested individual larger and older than he, but to Demetrios' astonishment, that didn't stop the prince's opponent from seizing him in a headlock and wrenching him to the floor. Laughing, Perseus slapped the sand to indicate he'd lost, and the blocky-chested man released him at once.

'Majesty,' he said without a trace of sycophancy.

Perseus dipped his chin by way of recognition, and in the same instant, launched a furious combination of kicks and punches that sent his opponent back several paces.

As if sensing Demetrios' surprise at the equality with which the pair treated each other, the instructor said quietly from behind him, 'There are no princes or lords in here, friend, or even kings. Every man is equal on the skamma. So it has always been.'

'I see,' said Demetrios, thinking, I might have a chance yet.

Perseus succeeded in throwing the blocky-chested man soon after. The victory seemed to be the end of the bout, for the two shook hands and separated. Seeing Demetrios, Perseus approached. 'What have we here? I thought you had snubbed me.'

'Forgive me, sire,' said Demetrios, his embarrassment flooding back. 'I went first to the gymnasium, thinking to find you there. Realising my mistake, I hurried here as fast as I could.'

'He would have been with you a little sooner, sire, if it hadn't been for the young fools in the changing room.' The instructor let out an evil chuckle. 'This one knows a few moves, mind. He left Melanthios mewling on the floor like a newborn babe.'

'Is that so?' Perseus' teeth flashed white. 'Melanthios has ever been a fool, wont to act before he thinks.'

'They thought I was lying about meeting you, sire,' said Demetrios.

'And if I know Melanthios and his friends, they didn't like a commoner stepping across the threshold either.' Perseus clapped him on the shoulder. 'Men like them never learn. In the storm of bronze, a man's station in life counts for nothing. It's what's in a man's heart, eh?'

'Yes, sire.' Pleased by this recognition, Demetrios said, 'You ready for another bout?'

'I'm standing here waiting. You're the one still clothed,' said Perseus, laughing.

Setting his chiton and undergarment by the door, Demetrios joined the prince on the skamma.

The instructor, who had been watching, let the end of his stick drop towards the floor. 'Begin!'

Demetrios' face pressed into the cloth covering the table. He exhaled, relishing the feel of the slave's hands rubbing down his back. He'd had massages before, but never this good. He and Perseus were lying side by side in one of the rooms adjacent to those set aside for wrestling and pankration. Three bouts they had fought, with Demetrios winning two and the prince one. The last contest had gone to Demetrios, but only by a narrow margin. Perseus had not taken the loss badly – 'I am only fifteen,' he'd said. 'Give me a year or two and I'll have the beating of you.'

He was right, like as not, Demetrios decided. Already skilled beyond his years, Perseus trained daily, whereas army duties meant *he* only practised once or twice every ten days. That was the luxury of being a prince, he thought, with only a trace of jealousy. Truth be told, Demetrios had been more envious until he'd realised the weight of responsibility falling on Perseus' young shoulders. All they had talked about since lying down was the war, and the treaty made with Rome, and the future.

'Did you find it difficult to accept that my father made peace with Flamininus?' Perseus' voice was muffled.

Demetrios felt a rush of anger. He had, and he did. Kimon and Antileon, and so many others had died fighting at Kynoskephalae. Others had fallen in the battles before that. Grateful that his face was hidden on the table, he answered evasively, 'I did, sire.'

'It's only natural. So many men were left at the Dogs' Heads.'

Unburied, thought Demetrios, shame stinging him that he had not honoured his slain comrades. The king's decision to avoid the mockery – by his Greek enemies – that would follow if he returned to the scene of his defeat was understandable, but a bitter medicine to swallow. At the first opportunity, Demetrios had decided, *he* would return to Kynoskephalae to try and find his friends' bodies.

'Father says that alliance with the Romans is better than being ground into the dust.'

'He's right, sire,' said Demetrios, hating his own words. 'That's what Flamininus would have done to us.'

'Given that the Romans are now our allies – hard as that is to stomach – Father says our best policy is to support them against a common enemy.'

'It's not something I could have imagined doing, but again, sire, the king is right.'

'The Seleucid emperor has ever been someone Father dealt with from a distance, cordially but with the knowledge that a day would come when war against Antiokhos was the only option. Knowing that we were weak, his fleet took the Hellespont last summer. This year, his gaze will turn westward, to Macedon.'

'Will the Romans fight him too, sire?'

'Flamininus says they will – if you can believe him. Father declares him to be as hard to pin down as a snake, and just as untrustworthy. It would not serve Rome, however, to let us face Antiokhos alone. If Macedon fell, gods forbid, the Seleucids would swarm into Greece like a plague of locusts. Flamininus' work to set Rome up as the dominant force here would be undone in an instant. The legions will resist any attempt by Antiokhos to invade, therefore, and we shall stand with them.'

Tartaros, thought Demetrios. I could end up in the battle line beside men who murdered my friends.

'Will you fight with me?' Perseus' voice was clearer – he had lifted his head off the table, and was looking at Demetrios.

There was only one answer to give, thought Demetrios. Meeting the prince's gaze, he said proudly, 'That would be my honour, sire.'

Melanthios and some of his friends were still boxing when Demetrios' and Perseus' massage had finished. The prince made a point of taking an embarrassed but then delighted Demetrios into the room, and when quiet fell, loudly announcing that this brave phalangist, who had been at Atrax and Kynoskephalae – 'None of you were there,' Perseus had added, his voice dripping with scorn – was his friend. 'Pick a fight with Demetrios, and you pick a fight with me,' he said, his gaze resting on an unhappy-looking Melanthios. 'Well?'

Melanthios dropped his gaze, and Perseus laughed.

Demetrios felt twice as tall as he had entering the palaestra. Perseus was a true comrade, he decided. The demonstration of loyalty had been for him alone.

Perseus took his leave of Demetrios outside. 'Duty calls,' he said with a mock-mournful expression. 'Father has called a meeting of his senior advisers, and I am to sit in. Until next time, my friend. I'll send word, or come to see you in the camp.'

'I look forward to it, sire,' said Demetrios, smiling and raising a hand in farewell. His belly rumbled, and he decided to wander in search of some food. A cup of wine wouldn't go astray either; he wasn't on duty until the evening.

Someone tugged at his arm. 'Help, sir.' The piping voice belonged to a squint-eyed urchin. Used to cutpurses, Demetrios brushed away the brat's grasping fingers. 'Away with you.'

The urchin bobbed from foot to filthy foot. 'My mother, sir. She's fallen over and hurt her hip.'

'Get her up yourself.'

'I tried, sir, but I'm not strong like you.'

'Get your brothers and sisters to help.'

'The little 'uns are no use – they're only three and five.' The urchin's chin quivered. 'All the neighbours are out.'

Demetrios' conscience pricked him. 'Where do you live?'

A skinny arm pointed to the alley opposite. 'Just down there, sir, not fifty paces. Please. Two moments it will take. My mother will be forever grateful.'

A glance up and down the street – there was no one else in sight – made Demetrios decide that the urchin's approach was genuine. He followed the boy into the narrow, dim-lit alley, grimacing at the inevitable smell of human waste and rotting food. Broken pottery moved under his sandals; so did more squishy material he scarce dared to look at. A one-eared cat, disturbed by their passage, picked up whatever it had been eating and vanished into the gloom.

Twenty paces in, Demetrios halted. He hadn't seen a single doorway. 'Where is your house?'

'Just a little further, sir.' The urchin's tone was wheedling.

Demetrios had heard a thousand falsehoods tumble from the lips of street brats. 'You're lying,' he said, turning.

'Philippos – is that you?' A woman's voice. She made to speak, then groaned, as if in pain.

Demetrios peered, could see no one.

'Philippos?' called the woman again.

'It's me, mother. I brought a kind man to help.' The urchin regarded Demetrios with a pleading expression.

The boy's called Philippos, thought Demetrios. He's trying to do his best for his mother. Cursing himself for being distrustful, he waved a hand. 'Lead on.'

They passed an opening to the right. Dark, narrow, Demetrios didn't even glance into it.

'It's here, sir.' The urchin came to a stop by an open door.

Demetrios peered into the hovel, but could see no one. 'Where is your mother?'

'In the back room. I'll show you.' The urchin slipped past, and before Demetrios could react, slammed the door in his face. There was a heavy thump as a locking bar fell into place.

Baffled and annoyed, Demetrios pounded on the timbers. 'What's going on, boy?'

'The man said he'd hurt my mother if I didn't obey,' came a muffled voice.

'Eh?'

'Had a nice tryst in the palaestra with your lover?'

The hairs on the back of Demetrios' neck stood on end. He turned, seeing a figure silhouetted against the light from the street. A figure that must have been lurking in the opening he'd ignored. A figure that blocked his way out. 'Empedokles,' grated Demetrios. 'I should have known it was you.'

'You should. Trusting fool.'

'Where's the woman? Tell me you haven't cut her throat.'

A snort. 'What do you care if I have or haven't?'

He's murdered her, thought Demetrios with real alarm. Left her

333

body in the gap where he was hiding. Demetrios shot a look over his shoulder, but the alley appeared to end in a high wall. The only way back to the street was past his enemy, who meant him real harm. His eyes searched the ground for a weapon – a length of wood, a large lump of pottery – anything.

Empedokles came closer. 'Who's the pillow-biter, and who's the chiton-lifter? That's what I want to know. Most would think Perseus the dominant one, being a prince and all, but maybe he can't get hard enough.' Empedokles made a fist and jerked his left forearm up from the elbow, mimicking a phallus, and then let it droop towards the ground. In a falsetto voice, he said, 'Maybe Perseus likes to play the girl. Maybe he likes the big strong phalangist to ravish him—'

'Shut your filthy mouth! The prince is not like that. Nor am I.' Demetrios stooped and picked up a triangular shard of clay. It fitted snugly into his right palm; when he made a fist, the pointed end protruded far enough from between his second and third fingers to form a 'blade'. It wouldn't kill, but rip it hard enough across Empedokles' face and he'd have a good chance of winning the fight.

'You would say that.' Hands low by his sides, Empedokles came even closer. 'Want to protect your lover, don't you? No one wants to think every tongue is wagging about them. Arse-lover, they call you in the speira. Nipple-teaser. Cocksucker.'

Demetrios' fury surged, and he lunged forward, clenching the pottery shard.

Light flashed off the blade that had been hidden in Empedokles' right fist.

Committed, powering forward, Demetrios could only try to grab Empedokles' wrist. He missed. Pain such as he'd never felt erupted from the bottom of his ribcage. He's stuck me, thought Demetrios. I can still take him. His left hand went down, gripping Empedokles' right, and he tried to tug the blade free. Oddly, his strength had gone.

'Tartaros awaits,' hissed Empedokles in his ear. He shoved hard, driving the sharp iron deeper.

The agony was so exquisite now that Demetrios cried out. He felt his legs buckling. Tried to punch Empedokles in the face with the shard and succeeded only in brushing it against his hair. Demetrios' vision dimmed, then brightened as Empedokles tugged free the blade.

334

A warm fluid sensation ran down Demetrios' belly onto his left leg. I'm bleeding, he thought.

Empedokles stabbed him again.

Demetrios groaned. 'Gods, that hurts.'

'Good.' Empedokles thrust for a third time.

Demetrios' legs folded. He found himself on his back, barely noticing the stench or the pottery pressing into his flesh from underneath. High above, between the roofs, he could see a strip of glorious blue sky.

The sky vanished as Empedokles crouched over him. 'I should have done this long ago,' he said, sliding the blade into Demetrios' chest.

The pain took Demetrios, and he fell.

A voice called, a familiar one.

Demetrios' eyes widened. Philippos? he thought, wondering. Philippos?

CHAPTER XXXIV

Philip was at breakfast in the courtyard nearest his private quarters in the royal palace. Watered and tended daily, the trellised vines were lush with growth. Hidden from view, a fountain pattered to itself. Down one end of the covered walkway, a slave pushed a twig broom along the mosaic floor. Overhead, an early lark trilled its excitement at the change in seasons. Philip's daughter Apama ran here and there, shrieking with joy as her nurse play-chased her.

Philip's pleasure in watching Apama was tempered with sadness at the thought of his son Demetrios, far away in Rome. Alone. Without friends.

Perseus, sitting across the table from him, saw the direction of his gaze and said, 'You miss Demetrios. So do I.'

'I do,' said Philip wearily. 'I had to send him – Flamininus would not have settled for peace if I had refused.'

'You did what you had to, Father, and Demetrios' last letter said he was being well treated.' Perseus frowned, thinking, and added, 'But I suppose it would, wouldn't it? A Roman stood over him while he wrote it, like as not.'

'You're learning, my son,' said Philip, able to take a little satisfaction from this, even with the grim reality of Demetrios' absence staring him in the face. 'Trust nothing unless you have seen proof of it with your own eyes, or heard it from someone who you can entirely trust. And people like that are few and far between.'

'You,' said Perseus.

'Yes.'

'Menander.'

'Correct.'

'My friend Demetrios – the phalangist who saved your life.'

'You can't be sure of that yet, but given what I know of him, I'd wager you're right.'

'Not my mother,' said Perseus, earning a rueful nod from Philip. 'The generals Nikanor and Athenagoras?'

'Thank the gods, yes.'

'Demetrios swears that he would trust his file-leader Simonides and the second-ranker Andriskos with his life.' Again Perseus checked himself. 'He may believe that, but I have not seen proof of it. Worthy men they are, no doubt, but not in the same league as Menander, for example.'

'Good,' said Philip. 'Anyone else?'

'Flamininus?'

They both laughed.

'There are no others that I can think of,' said Perseus.

'D'you see how lonely a position it is, being king? Oh, I am surrounded by men who praise my every move, who'd swear that my farts smell of roses, but let me tell you, Perseus, when it comes to the simple truth, rare is the man who can speak it to my face. The skill is in being able to judge who is lying to please you, or to ingratiate themselves' – here Philip thought uncomfortably of his admiral Herakleides – 'and who is being loyal, who is doing what's right.'

Perseus sighed.

Philip laughed and tossed a hazelnut at him. 'You have years to learn, my son. I intend to be a greybeard when the Fates cut my thread.' May the gods grant that be true, he prayed.

'We can't trust Antiokhos, that is certain. Do you think he'll invade this summer?'

'He'd be a fool to do so before seeing which way the land lies. Flamininus is to make public the terms of the peace treaty at the Isthmian Games, less than two months hence. Antiokhos' spies will have told him that, and he's not prone to rash decisions. The Seleucid fleet won't sail before the games, if it's to sail west at all.'

'What of the Aitolians, Father? Is their anger towards Flamininus and their hatred of you great enough to approach Antiokhos?'

The boy had been listening at the council a day prior, thought Philip with satisfaction. He was coming on fast. 'The Aitolians would sell their own mothers, but only at the right time. To move against Rome now would be premature. Flamininus' legions remain in Greece, and could crush the Aitolians the way a man stamps on an insect. The treacherous dogs are unhappy enough – I hear it from my spies every day – but they will continue to pay lip service to Rome for the time being.'

'It seems we too must always wait and watch,' said Perseus, his impatience making him sound like a little boy.

'Listen to youth,' said Philip, remembering his own impetuosity. 'You may not know it yet, but to wait and observe is preferable to fighting a constant war.'

'My head tells me that is true, Father, but my heart wants another battle. Like the one at the Axios.'

Philip's smile was indulgent. 'You shall have opportunities like that again, never fear. Think of the Dardanians like a dim-witted wrestler, who forgets each defeat after a few days. Picking a fight with his old enemy, he's surprised to be beaten, but then it slips his mind, and so it goes on. Give the sheep-humping Dardanians time, and they'll cross the border again. I guarantee it.'

'Can I command the force sent against the next incursion?'

Gods, but they grow up fast, thought Philip. Once it was could he stay up to have dinner with me. Then he asked for a real sword. Now he wants to lead my troops into battle. 'Maybe.' He held up a hand as Perseus shouted with delight, and said, 'I did *not* say yes.'

'You didn't say no either!' cried Perseus.

Hobnails rang off the floor, and Philip turned his head. 'Even at this early hour, duty calls.'

A stolid-looking officer of the guard appeared. Spying the king, he approached with a deferential look. 'Apologies, sire, for interrupting your meal.'

Philip waved a hand. 'I had finished. Speak.'

'A messenger has come from Carthage, sire.'

Philip's eyes darted to Perseus, and back to the guard. 'Go on.'

'His ship docked at dawn, sire, and he came to the palace without delay. Says he bears a letter from Hannibal. I tried to make him give it me, but he refused. "I am to pass it into the hand of Philip himself and no one else," he said, all high and mighty.' The officer glowered.

'I think I have met this man before,' said Philip with a smile. 'Show him in.'

The king's instinct was correct. When the officer appeared, two of his men flanking the messenger, there was no mistaking the tall, thin figure with black hair and green eyes.

'Hanno, son of Malchus,' said Philip warmly. 'We meet again.'

The guard officer looked astonished. 'You know him, sire?'

'I do.' To Hanno, the king said, 'Welcome.'

'The honour is mine, sire,' replied Hanno with a deep bow. He cast a look at Perseus. 'Is this your eldest son?'

'Indeed. Perseus, meet Hanno, soldier and trusted follower of Hannibal Barca. Veteran not just of the Trebia and Lake Trasimene, but of Cannae as well.' Philip had made sure Perseus' tutors taught him the details of Hannibal's extraordinary campaign in Italia.

'I would like to hear of that battle,' said Perseus, his eyes shining.

'Mayhap we will have time to speak of it, sire,' said Hanno, inclining his head. 'First, however, I must deliver this to your father.' Reaching into his purse, he took out a rolled parchment and stepped up to pass it to Philip.

Using a table knife, the king sliced the seal and unrolled the letter.

Greetings once again, O King of Macedon.
Here in Carthage, Rome pressures my enemies
to move against me. Very soon I must leave,
never to return. It saddens me that after all
my efforts, few of my people will mourn my
departure. Regretfully, I must inform you that
I will not be sailing to join you in Macedon.
Word of your defeat at the Dogs' Heads
reached me a little time since. It is a tragedy
for us both that Flamininus emerged triumphant.
Nothing would have given me more pleasure than
to serve as your general. and to lead your army
to victory over Flamininus. I doubt not that you,
a valiant leader, wish to continue your
fight against Rome. Yet the heavy casualties
your army suffered, and the territories you lost
mean that any possibility of this will
take years. Perhaps many years. Time is not a
luxury I possess, regrettably. Two-score years

and ten I have seen. Only the gods know what
span remains for me, but I must use it to fight
the Republic. I shall therefore be offering my
services to Antiokhos III, the Seleucid emperor.

Philip's vision blurred with rage. This was not wholly unexpected news, but seeing it written down made the blow even more hammer-like. Crumpling the letter without reading the final few lines, he glared at Hanno. 'He's not coming.'

The regret was plain in Hanno's face. 'No, sire, but Hannibal is sorry that he cannot.'

'Sorry! Sorry is not the same as the presence of the world's finest general. Sorry is not thousands of fresh troops for my army.'

'It is not, sire,' agreed Hanno.

'You must have known that coming here with this message risked your life,' hissed Philip. 'That reading your master's spurning of me, I might have you executed.' He jerked his head, and the officer and the bodyguards closed in on Hanno.

Hanno did not stir. 'Hannibal did not want me to come, sire, for just that reason. "Philip is a man of high temper," he said. I said that I'd found you to be a fair man. A man of honour. The honourable thing was to bring you the letter myself, to look you in the eye and apologise that Hannibal is unable to join you. I am glad to say that he granted me permission to do so. I've done my duty – now you must do yours, sire.'

'Father—' Perseus began.

Philip cut him off. 'Curse you, Hanno son of Malchus,' he said without heat. 'You give me no choice at all. I cannot blame the messenger for what he carries, not least because he has acted with honour himself. You shall leave here unharmed. Before you go, you shall enjoy my hospitality.'

Hanno made a deep bow. 'Gratitude, sire.'

'I don't suppose I can persuade you to join my army? I'd make it worth your while.'

'You show me great respect, sire, but I must refuse. I have served Hannibal for more than half my life. To leave him now, when his fortunes are on the ebb, would seem traitorous to me. I'm his man until I die.'

340

Philip laughed. 'I suspected that was the case. Very well. You shall return to Carthage and your master. But you'll also stay a night in the palace, and dine with me and Perseus here. That's my only condition.'

'A condition it would be my pleasure to endure, sire.'

'Until later then,' said Philip. To the guard officer, who seemed disappointed by Hanno's sudden elevation in status, he said, 'Find this man the best quarters in the guest wing. See that his every need is met.'

Smiling, Hanno was guided away.

Philip glanced at Perseus, who looked delighted by his response, and said, 'If I had ten thousand soldiers like this man, Kynoskephalae would have been my victory, not Flamininus'.'

'I don't know why, but I can tell, Father. There's an air about him, a confidence – it's hard to describe.'

He's turning into a fine judge of character, Philip decided, pleased.

Footsteps from the entrance to the courtyard drew both their attention.

'Perhaps Hanno has changed his mind?' joked Perseus.

'I doubt that,' said Philip. 'It will be another messenger.'

It wasn't.

Another guard officer, more junior than the one who'd brought in Hanno, appeared. His gaze slid first to Perseus, then to the king. 'Apologies, sire, for interrupting—'

'Yes, yes, we've been through all that,' said Philip. 'What is it?'

'There's a young nobleman requesting to see the prince, sire.' Again the officer's eyes moved to Perseus. 'Melanthios, he's called.'

'You know someone by that name?' asked Philip.

'Yes,' said Perseus, frowning. To the guard, he said, 'What does he want?'

'He would only say that it was urgent, sire. Very urgent.'

Perseus exchanged a look with his father, who nodded. 'Bring him in,' Perseus ordered.

'What could this be about?' asked Philip, intrigued.

'I have no idea, Father. Melanthios is a boor and a bully – he's no friend of mine. Yesterday, he and his friends picked on Demetrios at the palaestra.' Perseus related the rest of the story.

'Demetrios is a good man and no mistake,' said Philip, chuckling. 'I'd pay a gold coin to have seen him throw Melanthios.'

341

Before long, the junior officer returned with a limping Melanthios in tow.

'Approach,' said Perseus.

Melanthios hobbled closer. Ten paces from the king, he stopped and bowed. 'Sire.' With an awkward glance at Perseus, he repeated, 'Sire.'

'Melanthios,' said Perseus, with one word conveying superiority, dislike and a little surprise. 'What in Tartaros brings you here?'

'I bear sad news, sire.' Melanthios looked to the king for approval.

Wondering what Melanthios could know – given Perseus and he were not friends – Philip waved a hand. 'Speak.'

'The phalangist from the palaestra, sire . . .' Melanthios hesitated.

'Demetrios, yes,' said Perseus, a trace of concern in his eyes. 'What of him?'

In a quiet voice, Melanthios said, 'He's dead, sire.'

'Dead? He can't be,' cried Perseus. 'I bade him farewell on the street not a day since!'

'I'm sorry, sire,' said Melanthios.

'Did you have anything to do with it?' Perseus was on his feet, shouting.

'No, sire, I swear it!' Melanthios' face was terrified. 'My friends and I, we were all together still when you and Demetrios left. Not long after, we were in the changing room when there were shouts outside. We ran naked onto the street, and found your friend lying in a pool of blood down an alleyway opposite.'

Saddened, for Demetrios had been a loyal follower, Philip glanced at his son. Perseus' face was white as snow, apart from twin pricks of red at his cheekbones.

'Go on,' whispered Perseus.

'He was already close to death by the time we arrived, sire. Someone fetched a surgeon from the agora. He tried to stem the bleeding, but it was no use. We carried him into the house of an old woman who lived close by, and made him comfortable. The surgeon stayed with him.'

'Did he speak? Did he wake . . . before the end?' demanded Perseus.

'They said not, sire. I came to visit in the evening, and he had died.'

'You should have sent word to me!' In a heartbeat, Perseus was round the table and screaming in Melanthios' face. 'I would have had the best surgeon in Pella tend to him!'

'Forgive me, sire,' babbled Melanthios, cowering away from Perseus.

'I wondered if I should, but after the way I'd treated him, I thought you would blame me for what had happened. Also, the surgeon who examined him said no one living could stop him passing to the underworld. He'd been stabbed in the guts, twice, and in the chest. No one can survive that kind of blood loss, the surgeon said, sire.' Melanthios hung his head. 'I'm sorry.'

Philip did not intervene. This was a real test for his son.

Breathing heavily, Perseus stepped back from Melanthios. 'Why did you decide to come and tell me?'

'I couldn't sleep all night thinking about it, sire. I went to the Temple of Asklepios at dawn to seek guidance. The only thought that came into my mind was that you should know. He was your friend, and so . . . here I am, sire.'

'What of the whoreson who murdered him?' asked Perseus.

'He ran away before anyone could stop him, sire. It seems he murdered a woman too. Wondering if anyone had heard the fight, I went straight from the temple this morning to the house of the old woman into whose house we carried Demetrios. She told me that she had heard the fight, and that Demetrios said "Empedokles" at least twice.'

'Empedokles,' said Perseus, his expression flat and hard.

Philip caught his son's eye. 'You know who that is?'

'Demetrios had a comrade by that name. A man who made his life a misery from the first day he joined the phalanx.'

Philip's expression grew calculating. 'In that case, we had best have a word with this Empedokles.'

When Empedokles was hauled into the small, windowless room where Philip and Perseus were waiting, he looked terrified. Tossed to the flagstones by the two soldiers who'd half carried him there, he lay face down, trembling.

'Get up.' Perseus' voice cracked like a whip.

Empedokles pulled himself to his knees. His eyes moved from Philip to Perseus. 'Majesties,' he muttered.

'D'you know why you are here?' demanded Perseus.

'N-no, sire.'

Philip would have struck Empedokles then, for it was clear he was lying, but Perseus did not. Instead he said to the officer who'd come in with the soldiers, 'Did you search his belongings?'

'Yes, sire.' The officer held out a plain, bone-handled dagger. 'It's been washed, but there are traces of blood on the hilt.'

Empedokles' throat worked.

'A friend of mine was slain outside the palaestra yesterday. Demetrios, he was called,' said Perseus. 'He was heard to call his killer "Empedokles". Strange, is it not, that you and Demetrios served in the same file?'

'C-coincidence, sire,' said Empedokles. 'There are many men with my name. I can think of at least three others in the same speira—'

Interrupting, Perseus said, 'How many of them had a long-running enmity with Demetrios? I'll guess. None.'

Empedokles turned to the king. 'Your son is mistaken, sire. I'm innocent—'

'Talk to Perseus,' said Philip harshly. 'He's in charge.'

'An old feud with Demetrios. A witness who heard him call you by your name. A bloodied knife among your possessions,' said Perseus, calm as a lawmaker in court. 'These reasons would make most men call you guilty, but I want to hear it from your lips. Admit you murdered Demetrios, and I will give you a quick death. Deny it, and this man. . .' Perseus indicated the man standing with his back against the wall. Shaven-headed, stripped to the waist, as muscled as a prize bull, his job needed no explanation. The fearful-looking implements hanging from nails did that: pliers, blades, hammers and even a saw. Perseus went on, 'This man will extract the truth from you. Over a long time. Not hours – days. He tells me you might last a month if we're careful.'

The only sound in the little, airless room was Empedokles' frantic breathing.

Philip had been present at many such situations; he knew this was Perseus' first. He watched his son sidelong, expecting him to shout again, or to threaten Empedokles further, but to his delight, Perseus simply folded his arms and waited.

It took perhaps thirty heartbeats for Empedokles to crack.

'I did it, sire. I did it,' he said in a low voice.

Sorrow flashed across Perseus' eyes; then they went ice-cold. '*What* did you do?'

'I killed Demetrios, sire.'

'With a knife.'

'Yes, sire.'

344

'Was he armed?'

'No, sire.'

'So you murdered an unarmed comrade – a man who had stood in the file with you at Atrax and Kynoskephalae?'

'Yes, sire.' Empedokles began to weep.

'You miserable creature,' said Perseus contemptuously. 'You are not fit to clean Demetrios' equipment, let alone to decide that he should die. There is only one suitable punishment for you.'

Empedokles' head lifted. His expression wavered, terrified, pleading, disbelieving, as he wrung his hands at first Perseus and then Philip. 'A swift death you promised me, sire. Let it be a quick death.'

'I lied,' said Perseus with a laugh. 'You are without honour, and deserve to be treated with no honour. I am of a mind to give him to the bronze bull, Father.' Over Empedokles' wails, he added, 'Would you object?'

Impressed by his son's composure, and a little shocked by his ruthlessness, Philip shook his head.

Philip did not go to watch Empedokles cook to death inside the bronze bull. An instrument of torture devised more than three centuries before for the tyrant Phalaris, Philip had inherited one from his stepfather, whose advice had caused him never to have it used. A great bronze rendering of a bull with a door in its side, the machine could hold a crouching man inside. Placed over a fire, which could be slow-burning or fast, it roasted the prisoner within. Specially fashioned tubes in the bull's nostrils were supposed to convert the victim's screams into bellows, but Philip's stepfather said they did a poor job.

Philip had seen enough men depart this life, in particular of recent months. Although he was glad that Empedokles was to die – Demetrios was a sore loss, and deserved to be avenged – he had no desire to listen to Empedokles' screams. He'd heard some before they had taken the murderer away; Perseus' self-control had weakened a little, and he'd smashed one of Empedokles' knees with a hammer. 'That's for my friend,' he had snarled.

I shall leave him to it, Philip had thought in that ear-splitting shriek of a moment. My son has become a man. When the time comes, he will be fit to rule Macedon.

Life could be worse, Philip decided. Yes, he had been beaten by

Flamininus, and lost thousands of his men, but he remained king of Macedon. A recent exchange of letters with Flamininus had bolstered his position. It hadn't all been good news – in the first communication, Philip had had to accept the loss of the Fetters. Flamininus had no major objections to them remaining Macedonian, or so he said – at first Philip hadn't been so sure – but it seemed the Senate insisted on the fortresses being occupied by Roman troops. Writing back to express his disappointment, Philip had suggested that after a period of time, dependent on his loyalty to Rome, his soldiers might be allowed to reoccupy the Fetters. 'A reasonable proposition,' Flamininus had replied. 'I for one would have no reason to argue against it, for the Aetolians need constant monitoring. I can think of no one better to do that than you.'

Philip had taken great heart from this support. Rome might dominate Greece now, but it was keen to see his position remain strong, and not just because of the Aetolians. 'Antiochus,' wrote Flamininus, 'is a major threat.'

'He has ever been so,' Philip had replied. 'I have eyes in his camp – I know his every move. If he sets sail for Greece, my army will be ready.'

'Your determination heartens me,' Flamininus had written back. 'Know that the legions will stand beside your soldiers. Together we shall throw the Seleucids back into the sea.'

Philip's two greatest concerns closest to home – the Aitolians and Antiokhos – had effectively been negated. Even with Hannibal's aid, the Seleucid emperor could not prevail against his phalanx and the legions combined. Nor could the perfidious Aitolians. Thanks to Philip's efforts, Flamininus, and through him, the Senate, now regarded him as a faithful ally. True, he was paying reparations and his son Demetrios was a hostage, but the signs for the future were good. Years it might take, Philip decided, but I can wait.

Give it time, and the Romans will come to trust me entirely.

That is when I shall strike again.

CHAPTER XXXV

Isthmia, near Corinth, spring 196 BC

Flamininus' mood was buoyant. Triumphant. Ha, he thought. How apt. My physical triumph will be in Rome, perhaps a year hence, but the real one will be here, today. He was in his tent, which he'd ordered pitched outside the stadium where the Isthmian Games were held every six years. Its location went against convention – those attending the games were supposed to set up camp in a designated area some distance away – but Flamininus was unconcerned. No one would dare object to his tent or to the presence of large numbers of his troops. The gods wouldn't be angered either – almost the first thing Flamininus had done upon his arrival was to have delivered to the nearby sanctuary of Poseidon an extravagant offering of a dozen bulls. That would see the games' patron happy. The other deities continued to favour him too: Cynoscephalae and the subsequent peace treaty, which contained Flamininus' every recommendation, were proof of that.

Hosted by Corinth at a site ten miles to the east of the city, the Isthmian Games had been held for at least three centuries, and were outrivalled only by their Olympic cousins. Flamininus' journey here had been memorable. Like most Romans, he had never attended an Olympiad, or the Isthmian Games. He had known something about the festivals, but had never quite imagined their scale or splendour. Or, he thought wryly, their filth. The piss and shit of tens of thousands of people was not inconsiderable.

He had known that many would attend the games, but hadn't quite appreciated in what numbers. The roads here had been thronged with carts, horses, mules and people on foot. If it hadn't been for his accompanying cavalry, which had cleared his path, he'd still have been trying to reach the site. The travellers were almost exclusively men, on their own, in small groups and large. Now and again, Flamininus spied

347

bands of women, come to take part in the music and singing contests, and well guarded by male relatives.

There were men from Argos, Elis and Messenia, simple, rough but good-natured types who joked and laughed with everyone. Proud, red-cloaked Spartans, ignoring the other road users. Athenians, with their noses in the air, also imagining themselves better than all others just because of where they came from. Boeotians and Locrians, Thessalians and Achaeans, and men from a dozen smaller city states and regions. Macedonians, who glared first at his cavalrymen, and him after.

There were even a few Romans – allowed to enter the Isthmian Games these past twenty-five years or so – unsurprisingly, they cheered to see Flamininus. He'd stopped to talk with these athletes – chariot drivers, boxers and wrestlers – and called on Fortuna to favour them all. He'd even sent Potitius to lay down some coin on the strongest of them with the bet takers. Any winnings he might receive would be tiny in comparison to the wealth of Greece soon to be at his disposal, but few things pleased Flamininus more than a wager come good.

He had arrived the day before the games opened, and for the first time in many years, had wished to be anonymous. Although many might have come to hear his words on the morrow, the majority had come because this was one of the biggest events to occur in all Greece. The sense of occasion was undeniable, and Flamininus longed to wander about the temporary town of tents that had sprung up close to Poseidon's temple and the stadium. He didn't want to drink himself insensible at one of the many wine stalls, or gorge on the incredible array of foods – meats, cheese, bread, pastries, honey, fruit, olives – on offer. Nor did he wish to lie with a whore, have his future foretold, or buy trinkets.

What Flamininus would have enjoyed was to soak up the Greekness of it all, and to wander the athletes' area, just to see them oiling their muscles, or running up and down, and mock-wrestling. To watch as the grooms exercised the horses, and prepared their chariots. He had grown up on tales of the Olympics; nothing like it or the Isthmian Games existed in Italia. It was frustrating, therefore, to be effectively confined to his tent. The conqueror of Macedonia could not be seen to act like a moonstruck youth, he had decided, nor even to walk among the crowds. After his speech tomorrow, it would be different, and in the coming days, Flamininus planned to attend chariot and horse races, and to watch athletic and boxing contests. Of particular interest to him was the *hippios*, the four-lap footrace special to the Isthmian Games. He would also visit the athletes' camp, and speak with some of the winners. Soaking up the spirit of the games, he would come away the richer for it.

Flamininus smiled, and set aside his plans. Today, nothing was more important than his speech. This was his day, the culmination of long years of climbing the political ladder, securing the consulship and after, command of the war against Philip. Victory had been secured over Macedonia. Whether they knew it or not, the Greeks had been brought to heel. He would make much of their freedom, but from this day onward, the Republic would cast a long shadow over Greece, and it was all thanks to him. To me, he thought. Titus Quinctius Flamininus.

No one was going to spoil his enjoyment of this, the pinnacle of his career. Not Lucius, who, still in disgrace, he had forbidden from entering his tent. Not even Galba would ruin the occasion. 'Ah, Galba,' Flamininus murmured. 'How I longed to become the conqueror of Greece. How I burned to be free of you. How sweet it is that these two desires shall be granted on the same day. Today.'

'Master?'

Flamininus smiled. Even Potitius could make him smile today. 'You have paperwork for me?'

'No, master. It's all been dealt with.'

Surprised, Flamininus looked around. 'Surely not?'

'Knowing that this was your day, master, I worked late into the night to see it done.' Potitius' lips opened, as if to lick; he paused, then closed them again.

'Well done,' said Flamininus, pleased on two counts. He made an uncharacteristic, impulsive decision. 'Tell me – do I seem ready?' Turning, as had been the norm with Pasion, he allowed a stunned Potitius to appraise him.

'Yes, master. You look . . . imposing.'

Feeling even more important, Flamininus stood a little taller. 'And my hair – is any out of place?'

Potitius walked around him; he brushed and patted at the top of Flamininus' head. 'A few hairs there, master. Nothing more.'

'What about marks on my armour?' Flamininus had ordered his

body slave to make his sculpted breastplate – fashioned especially for today – shine like the sun, but he was concerned that the fool had marked it while helping Flamininus to put it on.

Tongue protruding with concentration, Potitius used a strip of cloth to polish here and there. 'It's magnificent, master,' he declared. 'Worthy of a triumphant general.'

'The knot on my belt?' Befitting his status, Flamininus had a red sash tied around his midriff, over his armour.

Potitius adjusted it a fraction.

'I think I'm ready,' Flamininus pronounced.

'You look as if you've descended from the heavens, master.' Potitius sounded genuine.

Flamininus made his second on-the-spot decision of the day. 'You have served me well. When we have returned to Italia and life has returned to normal . . . in say, two years, you shall have your freedom.'

Potitius licked his lips, and then he began to cry. 'Thank you, master. Thank you.'

'Come now,' said Flamininus, feeling awkward, and behind that, a rush of guilt about Pasion. 'There's no need for a display.'

'No, master.' Potitius composed himself. 'Your commanders and officers are ready.'

As they should be, thought Flamininus. At other times, he would have let them sweat in the sunshine, but he was eager for proceedings to begin. 'Good. Let us go then and free the Greeks.'

Emerging from the tent, he walked towards a large group of waiting legates, tribunes and staff officers. Not a man of the scores of senior officers in his army appeared to be absent. They all want to bask in the glory, thought Flamininus. He didn't begrudge them. Apart from Galba, that was. His enemy, spindly legged as a stork, was watching from a position close to the front of the assembly. Enjoy it while you may, Flamininus gloated silently. Your world is about to turn upside down.

Preceded by a nervous-faced Corinthian official and a maniple of principes – Flamininus had insisted on Felix's unit – he and his officers entered the crowds around the stadium, which held nigh on ten thousand people. Preoccupied with his preparations, Flamininus had paid little attention to the announcements and cheers that had been emanating from the brick-built structure all morning.

A vast mob milled about; they were the usual mixture of those who'd come late and missed a ticket to see the official opening of the games, and those who'd come just to partake in the festive atmosphere. The vendors who plied a living wherever large numbers of people came together were present in droves. Fried-pork sellers and wine merchants, including an enterprising Plataean who had brought in vast stores of amphorae, and appeared to be making a killing as a result. Pastry makers. Bakers. Men offering olives, cheese, nuts. Bet takers and whores. Cutpurses, snot-nosed children and cripples begging for coins. Few appeared to know that Flamininus was here, or to care.

That might have irritated him usually, but not today. Inside the stadium, thousands of people were waiting for the games to begin, but there were also representatives from every city state in Greece. All these were here to witness his speech, his long-awaited speech that would reveal the terms of the peace treaty with Philip. The treaty that had come about because of *his* victory at Cynoscephalae.

The Corinthian official came hurrying back to inform Flamininus that the jugglers, acrobats and actors sent in to keep the audience amused had finished. Everything was in place. It would have pleased Flamininus to have first sent the maniple of principes into the arena for a display of martial valour, but that might have angered the Greeks, and on this of all days, he did not want that to happen. Leaving his soldiers by the entrance bar a personal escort of twenty, and guided by the sweating Corinthian official, he made his way up the tunnelled staircase that led to the best seating.

The clamour of earlier had been replaced by an air of anticipation. As Flamininus emerged into the stadium proper, which had been decorated with garlands and flowers, gasps and cries of, 'He's here!' went up. Smooth-faced, giving nothing away, Flamininus sat down, soon after joined by his legates and tribunes. Less high-ranking officers had to make do with seats further up the stands. His escort of twenty principes remained standing on either side, taking up positions on the steps that led up and down between the rows of seating.

A hush fell.

Flamininus' gaze wandered from left to right, around the entire stadium. It gave him supreme pleasure that every face was watching him. *Him*. Not you, Galba, he thought, turning round to give his enemy a broad smile. Galba, normally the master of masking his feelings, scowled.

The Corinthian official asked was Flamininus ready.

He nodded, watching as the official signalled to someone on the sand. He in turn cried a command and a moment later, a herald and a trumpeter paced into the centre of the well-raked arena.

Total silence descended.

Flamininus closed his eyes, and thanked Jupiter, Mars and Fortuna, his favoured gods, for their help and guidance.

The trumpet sounded, a long, glorious set of notes.

Unrolling the parchment in his hands, the herald cried, 'The Senate of Rome and the general Titus Quinctius Flamininus, having beaten King Philip and the Macedonians in war, declare the following peoples to be free, exempt from taxes, and subject to their own laws: the Corinthians, Phocians and Locrians, the Euboeans, Magnesians and Thessalians, the Perrhaebians and the Achaeans of Phthiotis.' These were the peoples who had been Philip's subjects.

To Flamininus' astonishment, no one spoke. There were no shouts of delight – or anger. Glancing at the nearest Greeks, he realised that they were so shocked by the announcement that they didn't know how to react. Men were questioning their neighbours – 'Did you hear what I did?' 'Am I dreaming?' – and when the herald made to walk off the sand, scores of voices demanded that he repeat his proclamation. And so, to Flamininus' amusement, the announcement was read out again.

This time, the message sank in, and the audience's reaction was wild. Such cheering as Flamininus had not heard since the declaration of Scipio's defeat of Hannibal at Zama went up. Men embraced each other and wept openly. Some danced where they stood. Others saluted Flamininus and called down the blessings of the gods on him. Exulting in the attention, he gave them gracious nods in return.

Alone among the audience in not seeming pleased, he spied the Aetolian representatives, among them Phaeneas and Alexander, with whom he had tangled before. Sour-faced, venomous even, they threw frequent glances in his direction. Many would not have noticed the absence of mention of the Fetters, would not have realised that this meant the fortresses would continue in Roman hands – but the Aetolians had. Flamininus cared not a whit: in fact, he was pleased. Let the fools resent Rome, he thought.

We are their masters now.

The games began soon after, but few in the audience paid much attention to the chariot racing or the athletic contests. Flamininus also paid
little attention to the display; he was considering every part of his plan
to deal with Galba. It was a delight that the man was sitting behind
him, blithely unaware.

Even better was the manner in which Galba sought him out when
the games came to an end for the day. Surrounded by euphoric Corinthians and grinning Euboeans, next handed a garland by a Thessalian
and hugged by a pair of Phocians, Flamininus was slowly making his
way towards the stairs when Galba appeared by his shoulder.

'We need to talk.'

'Indeed we do,' said Flamininus in a friendly tone.

Galba shot him a suspicious look. 'Now.'

'An excellent idea – I was thinking the same thing.' Flamininus
smiled as a Magnesian showered him with thanks. When the man
made to give him another garland, he shook his head and indicated
Galba.

Unable to refuse for fear of offence, Galba muttered something ungrateful and allowed the Magnesian to place the flowers around his
neck. They walked on. 'The riches of all Greece will start to flow into
Rome's coffers now,' Galba said in Flamininus' ear.

'Indeed they will,' said Flamininus, thinking, I'll be as wealthy as
Croesus.

'I want my money.'

'Let us talk somewhere quiet,' said Flamininus warmly. 'I have some
better than tolerable local wine.'

With an irritable nod, Galba agreed.

It took longer than expected to reach Flamininus' tent. The crowd
outside, which had scarcely noticed him during his walk to the stadium, erupted as he made the return journey. Buffeted by claps on the
shoulder, wearing half a dozen garlands, kissed on both cheeks a hundred times, and thanked a thousand times if it was once, Flamininus
enjoyed the experience thoroughly. Galba, on the other hand, looked
as if he'd rather be anywhere else.

Reaching Flamininus' tent, they entered, leaving everyone else outside. Telling his officers that he would see them at the planned feast later, and that he had an important matter to discuss with the legate Galba, Flamininus led the way to his private quarters.

Filling a cup from a silver jug – a Greek one, from Thessaly – he offered it to Galba. 'Wine?'

Galba hesitated.

Flamininus laughed and poured a second for himself. Quaffing a large mouthful, he glanced at Galba. 'Satisfied?'

Looking a trifle embarrassed, Galba took the cup.

'To victory over Philip, and the freedom of the Greeks,' said Flamininus, raising his own.

Galba repeated the toast, and they drank.

Make your move, thought Flamininus. Walk into my trap.

'About the money you will pay me,' began Galba.

'Go on,' invited Flamininus.

A trifle surprised, Galba issued a list of demands. Appreciating that not all the treasure that came into Flamininus' hands would be coin, he already had valuers in place to assess the goods' worth. He had made arrangements with a shipping agent in Athens – that was the port his share was to be sent to.

When Galba was in full flow, and seemed confident that he was to be paid, Flamininus held up a finger. Galba didn't notice, so he coughed.

Galba paused; he frowned. 'Have you not been listening? Must I repeat myself?'

'No, no. I have heard every detail. It's just that I have no intention of paying you. Oh, you can keep what I gave you before – a goodwill gesture, if you like, but not a single drachma more will you receive. From this moment, our agreement is over.'

Galba's eyes bulged. 'What?'

'You heard, you old goat.'

'The Greeks' acclaim has gone to your head, as I thought it would. You arrogant fool,' said Galba, his voice shrill with scorn. 'The Senate shall hear of your dealings with the Aetolians. I will see you condemned as a traitor. Your life will be ruined when I am done with you. Ruined!'

'Are you done?' asked Flamininus sweetly. Lifting a parchment from his desk, he said, 'D'you know what this is?'

Suspicious, Galba tried to grab it, but Flamininus stepped backwards, out of reach. 'This is the testimony of a one-armed legionary by the name of Pennus.'

'There are a thousand maimed fools like him on the streets of Rome,' said Galba, curling his lip. 'What have you paid him to say?'

'I have not just his statement, but that of five of his comrades, as well as his centurion's.' The last had been obtained after a beating and the threat of worse, but Galba didn't need to know that, thought Flamininus. He continued, 'They were all present at Celetrum.'

Galba's face turned the colour of a newly dead corpse. 'Celetrum.'

'Ah, you remember it,' Flamininus gloated.

'Celetrum,' said Galba again, like a simpleton.

'Indeed. A town where you stole a fortune that belonged to the Senate and people of Rome, and here's the proof.' Flamininus waved the parchment. 'And before you get any ideas, Galba, know that this is a copy. The originals lie in the strongbox of a trusted friend in Rome. If anything untoward should happen to me, he will send the lot to the Senate.'

Galba's shoulders hunched. 'What do you want of me?'

'Why, not a thing,' replied Flamininus. 'You shall never speak a word of what you know about me, and I shall keep silent about the fortune you stole. Oh, and as I mentioned, I won't be paying you any coin either.'

The poisonous look that Galba shot him then was worthy of Medusa.

'Are we in agreement?' Flamininus rested his hand on the desk beside the dagger he had left there for this exact purpose. I will happily kill you now, Galba, he thought, and come up with an explanation afterwards.

Galba's eyes darted from Flamininus' face to the dagger, and back. 'Yes.'

Flamininus couldn't help himself. 'Who is the conqueror of Macedonia and Greece?'

Silence.

Flamininus' fingers closed on the hilt.

'You are.'

'Good.'. With a jerk of his head, such as he'd give to a slave, Flamininus added, 'You may go.'

Like a whipped dog, Galba slunk from the room.

Apart from the victory at Cynoscephalae, Flamininus couldn't remember a happier moment in all his life.

He wasn't finished with Galba, however. Not yet. The snake might have been crushed, but he wasn't dead, and he would already be plotting a way to get back at Flamininus. A final lesson needed to be delivered, in the most brutal of fashions.

Waiting until Galba was gone, Flamininus summoned the officer of the guard from outside the tent. 'I have a task for you,' he said in a confidential tone.

CHAPTER XXXVI

It was the evening of the same day of Flamininus' declaration at the Isthmian Games, and Felix and his old comrades were sitting around, as they had so many times over the years. But rather than get pissed, as every other person in Isthmia, Roman or Greek, appeared to be doing, they were holding a council of war.

Felix had been surprised to be summoned by Flamininus just a short time before. The general's request had stunned him, but a heartbeat later, he'd agreed. Felix only wanted to take one man with him, and he'd decided on Clavus, who had proven his loyalty before. Sparax had long ears, however, and he'd caught the word 'Galba' when the pair were hunched together by the fire. Demanding to know what was going on, he had made enough noise to start attracting other men's attention. Just to shut him up, Felix had let him in on the secret. Of course then he'd had to tell Dordalus as well – he couldn't leave out the last of his former brothers-in-arms.

Sparax's reaction was like that of a three-year-old handed a huge honey pastry. He could not stop grinning. 'The only thing better,' he declared, 'would be to kill Onion Head.'

'No, this is better,' said Clavus with an evil grin. 'Far better.'

Late in the night, in the darkest hour when men are wrapped in their blankets, dreaming, and even the sentries' eyelids droop, Felix and his three friends stole between the rows of tents. It was fortunate that not all Flamininus' legions were present, meaning the camp was small. Only the Eighth had been delegated to travel to Isthmia; the other legions were at Elatea and important locations such as Chalcis and Demetrias. A strong detachment had also been sent to garrison the Acrocorinth, which lay south of the city of Corinth, ten miles to the west.

The friends' faces, arms and legs were blackened with ash from the almost-dead fire. Nice and slow, we'll take it, Felix had warned, and none of us will twist an ankle. Better to move this way than along the avenues and risk being seen by the one sober, still-awake officer in the camp. No one argued.

Their mission, while sanctioned by Flamininus, was illegal. If the comrades were apprehended before it, they'd probably escape with a light punishment – the four had agreed to stick to the same story, that they were going to rob wine from the legion's stores – but if caught in the middle of doing what Flamininus had asked them to, matters would take an altogether more unpleasant turn.

Because of this, Flamininus had not made his unusual request of Felix an order. 'If you're discovered, I will not be able to save you,' he'd said. 'You must do this of your own free will.'

Felix had agreed before Flamininus had even finished speaking, and despite the risk, Clavus hadn't taken much persuading either. Nor, as Felix had been pleased to discover, had Sparax and Dordalus. 'It can't be ath dangerous ath Atraxth,' Sparax had joked. 'Nor plenty of other battleth we've been through.'

That said, thought Felix, halting as a man in the tent they were passing coughed himself awake, they were still in danger. The sight of their ash-covered faces would alert even the drunkest officer. To be sure that there would be no consequences, they needed to pass unseen all the way to their destination *and* back. The cougher muttered and lay back down. He had been drinking, for within a dozen heartbeats, he was snoring again. Signalling that they could continue, Felix padded on.

Reaching the camp's central crossroads, he stayed in the shadows and peered over at the senior officers' tents. Most of the army had missed Flamininus' declaration, but every senior officer had come to witness it. Their tents were what Felix was staring at; he knew the one they wanted because Flamininus himself had told him.

There was no one in sight on either of the main avenues. Incredibly, there were no sentries visible outside the pavilion that comprised the temporary headquarters either. Only outside Flamininus' great tent could Felix see anyone, and that was just four men. Two were leaning forward on their grounded shields in a posture so familiar that Felix knew they were asleep. The other two weren't much better, barely stirring even when an owl called overhead.

Indicating that he would go first, Felix stole across the avenue to the senior officers' tents. No alarm was called. No voice shouted at him to stop. He waved at his comrades, and Clavus crept over next. Sparax and Dordalus made it without incident as well. They grinned at each other, their teeth the only bright parts of them.

Eyes peeled for sentries, Felix led the way along the line of tents. The noise of snoring and occasional farting was just as bad here as it had been outside those of the ordinary soldiers. Antonius had been fond of saying that every man looked the same when he was taking a shit. They all sounded the same when asleep too, Felix decided, amused.

Seven tents in, he stopped. 'This is the one,' he mouthed. There was still no sign of any sentries, and he thanked the gods for Flamininus' order that had seen every man bar his bodyguards and the soldiers deputised to man the walls given the night off duty. 'It will help you,' he'd said to Felix with a wink. 'Not that I have any idea what you're planning.'

Three of them were going inside. Felix was one, obviously. None of the others would volunteer to stay behind, so he'd made them draw lots. Sparax was disgusted to end up with the short straw; even now, he was glowering. 'Stay alert,' Felix mouthed. 'Whistle if you see anyone.' Still scowling, Sparax nodded.

Felix knelt and lifted the tent panel enough to peer inside. Accustomed to the dark, he was able to pick out a table and dining couches. Sure there would be no one in this chamber, he glanced at Clavus and Dordalus, and then, with one of them holding up the leather, crawled under. The arrangement was that he should check it was safe before they entered. Rising to his feet, Felix tiptoed around the dining room, grateful for the thick carpets underfoot. Through the doorway, he found a reception area, which was also empty. That was good enough. Back he went to get the others. Once all three were inside, they took off their neckerchiefs and tied them around the lower halves of their faces. Daggers ready, strips of cloth for gags in hand, they crept in single file towards the sleeping quarters. Felix knew where to go because Flamininus had explained the tent's layout to him.

They found the first sleeping slave in a small office. Felix didn't hesitate. The slave woke with Felix's hand over his mouth and a dagger at his throat. Clavus was whispering in his ear to stay quiet if he wanted to live. Terrified, the slave did not move a muscle. An instant later,

Dordalus had gagged him, and a dozen heartbeats after that, he had been trussed up like a hen for the pot.

A second slave outside the bedroom met the same fate. Wide-eyed, he nodded when Clavus repeated his warning. When Felix leaned down to ask if there was anyone else in the bedchamber but its main occupant, he got a shake of the head.

Felix's heart sang. 'Ready?' he mouthed at the others, who grinned their assent.

Dagger at the ready, Felix lifted the fabric partition and entered the room. The air inside was stuffy – a mixture of sweat, farts and sour wine. A bed dominated the space; on it, he made out a prone shape. Ten paces, and Felix was standing over the sleeping man. Gods, how he had longed for a moment like this, but never thought to see it. Clavus took up a position on the other side of the bed; Dordalus was at its foot.

'Galba,' Felix said in a low voice.

The figure stirred, and settled again.

'Galba, you piece of shit,' muttered Felix.

Galba's head lifted off the pillow. 'Wha—'

Placing his dagger tip under Galba's left eye, Felix eased the legate's head back down. 'Apologies for disturbing your rest, legate,' he said quietly. 'We won't take up much of your time.'

Petrified, Galba did not resist as Felix gagged him as he had done the slaves. Clavus and Dordalus pulled back the covers and bound the legate's hands and feet with strips of leather. Methodically, then, and in complete silence, the three began to beat Galba. To Felix's regret, they didn't deliver the kind of punishment *they* might have received, because that would have killed him. 'He must not die,' Flamininus had ordered. 'Try not to break any bones either. Hurt the whoreson enough that he'll be in pain for days, but don't cripple him. To Galba, the humiliation will be almost worse than the beating.'

Galba tried to roll into a ball, so Dordalus and Clavus tied his wrists and ankles to the legs of the bed. They continued thrashing him. Little sounds of pain escaped Galba's bound mouth. Whimpers. Moans. Then he began to weep. When Felix noticed, he was glad.

Not long after, Galba had wet himself, and stopped struggling. With great reluctance, Felix signalled to the others. 'Any more, and we'll kill him,' he whispered.

Clavus and Dordalus looked disappointed, but they stood back.

Felix stooped to place his lips against Galba's ear. 'We come from Flamininus, in case you hadn't guessed.'

Galba went rigid.

'Regard this as a polite message. You will never again interfere with Flamininus' business. You will never obstruct him in the Senate, or anywhere else. In fact, you will avoid him at all costs. When it can't be avoided, thanks to your duties here in Greece, for example, you will defer to him in every way. Make but a single transgression, and we will return. Our next visit will not be so pleasant.' Flamininus had given no further instructions, but Felix wasn't done. His revenge was not yet complete.

He reached down, and lifted Galba's sleeping tunic. Pulling aside the undergarment, he laid his blade under the legate's wizened scrotum. Galba trembled, and Felix said, 'You will forget that we were even here. You will not seek me and my comrades out, or make any attempt to find us, because if you do –' and here Felix moved his wrist so that Galba's balls were balanced on the dagger '–we, or some of our *many* comrades will come back and cut these off. After that, we'll slit your scrawny throat. Do you understand, *legate*?'

Galba's head went up and down, very quickly.

Felix stared into his eyes from a hand's breadth away. He saw the kind of mad terror he'd seen before, in panicked men who were trying to flee the enemy, whose minds were empty of everything except the burning desire to live. Long and hard he stared, to be sure that Galba had been scared witless.

A foul smell hit Felix's nostrils; Galba had lost control of his bowels. It was enough. Stay any longer, Felix decided, and the malicious legate's heart might give out. That would have been satisfying, but it went against Flamininus' orders, and he preferred the knowledge that Galba would live the rest of his life with the memory of being utterly humiliated by ordinary legionaries.

Justice had been served, Felix decided.

He went to report to Flamininus the next morning. Announcing himself at the entrance to the general's tent, he was admitted at once. It was hard to believe the change in his fortunes, thought Felix. Little more than a year before, he'd been tied to the back of a wagon and flogged.

Now, with his revenge on Galba complete, he was being ushered into Flamininus' presence. Flamininus, his new ally.

They entered an airy chamber, carpeted, Greek statues lining the sides. The general sat alone at a table laden with food: bread, pastries, olives, cheese and greens.

'Optio Felix Cicirrus to see you, sir.' The officer who had accompanied him saluted and withdrew.

Felix came to attention. 'Sir!'

'At ease, optio.' Flamininus beckoned, indicated a second stool. 'Sit. Join me.'

'Sir, I—'

'Come, I won't have it any other way. You are the man who delivered Galba to me on a plate, as it were.' Flamininus indicated the platters before him, and chuckled. 'How is Galba?'

Felix sat, grinning. 'I don't think he'll be eating right now, sir. He will be black and blue by this evening.'

'That's terrible,' said Flamininus mock-solicitously. 'Did he listen to your message?'

'He did, sir. I'd stake my life on it.' Felix described what had happened in full detail.

'How . . . satisfactory.'

If Flamininus had been a cat, thought Felix, he'd have been purring.

'Eat. Break your fast,' urged Flamininus. 'Try these honeyed pastries, they're my favourite. My cook – a princeps like yourself – makes them every morning. You'd find it hard to find better ones in Rome.'

A taste, and Felix agreed with him. He ate one, and then, with Flamininus continuing to offer the plate, a second. 'Gratitude, sir.'

'After what you did for me, it's a trifle.' Flamininus' face grew more serious. 'We must talk about the future. I know you wanted some leave, that you might take a gravestone to Cynoscephalae and honour your brother suitably.'

'Yes, sir.' Felix's heart squeezed.

'I'll have the paperwork drawn up today. Take your tentmates as well. A month should be enough time?'

'Yes, sir. Thank you, sir,' said Felix, astonished. He'd not expected to be rewarded so soon, nor to be given that amount of time. To be allowed to have Clavus, Dordalus and Sparax accompany him was also wholly unexpected. There would be time and enough help, thought Felix with a flood of emotion, not just to see a tomb erected for Antonius, but perhaps to do the same for some of their fallen comrades.

'One of the finest stonemasons in Greece works out of Corinth. He's expecting you – he has been paid to deliver you whatever plaque you desire. An army wagon is at your disposal as well, to carry the stone to the battlefield.'

Felix's throat closed; moisture pricked his eyes. 'The gods bless and keep you, sir,' he whispered.

'It's nothing more than you deserve,' said Flamininus warmly. A bulging purse appeared on the table. 'This is yours too – that's an order.'

Again Felix muttered his thanks.

'When you return, do you see your future in the army, past your term of service, say?'

Since Antonius' death, Felix had struggled to find purpose. He felt differently now. His revenge on Galba had given him a sudden new lease of life, and now it seemed the general saw a future for him. Felix's spirits rose further; the idea *was* tempting.

'Well?' asked Flamininus.

Stay in the legion and your luck will never hold, Felix told himself. Sooner or later, someone will recognise you, will remember that you were dishonourably discharged after Zama. He bowed his head. 'I can't, sir.'

'Why ever not?' demanded Flamininus. 'Soldiers like you are one in a thousand. I can see you making centurion within three years, and senior centurion within five to seven.'

Felix couldn't believe his ears. 'Really, sir?'

'Really. What do you say?'

Felix looked at Flamininus, decided that he was worthy of trust, threw caution to the wind, and said, 'I fell asleep on sentry duty after Zama, sir.'

Flamininus frowned. 'Why are you telling me this?'

Felix couldn't help himself. It all poured out. His experiences of the war against Hannibal. Matho's brutality. The battle of Zama. Killing the elephant. Life in the camp outside Carthage. Ingenuus' discovery of the wine. Drinking so much that he and his comrades had dropped off, allowing the prisoners to escape. The fustuarium, and beating Ingenuus to death. Being hounded from the legion by Matho. The brothers' miserable life back in Italia, and their decision to re-enlist when war was declared on Macedonia.

Felix left out no detail, except his encounters with Matho. Those dark secrets would go with him to his grave. A grave, he thought as Flamininus stared at him, that he might be filling sooner rather than later. Yet despite the fact that he had laid his head on the execution-er's block by revealing all, Felix felt an enormous weight lift from his shoulders. It was a relief to have come clean at last.

Silence fell when he'd finished, and as it dragged on, Felix con-cluded that Flamininus was no different from Galba. It would be the fustuarium again. Despairing, Felix bent his head.

Flamininus began to laugh.

Felix looked up, amazed.

'By all the gods, that's a story and a half, and no mistake.'

He's toying with me, thought Felix, the last of his hope vanishing.

'Let me deal with it.'

Still convinced that Flamininus would have him executed, Felix didn't understand. 'Sir?'

'I have just conquered Macedonia, optio. Pardoning a valiant legion-ary – you – is a small matter in comparison. Fear not. Your name will be cleared. Your achievements at Zama and Cynoscephalae will not go unrewarded either.'

Felix cracked a nervous smile. 'I don't know what to say, sir.'

'You can thank me for a start.'

Panic flooded Felix's every vein. 'I'm sorry, sir. A thousand thanks – I will forever be in your debt.' He looked at Flamininus to find the general smiling at him.

'Peace, optio. I took no offence.'

Felix nodded. 'Gratitude, sir.'

'Philip has been vanquished, but the threat of Antiochus looms on the horizon. Another war is likely, if not this year, then within the next two or three. Men like you and your brother won the battle at Cynoscephalae. Hard men. Brave men. Rome needs you. *I* need you. Tell me you'll stay.'

Felix had never seen a ghost, but he could sense Antonius at his shoul-der, grinning in encouragement. He had never been surer of anything in his life.

He met Flamininus' gaze, and said, 'I'm your man, sir.'

AUTHOR'S NOTE

L ittle known nowadays, the war between Rome and Macedon (200-197 BC) was a conflict of huge importance, forever changing the Mediterranean world. It's not exaggerating to say that it influenced the future history of Europe.

A quarter-century before the war, no fewer than five powers had existed around the Mediterranean: Rome, Carthage, Macedon, Syria and Egypt. By 168 BC, this had been reduced to just two: Rome and Egypt. With stunning speed, the Roman Republic had moved from regional power to superpower. Many would argue that its path to empire was inevitable from this point onwards.

In order to help differentiate Romans from Macedonians/Greeks, I have used anglicised Roman words and anglicised Greek words when talking from the relevant characters' points of view. One of the exceptions is Philip himself. By rights, I *should* have called him Philippos, but he is known to history as Philip, and I felt to call him anything different would confuse. The broad brush-strokes of the story within these covers is true; so is much of the finer detail. Philip V of Macedon was a complex, mercurial character, at once capable of tactical master-strokes and major miscalculations, of extreme cruelty and insane courage.

His early successes were due in part to his stepfather, Antigonus Doson, who had left the kingdom in a strong position; his Common Alliance had stabilised the Greek city states and protected Macedon. Their relationship is unknown. Philip probably didn't send any soldiers to Zama, but he is known to have made fun of Flamininus' Greek allies at Nicaea, and his diagramma changing the age of conscription into the army happened. No hothead when it came to decisions of vital importance, he is recorded as having been reluctant to fight the battle at Cynoscephalae because of the terrain. Philip had spies in Rome; I like to think that Flamininus might have had the same throughout Greece, but have no proof.

There is no evidence that Galba was as devious as I have made out, nor any that he blackmailed Flamininus. He took part in the first war with Macedon, with not a great deal of success. His theft of money from Celetrum is my invention, but I took the idea from Marcus Acilius Glabrio, who *was* prosecuted for stealing war booty in the war against Hannibal.

Flamininus was that rare creature in Republican Rome: someone who acted at times like a king and got away with it. He was a man of contradictions: loving all things Hellenic, speaking Greek, yet overseeing the death of Macedonian and Greek independence. The level of intrigue and the rivalry between Flamininus and Galba is my invention. His elder brother, Lucius, was known as a degenerate; in 184 BC, he was expelled from the Senate.

Minucius Rufus, Scipio Africanus and Caius Cornelius Cethegus were all politicians of the period. Marcus Claudius Marcellus was elected consul towards the end of Flamininus' campaign in Greece. Polykratia was Philip's concubine; his wife was Penelope, his children Perseus, Demetrios and Apama. Amynander of Athamania was a real man; so too was the Spartan king, Nabis. There is some confusion about the timing of Philip's deal with Nabis – whether it was before the embassies were sent to Rome or after. I went with the latter. The generals Athenagoras, Leon, Herakleides of Gyrton, Nikanor and Philokles all served Philip. Agelaos of Nafpaktos – Naupactus to the Romans – did predict the fate of Greece at Rome's hands. Brakhylles of Boeotia, Phaeneas of Aetolia, Nikostratos and Aristaenos of Akhaia and the commander Androsthenes were real characters; so were Lucius Calpurnius and the Roman commissioners Publius Lentulus, Publius Villius, Lucius Stertinus, Lucius Terentius and Gnaeus Cornelius.

A word about Roman soldiers of the time. Metalled belts may not have been common in the Republican period, but they were known, as finds from Numantia in Spain have shown. Legions were probably numbered in the third century BC, but we don't know much else. The empty gateways of marching camps were filled at night with stacked cut timber. To my knowledge, no Roman arming cap has been found, but they must have existed. Without one, concussion is inevitable – and a number of examples have been found in other contexts, for example the Thracian lambswool one I described Felix wearing.

The Roman gladius hispaniensis was lethal, and it wasn't just a stab-bing weapon. Livy describes how scared Philip's soldiers were of these blades, because of the ease with which they removed limbs. Optiones were sometimes positioned at soldiers' backs; they used their staffs to push men forward. Centurions are recorded as having called their sol-diers 'boys' as well as 'brothers'. Sacrificing animals before battle was the norm, although it took place later than I portrayed, i.e. on the morning of the battle. I didn't make up the scene with the twenty-one bulls, but stole it from thirty years later, when the general Lucius Aemilius Paullus was about to fight Philip's son Perseus at Pydna – see Livy Book 44! The practice of advancing towards the enemy in silence is recorded during the Principate; it may have been used earlier.

It is worth mentioning Felix's dreams here. Post Traumatic Stress Disorder, PTSD, was almost unknown in ancient times – the evi-dence to suggest otherwise is scant. The reasons for this must have been manifold but serve to show us how different ancient peoples were – we want to think that Romans were like us, but in so many ways, they weren't. Two thousand years ago, life was brutal. Death was ever-present – think infant and child mortality rates of 40–60% by the age of ten, and a life expectancy of under thirty for women (thanks to childbirth), and about forty for men. Slavery and horrific public executions were normal throughout the Mediterranean; so too was widespread slaughter in war. In other words, the average person, whether Roman, Macedonian or Greek, was used to a great deal more violence and death than pretty much anyone is today, and was, in my mind, therefore less likely to suffer from PTSD.

To illustrate this further, I refer to the scene when Flamininus re-members how it is better to use an implement to strike a slave rather than his fist, in case he should injure himself. This comes directly from Galen, the Roman-Greek surgeon who spent his life helping the human condition – yet even he thought it acceptable to strike a slave. Evidence from slaves could not be used in court unless extracted under torture.

The Macedonian phalanx was a formidable battle formation. By the time of Philip V, cavalry had reverted to their earlier role, that of being subsidiary to the infantry. The structure of the phalanx is, like so much to do with the ancient world, open to debate. Thanks to the Greek historian Polybius, we are fairly sure that the basic 256-man unit (16 men wide, 16 men deep) was called the *speira*. Four *speirai* formed a battalion, which may have been called a *chiliarchy*, and four *chiliarchies* formed a *strategia*. Philip's phalanx was often referred to as having a strength of 10,000 men; Connolly and others have suggested therefore that his two *strategiai* each had *five* chiliarchies. Some of Philip's units were called white shields and brazen shields; copying Connolly, I decided to make these full strategiai in size. There is almost no historical evidence for phalangists engaging in training; the exception is Philip V, who insisted his soldiers train during this war. Trumpets were used to relay commands at distance, as with the Romans. Like the legionaries, Greek soldiers wore hobnailed sandals. A white flag was used to signal the advance.

Philip's helmet with ram's horns is attested. Pankration was a brutal sport, much respected by all Greeks; Spartans were known for their gouging. Harpastum was a Roman ball game, but contrary to the 'information' on many websites, no evidence survives for it being a brutal game played by legionaries. Galen said the game involved an element of wrestling, but unlike running or horse-riding, entailed no danger. Greek drinkers diluted their wine less than the Romans. It's not known if 'million' was used by the Romans, so I used the term 'a thousand thousand' instead. Romans used inches, feet and miles (the last was only a little smaller than the Imperial mile). Greeks used feet – different to the Roman one! – and stades.

The toys I described have not all been found in a Greek or Roman context, but they are items that date to at least two thousand years ago. The lemons known in Rome at this time were not the same as today's fruit (scientific name *citrus limon*) but rather the citron (*citrus medica*). Hesiod's *Works and Days*, a lovely little treatise on agricultural life in ancient times, still survives. Alcaeus' barbed poem about Philip is real too. Glassware was rare at this time; not until the late Republic did it become common. The quantity of wealth taken from Greece after Flamininus' victory, and fifty years later, after the sack of Corinth, is staggering. Estimates place it in the tens of billions of pounds. Many thanks to Jon Wood, editor of this book, for mentioning the bronze bull to me. It's not an invention, but something recorded as having been used in Sicily. Gratitude also to my good friend Giles Kristian for the phrase 'blade death', which comes from his absolutely magnificent novel, *Lancelot*.

Despite what some people believe, people in ancient Rome cursed just as much as we do today – perhaps more so. Proof exists in the plentiful, lewd graffiti in Pompeii and bawdy Roman poetry. You might be surprised to know that the 'C' word was one of the commonest swear words. So too was 'cocksucker'. 'Fuck' is less well attested, but there is a Latin verb *futuere*, which means 'to fuck'. My more frequent use of the 'F' word compared to the 'C' word is nothing more than an attempt to spare blushes.

The Greeks were fond of swearing too. I liked the expressions 'dusty footed' and 'tent sulker' too much not to use them. Although the word 'barbarian' is often thought of as Roman, it derived from the Greek *barbaros*, which means foreigner, or someone who doesn't speak Greek. I love the theory that the word might have come from how non-Greek speakers sounded: 'bar-bar-bar'.

The ancient texts are indispensable to an author of Roman and Greek historical fiction. Without Livy, Pausanias and, to a lesser extent, Polybius, Hesiod, Xenophon, Aristophanes and Diodorus, my task of writing this book would have been nigh-on impossible. Their words must be taken with a pinch of salt, but they are vital when describing events that took place more than two millennia ago. I own many texts; I also make extensive use of the Lacus Curtius website, which has English translations of surviving texts. My thanks, therefore, to Bill Thayer of the University of Chicago, who runs it. Find Lacus Curtius here: tinyurl.com/3utm5.

The modern texts on my desk when writing *The Falling Sword* include *A History of Greece* by J.B. Bury and R. Meiggs; *Roman Military Equipment* by M.C. Bishop and J.C.N. Coulston; *Greece and Rome at War* and *The Greek Armies* by Peter Connolly; Conway's *The Age of the Galley: Greek and Roman Mythology* by D.M. Field; *Ancient Greece* by Robert Garland; *The Complete Roman Army* by Adrian Goldsworthy; *Atlas of the Greek World* by Peter Levi; *Roman Conquests: Macedonia and Greece* by Philip Matyszak; *A Companion to Greek Religion* edited by Daniel Ogden; *Everyday Life in ancient Greece* by Nigel Rodgers; *The Hellenistic Age* by Peter Thonemann; *Philip V of Macedon* by F.W. Walbank (without this superlative text, I would have been utterly lost); *Warfare in the Classical World* by John Warry; *Taken at the Flood* by Robin Waterfield (whom I am also grateful to for his help with planning a visit to Albania). Publications by Osprey and Karwansaray are often helpful, and I couldn't do without the *Oxford Classical Dictionary* (thanks to my father for that!).

I do other things apart from writing novels. Check out the digital short stories I have recently written: *The March* follows on from *The Forgotten Legion*, and reveals what happened to Brennus; *Eagles in the Wilderness* is about Centurion Tullus of the Eagles books. Don't worry if you haven't got an e-reader: all you have to do is download the free Kindle App from Amazon, and you can read the stories on a phone, tablet or computer. If you'd like to visit Pompeii and Herculaneum with me as a guide, look up the amazing Andante Tours (https://tinyurl. com/yc4uze85) and if you like cycling with an historical twist, look up Bike Odyssey (https://bikeodyssey.cc/guides/) and Ride and Seek Bicycle Adventures (https://rideandseek.com/). Both these companies run epic cycling trips (Hannibal, Lionheart, Julius Caesar) that I am involved with as an historical guide.

Many of you will know that I support the charities Combat Stress, which helps British veterans with PTSD, and Médecins sans Frontières (MSF), which sends medical staff into disaster and war zones worldwide. If you'd like to know more about one of the money-raising efforts I made with author friends Anthony Riches and Russell Whitfield, look up 'Romani walk' on YouTube. The three of us walked 210 kilometres in Italy, wearing full Roman armour. The documentary is narrated by Sir Ian McKellen – Gandalf! Find it here: tinyurl.com/ h4n8h6g – and please tell your friends about it. I love Christian Cameron's historical novels; I hope some of you noticed my homage to his character, Arimnestos.

More recently I have been helping Park in the Past, a community-interest company that plans to build a Roman marching fort on the English–Welsh border near Chester – I hope you noticed the book's dedication. It is the most amazing project. Find it here: parkinthepast. org.uk. Thanks to all of you who continue to donate, support and help with the fundraising. Two readers who've been especially supportive appear in this book: Philippos is based on the inestimable Bruce Phillips, one of life's true gentlemen, and Livius is based on the wonderful Lesley Jolley – both were supposed to die in *Clash of Empires*, but I liked their characters too much. Sorry you had to die in this book, Bruce and Lesley! Kimon and Antileon are affectionate depictions of two old friends, Killian Ó Móráin and Arthur O'Connor. Here's to another three decades of comradeship. Another character from real life is Clarus, also called Quinton Johansen, the winner of a competition that raised funds for Park in the Past. I am grateful to the ever-generous Robin Carter of Parmenion Books (check out his website), and the many books he has donated to 'the cause'.

And so to my editors at Orion Publishing, Jon Wood and Craig Lye, and more recently, Ben Willis. Huge thanks to you for your tireless work, keen energy and encouragement on every step of the way. I'm indebted to all my foreign publishers, and in particular the team at Ediciones B in Spain – gracias! Others must be mentioned too: Charlie Viney, my wonderful agent and friend, Chris Vick, masseuse extraordinaire, who ensures that my back doesn't seize up. Thank you both.

I cannot forget you, my fabulous readers. You keep me in a job, and I am always appreciative of that. In December 2018, I celebrated being a full-time author for ten years. It's all thanks to you! Please keep sending your emails and comments/messages on Facebook and Twitter. Look out for the signed books and Roman goodies I give away and auction (for charity) via these media. I should mention that after you've read my books, leaving a short review on websites such as Amazon, Goodreads, Waterstones and iTunes has never been more important. Historical fiction is currently a shrinking market, sad to say. Times are tougher than they were when I was first published in 2008, and an author lives and dies on their reviews. Just a few minutes of your time helps me more than you know – thank you in advance.

Last but not least, I want to thank my wife Sair and my amazing children Ferdia and Pippa for the huge quantities of love and joy that they bring into my world.

Ways to contact me:

Email: ben@benkane.net

Twitter: @BenKaneAuthor

Facebook: facebook.com/benkanebooks

Also, my website: benkane.net

YouTube (my short documentary-style videos): tinyurl.com/y7chqhgo

GLOSSARY

Acarnania/Akarnania: an isolated area of north-western coastal Greece, allied to Macedon.

Acrocorinth/Akrokorinth: the mighty Macedonian fortress sited at the neck of the Peloponnese; one of the 'Fetters of Greece' (see separate entry), it controlled access to the mainland.

Aegean Sea: the body of water between Greece and Asia Minor.

Aetolia/Aitolia: a city state in west-central Greece; an implacable enemy of Macedon.

agora: a Greek term for the place where people gathered. Typically in the centre of towns or cities, its Roman equivalent was the forum.

Ambracian Gulf: an enclosed bay between Epirus (modern-day Albania) and Acarnania.

Anticyra: a port on the northern coast of the Gulf of Corinth; part of Phocis.

Antiochus III/Antiokhos III: the Seleucid ruler of Syria, a vast kingdom that had emerged after the death of Alexander the Great. An energetic and clever ruler, he reconquered large areas lost by his forebears. It will come as no surprise that he was on both Philip's and Rome's radar, as it were.

Antipatreia: modern-day Berat, Albania.

Aous, River: the modern-day Vjosa river.

Apollonia: a city sited at the mouth of the River Aous; it allied itself with Rome in 229 BC and served as the main base for the military campaigns against Macedon.

Ares: the Greek god of war, embodiment of the destructive but often useful aspects of war; his sons were called Fear and Terror.

Argos: a city state in the eastern Peloponnese.

asses (sing. as): small copper coins, each worth a sixteenth of a denarius.

Asia Minor: modern-day Turkey.

Asklepios/Aesculapius: the god of medicine. A major shrine to the god, the oldest in Greece, existed in Trikka, modern-day Trikala.

aspis/aspides: the small, round shield used by Philip's

phalangists. Sheathed in bronze with a wooden core, the face was usually embossed. In shape it was a little concave, and about eight palms in diameter. The aspis was controlled with a band for the left arm, and a neck strap. Modern reconstructions weigh about 5 kg.

Athamania: a small region to the east of Epirus and the west of Thessaly.

Atlas: one of the Titans who rebelled against the Olympian gods, he was condemned to hold up the sky for eternity.

Atrax: a vitally important Macedonian fortress situated in the Thessalian plain, east of Gomphi, and site of a defeat for Flamininus' legions in autumn 198 BC.

Attalus/Attalos I: king of Pergamum from 214–197 BC, and loyal ally of Rome.

Attika/Attica: the territory belonging to the city of Athens.

Axios, River: the modern-day Vardar river.

Bacchus: the Roman god of wine.

Bargylia: a town in western Asia Minor, north of Bodrum in modern-day Turkey.

Boeotia: a region of central Greece. Pronounced 'Bee-o-sha'. One of the most stylish and recognisable helmets from ancient times was the Boeotian, worn by cavalrymen.

Brundisium: modern-day Brindisi.

Bruttians: the inhabitants of Bruttium at the toe of Italy, roughly modern-day Calabria.

Caecuban: a type of Roman wine. See also the entry for wine.

caltrops: the ancient precursor to the spiked chain used by police today to stop speeding vehicles. A four-pronged piece of iron varying in height from 5-15 centimetres, it was designed when thrown to land with one point uppermost. The Romans used them at the bottoms of ditches and on the battlefield.

Capua: one of the most important cities in Republican Rome. Now a small town north of Naples.

Carthage: founded by Phoenicians as a trading settlement in the eighth century BC, it developed into a mighty city state with territories covering the entire western Mediterranean. It fought three great wars against Rome, losing all of them; at the end of the last (149–146 BC) it was razed to the ground. Note: its fields were *not* salted.

Carthaginians: natives of Carthage.

Celetrum: modern-day Kastoria, in north-western Greece.

Cenchreae/Kenchreai: one of two ports serving the city of Corinth, it was situated on the eastern side of the isthmus linking the Peloponnese to the Greek mainland. Ancient ruins can still be seen there today. See also entry for Lechaeum/Lekhaio.

Centuriate (in Latin, *comitia centuriata*): a remnant of Rome's earliest political structure, it was largely defunct by the late third century BC. Its members were, for the most part, farmers.

centurion (in Latin, *centurio*): the disciplined career officers who formed the backbone of the Roman army. See also the entry for legion.

century: the main sub-unit of a Roman legion, led by a centurion. It numbered eighty men. Each century was divided into ten sections of eight soldiers, called contubernia. Two centuries formed a maniple, a larger tactical unit. See also the entries for contubernium, maniple and legion.

Chalcis/Chalkis: a Macedonian fortress and the main city of Euboea. One of the three 'Fetters of Greece'. See also the entry for Fetters.

Chalkedon: a town on the Bosphorus straits.

chiliarchy: one of the sub-units of the phalanx, comprising 1024 phalangists. See also entries for phalangist, phalanx, speira and strategia.

Chios/Khios: an important Ionian town on an island of the same name; situated off west-central Asia Minor.

chiton: the tunic worn by most Greek men. One large piece of wool or linen, it was folded in half and pinned at the shoulders and the open side.

Companion cavalry: although no longer the shock force of Alexander's day, these horsemen were some of the finest ancient cavalry. Their horses wore only saddle blankets. Wearing bronze or padded linen breastplates and Boeotian helmets, the Companions were armed with the xyston, a thrusting spear up to five metres in length.

consul: one of two annually elected chief magistrates, appointed by the people and ratified by the Senate. Effectively rulers of Rome for twelve months, they were in charge of civil and military matters and led the legions to war. Each could countermand the other and both were supposed to heed the Senate's wishes. No man was supposed to serve as consul more than once, but in times of need this was disregarded.

contubernium (pl. contubernia): an eight man sub-unit of the century. The legionaries in each slept in the same tent, and shared duties.

Corinth/Korinth: the city sited on the narrow isthmus of land between the Peloponnese and mainland Greece.

Corinthian/Korinthian Gulf: the long, slender body of water between the Peloponnese and mainland Greece.

corona muralis: a prestigious silver or gold award given to the first soldier to gain entry into a town under siege.

Cretan: a man from the island of Crete/Krete.

Croesus: a sixth-century BC king of Lydia in western Asia Minor who was famed for his wealth.

Curia: the Senate house in Rome, found in the forum Romanum.

Cynoscephalae: the 'dogs' heads', a range of hills in Thessaly. The exact site of the battle in 197 BC is uncertain. A recent article in *Ancient Warfare* magazine posits the location near the modern village of Zoodochos Pigi. I visited the village in July 2018, and found the theory to be reasonable, but in the absence of archaeological evidence, it remains just that – a theory.

Dardania: a land bordering north-west Macedon (modern-day Kosovo); populated by the wild Dardanian tribes.

Demetrias: a Macedonian fortress on the Pagasean Gulf; one of the three 'Fetters of Greece'. See also the entry for the Fetters.

denarius (pl. denarii): the staple coin of the Republic from its introduction around 211 BC. Before this, the Romans had used some of their own coins, notably the as, as well as Greek coinage from the cities of southern Italy.

Dio/Dium: a Macedonian coastal town, it was also at the foot of Mount Olympos.

Dionysos: the Greek god of wine, intoxication, ritual madness and mania, he was Bacchus to the Romans.

Dipylon Gate: the double gateway in the north-west section of Athens' great wall.

drachmae (sing. drachma): the staple coins of ancient Greece. The word's origin is *drachm*, which means 'a handful', or 'a grasp'. Made of silver, they were minted by numerous city states. There were six obols in a drachma.

Egypt: after Alexander the Great's death, Egypt was ruled by the Ptolemies. By the late third century BC, it was in a weakened state but would totter on for another 200 years.

Elatea/Elateia: a city in ancient Phocis, it remains a town to this day.

Elysium/Elysian Fields: the part of the underworld for heroes and those who had led a righteous life.

Epirotes: men from Epirus, a region west of Athamania and Thessaly, and south-west of Macedon, equating to parts of modern-day Albania. Most of its tribes supported Rome against Philip.

epistates: a superintendent or overseer.

Esquiline Hill: one of the seven hills of Rome.

Euboea: a long island to the north of Athens and Boeotia. Pronounced 'Yew-be-a'. The important fortress of Chalkis was on Euboea.

Fetters of Greece: the three

fortresses of Akrokorinth, Chalkis and Demetrias (see relevant entries). Named by Philip V for their ability to keep Macedon safe from Greek hostility.

Fortuna: the goddess of luck and good fortune. Like all deities, she was notorious for her fickle nature.

forum: the public space at the centre of Roman towns. Bordered by covered markets, civic buildings and shrines, it was where people met to do business, converse and witness court cases and public announcements.

fustuarium: a punishment meted out to legionaries for reasons including falling asleep on sentry duty, stealing from a comrade, desertion in the face of the enemy or taking off one's sword while digging a ditch. The guilty individual was beaten to death by the men of his contubernium, with either bare fists or sticks.

Gomphi: a Macedonian fortress that protected Thessaly from attack to the west.

Gonnos/Gonnus: a town in northern Thessaly, close to Tempe.

Gorgon: in Greek, 'Gorgo', a mythical monster whose gaze turned people to stone. Her head was often depicted on Greek warriors' shields.

gugga: a Latin term of abuse for Carthaginians, found in one of Plautus' comedies. It possibly means 'little rat'.

gymnasium/gymnasia: constructed by the state, found throughout Greece, these were building complexes with dressing rooms, training quarters and special areas for contests. Lectures on philosophy and literature were also held in gymnasia.

Hades: the underworld for both Romans and Greeks. Elysium, paradise, was part of the underworld. So was Tartaros. I created a difference between Romans and Greeks by having the former use 'Hades' and the latter 'Tartaros'. In reality, this would not have happened.

Hannibal Barca: most famous son of Carthage, he remains one of history's finest generals. Having initiated a war with Rome in 218 BC, he marched an army from Spain to France and over the Alps to Italy. Although he inflicted massive defeats on the Romans, most notably at Lake Trasimene and Cannae, he never forced the Republic to surrender. Zama was his only major defeat; after it, he helped to rebuild Carthage.

harpastum: one of the ball games played by the Romans. See also author's note.

hastatus (pl. hastati): one of 1,200 young legionaries who stood in the first rank of each legion. The hastatus wore a bronze breast and back plate (the pectorale), a single greave, a triple crested helmet, and carried a shield. He was armed with one or two javelins and a sword.

Hellespont: the modern-day Dardanelles.

Hephaistos: the Greek god of blacksmiths, metalworking, carpenters, craftsmen, fire and volcanoes. His Roman equivalent was Vulcan.

Hera: Greek goddess of royalty and marriage.

Hercules/Herakles: the divine son of Jupiter/Zeus, famous for his strength and twelve labours.

herm(s): stone cult objects revering Hermes. Square columns topped by a bust of the god, with an erect phallus halfway down the stone's height, they were often used as milestones and boundary markers.

Hermes: messenger of the gods; a deity worshipped by shepherds and travellers.

Hispania: the Iberian Peninsula.

hoplite: soldiers in ancient Greece. Citizens of city states, they were armed with spears and shields, and fought in a phalanx. Their spears were much shorter than those of Macedonian phalangists.

Iasos: a town in coastal south-western Asia Minor.

inch: Roman linear measures were based on the pes, the standard foot. The pes was divided into 12 inches or 16 digits, the length of both being the same.

The modern equivalent is 11.65 inches/296 mm.

Illyria: parts of modern-day Slovenia, Serbia, Croatia, Bosnia and Montenegro.

javelin: the famous Roman pilum (pl. pila). The third-century BC version was more primitive than that of the Principate. It consisted of a wooden shaft some 1.2 metres long, joined to a thin iron shank topped by a barbed head. The range of the javelin is thought to have been about 30 metres, with an effective range of half this distance.

Isthmia: a town on the Peloponnese, south-east of Corinth, and site of the Isthmian Games (see separate entry).

Isthmian Games: one of the four Panhellenic Games, competitions observed by all Greeks. Originating in the sixth century BC, they took place both the year before and the year after the Olympic Games. Events included chariot races, pankration, wrestling, boxing and musical and poetry contests. Women were allowed to enter the last two.

Istros, River: the modern-day Danube river.

Judaean: someone from Judaea, modern-day Israel.

Jupiter: often referred to as 'Optimus Maximus' – 'Greatest and Best'. Most powerful of the Roman gods, he was responsible for weather, especially storms.

kausia: a Macedonian flat hat worn by men.

kopis: a curved, single-edged sword used by Greek soldiers.

Kleonai: a town situated between Argos and Corinth on the Peloponnese.

krater: a large, two-handed vessel for serving wine.

Kyklades/Cyclades Islands: an archipelago in the Aegean, close to the Turkish coast. About thirty are inhabitable. In the third century BC, they were variously ruled by Macedon, Egypt, Pergamum and Rhodes (see relevant entries).

Larisa/Larissa: a town in central Thessaly. Today it is Greece's fourth most populous city.

Lechaeum/Lekhaio: the western port for Corinth, it was connected to the city by a pair of strong walls. See also entry for Cenchreae/Kenchreai.

Latin: not just a language, but a people.

legate (in Latin, legatus legionis): the officer in command of a legion. A man of senatorial rank, most often in his early thirties. The legate reported to the general commanding the campaign.

legion: the standard large unit of the Roman army. In the mid-Republic, it was made up of 4,200 legionaries: 1,200 each of the velites, hastati and principes, and 600 triarii. 300 cavalry were also attached to each legion.

lembi (sing. lembus): Illyrian galleys, often used by pirates. Small and manoeuvrable, they were powered by about fifty oars, and did not have a sail.

Leukas: an Acarnanian settlement on the modern-day island of Lefkada, off western Greece.

liburnian: a small galley with either one or two banks of oars used by the Illyrians and Romans for raiding and patrolling.

Locris/Lokris: a small region in central Greece, much of which lay on the Malian Gulf, facing the island of Euboea.

Macedon/Macedonia: formerly of little importance, the kingdom rose to pre-eminence under Philip II, father of Alexander the Great. By Philip V's time, its glory days had long gone, but it was still the dominant force in Greece.

Magnesians: inhabitants of Magnesia, part of the Greek coastline south of Thessaly.

Malian Gulf: a gulf in the western Aegean Sea, and part of the coastline of Locris. Thermopylae lies on its southern aspect.

maniple: a sub-unit of the legion adopted around 300 BC. It's unclear exactly how many legionaries were in a maniple, but most academics agree a double century was probable. The maniple disappeared in the Marian reforms of the late second century BC.

Mars: Roman god of war. All spoils of war were consecrated to him, and few commanders would go on campaign without having visited Mars' temple to ask for his protection and blessing.

Myron: a Greek sculptor of the fifth century BC, famous in antiquity, still renowned. Only two representations of his work survive, one of which is the Discus Thrower, copied in Roman times from the bronze original.

Nemea, River: a waterway west of Corinth. As far as I can discover, the river is still called the Nemea today.

Nicaea/Nikaia: a town on the Malian Gulf close to Thermopylae.

Numidians: people from Numidia, an area that included parts of modern-day Algeria, Tunisia and Libya. Their riders were some of the finest cavalry in the ancient world.

obol: a low denomination coin made from copper or bronze. The name derives from a word meaning 'spit'. Six obols made one drachma.

Olympos, Mount: the highest mountain in Greece. Situated between Thessaly and Macedonia, it was home to the gods.

optio (pl. optiones): the officer who ranked immediately below a centurion; the second-in-command of a century. See also the entry for legion.

Orestis: an area of western Macedon, roughly the Kastoria region of modern-day Greece.

Ostia: built at the mouth of the River Tiber, this was the port of ancient Rome. I thoroughly recommend a visit to this amazing archaeological site.

Ottolobus: possibly near modern-day Lake Malik in Albania.

Paean: a song addressed to the gods, used by Greeks in personal, civic, political and military situations. I love the novelist Christian Cameron's use of it. (If you haven't read his books, please do!)

Paestum: a Greek-speaking city in southern Italy, founded as Poseidonia around 600 BC. At the time of the events in this book, it had only been under Roman influence for about a century. The splendidly preserved Greek temples still to be seen there are a wonder to behold.

palaestra: a private training school for boxing and wrestling. Often part of a gymnasium, an exercise and training facility for athletes.

Pallene: a town on the Peloponnese west of Corinth.

pankration: a Greek combat sport that allowed boxing, kicking, wrestling throws, strangleholds and pressure locks. Although brutal, pankration was an Olympic event.

Pelion, Mount: a summit on the coast of south-eastern Thessaly.

Pella: capital of Macedon. By the third century BC it was a magnificent city with a central grid complex of streets.

Peloponnese: the finger-shaped peninsula held to the Greek mainland by a narrow isthmus.

peltast: originally a term for a type of Thracian light infantry, by the third century BC it referred to a class of soldier used by many Greek city states. Armed with a crescent-shaped wicker shield (the pelte) and a bundle of spears, they were fast-moving, dangerous troops.

Peneios, River: the modern-day River Pineios in Thessaly.

Pergamum/Pergamenes: a kingdom in western Asia Minor formed after the collapse of the Lysimachian empire (which had been ruled by Lysimachus, one of Alexander the Great's generals). Governed by the Attalid family for a century and a half from the 280s BC, the kingdom allied itself with Rome against Macedon on numerous occasions.

Perrhaebians: inhabitants of Perrhaebia, the northernmost part of ancient Thessaly.

Perseus: eldest son of Philip V, later to be ruler of Macedon himself.

phalangist: a soldier who fought in the Macedonian phalanx. His helmet was often simple but could have a crest. His armour was a bronze cuirass or padded linen corselet, and greaves. He carried an aspis shield and a massive sarissa spear (see relevant entries), and he probably carried

a sword as well.

phalanx: long the staple fighting unit of the Greeks, this was akin to a battering ram, with thousands of men facing up to similar enemy formations while protected on the flanks by light infantry and/or cavalry. Adapted by Philip II and Alexander the Great to great effect, it formed the core of Philip V's army.

Pharsalos: a town in southern Thessaly. Today called Farsala, it was known to the Romans as Pharsalus, site of a famous battle between Julius Caesar and his Republican rival Pompey the Great.

Pherae/Pherai: a city in south-eastern Thessaly.

Phlios: a town on the Peloponnese, south-south-west of Corinth.

Phocis/Phokis: a region in central Greece lying between Boeotia and Locris.

Phthiotis: part of south-eastern Thessaly.

Plataea: a small city state north of Athens. Noted for being the only state to march with the Athenians to Marathon.

Pluinna: sadly, the location is unknown. The word may mean 'mountain', which doesn't help much in the terrain of Macedonia, Greece and Albania!

Poseidon: Greek god of the sea.

principes (sing. princeps): family men in their prime, these 1,200 legionaries formed the second rank of a legion's battle line. They were armed and armoured similarly to the hastati, with the notable exception of a mail shirt instead of a pectorale (see the entry for hastatus).

Ptolemy: the ruler of Egypt.

Rhodes: a natural trading centre thanks to its five harbours, it had territories among the Kyklades Islands and on Asia Minor.

sarissa: the long thrusting spear of the Macedonian phalangist. Between 4.5 and 5 metres in length, it was made of two parts that screwed together. Used two-handed, it had a heavy butt spike that served as a counterweight. In battle, the first five ranks levelled their spears at the enemy, which must have been a terrifying sight.

Scipio, Publius Cornelius: one of Rome's most famous generals. A youth at the outset of the second Punic war, by its end he was a shrewd and careful commander who had learned enough to beat Hannibal at his own game.

Seleucid empire: one of the kingdoms formed during the wars of the Successors, the bitter clashes between Alexander the Great's generals and followers. It was vast, reaching from the Mediterranean almost to India. By the late third century BC, it had just emerged from a difficult period thanks to the leadership of its new Seleucid ruler, Antiochus III.

Senate: the governing body of Republican Rome.

senator: one of 300 nobles from the senatorial class elected to stand in the Senate.

shekel: a silver coin used by the Carthaginians and many other ancient Semitic peoples.

shield: the Roman scutum (pl. scuta) was an elongated oval, about 1.2 metres tall and 0.75 metres wide. It was made from two layers of wood, the pieces laid at right angles to each other; it was then covered with linen or canvas, and leather. Republican scuta had a central wooden spine that ran from the top to the bottom. The scutum was heavy, weighing between 6 and 10 kg. A large metal boss decorated its centre, with the horizontal grip placed behind this. Decorative designs were often painted on the front, and a leather cover was used to protect the shield when not in use, e.g. while marching.

skamma: the softened sand found on the floor of wrestling rooms in palaestrae.

Sparta: also known to Greeks as Lacedaemon or Lakonia, which gave rise to the modern word 'laconic', the land of the Spartans spanned the central Peloponnese.

speira (pl. speirai): a 256-man strong unit of the Macedonian phalanx. It measured sixteen men wide, sixteen deep. See also Author's Note.

stadion (pl. stadia): a Greek

unit of measurement, roughly corresponding to 176 metres.

strategia (pl. strategiai): a 5,000-man strong unit of the Macedonian phalanx. See also Author's Note.

Stobi: a town in northern Macedon; today the site lies in the Republic of Macedonia.

strigil: a curved bronze instrument used by Greeks and Romans to scrape sweat and dirt off the skin.

talent: an ancient Greek unit that measured mass as well as money. Its weight is uncertain – it may have been anywhere between 20–50 kgs, but whatever the correct figure, a gold talent would be worth in excess of £1 million today.

Tarentine: someone from Tarentum, modern-day Taranto.

Tartaros: part of the underworld.

Tempe: an eight-kilometre defile in the mountains between Thessaly and Macedon. It was the easiest route between the two regions but could be easily defended.

tesserarius: one of the junior officers in a century, whose duties included commanding the guard. The name originates from the tessera tablet on which was written the password for the day.

Thebes: one of the most powerful Greek city states in the fifth and fourth centuries BC, it was burned to the ground by Alexander the Great and had shrunk to a shadow of its former self by the time of the war with Macedon.

Thermopylae: site of one of history's most famous battles. In 480 BC, King Leonidas of Sparta and his 300 warriors, together with 6,000–7,000 Greeks, held off a vastly larger Persian army for two days. When the enemy appeared behind them, most of the Greeks left, but not Leonidas and his 300.

Thessaly: a region of north Greece. Essentially plains enclosed by mountains except for the Pagasean Gulf to the east, in the third century BC it was mostly controlled by Macedonia; Aetolia held sway over smaller areas.

Thrace: a region populated by fierce, warlike tribes – the Thracians. Today it would lie in parts of Greece, Bulgaria and Turkey.

triarii (sing. triarius): the oldest, most experienced soldiers in a legion. These 600 men wore helmets, mail shirts and a single greave. They each carried a shield, and were armed with a sword and a long thrusting spear.

tribune: one of six senior officers in each legion. During the mid-Republic, these men were of senatorial rank.

Thronium: a town on the Malian Gulf east of Nicaea.

Tiber, River: the river that flows through Rome to the sea at Ostia.

Trebia: site in north-east Italy of

Hannibal's first major victory over the Romans in December 218 BC.

Triballians: a Thracian tribe who lived in the area where modern-day Serbia and Bulgaria join.

Trikka: modern-day Trikala, in Thessaly.

trireme: the classic ancient warship, which was powered by a single sail and three banks of oars. Each oar was rowed by one man who, on Roman and Greek ships, was freeborn. Exceptionally manoeuvrable, and capable of up to 8 knots under sail or for short bursts when rowed, the trireme had a bronze ram at the prow. This was used to damage or sink enemy ships. Small catapults could also be mounted on the deck. Each trireme was crewed by up to thirty men and around 200 rowers; it could carry sixty infantry, giving it a very large crew in proportion to its size. This limited the triremes' range, so they were mainly used as troop transports and to protect coastlines.

turma (pl. turmae): a ten-man cavalry unit. In the mid-Republic, each legion had a mounted force of 300 riders. This was divided into thirty turmae, each commanded by a decurion.

velites (sing. veles): light skirmishers recruited from the poorest social class. 1,200 were attached to each legion. Young men of perhaps sixteen to eighteen years, their equipment consisted of a small, round shield and a bundle of 1.2 metre javelins. They also wore strips of wolfskin on their heads.

vitis: the vine stick carried by centurions. It was used as a mark of rank and also to inflict punishment.

wine: it is unclear when viticulture first came to Italy. It was practised by the Etruscans but could also have been introduced by Greek settlers. At the time of this book, Roman winegrowing had not yet reached its peak. Alban, Caecuban and Falernian were some of the most famous types.

Zama: site of Hannibal's defeat at the hands of Publius Cornelius Scipio in October 202 BC. Today the probable site lies south-west of Tunis, close to the border with Algeria.

Zeus: the most important Greek god, and ruler of the other deities. He was revered as the god of thunder and of the sky. Soter means 'the Saviour'; it was a title given to many gods.